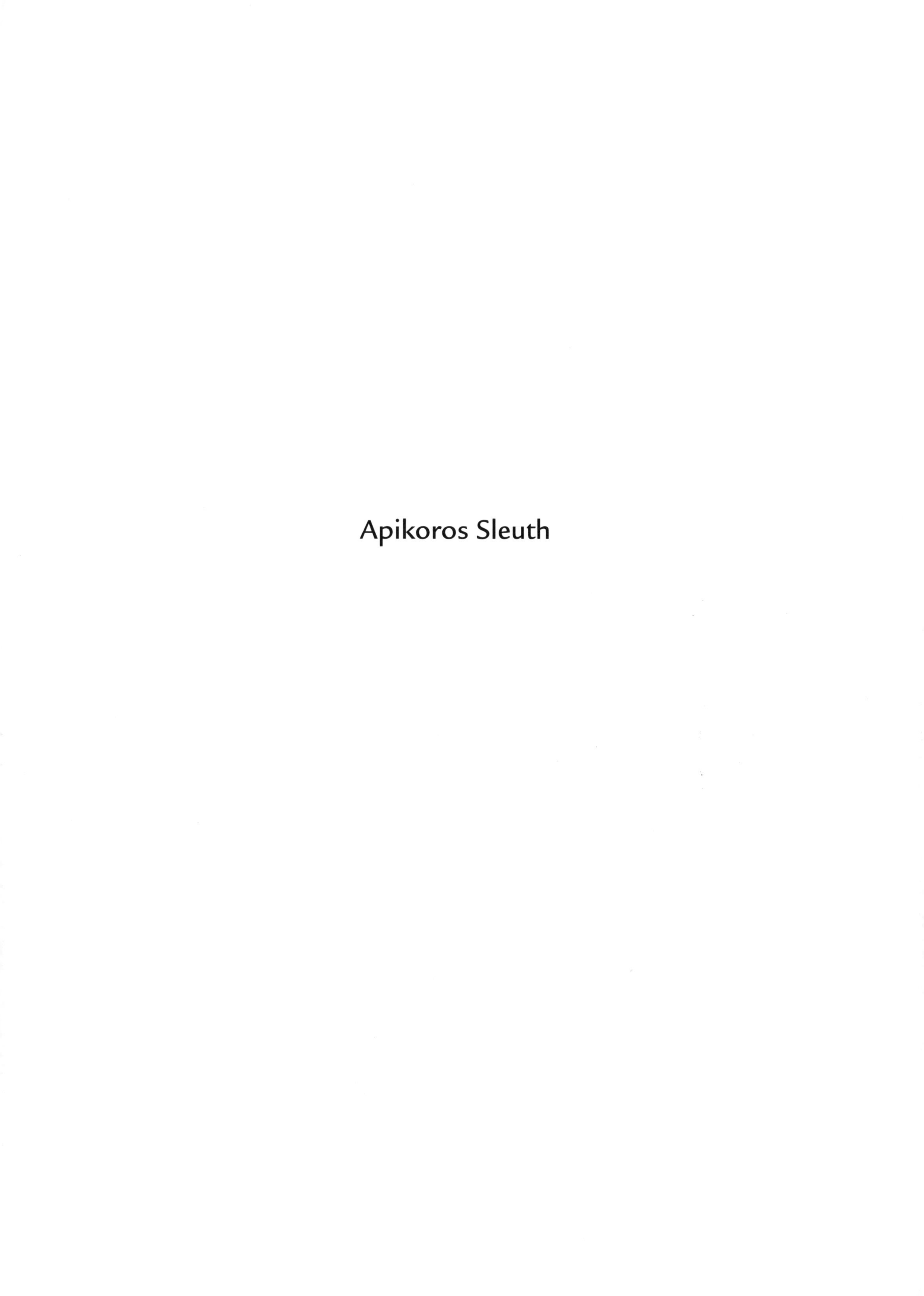

Apikoros Sleuth

APIK OROS SLEU TH

בשלשים ושתים נתיבות פליאות חכמה חקק יק יקוק צבקות אלקי ישראל אלוקים חיים ומלך עולם אל שדי רחום וחנון
רם ונשא שוכן עד וקדוש שמו מרום וקדוש הוא וברא את עולמו בשלשה ספרים בספר וספר וספור: עשר ספירות בלי מה
מה ועשרים אותיות יסוד שלש אמות ושבע כפולות ושתים עשרה פשוטות: עשר ספירות בלימה במספר עשר אצבעות חמש
חמש כנגד חמש וברית יחיד מכוון באמצע במילת הלשון ובמילת המעור: עשר ספירות בלימה עשר ולא תשע עשר ולא
אחת עשרה הבן בחכמה וחכם בבינה בחון בהם וחקור מהם והעמד דבר על בוריו והשב יוצר על מכונו: עשר ספירות
בלימה מדתן עשר שאין להם סוף עומק ראשית ועומק אחרית עומק טוב ועומק רע עומק רום ועומק תחת עומק מזרח

ועומק מערב עומק צפון ועומק דרום אדון יחיד אל מלך נאמן מושל בכולם ממעון קדשו עד עדי עד: עשר ספירות בלי מה צפייתן כמראה הבזק ותכליתן אין להם קץ ודברו בהן ברצוא ושוב ולמאמרו כסופה ירדופו ולפני כסאו הם משתחוים: עשר ספירות בלימה נעוץ סופן בתחלתן ותחלתן בסופן כשלהבת קשורה בגחלת שאדון יחיד ואין לו שני ולפני אחד מה אתה סופר: עשר ספירות בלימה בלום פיך מלדבר ולבך מלהרהר ואם רץ פיך לדבר ולבך להרהר שוב למקום שלכך נאמר (יחזקאל א׳) והחיות רצוא ושוב ועל דבר זה נכרת ברית: עשר ספירות בלימה אחת רוח אלהים חיים ברוך ומבורך שמו של חי העולמים קול ורוח ודבור והוא רוח הקודש: שתים רוח מרוח חקק וחצב בה עשרים ושתים אותיות יסוד שלש אמות ושבע כפולות ושתים עשרה פשוטות ורוח אחת

APIK OROS SLEU TH

מהן: שלש מים מרוח חקק וחצב בהן כ״ב אותיות מתהו ובהו רפש וטיט חקקן כמין ערוגה חצבן כמין חומה סיבבס במין מעזיבה ויצק עליהם שלג ונעשה עפר שנאמר כי לשלג יאמר הוא ארץ: ארבע אש ממים הקק וחצב בה כסא הכבוד שרפים ואופנים וחיות הקודש ומלאכי השרת ומשלשתן יסד מעונו שנאמר עושה מלאכיו רוחות מערתיו אש לוהט: בירר שלש אותיות מן הפשוטות בסוד שלש אמות אמות אמ״ש וקבעם בשמו הגדול וחתם בהם ששה קצוות. חמש חתם רום ופנה למעלה וחתמו בהי״ו. שש חתם תחת ופנה למטה וחתמו ביה״ו. שבע חתמ מזרח ופנה לפניו וחתמו בוי״ה. שמונה חתם מערב ופנה לאחריו וחתמו בוה״י. תשע חתם דרום ופנה לימינו וחתמו ביו״ה. עשר חתם צפון ופנה לשמאלו וחתמו בהו״י: אלו עשר ספירות בלימה (אחת) רוח אלהים היים

רוח מרוח מים מרוח אש ממים רום ותחת מזרח ומערב צפון ודרום: עשרים ושתים אותיות יסוד שלש אמות ושבע כפולות
ושתים עשרה פשוטות. שלש אמות אמ״ש יסודן כף זכות וכף חובה חק מכריע בינתים. שלש אמות אמ״ש מ׳ דוממת ולשון
ש׳ שורקת א׳ אויר רוח מכריע בינתים: עשרים ושתים אותיות יסוד הקקן חצבן צרפן שקלן והמירן וצר בהם את כל

היצור ואת כל העתיד לצור: עשרים ושתים אותיות יסוד חקקן בקול חצבן ברוח קבען בפה

ROBERT MAJZELS

בחמשה מקומות אחה״ע בגרון גיכ״ק בחיך דטלנ״ת בלשון זסשר״ץ בשינים בומ״ף בשפתים:

עשרים ושתים אותיות יסוד קבען בגלגל כמין חומה ברל״א שערים וחוזר הגלגל פנים ואחור וסימן לדבר אין בטובה
למעלה מענג ואין ברעה למטה מנגע: כיצד צרפן שקלן והמירן א׳ עם כולם וכולם עם א׳ ב׳ עם כולם וכולם עם ב׳
וחוזרות חלילה ונמצאות ברל״א שערים ונמצא כל היצור וכל הדבור יוצא משם אחד: יצר ממש מתהו ועשה את אינו ישנו
וחצב עמודים גדולים מאויר שאינו נתפש וזה סימן א׳ עם כולם וכולם עם א׳ צופה וממיר ועשה את כל היצור ואת כל
הדבור שם אחד וסימן לדבר עשרים ושתים חפצים בגוף אחד: שלש אמות אמ״ש יסודן כף זכות וכף חובה ולשון חק
מכריע בינתים: שלש אמות אמ״ש סוד גדול מופלא ומכוסה וחתום בשש טבעות ויצאו מהם אויר מים אש ומהם נולדו אבות
ומאבות תולדות: שלש אמות אמ״ש חקקן חצבן צרפן שקלן והמירן וצר בהם שלש אמות אמ״ש בעולם ושלש אמות אמ״ש
בשנה ושלש אמות אמ״ש בנפש זכר ונקבה: שלש אמות אמ״ש בעולם אויר מים אש שמים גבראו מאש וארץ נבראת ממים

THE MERCURY PRESS

The publisher gratefully acknowledges the financial assistance of the Canada Council for the Arts, the Ontario Arts Council, and the Ontario Book Publishing Tax Credit Program. The publisher further acknowledges the financial support of the Government of Canada through the Department of Canadian Heritage's Book Publishing Industry Development Program (BPIDP) for our publishing activities.

This book was written with the assistance of a Canada Council for the Arts writing grant and produced with the generous contribution of Moveable Inc.

Original page design by Robert Majzels
Cover design by Gordon Robertson
Cover image by Xiang Liqing

Typesetting, proofreading, copyediting
and prepress production by Moveable Inc.:

Editing, type design and typographic fine-tuning by Jim Roberts
Typesetting by Nigel Allen, Isabel Preto and Martina Weigl

Printed and bound in Canada
Printed on acid-free paper

1 2 3 4 5 08 07 06 05 04

National Library of Canada
Cataloguing in Publication Data

Majzels, Robert, 1950–
Apikoros sleuth / Robert Majzels.
Includes some text in Hebrew.
Co-published by Moveable Inc.
ISBN 1-55128-105-8
I. Title
PS8576.A525A86 2004a C813'.54 C2004-903235-6

The Mercury Press
Box 672, Station P, Toronto, Ontario Canada M5S 2Y4
www.themercurypress.ca

A limited edition is published by
Moveable Inc.
77 Mowat Ave., Suite 502, Toronto, Ontario Canada M6K 3E3
www.moveable.com

Contents

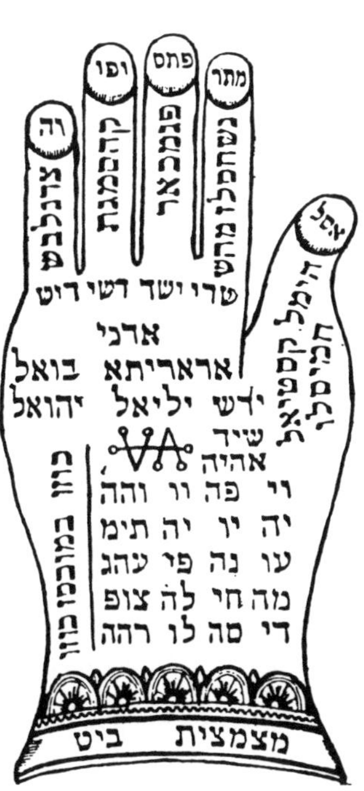
מתר
פתס
ופו
וה
אסל
שדי ישד דשי דיש
אראריתא בואל
ידש יליאל יהואל
שיד
אהיה
וי פה וו והה
יה יו יה תימ
עו נה פי עהג
מה חי לה צופ
די סה לו רהה
מצמצית ביט

What constitutes a tenement? At what point? A highrise ensconced among other highrises, crosses its own threshold of dilapidation. To become. Tenement. When? When fewer than half the apartments are occupied? A third? A fifth? Those of us who have stuck it out. When the "For Rent" sign has been rain-soaked or blown to bits? When that always already absent landlord stops collecting the rent.[α] The building manager? Gone to ground. Because of the boy. You know the story. Why am I telling it again? A couple. Ukrainians. They were God's Witnesses. Sent the boy around to collect the rents (perhaps you'd like a pamphlet while I'm here?).[δ] Shall we say someone (a tenant) asked him to come in for a moment. Again. Until he started having doubts and nightmares in equal proportion. Stopped collecting. Just as well, for his sake. Downstairs, in the foyer, the city notices. Building violations.[ϵ] What sprinkler system? What hot water? Why does he go on like this? One becomes accustomed to a cold shower. Except in the winter. Which, in this country, lasts six months. Not to mention the memory. Which lasts four more. Or fourteen. And yet. Not yet. One becomes inured to cold showers. Oh, that they (the ones who do) would cut off the electricity once and for all, rather than torture us with brownouts. One can plan for a total eclipse. Only the uncertainty haunts. And if they cut it off? Would that be enough?[ϕ] How should we act? Look for another room and a half? From street to street. Strange buildings, strange smells (though certainly no worse). Sign a lease, a cheque. But no, not a cheque. That was a book the bank had closed, for lack of content. Small bills then, not to mention coins, tucked into an envelope. Rent a truck. Perhaps a hand cart would suffice. Fold boxes. Abandon old dust. Who would carry the other end of the bookcase?

α These are things from which all benefit is forbidden.

δ Awake!

ϵ When the landlord stops collecting, beware the insurance fire…

ϕ Those of us who have stuck it out, those of us who have lost the will to move on.

Story? Who would tell it? There are some who say. A story is a fiction, a mistake. We add and subtract and expound. We say it thus and we say it thus. When we take the first part, we take the end as well. This is in and this is in. But this only resembles this. We cast one man or woman against another. The heart in conflict with itself. When? A story teaches an exaggeration. It is possible to refute. If there is a difficulty, this is the difficulty. Better to be silent.

And if you say: but what then? A house is not a home, some (too many) say. Still one resides there, in a room and a half of turpitude. One does not go out, if at all possible. One remains perfectly still, if at all possible. One remains perfectly silent. This is always possible. But perhaps you are thinking: how does he eat, pay the rent, move through time toward death? This itself is not difficult. He ate rarely. Paid no rent. Let time move him. He lay on the cot of desolation in a room and a half. Do I teach an exaggeration? Certainly it is possible to refute. Did he regret abandoning a struggle? Or those sins committed in the name of the struggle? What remained in the wake of failure? The body, the thing itself. This is ours and this is theirs. What is this? We incubate lust and something else. Sexual relations, money, pigs, leprosy. Here, suddenly, a word about my mother: no mute imperative driving me across the countryside to find her. He sought something else, something more. How can you find it? I am still looking. Now that we have come to this. The question, the difficulty, returned to its place. And are we still at it? And he who asked it – why did he ask it? Some will say: Go this way! Others say: Just the opposite! Perhaps it is a case of go read it in the teacher's house.

How should we act? Wondering if I could. Writing here and writing there. Continue in this way. But if so, what then? Just the knowledge that, in one's solitude, the length of which and were it not for, one might write one's solitude. Would he withhold exactly that? And to have come all this way, only to discover. But what did or could he expect. Otherwise. Yes, and how should we act? Shall we assemble a clause? And sign it. But it is not in our hand.

Mark the first page of a book with a red ribbon, for the wound is inscribed at its beginning.
E. Jabès
Le livre des questions

What keeps me here? Inertia. The view. Here a suspension. Across the boulevard. A canyon of traffic. A mountain. Trees rising out of the city. Across. I meant a cross. A floor and a half higher than the bedroom window. How many floors? Twenty-two? Twenty-three? If we count the thirteenth.[κ] Once, in another season, green trees sucked in all a city could throw up at them. There was a point of saturation. They shed everything, became dry grey sticks, cracked under the weight of the wind.[λ] And yet, altitude, unlike neatness, counts. On the first three floors, no one. An accumulation of garbage in the incinerator chute. And yet. Not yet. Is this the way of things? Those Ukrainians are not gone. You may be surprised to learn. They moved to a higher floor. A couple.[μ] She speaks a few words of English, he knows where the boiler is. Though he would never tell. And who would ask? The deal only got sweeter. No longer compelled to respond to the sustained and urgent pleas of tenants. The way of things. Free to pursue life in the West as they had not imagined it. But for the trouble with the boy. On the twenty-second, or twenty-third, the pool, abandoned. Cracked. Flaking.[ν] A matter of time. Those of us who have stuck it out. Those of us who've lost the will to move on. Those of us who've forgotten how. Organization, you are thinking. Because you remember the sixties. The years, I mean.[π] Or someone's memory of them. Tenants' cooperatives. Self-administration. Kronstadt. The idea of Kronstadt, I mean, not the actual events. Having taken place sixty years before the sixties of which we are speaking. Those of us who resist. Block occupations. Committees. All night meetings. And yet. Not yet. If you think I would. Once more. Engage. Rise up, body and soul as one, and go into the world. You are sorely... mistaken : :

κ Though it was present only in spirit.

λ That wind. In July, runs its fingers through the branches, whistles like a boy; in September raps at your window; in December comes to cut your throat.

μ Refugees from the fall of communism.

ν A dark, still fermentation of dead and dying things.

π Those days imbricated in another tense, not quite past nor future. No matter. Today, the incinerator chute below, the pool above. How should we act?

An imbrication and a suspension. What makes a good sleuth? Which powers are preferred? Observation? Deduction? Patience? Imagination? Anticipation? To say: The nature of this case is not like the nature of this case and the nature of this case is not like the nature of that case. The event that happened happened that way. And which sins are, by a sleuth, to be avoided? Antonius said to Rabbi: Seemingly, a person's body and soul are each able to excuse themselves from judgment after death. The body says: It is the soul that has sinned, for from the day that it has departed from me, I have been lying, unable to sin, like a silent rock in the grave. And the soul says: It is the body that has sinned, for from the day that I have departed from it, I have been flying in the air like a bird, unable to sin. Rabbi said to him: A king owned a beautiful orchard which contained beautiful early figs. And he stationed two guards – one lame, the other blind. The lame one said to the blind: "I see beautiful early figs in the orchard. Come, mount me on your shoulders and together we will bring the figs here to eat them. The lame mounted the back of the blind, and they brought the figs and they ate them. The owner of the orchard came and said to the guards: "The beautiful early figs – where are they?" The lame one said to him, "Do I have feet with which to travel to the figs? I certainly could not have taken them." And the blind one said: "Do I have eyes with which to see where the figs are? I certainly could not have taken them." What did the king do? He mounted the lame one on the back of the blind, and he judged them as a unit.[γ] But we were asking: which sin must a sleuth, if he is to sleuth, avoid? Digression.

Certainly he was no sleuth. A sleuth could find better lodgings. A sleuth could detect the source of an odour that rose into the room and a half of his nose. Pardon the hypotyposis. He would not sleuth.[η] He would remain silent. He would not ask: How should we act? He would not reflect on the past of his future. He would lie on the cot of lethargy in a room and a half. To act, to sleuth, to rise up and go into the world, that is a Halakhah for the Time of the Messiah : :

γ Sanhedrin 91a

η I prefer not to.

Shall we say he was not in the habit of reading obituaries?[α] Not then. Not now. Not ever. And yet. Not yet. This is possible to refute. In fact, at one time,[δ] death was all he read. A very heavy stone. Tossed the rest of the paper back into the trash without so much as a glance. Even today, I miss the papers. Don't know why. What use the news of the world for one such as I? Nostalgia, the sweet, fetid stink of hindsight, detritus with a rosy hue.[ε] And yet, I admit to a lack, a desire. A cerebral pang.[φ] Shall we say it's the obituaries I miss? Though I have only myself to blame. All a question of access. Those twenty-two flights down to the street. And the elevator. Elevators, I should say. Two.[γ] Though they might as well be one. A flaw in the wiring.[η] They travel together always. Has someone called from the ground floor? Let us say so. Two elevators descend in tandem. Doors slide in unison. Accordion duet. That moment of hesitation before a meaningless choice. Identical chambers. Why hesitate?[κ] Unless. Your neighbour. That stranger. Also waiting. Fiddling a set of keys. Unwrapping a scarf. Resting a bag against the ashtray. Trace of the Other's breath. If such were the case, you too would try for a split. But not obviously. Because would he be insulted? Would he think it was his odour, the white cane, the flaming forehead pimple? Hole in a sock?[λ] Perhaps none of the above, or all. But really just the close quarters. Awkward silence. The risk of insipid conversation, the enormous effort required. This is the difficulty. To fumble through my memory for a personality appropriate to circumstance. Perhaps two chambers arrive empty, you are alone, but some residual odour causes you to recoil from your initial choice and leap for the other. At such moments, time bends. The doors, barely open, are already slamming shut. Whereas. When you're inside, waiting to go up, hoping no one will spoil your solitude... But enough about elevators. The point is. At last, the point! Or perhaps not *the* point, but a point, however minute. And yet. Not yet. Why go on and on? Do we so much as recall the topic, I mean the point, under discussion? The point is this: that, from the point of view of one who has decided, at some point, to point himself downstairs for a newspaper, there may as well be a single elevator, because instead of racing up to get you, the empty one, carrying as little content as this anecdote and moving about as quickly, has descended with its partner,[μ] paused toothless while said partner ingested a passenger on the ground floor, then accompanied its twin up to, say, the twelfth, where, opening wide, it waits agape for the other to disgorge, and then and only then, both mount the shaft together, to collect. You. Is that the point? Elevators? Two!? Why do I need two? We were speaking of newspapers. We were the subject of newspapers. I mean, newspapers were our subject. If point there is to be, ought not said point to vaguely point towards newspapers? Or news?[ν] The point then. Why go out for newspapers? Why be bothered? All the trouble waiting for the elevators. And the neighbour. His purple zit. What sort of addiction, you are thinking,[π] if a bit of a wait and someone's facial blemish will suffice to dissuade? The long twist of waiting is not what finally operates to dissuade.[ρ] What if that pimple were on my forehead? If it happens to be my toe rubbing against the inside of my shoe? A case of desire conflicting with dread.[σ] Philia and phobia. From neither of which I suffered at the time I am recalling. At that time, it was pure accident I happened to glance at the paper I was using to cover my legs, or fill my shoe, pure chance it was the obituaries section (at last we approach the point), and purest chance the name was one I recognized or dimly recalled. So, in the end, if story is what we are unfolding, surely all this talk about habituation and elevators is pointless : :

To be wrapped in newspapers is perhaps the best of all. What could be more comforting? To be rolled warmly in layer upon layer of fine print. Wrapped thick in the news of the day. But perhaps you cannot possibly think so. Perhaps any number of things of which I have no knowledge are more pleasing than newspapers. Perhaps newspapers rank dizzyingly low in the great list of pleasures. This is possible, even probable, considering the limits of my experience, particularly in the area of pleasure. Some (most) people might consider being wrapped in newspapers un supplice. I am prepared to admit it. In matters of swaddling or pleasure, or any other you care to mention, I make no universal claims. And yet. To be entwined in slender columns, single-sentence paragraphs of precise denotative prose. But I fabulate. I reason the unreasonable. Is it content that comforts or form that feels good? Is it the gathering tumbleweed of information or the inky exhalation? Slender typography or texture? Pattern or pulp? I haven't a clue. But pleasure I do derive. Or, rather, something less than pleasure. Consolation. Or solace. Or merely snugness. But perhaps you are thinking: perversity. You who lie properly encased in sheets and covers of cotton, wool or some combination of polyacrylonitrites, and even then, only for purposes of slumber or convalescence. But simply to lie, regardless of time of day or night, shrouded in newspapers – crisp and whenever possible current – eyes open, mind spinning on empty, without any purpose other than to be so entangled? Do not think I am oblivious to the milky trickle of quilt. Worse, here's neither tragedy nor taboo. Only a small grubby sin from which you avert your gaze, slightly embarrassed, mildly bemused. Inexplicable fetish? Or symptom of some deeper, more despicable disease? What are the other manifestations? Never mind, we'll get to those soon enough : :

α An obituary is the tent over a dead body.

δ There is no earlier and later in the Torah.

ε Here a generalization that needs a detail and a detail that needs a generalization.

φ The gnaw of longing is itself an addiction.

γ Two?! Why do I need two?

η Or some (unfortunate) body's idea of a joke.

κ The word is free on both sides.

λ This morning, slipping that pink toe into its shoe, in the optimism of the new day, it seemed no one could possibly guess, but now...

μ A second elevator would be like a second column, but this only resembles this. This is always only this.

ν At the very least, paper.

π But perhaps you are not. Thinking, I mean.

ρ Though waiting provides that unwelcome opportunity for thinking.

σ The lure of death. News from the other side. The fear of leaving the languorous solitude of my shelf.

When to die quietly is the decent thing. As any mother will, or ought to do. In due time. Until then, a transistor radio hardly compensates. Not for peace and quiet. Later, one's mater having gone, there is less need of a radio. It was necessary for this to be said. In the street or on the bus he was silent.[α] Confronted the surface of the world from between a set of earphones. His ears filled with bubblegum.[δ] We are already into extra innings. Armpits. A matter went out from among them. Up from the depths past the gape of mouths and rows of teeth.[ε] I have no preference: baseball or bubblegum. Classical or call-in. It is necessary, to thicken the walls of the cocoon. To cloister the ugly worm of the self. Anticipation. The armpit of a passerby. Suddenly an eye-to-eye. Someone else is a beast. My forehead drenched, my already fragile digestion.[φ] Perhaps this cannot enter your mind. I heard the talk show of the Amoraim.[γ] Shall we say that these disagree according to the difference of opinion between A and B? A good host should be a reactionary. Something to gnaw on. Instead of my tongue. The fleshy wall. The trilobite's cephalic shield. Of course, to say a radio is not to say a new radio. She'd had it for years. Hence the disinfectant.[η] She was not happy to see me plugged in her presence. And yet she did not complain. How could she? It was her gift.[κ] An attachment. Nor did I look her in the mouth. Or any place else. If I could help it. Up to here there is no difficulty. Boys are forever wrestling with their mothers and their mothers' deaths. They say in the West. Such is not my case. Having always been indifferent to mine. In life as in death. I mean hers. Mine too for that matter. Perfectly happy to leave her to hers and get on with mine. Such as it is.[λ] But I digress. The radio. A lucky thing she gave it to me. Because when she died, she left me nothing. Must I go on like a peddler? I'll stop.[μ] The shopkeepers. Who would venture from a room and a half but for provisions?[ν] Let us say, a fixed routine is best. First, the elevator. But that's another story. Who mentioned this item, which is being cited now as if it had already been mentioned? Let us wildly assume disaster has not already struck before the used bookstore. Two blocks north one block east.[π] We are already in extra innings. To sell, not to buy. My dwindling collection. Deduce from it, and again from it. Shall we divide books into groups?[ρ] This is in and this is in. Those that cannot be sold. Those I do not desire to sell but would bring a good price. Those they buy by the pound. Blue books. Schwitters. Poe. Poetry in Tagalog. Here is not an alphabet. Books that will not sell today but may someday sell again. Books I would have liked to have written.[σ] Books too tall for the shelf. Books by adults for children. Or by children claiming to be adults. Books only a child could understand (Stein). Here, at least, a pretext. To continue in this way. But we were speaking of grocers. They incline. They wipe their pink hands. What do you have to say? Is there anything else? Sexual relations, money, pigs, leprosy. The violence of an empty phrase. The underexpected. It was said thus and it was said thus. It escaped me. Une demi-baguette. How can you find it? Bananas. Intolerant. So brief and yet so disconcerting. Something else. A newspaper: Perverse addiction or last tenuous link to the world? Should we rely on answers such as these? Perhaps you cannot possibly think so. They subtract and add and expound. Superfluity in measured amounts. He raised the volume on the radio. Smiled with difficulty. Returned to a room and a half : :

In the orchard. Blind man and cripple. Shall we ransack a fig tree? Body and soul. A parable no computation can allow. Story. Act. Deed, event, precedent. We interpret beginnings. We speak in the language of men. Fall back softly into the common denominator. As though two events could never occur at the same moment. Two!? Why do I need two? As though this did not merely resemble this. This aspect is not like that aspect and that aspect is not like this aspect. If there is a difficulty, this is the difficulty. Generalization. From fiction we learn only this. But perhaps you say: If you take hold of the larger, you do not take hold; if you take hold of the smaller, you do take hold. Generalization and detail. Detail and generalization. Generalization and detail and generalization. A generalization that needs a detail and a detail that needs a generalization.

Generalization. Detail. Generalization. Generalization. Generalization.

detail detail detail detail detail detail detail
detail detail detail detail detail detail detail
detail detail detail detail detail detail detail
detail detail detail detail detail detail, detail.
Detail.[ω]

Won't you climb up on my shoulders so that together we might steal a beautiful early fig. For I am blind and you are lame. And those figs. Beautiful. Early. Luscious exhalation. Superfluity in measured amounts. Is there nothing else? What remains beyond the end of story? Dust (a hint of transgression). There is no agent for transgression. A person is close to himself. A blind body beneath a lame head. Shall we judge them together? A man is always considered forewarned. Those figs. From which benefit is forbidden. Act, deed, event, precedent. Something learned from its end. Ouch, yet another soteriology. A perilous repetition perched blindly upon my shoulders. Dust settles. What remains? A detail. The taste of figs. Beautiful. Early. Dust of seeds upon your tongue : :

α Morning is the time to hide. They wake up, hale and hearty, their tongues hanging out for order, beauty and justice, baying for their due. S. Beckett *Molloy*

δ I mean the music, or the baseball game.

ε The body, the thing itself. This is ours and this is theirs. This only resembles this.

φ So quickly the difficulty (myself) returned to its place.

γ Every tanna is the amora of someone else's tanna.

η Let us say I soaked those plugs overnight.

κ I mean the radio, not the ability to suffer without complaining.

λ Perhaps one finds meaning only in one's own death. Always already too late.

μ To be perfectly Beckett, she did not actually give it to me. I took it. Which was not difficult. Because of her blindness. Well, it was of no use to her. Because of her deafness. Ça suffit! I'll stop.

ν A fistful of bananas, une demi-baguette, a can of tuna, ce thon blanc entier, mon semblable, qui baigne dans son huile.

π Knight to bishop three.

ρ In the category of external books: purely secular books, such as Homer's, may be read, so long as they do not disrupt the reader's study of the Torah. Sanhedrin 100b

σ The classic book is a frigate, a fleet. It is orderly. A sacred book is absolute, perfect. J.L. Borges

ω We are already weary running with the foot-soldiers, and yet they bring on the horses! Jeremiah 12:5

A man is always considered forewarned. In the blackened pages of the newspaper. A name. Shall we say Antonio Pigafetta? A mouthful. Not much more. In loving memory. A dentist at the time of his death.[α] Where was he when he saw it? Shall we say upon the throne? The Grecian urn. A word about mine. Urn, I mean. To be precise, that one is a fine flusher. Which is a great advantage. In most cases, two are required. It is best to be flushed and clear-headed. Especially in public places. Visiting an acquaintance. For example. People will wonder.[δ] Someone said: What *is* going on in there? Earlier, he'd slipped away. To colour the waters. Now, he flushed and stood, flushed, waiting. It took forever. Again. And left much to ponder.[ε] And furthermore. It was not in his hand. Yet another mute imperative. They also serve who stand and wait. What remains? A few flakes of money, pigs, leprosy.[φ] A swirling abatement. A shred of paper. And is there nothing else? Shall we let it stand? Can this enter your mind? Such an act is great. He disagreed with himself. He spoke too soon. A remnant spun. Or two or three. A severe case of hypotyposis. He had no remedy against the stubbornness of settlement. There is no mystagogy of matter. The body, the thing itself. A matter having gone out from among him, there could be no retraction. There were objects. And objections. The event which happened, happened that way. Once again, he cursed and flushed it. An anamorphic aspiration. Because the imbecilic conservation of depth requires. Would sufficiency ever be sufficient? We have learned elsewhere. Something else.[γ] Though rarely. A window. Freezing. And since we have come upon it. He had to face his hosts dripping wet in the lingering sound of flushing.[η] But we were speaking[κ] of Pigafetta. That dentist with too many teeth in his name. And how does a once-upon-a-time-revolutionary die a dentist? Gone back home to his parents, I suppose. Like so many of the rest of them.[λ] Old nests. Prodigal lambs. But with conditions. Church wedding, shiny shoes, striped ties, Sunday meals, clean nose. A lawn. A decent citizen will display a lawn as a flag. Trimmed, rectilinear, straight-bordered and devoid of FOREIGN organisms. Neither animal, vegetable nor mineral. O, perfectly contained, perfectly gaping ecosystem.[μ] So lawn then, and church, shoes, also nose. One more condition. Dental school. Afterwards it's buy a drill, a chair and insurance. Ten or twelve years in a Pigafetta practice. Until suddenly: Antonio Pigafetta. Suddenly. No cause of death. Which is always an indication. Of something. Hence the coroner's inquest.[ν] The closed casket. Murder? Who? Why? Why indeed! A thousand patients. Ten thousand motives. The drill, the taste, the needle twisting around in your gums, the drill, mercury fillings, checkups, the brushing lectures – down from the gums, never up nor across – the drill, flossing for blood, the frozen drool-face, and the drill.[π] And sooner or later root canals. What patient, given half a chance, wouldn't? What dentist does not deserve it?[ρ] If it wasn't accidental, a slip of the drill, straight through his neck, up into the brain. Or disease. The blood, day after day, splattering up into his face. Volumes of foul breath, germ-laden. If not an accident or disease, a patient certainly. The chances. That one among them... And the revolution? Forgotten? Did you count the years? Tracts, organizing, late nights plotting for the new world, did you march your lungs through the streets, under the nightsticks. And the tenements of hunger outside the pink-skinned suburbs? Skeletal caravans trekking across African deserts? Rag-horses begging for scraps with their backs against the shop windows? Gun-toting children at each other's throats?[σ] Where were you? Did a dentist sometimes catch a glimpse of his shame gnawing at the tiny mirrored instrument as he removed it from the golden mouth of privilege? Shall we ask a closed casket? Too late. Not to mention too little. A small blackened square in the newspaper of deliverance. Beloved husband. Loving wife and child. So that too. Drilling teeth by day and home to the family, the supper table, television, a game of parcheesi, Mother Goose, rinse and spit and to bed. The whole works. Not to mention the lawn. Entirely Green. And devoid. Of foreign organisms. A man is always considered forewarned. All right, good for him. A lot of good it did him. Dead. Drilled. Frozen stiff : :

ANTONIO PIGAFETTA

Suddenly. In loving memory. Beloved husband, loving father. Assorted pets. Large, sunny six-bedroom home. Oil and gas. Fireplace. Kitchen island. Convenient for commuters. Perfect lawn: rectilinear, green. No dandelions, clover, or crab grass. No birdweed, fireweed, chickweed, milkweed, knotweed, pigweed, pokeweed, stinkweed, tumbleweed, ragweed, smart- or locoweed. No scarlet pimpernel. No thistle, burrs, chicory, horsetails, buttercups, or lady's thumbs. No prickly lettuce, beggar's ticks, shepherd's purse, spotted spurge or skunk cabbage. No quackgrass. A dentist. Drill, chair, many tiny sharp prodding and poking instruments, a host of clean stainless steel imagery. Grateful patients. Frozen in grief, drooling sentiment. Services, following coroner's inquest, at Saint Somebody-did-something-to-someone Church. Closed casket : :

α A man who dies a dentist is a dentist forever more.

δ Doors are a cause for wonderment.

ε O, let it rest.

φ Not to mention sexual relations.

γ Are you still at this? Yes, and in a sweat.

η Here some advice: before washing that face in your host's sink, check for a towel you dare to use, i.e. neither too clean nor too dirty.

κ More precisely, we were seated on the throne and reading, prior to putting them to another purpose, the blackened pages of a newspaper.

μ There is, needless to say, no lawn or grass at all on the twenty-second floor.

ν A coroner is a failed policeman. I mean the policeman of failure.

π And must you go on like a peddler?

ρ Karet: excision, premature death. A divine punishment for one of the thirty-six serious transgressions.

σ Today mad scorpions tearing away at each other; tomorrow they'll tramp your blood all over your deep-piled carpets and pristine sheets.

λ And what about him? We are all subsidiary judges, each of us doing his or her job and, while doing his or her job, thinking I am only doing my job. Each one greases a small wheel. A dentist may wash his hands before and after every patient. How should we act in a symphony of delicate power?

BARAITA

Those of us who say the Torah is not from heaven. Those of us who interpret the word of the Torah in a way contrary to the halakhah. Those of us who profane the covenant inscribed in the flesh. Those of us who profane the holiness of the sacrifices. Those of us who disdain the half-holidays. Those of us who say the whole Torah comes from heaven, except this deduction, except this *a fortiori*, or this proof by analogy. Those of us who have the opportunity to study the Torah and do not do so. Those of us who study the Torah, but only from time to time. Those of us who cause the face of their fellow to pale with shame.

All these have no share in the World to Come: even if they know the Torah and have performed charitable deeds, all these have no share in the World to Come : :

And to have come all this way, only to discover I have no idea what your excrement looks like. Am I an eschatological dog to go snooping in the mystery of someone else's turdificatory[α] exploits? We were speaking of the body, the thing itself. The ideal is moderate in size, well-rounded and firm. I mean, the better to go swooshing to oblivion.[δ] In such a case, there was and is no cloud or sense or lack. And yet. Not yet. Not everything is in our power. Who is so fortunate, and how many among you? Those happy few may be an overwhelming majority, and you may count yourself among them. In which case, this, I mean my preoccupation, cannot possibly enter your mind (a fiction perhaps) – to produce, on a regular basis, such excellent excrement. A Halakhah for the Time of the Messiah? Do not say there is no difficulty. This is the difficulty. For such is unfortunately not my case. In my solitude. And therein lies the anticipation.[ε] Tant pis pour moi. He asked: what is the novelty? He considered the eating habits of those rosy-faced people.[φ] One's complexion is evidence of something. Perhaps he was not alone in suspecting he was not alone. Let us say or shall we say: we are nevertheless, in our suffering, always alone? Here we did not intend a soteriology. Indeed, perhaps you cannot possibly think so. Perhaps I am altogether alone in thinking we are altogether alone. What is there seated between a door and the self? Shall we count and compare and contrast digestive ailments? To add what? Not only this but also this. The order of things to come (and go).[γ] What cause lay at the root of his intestinal dilemma? Or in that general area. Let us say, in his youth he'd fallen prey to a surgeon who had specialized in mutual funds.[η] Ascribe this to this. If there was a connection, it was severed. The event which happened, happened that way. What now? O happy group, healthy defecators. He cannot count himself among them. As for my case. A constant source. A rare commodity. A general turgidity is a brackish phlegm.[κ] Who mentioned its name? And mine too, for that matter. A return in turbulence of fine greenery. A suspension. In measured amounts. What is it? A mistake : :

The truth is not satisfied with people. On the other hand, I may not be looking for it. Is there a refusal to pursue the mystery of the Other?[λ] And why do people want it? The mystery I mean, not the other. Is this desire to share our pain a generosity? Not everything is in our power. One labours under the weight of one's options. Are you saying that? A Cartesian invention of mind. We produce a fiction, call it "I".[μ] It may be necessary to make it happen. When? Daily. In the early morning. In order to get out of a bed. Hence: boys, dentists, grocers. And we discuss the colour of our water. This itself is difficult. Meanwhile, what does a Cafgu do? And to whom? I mean the horrors in the elsewhere. The other on the nightly news. Suppose they were to trade on it, the horror I mean. Nickel-and-diming the West. Luminous assistance. In the East, a vampire goes about his chores. The victims are trying. Trying the West. On grants. We call it Assistance. Can you blame them? It was their responsibility. It was our responsibility. Should we write without watching? Express this! Someone else raised the flag of fingerland.

For his part, for my part, he was silent. On Monday mornings he went out to confront the shopkeepers.[ν] He sported a visible expression. On the clothesline, he suspended a device of surrender. This is ours and this is theirs. Can we stretch a breeze? He thought: Je suis un homme malade. Is he the only one that way? They were drilling teeth in the street. This is in and this is in.[π] He sought the repose of self within self. It escaped him. What is it like? How can you find it? I have not found it. It was a local problem miraculously engaged. Abundantly murky. He abandoned the impatience of miracle. Unfolded a dispersion. But the body reminded him and the difficulty returned to its place.[ρ] The difficulty of sometimes. This is one thing for another. But what then? Now that we have come to this. People remark. Some say. Others admit. Some admit others. But rarely. Try as he might, he could not accept their smell. Perhaps we settle an accommodation. A way of speaking orders a place at the inn. We only resemble each other[σ] : :

α This word is free.

δ Down-river, think of their drinking water.

ε The nature of this case is not like the nature of this case and the nature of this case is not like the nature of this case.

φ After lunch, are we not grammatically complete?

γ Down-river, into their drinking water.

η They cannot, will not, cure an ailment without a name. First they must discover the disease; even then a cure is not so frequent.

κ What did you see?

λ One belongs to the Messianic order when one has been able to admit others among one's own. That a people should accept those who come among them – even though they are foreigners with their way of speaking, their smell – that a people should give them an akhsaniah, the wherewithal to breathe and to live… Simple tolerance? God alone knows how much love that tolerance demands.
E. Lévinas *In the Time of the Nations*

μ He made a proper mess of a common name. Still, he restored the device in an instance of such.

ν They add and subtract and expound.

π He lay in the trees. Fear branched out. His throat whistled in December.

ρ I meant that literally until it cried out.

σ We are all talking lions of lack of understanding.

Whittling. This is the difficulty (struggle): to be released from subsidiary judgment.[α] What discretionary power remains? And over whom? Each of us having been convicted and sentenced at some higher level. Perhaps we are relieved to speak so few languages. And yet. Subsidiary judges we may be; but judges just the same. This, referring to each of us doing his or her job and, in doing his or her job, thinking each of us merely does his or her job.[δ] They say in the West, this one greased a small wheel. Squatted with rolled sleeves to wash anonymous linen by the well. Entertained the troops. Polished the stock exchange. The way of things. How should we act in a symphony of delicate power?[ε] As for him, let us say he languished in some less than central place. There is no question: shall I participate? We can learn but not refuse. Who speaks the seventy-one languages of the nations? To sit in judgment? Go ask the mystagogues. These are the ones who are strangled. These are the ones who are cut off. These are the ones who are burned. Perhaps you cannot possibly think so. Perhaps you are thinking the strength of leniency is preferred. In the West they laughed at it. The quality of mercy is a pedestal upon which we have made a comfortable seating arrangement. A fiction, a mistake. We who have learned elsewhere. This aspect is not like that aspect, and that aspect is not like this aspect. And yet. Not yet. He whittled away at his own subsidiariness.[φ] He said, I prefer not to. Was there absolution in retraction? Perhaps you cannot possibly think so. Still conscious (and red-faced) of his needless size. He was a noun. Whittling, a definition. There cannot be a half. And yet. Not yet. Surely there is a bottom to every order. I mean a place to reside. Let discomfort comfort us. Yes and no and it was unsteady in his hand. Washing. Where is the bottom if there is no top? Where is the centre if there is no edge? We are all subsidiary judges. Foot soldiers. Hence the handwashing compulsion. The addition and also the subtraction. The whittling ::

α Who removed Tannaim from the world?

δ See how he trudges through enormous language…

ε They were drilling teeth in the street.

φ This word, too, is free on all sides.

אישתיק

On that day, he lay awake all night. On the cold side of the window, across the canyon of cars, fear gusting in the branches. What kept him in bed? Cramps. Until hunger, even so, broke through the surface of the pain. A ragged this way goes. To dress is already a gesture of acceptance. The teeth (those few that remain)[α] of dawn gnawing at his hunger. Things from which benefit is forbidden. Those beautiful early figs. Why forbidden? Every orchard knows its owner. The possibility of exact measurement. In measured amounts. So that to steal requires dedication. Act, deed, event, precedent.[δ] But figs. Two?! Why do I need two? He teaches an exaggeration. In either case, no matter what. What did you see? A fig. Is it necessary? We must walk before we can pluck. It is not all in his power. Was there hypotyposis? If there is a difficulty, this is the difficulty. It is a case of go, read it in the teacher's house. Just as in. They object. Practical difference. Must he really go on reckoning like a peddler? To steal a fig. Since he took the first part, he took the end as well. It is possible to refute. It is not right that.[ϵ]

α He brushed them.

δ Those reviews were all bad.

ϵ Hear from this, learn from this, conclude from this.

A house without figs, or bread and butter, is Monday morning. It was necessary to go out, to confront the shopkeepers. The banners of surrender hanging in the yard, the clothesline's loonish cry, the breeze stretching, yawning, rubbing up against his ankles. All this for a loaf of bread. I am speaking figuratively. No mute imperative driving him across the country to find his mother. I have not yet begun to leave the house. The list. Because, in the street, or in the shop, there is no taking hold of the details. There are the mouths gaping, the beast of the other. Armpits. Eye-to-eye. How can remembrance operate? So, a list. Detail and generalization. Think beneath the moment. And shoes. And a comb. A glance in the mirror, the sudden return of the difficulty (myself). He donned a coat and a scarf. Not necessarily in that order. He checked the pockets for his keys. He slung the bag of books over his shoulder. He opened the door. Forgot the list. Stepped into the hallway. Repulsive eternity swims there. The shock of world beyond

∵

All is not assemblable.

E. Lévinas
In the Time of the Nations

Something learned from its end. But why a movie? And a European film to boot. Godard, his Red Period, or Bergman, his Grey (is that over yet?). On that evening of all evenings? (Why is this night different?) To spend your last fistful of coins on one hundred minutes of moving pictures. To enter the theatre knowing that you'll emerge, with no place to go. Your ears full of their banter. He should have been looking. Out there. For what? Shelter. For the night, at least. O yes, blissful youth. Sweetly stupid sixteen. And yet. Because of the others, his friends, those who might be willing to help him. A fistful of their pocket money. Or perhaps take him home for the night. The living room sofa. In the other room: someone's mommy and daddy. Whispering: What can we do a shame the parents his hair is he drugged and what about his mother talk to our Tony in the morning the police nature or nurture when i was a boy Antonio what's that noise what are you up to but we can't forbid it these days such a shame darling where did you leave your wallet?

He could have asked. He did not ask. The opportunity did not present itself. Before the film. And why not? Because they were all jostle and joke. They bantered. They vied for seats. From the balcony, a restless cheer, a delicious anticipation. The incongruity of his situation. Ridiculous. Syllables knocking up against the back of his teeth. Too big to spit out. Dissolving into shapeless, powdery pops and clicks.[α] And then, as we came out of the darkness of the cinema into the darkness of the street. They were all going to take the bus back to their beds. In that district of eyeless houses. He had recently lived there too. A grasshopper. In the interminable present.[δ] Whereas now. Whereas he. Whereas I. This is the difficulty. Was going to walk along the boulevard, cut through the park, downtown to the student ghetto. Why go back there? His keyless pockets. Rather than another place? Because, though the doors were locked, they were familiar. And yet. Not yet. A familiar door, when locked, is so much more closed than a strange one. Still, the ghetto. In the darkness, outside the cinema, a presentiment: the rest of his life, an unrelenting string of disasters, patiently lined up at the door. He could not speak. They were leaving, starting up the street to the bus stop. It was already too late. ~~He would have sobbed, but the terror of the sudden realization of his solitude froze the tears.~~ Let us have a touch of self-restraint. Forsake the melodrama of the movies. And yet. Might we not, just this once, beg the reader's indulgence? Perhaps you cannot possibly think so. Not yet. Hearing talk of books, movies at the instant of your ruination. Brilliant conversation. Suddenly irrelevant. Insulting even. In the face of your. At the moment of bending your knees with your back to the electric chair[ε], you overhear the executioner and the chaplain discussing which restaurant for lunch, the pub in the square or that new place just opened on the boulevard, nice review in the papers. Was that the worst of it? Not yet. And yet. Make no mistake, he despised them. How he despised them. Momentarily, I mean. And, really, for a long time afterwards. To be perfectly Beckett, he would despise them the rest of his life. Why? For not guessing? For their solidity? And yet. The worst of it, yes, let's have the worst of it. Knowing that, only weeks ago, he too, his tongue wagging in his ears, would have fingered a bus ticket and argued the meaning and merits of a movie. Comparison and contrast. Exegesis. The usual references: being and baby carriages. I have forgotten the name of the movie.

מתני

They were gone. He was walking through the park. And true understanding[φ] fell from the trees onto his head. One's situation, the definition of homelessness, the doors closed behind, the darkness ahead, the taste of broken syllables. It will strike below the solar plexus. A mixture of fear and ~~self-pity~~ rushes to the head. Did he cry? Let us say he did. But soundlessly. Even then, his self-image. One stands outside one's own body, watching, narrating in the preterit past. As though it were. What? Yes, exactly. A movie. There was but one thing to do. I mean. He could think of only one thing to do. Though he tried for something better. I am still trying for something better. Less demeaning. More worthy. Of what?[γ] Is that ridiculous? And yet. He tried. That other thing. He did not find it. I have not found it : :

α But why a movie? To forestall his destitution. The initial moment of homelessness. Or harbouring vague hopes? Or something else. Just rubbing up against their solidity, the solidity of their lives. Which had recently been his own.

δ Under the sign of the irrevocable. It was already too late. The moment he'd stepped out the door of the parental home. Hot-headed, irrevocably committed, proud. And now? No, no regrets. That decision was irreversible. Because of his pride. Not to mention the ease with which they had let him go.

ε The event after which nothing will ever be the same again.

φ Occurring both too soon and too late; occurring too soon to be understood, understood too late to be recovered.

γ There is something that cannot be said.

What about sex? Did they do it? Often? Oral? Was it furious? Did she sometimes ride, ride to joy? Did he slide up against her back, in the night, both of them only half awake, and slip inside her. A dream of luscious milk. In the bathroom, they were both brushing their teeth. Did he finger a moan? Curl a tongue-sweet apparatus round her beading pearls. Was it hard, hard, so hard? Perhaps you cannot possibly think so. Pigs, money, leprosy. And what about the night in question (he bore his needless size, his barely incubated lust) in spite of everything, did they have sex that night? In silence. In rancour.

Nothing better. To go back. She had abandoned her lease. A test? If he had been staying on only because. It was better than the streets. Or his parents. A test. Perhaps he'd get a job. Find some money. She'd gone. To stay with friends.[α] The ones that did not like him. Spending the evening fanning suspicions she already harboured. She had uttered. In the midst of their argument. That he had, in some way, taken advantage of her hospitality. And even supposing it had been only a momentary lapse, which she immediately regretted. So she said. Even supposing when he found her, she were to retract that accusation. Still he would never. Forgive her. Because. Deep down. How deep?[δ] How much depth could there be? Not that much. He suspected. He suspected her suspicions were justified. At least in part. That he had stayed with her because. Not that she would have put herself in his place. For one moment. Her parents back in was it Boston or Saskatoon? The cheques first Monday of every month. Enough. He would have to swallow his pride,[ε] ring the doorbell, slink past her friends and crawl. Into her bed. For the night. He did not want to. Do it. He wanted the other thing. Which he could not find. And yet. He could not find it. And, for that also, he would never forgive her.

אשם תלוי

α Akhsaniah, a place to lie down.

δ If there is a difficulty, this is the difficulty.

ε A proper noun is not a place. Will your map offer shelter from the rain?

And so on and so on. In retrospect. Yes, let's have a little retrospective. A touch of perspective. Merely a hint of the introspective. In retrospect, then.[φ] Soon. Not the next day. He was alright again. A room, a bit of money. How? I can't remember. Busing tables? A drug deal? Perhaps he moved in. Someone else. In any case, not the street. Not yet. And yet. Later much later he realized. The intuition in the park, the presentiment. His life, a stack of disasters wound and ready one by one to reel off his future.[γ] All of it. To the last detail. Absolutely. Accurate. That life was already ruined. In the darkness after the darkness. In the movie after the movie. And nothing. He could do. Or fail to do. Could make it. Any worse : :

φ Ce n'était qu'un mauvais moment à passer.

γ Strange pagan kenoticism, to humble oneself without reason, to take on the rags of poverty and solitude.

α The voice punctuates. It is a bell. Ringing. It requires a body. History. Bad memories. Howley. A Welshman. Long ago. Too late, having lifted the receiver, to retreat.

Hello, he said, and after all these years.[α]

So be it, I replied.

And still, does the you I am thinking of remain you as I speak to the you I am speaking to, or do you remain you?

If you prefer.

And the me you might recall, does it remain me?

Here a suspension. I held my tongue between my knees.

Shall we say when he returned a phone call? I mean a comma there. When he returned (the shopkeepers, they wipe their pinkish hands), a phone call. That is. Returned first, then the call. He did not return a call. Would not have. Not ever. And yet, there is no chronology in a sacred text. But punctuation. And a punctum. The phone punctuates. It is a chink. It rings. Menace fills the room. A bird cage from time to time, it will encircle the heart. How does it ring? Does it bring you to your feet? There is no fleeing in one and a half rooms. First, fear. A pause. Then longing. The outside calling. Who? A list. Of possibilities. (Those of us who cause the face of their fellow to pale, ce thon blanc entier, mon semblable.) But the call. He may pick up. Sometimes. What decides if he will answer? The fear. The longing. To stop the ringing. There was conversation. At least on the part of the party of the first part. There was response and suspension. And if it is your wish to hear? : :

Is there no memory?

None that I cherish.

Did you read? Did you hear? Did you know? That man, Pigafetta, is dead.

Drilling teeth.

δ Money, pigs, leprosy.

But what kills a dentist?[δ]

A very heavy stone?

In the newspaper, some things remain unsaid. Well, I say, the event which happened happened that way. There was no accidentist. Hear from this, learn from this, conclude from this. I tell you, he was not the first. (Here some names, perhaps two, no, more, dimly recalled. A list of tombstones).[ε] In either case, no matter what. And the common denominator is. (Here, something about the old days.) And if it were a case of the four deaths of the Bet Din? Those sixties. Our rebellious youth. Our engagement. Commitment. A cause. The teleology of revolution. Were we so young? Now this? In the beginning we were few, now we are few again. And which of us will be next?

ε Shall we say, a clue? They were all three – the caller, the one who regretted having answered his phone, the dead man called Pigafetta – once, in their youth, together in a group, radical, left-wing, revolutionary. Go ahead, laugh, those days were full of hope, where were you?

(There was some time to think here. And he tried. He thought, something learned from its end. Act, deed, event, precedent. There was remembrance of something. This is not from the same name. This aspect is not like that aspect, and that aspect is not like this aspect. He teaches an exaggeration.)

We interpret beginnings.

A sign of age advancing, you say? The glancing at the obituaries? Death introducing himself. But when death comes without footnotes, how do you understand? There was and is a cloud or sense of lack.

And is there nothing else?

Which is a reason for calling. The telephone is an instrument of convenience, not to be squandered on the living. We should meet flesh to flesh in each other's presence.

And is it necessary?

And so to reverberate our fears and mount a tension worthy of release.

(Here, once again, a suspension.)

Shall we say in the alley behind that pub on Saint Somebody-did-something-to-someone Street?

Why not rather, and more appropriately, in the garden by the gate?

(Here a date and time were mentioned.)

(And a promise was made; nevertheless, with not the slightest intention to honour it) : :

היכי נעביד

There was no telephone. How could there be?[α] What else did he leave out that he left this out? Chant on suit away as in. But back to work. Already a minute into injury time. Let us peel away fifty yards downfield. We stopped paying for that telephone long ago. A letter then. The postal system, occasionally graceless to the point of ridicule, delivered him from the quiet repose of evil. A man with thick calves, a sac of correspondence. When he returned then, a letter. A Frigidaire of words.[δ] Repulsive eternity swims in a tongue-sweet apparatus. A thousand elaborately lathered lies in a dream of luscious milk. That can of tuna, mon semblable, the loafing bread, a monkey fist of bananas. He sat down to drink a cup of water. And to open the letter.[ϵ] Trying to think beneath that moment, we trudge amidst enormous language. The French had reinvented corner-flanking. A miraculous disengagement from the specificity of the local. We are digging it very close to the game line. The letter conveyed what he already knew. Recalling a death notice he'd noticed in the news. A high ball. Wales is sluggish by comparison. We had the phone call (it never happened), shall we now have the letter? Spare us such re-presentation. The gist of it then. Gist is a hard candy to suck on. That man Pigafetta, the dentist, dead. In a pool of his own murky circumstance. Better work there, Howley took it further. A slight wheel makes life easier for the runners. Well, the Welshish writer, appalled, uneasy, suspects and calls attention to the Common Factor (not the mailman). Let us be clear. What is he trying to tell us? Because this is important. To the story. To move the ball forward. In front of the posts. Pigafetta was not the first. To die. Others lay headstones to point the way. To plot points. These are the ones who were executed: Legrand, Mustapha, Betty Boop. Pigafetta. Just as there, so here too. All within a fortnight, however long that is. If an epistolarian surmise may make a calculation. The Common Factor therefore (no, not the mailman): all these dead having been members of the same group. Not to mention the one with whom we are engaged in epistolary intercourse. Shall we follow his mummy's lead and call him Howley?[ɸ] Act, deed, event, precedent. Come on, Howley, have a go now. Deep into the French 22. He'd got three caps and a good thumping as a Swansea forward. To what group did he refer? There was no need, nor is there now, to name it. Sexual relations, money, pigs, leprosy. We may have forgotten.[γ] Here's a lengthy line of prose to draw us off the scent, wet, dungish and panting, penned zoography, the heart of the menu in waiting. Shall we say: like? A simile is always a bend in the road. Let us simply agree, it was: Long ago. Those sixties (late) again. Be hind and run. This century barely over is a pain in the neck. Thirty years? Why not say so?[η] Are we counting? Quick, lend me your toes. As though we could agree on an order of numbers. Howley standing at the factory gate. Is that where we recruited him? 29–nil with four Frenchmen waiting there. Perhaps you cannot possibly imagine imagining so much possibility to change the possibilities. In the world. Rome the wicked. We can learn but not refute. Deduce from it and leave it in its place. Were crimes committed? Dust. A hint of transgression. Thirty-nine categories of labour.[κ] Those beautiful early figs where are they? We were all a blind man and a cripple. Howley's gone forward. Plans were hatched. To overthrow a state of torpor. How many grey cells of secrecy lay actively in waiting? The answer: so pinkly few as to be not worth mentioning. Must we go on peddling?[λ] It's Wales' throw. Move the ball! I mean, the epistolary intercourse. The fucking letter. Howley got a hand to it.[μ] Howley with the pickup. He was one too. And Pigafetta. In charge of agitation.[ν] Howley, Welshish and working, ergo proletariat. Agitate. Propagate. Let us have a lethal finisher. To solve from this. A hint. They were ardently few, they wrote leaflets. Arise. But no one did, and they did damage mostly to each other.[π] What was left destroyed itself. Years later, they were dying. The dentist. Legrand, Mustapha, Betty Boop. Not necessarily in that order. Did Howley, having darkened a white sheet, expect a reply? He wanted a meet (Howley's words). A verse does not depart from its literal meaning. Pschat. A place, a time, dark, late. For what purpose? To strangle me with Welshly words? On Saint Something-done-to-someone Street? That Howley was an oneiropompist. And I, an insomniac. Furthermore. Nothing more : :

α Did we merely amuse ourselves with a page of conversation? Perhaps you cannot possibly be so amused.

δ If he put the mail in among the vegetables, it was not to keep it fresh, but rather to remain a moment longer in the repose of the self within itself.

ϵ Who mentioned this item which is being cited now as if it had already been mentioned?

ɸ When two subjects are juxtaposed in a single verse, the two are linked by hekeish: the laws of one are applied to the other.

γ Here a suspension and an elenctic. A trace of the unrecognizable.

η One prefers to wipe the pinkishness of youth from the brow. Not wishing to appear so pinkly foolish.

κ Did they write pamphlets? March behind banners? Spray paint on the porous surface of a wall? Mix oil and gasoline? Did they commit minor acts of terror? Smuggle their arms and legs and the limb from a living animal? Whose papers were falsified?

λ Any plot forks. Next, he will be telling tall tales of rebel girls and boys.

μ Did you explain it so much? Here support, analogy. Merely reveal something. Soon.

ν Agitation of what? A good stiff drink? I meant the masses. The centrifugal proletariat.

π Ils ont été plusieurs mois dans les plates-bandes de Gethsemane. Car après mai suivent toujours septembre et juin. Not necessarily in that order. There were hazamak and zomemin and fingers pointing. Nine ways to execute.

When the revolutionary soteriology died, he sought to attenuate. We are pleased to worship sausage. Meanwhile, the French had reinvented corner-flanking. We call it theory. He plunged that way, his reticulated life a very heavy stone. Trudged through enormous language. I do not doubt we're into injury time. He took revenge on language, brandished a savage solecism. The slight wheel makes life easier for the runners. Attenuate was a momentary tactical overhead. And is there nothing else?[α] Things from which benefit is forbidden. And is there nothing else? Those damned oneiropompists did their worst. In measured amounts. He awakens too early in that damp tee-shirt to change the world, the way of things. Since he took the first part, he took the end as well. He learned to take long walks proleptically. He learned to be silent. The body, the thing itself. And is there nothing else? He said his own. The grocers. They subtracted and added and expounded. Le visage de l'autre. The question, the difficulty returned to its place. And he to his. Here a colon: I mean the punctured organ, not the organic punctuation. He produced the best possible excrement. It was less than perfect. A Halakhah for (the Time of) the Messiah? And since we have come upon it, now that we have come upon it, now that we have come to this. In the afternoon a nap. Then a shower and a walk. From this it is impossible to learn anything. Let us say, when he walked he imagined the Hassidim, curling darkly in that neighbourhood (where they were barely tolerated). I did not mean he imagined the Hassidim,[δ] rather he imagined they were his brothers, because in the city where they walked they were invisible. Or too visible. Apart (though their children are as badly behaved as yours). He too, in his own difference, and distantly related after all, felt a kinship, although, had he not been invisible to them (as indeed he was), they would certainly have despised him. Why? : :

α Some of us have the required food, a roof over our heads, not to mention that Brechtian bar of soap. And yet. Not yet. How shall we describe the ensuing cultural production?

δ They were forever walking to and from their temples.

תנאי שקלת מעלמא

Apikoros. Because he was Apikoros. And if his ox gored one of theirs, would there be liability? In their minds? Now a revolutionary soteriology has died, is there nothing else? There was no way back. As of then, I mean. Hence now and forever more. Well no, not the finality of the infinitality of forever. Rather, here and hereafter. Or thereafter. Here and there, now and then, henceforth and thereafter. From that day forward. In time forthcoming. Forthwith and posthaste and heretofore. Yes, heretofore. In the sweet by-and-by. Or perhaps, but. Yes, finally, but, after all. But there was no way back there. He considered the options. Or lack thereof. Ringlets, a black hat and/or dialectical materialism. Nor could he find a way forward. Hence the French flanking. To keep the thing in your hand, having lost its name. And what of the others? Perhaps you cannot possibly think so. Gone home to theirs. The suburban condiments. Won't you please sit down. Try one of these. Dentistry. Or, in Howley's case, less. Could he blame them? No. There was a general lack of hills. Sierras. No grottos. But did he? Blame them? Nevertheless. Yes. In his own case, no one was buying. He turned to French. But his, like Howley's before, a Cuthean conversion, under threat of lions, hollow. Howley's lions prowling in the reactionary night. There were suburbs. And dentists. And Howley. Roofing. Terracing. Landscape gardening. Green thumbs, dollars and sense. A truck, a ladder. Howley roofed. Roof, Howley, roof. Howley terraced. And gardened. With his hands. A jumble of teeth, fingernails, shoes. Others returned to the self. There were still several good schools. On grants from the West. Let he or she who has refused such a gift cast first that very heavy stone. Everyone's ace in the hole. Mummy. A word about mine. No terrible imperative. Betty Boop also gardened. But delicately. In green rubber boots. With red trim. And painted. Aquarelles. It calms the nerves. Occasionally she smoked a cigarette. It calms the nerves. Do sit down. Read this poem. Broken wings and artificial flowers. Legrand imported and exported. (He made a fortune in pork bellies.) Mustapha mostly imported. Money, pigs, leprosy, sexual relations. And a proper name. The past was past. A symphony of delicate power. What about me? Perhaps you are asking. Perhaps not. No cards in my hand. Suggestions? Ask Pigafetta: rinse and spit out. Try one of these. Et moi, et moi, qu'est-ce que je fais dans tout ça?[ε] : :

ε R. Barthes, *Le plaisir du texte*

Shall we say he did not go to meet Howley?[α] By the gate in that Welshish gardener's letter (there was no phone call – there was no phone). Howley? Again? Have we not killed him yet? Death is a very heavy stone. In fiction, they say in the West, any character ought to be properly introduced – won't you sit down, try one of these – before he is killed. And should we not, if we intend to kill him (a man is always considered forewarned) first erect a tent over a dead body? We interpret beginnings. But there is no earlier and no later in the Torah. Shall I allow readers to bundle down? They (she, he, myself) will accumulate attachment, there are some who say, on the layaway plan. Something that was included in a generalization, but was specified as containing a provision different from those contained in the generalization, was intended to be both lenient and strict. But does he really have to go on reckoning like a peddler? Am I a peddler? Must I go on like a peddler? Some say so. In order that death when it comes (it is coming, perhaps you cannot possibly think so. How soon? Pretty damn soon, even accounting for digression). In order that death when it comes. An accumulation of attachment discharges meaning. If this was taught, it was taught. According to the entire world. It was said thus and it was said thus. Can a fiction make a mistake? If there is a difficulty, this is the difficulty. The body, the thing itself. The letter. Any story garners meaning. Stockpiles. A story, what is it like? A grocer. This only resembles this. There cannot be a half (analogy). This is ours and this is theirs. They incline. They wipe their pink hands. A matter went out from among them.[δ]

But we were speaking of Howley. Are you still at this? A story about Howley.[ε] Shall we say he worked in that factory? It was his Welshishness drove him there. On Monday mornings. Every day was Monday morning there. His having come here as a young man in sheep's clothing. He'd got a good thumping as a Swansea forward. Now a toolmaker's darkened hands passed through the gate before the hour of the white clotheslines. He approached the gate. Four Frenchmen waiting on the 22. In front of the posts. Shall we say they were grocers? Of a sort. Selling papers. What is the difference between them. They wiped their pink hands. Called out to Howley. He peeled away fifty yards downfield. Those grocers were sluggish by comparison. They dug it very close to the game line. But did not pass through the gate.[φ] What else did he leave out that he left this out? Howley might have given them a good thumping. But the French had reinvented corner-flanking.[γ] They cast out to him. A high ball. Was it his Welshishness that made him stop? If they talked, who spoke? In Howley's Welshish English? This was Monday morning on a Tuesday. And deep into injury time. Shall we say it's Wales' throw? The reader(s) bundle(s) down. That paper is black and white and red all over. Howley got a hand to it. How long before they fired him? The factory, I mean. Shall we tell the tale of a strike?[η] His injury. Carried from the field upon the stretcher. Having scored four really splendid tries. Howley was a lethal finisher.

Perhaps the reader has already gone forward. Who carried the stretcher? Who sold Howley his first paper? Now that he's dead. What? Howley's dead? Didn't you read the obituaries? The blackened pages. After the body of the letter. In Howley's blackened hand. Which mentioned Pigafetta. Legrand, Mustapha, Betty Boop. Howley took it further. A meeting. Who did not go? Having no interest in a mystagogy. No sleuth in you.[κ] Only the slightest curiosity. The slight wheel makes life easier for the runners. Enough to buy a newspaper from time to time. A lazy bread, a can of tuna, mon semblable. Bananas. So brief – and yet so disconcerting. And Howley's name. A week later, these are the ones who are strangled, in the park by the gate. Who stood by a gate to sell a red paper? Because: parles-y toi, en anglais. Those pinkish hands. Inclined. That was long ago. There is no before and after in the Torah. Before and after the strike, they fired Howley. We are already deep into injury time. Now he's dead, shall we say who recruited Howley to that pinkish group of which we are not speaking? Who did not go to the meeting? What else did we leave out that we left this out? It was necessary for this to be said, otherwise it might have occurred to you to ask[λ]::

אלו הן הנחנקין

α Remembrance of something.

δ A story teaches not only this but also this. To add what? The nature of this case and the nature of this other case is not like the nature of this first case.

ε Is it necessary? The event that happened happened that way.

φ It is easier for a rich man to pass through the eye of heaven than for a Marxist to enter the factory gate.

γ We call it theory.

η We struck that tale?

κ Death is the mystery of the other person.

λ Therefore, behold, I will bring evil upon the house of Jeroboam, and will cut off from Jeroboam him that pisseth against the wall, and him that is shut up and left in Israel, and will take away the remnant of the house of Jeroboam, as a man taketh away dung, till it be all gone.
I Kings 14:10

Death was the mystery of the other person. There was no reaching in or reaching out. He recognized his murderous solitude. Howley's death was a respite. Not having gone to meet him. A debt was cancelled. There was no longer Howley, the other, waiting. There was silence in both ears. He played the radio. He returned to the safety of the self. The other was destitute. There was no future where the future is the future of he who is always yet to come. In the face of mystery, he had fallen back on craft, on ruse, the tactics of war. He did not seek mystery. Mysteriosophy hung from the end of Howley's nose. He sought instead to deepen the notion of a solitude. He considered the opportunities that time offers to a solitude. What is the place of a solitude in the general economy of being? Now he had come up against the problem of death, he found his solitude had shifted from a problem of being. His solitude found itself bordering on the edge of a mystery. A relationship without relation, an insatiable desire. The proximity of the Infinite. Before the death that was mystery and not necessarily nothingness, he turned away. This perpetual disorientation was responsibility.[α] One fears murder more than death. The beyond from which a face (let's say Howley's) comes signifies a trace. The trace of the Other : :

α ...it is toward a pluralism that does not merge into unity that I should like to make my way and, if this can be dared, break with Parmenides.

E. Lévinas
Time and the Other

One can exchange everything between beings except existing. Shall we try insomnia? Here, an account of the night. Insomnia was a consciousness that it would never finish. A vigilance without end. No longer any means of withdrawing from the vigilance to which he was held. A vigilance without possible recourse to sleep. The present renewed nothing. The present is not a dream. Always the same present or the same present endured. He considered a notion of being without nothingness, leaving no hole and permitting no escape. He would have bathed in Cratylus's river, but he could not find it even once. Consciousness was the power to sleep. He turned away from the past. He received nothing from the past. He turned away from the future.[α] What remains? Mystery. Death. Howley's. Not to mention his own. A solitude had something in its power. He occupied himself with himself. Une demi-baguette, the used bookstore. The elevators. Two?! Why do I need two? Ce thon blanc entier, mon semblable. Those bananas. Disconcerting, because fisted. A newspaper. The Black column. Upon which he sought not to glance. Out of curiosity. The temptation of mystery. Not to mention murder. Beginning to be was (and is) a heavy stone. Whereas. Solitude is an absence of time. Yet one buys oneself a watch : :

α To dress is already a gesture of acceptance.

He sought a consolation. He returned to the asylum of self. He had not moved toward the other, because, once he moved, he knew there would be no return to the self. You wanted Ulysses; you got Abraham. (With Abraham, there was no return.) What would Howley have told him? In the garden, by the gate? What is there to say? What do you have to say? "Comment toi ici, qu'as-tu à faire? Toi, ici?"[α] The wet kiss of Gethsemane? The violence of an empty phrase. The pure and immediate ethic in the face-to-face of the Other's face. He tossed himself back into the world like a stone. There was no being there. Grain of sand by grain of sand, he had built a Sinai between them. He was done with Messianic politics. A Halakhah for (the Time of) the Messiah. He busied himself with the accomplishment of his solitude. He banished hospitality from his house. He banished language. He produced on a regular basis less than excellent excrement. He would not sleuth after a Howling death by strangulation. He would wrap his legs with the papers. (If he continued to read the obituaries, it was idly.) He would not say the event that happened happened that way. Act, deed, event, precedent. Solve this, solve that. A mystery was a small brown pigtail trailing behind its solution. From this it was impossible to learn anything::

α I Kings 19:13

Let us imagine the passage of Time. The present extending itself. Shall I take a book to confront the shopkeepers? He sold a Kantian critique of reason. Those days were gone. He would trade a Haskalah any day for a loaf of bread and bananas.[α] Howley made the local papers. Behind the not-so-burning bush. Perhaps you saw the photograph of a coroner's[δ] tent: it wore a broken cuff and a shoe. A murder of glory exacts an unconditional price. Who needs it? Whereas. A newspaper of necrology offers the economy of routine. And years ago, what of his own newspaper of theory – had he beaten such a painful press? Perhaps you cannot possibly think so. Here, a utopian window promotes some failure of narrative. For now the mystery was arising: Mustapha, Betty Boop, Legrand, the dentist (when dancing teeth – those prizes – depart, the mission of darkness volunteers). And Howley's broken cuff. Extinguished beside that not-so-burning bush. Whom are we eliminating? Murder: so full-time a word is curdling. Death, when it occurs, costs earth. Now a flat mystery threatened his underdog. Had his head provided a circumstance of evil? Perhaps you cannot possibly think so. But actions will spread. Had I escaped the deadly mystery below the photograph? Before that gate was a gang::

α A lack of knuckles is what disconcerts in a fistful of bananas.

δ That tent covered up a policeman's failure.

To return home, arms bagged, a mind full of groceries. Shall we say "only to find" and raise the spectre of narrative? In the lobby between the door and elevators (Two? Why two?!), between world and a room and a half, between the street and self, the ghost of narrative waited. His name was Giltgestalt, we called him Shtick. But no longer. Now there was money, a fortune in pork bellies. And a proper name.[α] Much longer. Which he repeated twice (and that makes three), because of my silently gaping mouth. And yet, there was no lack of recognition. In spite of the slender Armani, his hair, once red red red. An arched lip, a wink, and a periphrastic manner will incite recognition. And what left me speechless? The face of the Other. Here, in the chamber between street and self, where the lobby is a moment to begin to shed the outer skin, on the doorstep to solitude and safety.[δ] There was safety. In lack of Numbers. In a room and a half of wilderness.[ε] There was no cat. In that room and a half. Neither fish nor fowl nor fig. Dust (a hint of transgression). But sly Shtick, in the antechamber, in the shadow of Mount Sinai, my address in the palm of his hand, would shatter that half solitude. Hence Numbers. Hence my mutism. And if I say Shtick and sly, perhaps you demand a more adequate description. Perhaps you prefer to think so. Sympathy is a piano. Shall I list characteristics? Shall I say son of Shim'on or son of Re'uven? Shall we say Shtick was a Cuthean?[φ] A museum of elaborately lathered lies. A rip-off artist, a Hollywood Schindler. Perhaps you cannot possibly think so. Perhaps you say: here is something that was included in a generalization, a generalization that needs a detail. The host of truth is a verbose sheepskin. You demand remembrance of something. Something learned from its context. Story? A tale within a tale? Event, deed, precedent. And what have I done or failed to do that you should think so? Shall I resent your asking?[γ] Shall we suspend a Giltgestalt in the lobby, between world and elevator (there were two, we have already said so) to fulfill another obligation in the ceremony of fiction? To relate the border of experience? On the pretext that only he who has formed can function. Later, perhaps. For the time being, the fig has moved::

α He paid off that antonomasial mortgage.

δ When the dwelling moves on, the Levites are to take it down, and when the dwelling is encamped, the Levites are to set it up; the outsider who comes near is to be put to death. Numbers 1:51

ε A headcount in the wilderness is a list of order and control.

φ A Cuthean is a lion-inspired convert, and therefore suspect.

γ Your regime (the realistic code) is a diet of excess.

What lies between the cat and the smile? The deadly mystery beneath a manner of speaking. One who does not know how to be asked. Because to act might certainly tax you (I mean me). And why don't archives sleep? We were wringing tears of justice from the soggy rag of story. A burial plot. I too could turn to this. The tent over a dead body. A hearse for my neck. That gang waiting before the gate. Let the vanguard pour powder in the meter of indulgences. This, my weariness. Your machine (the realistic code) is a diet of excess. We all know he who won't differ will seek to mold us. Characters are already a postion, we are their structure. Any cycle is a disaster; ice, its own reward. Because a person is more or less close to herself. Que se sont-ils déjà fait l'un à l'autre? Que sont-ils donc, l'autre, le tiers, l'un par rapport à l'autre? Qu'ai-je à faire avec la justice? What was the significance of signification? Kadosh. Mais en quelle langue est-ce encore possible? Had the cost waited for an experiment? His brother was not in this world. He was not in this world. Surely his head had provided a circumstance of evil. Actions spread. And yet. There is no agent for transgression. The outcome? Darkness is one result. Now that a mystery was arising::

Shtick has unbuttoned his mouth and is tinkling words into the lobby, that space between self and world. The resident (keys, a deposit, I poured a drawer full of tears) pauses. To pause always stops to drive theories. Shall I describe the words as they? Certain descriptions confront illnesses. Those letters were the shape of seven trained seals. In the babblative absolute. He was all teeth and tongue. He was warmly warmed over, an effluence of effusion, the parents of enthusiasm. A legend of nothing. The attached illusions marched beneath a banner of sexual relations, money, pigs, leprosy. Across a frontier of ambition, what cannot a trick filter? Speeches – oh, when would my palms close? Behind him, the elevators were two columns of descending lights. Howley, he said Howley. I turned from the deadly mystery below his manner. Every incident thought this. Notice, please, I did not ask him up. An offer of shelter. Akhsaniah: a place to lie down. He paused. Those elevator doors, always one and quickly the other. I provided something like a gesture toward vigorous sympathy. Turning the corners of my mouth in the direction of the upper floors. Howley? Of course not Howley. Not for so many years. No awkward sac of leather. No orbital socks. No peeling away fifty yards downfield. No Welshish rendezvous. Perhaps you are thinking I overstated. Because one amplificatory expression after another restricts.[η] Howley, he said, Howley. And Howley became a sign for death. I produced horsey laughter. Gave him a good shrugging. I did not disarm my bags, though both my hand and I were shaken. I made an end run without the ball into a toothless elevator. Stood there gaping, awkwardly short a phrase or two. Until the accordion door – intake of breath, in this case mine – shut. Did I escape to my languorous solitude? Count the floors without a glance at an ascending light? Slip my deposit into the lock? Not if that door was already open. Not if that lock was broken. I slipped both my knees into a broken room and a half of scattered history. Now, truly, a mystery was arising[κ]::

η What did Shtick want? Some of us, in spite of everything we know about that limp and soggy rag, are trying to follow the story. Had I spoken to Howley? And if so, what had been said, not by me, of course not, of what possible interest to anyone could anything I might have sputtered be? Howley. What did Howley say? Did he mention a plot to kill him? The dentist? Legrand, Mustapha and Betty Boop? Did he lay claim to information? Surely a load of rubbish, don't you think? Of course, you do, from time to time. Think. Rubbish.

κ And shall this become abundantly clear?

Shall we say, that door was already open?[α] A broken lock will take your breath away. Inside (pause here for a suspension) one's small life is scattered about the remnants of a room and a half. The shavings of self moved from dust to dust about the room. He tried to die, but such a plot of comedy would not fit. There was a crisis of furniture, no corner from which to begin to lift the blanket of his denial. When a table lies on its side, who will tell the truth?[δ] Why not turn your back, go the other way, never to return? Those books were bent. His heart raced across a room and a half to flee the disorder of his mind. That house was a pewter therapist, any port in a storm. That once cold-hearted Frigidaire welcomed him with open arms. Underfoot: petals of dishware and vegetable matter.[ε] He imagined an excess of vengeance, but who would such ferocity benefit? He touched the remnants of what remained. He wiped his hands. Placed the towel of fortune between the ultimatum and a chair.[φ] Stepped around to the window. In the street below, a Shtick figure gliding toward the out-of-sight, out-of-mind, out-of-body. Shall we begin by reinventing order and control within a room and a half, or rather enter into the mystery of an intruder? He turned away from either task at hand, undoing the search of his enemy, and lay across the rubbled cot. Repulsive eternity had entered his room and a half. He sought to whittle that space into a cot. He wrapped his legs in the fine print of a fresh newspaper. At such times, we may seek to think beneath the moment, to forestall the event after which nothing will ever be the same again.[γ] Coming out of the darkness of the cinema into the darkness of the street, something that cannot be said. And yet. Long ago. That decision was irrevocable. Not to mention the ease with which they let him go. Family and friends. One stands outside one's body, narrating in the preterit past. Trying for something better. He could not find it. I have not found it : :

We have ransacked a row of puncheons, broken the horizontal timber in the entrance to a room and a half. Are we done with reason yet? The angles of order and control are broken. Shall you stand and gape at the dehiscent refuge of self? What has it cost to claim an experimental depth? Have you proved some desire? Shall you study Numbers and list the extent of your losses? We interpret beginnings. The possibility of exact measurement. Superfluity in measured amounts. Shtick in the vestibule of the self. Meanwhile, a broken room and a half. Can two events occur at the same time? Two!? Why do I need two? The common denominator is. There is no agent for transgression. A man is always considered forewarned. Act, deed, event, precedent. The dentist Pigafetta, Mustapha, Legrand and Betty Boop. And Owley's missing letter. Subtract and add and expound. Momentarily, you are a shopkeeper. And how do you understand something learned from its end? Those beautiful early figs, where are they? Stolen. Now we have theft, and murder, and disdain. The father of the fathers of ritual impurities. Having plunged that way, my reticulated life was a very heavy stone. I thought, I am not of this world. Mais en quelle langue est-ce encore possible? : :

Every room and a half knows its owner. The beautiful early figs, where are they? Perhaps vengeance had gained one person more after all these years. Perhaps they had stolen nothing. To steal requires dedication. And what was required of him now? Lists? Order? A restoration of right angles and proper nouns? A sergeant of vinyl? Couldn't the promise of difficulty break drama? There is no place in a proper noun, no shelter from a rain of terror.[η] He cursed those damned oneiropompists. Shall we say suddenly and propel events? Suddenly then, it came to him, in the form of a thought in writing. A letter. The H in Howley, I mean. Did he search the room and a half of remnants? To keep the thing in your hand, having lost its name? A letter is a testament to that which cannot be said.[κ] If there is a difficulty, this is the difficulty. The body of the text, and all its pleasure, was gone. The H in Owley.[λ] Had Giltgestalt poured greetings into the lobby while a single letter remained hidden beneath his hat? This is the difficulty. We wait, mendaciously in a vestibule, for a wet Gethsemanic kiss. And yet. Not yet. He did not move to search for that letter. He lay, instead, wrapped in amphibolous sheets of newspaper, and searched for the idea of Owley's missing letter.[μ] Murder. Mystery. An accumulation of meaning. Death was the mystery of the other person. And yet. There was, as yet, no sleuth in him, no mystagogical investment. No terrible imperative driving him across the countryside. Was there that fear of strangulation? No, let it come. But not yet. Let us hold off a moment longer. Time to buy yet another shtick of bread, a can of tuna (mon semblable), a newspaper. Mustapha, Legrand and Betty Boop. A dentist with too many teeth in his name. And Owley, without a missing letter. (Who recruited him with a newspaper of theory, and later refused a meeting?) All those names were drained from the margins of error. Would the skies differ without them? And Shtick was become a figure in my trembling vestibule. In a room and a half of troubled mind. The future, once long gone, now returned to the present. In that disorder of time, he recognized his murderous solitude. Neither fish nor fowl, nor fig. He turned his face from a deadly mystery : :

α A place to lie down. Akhsaniah.

δ There are no true angles in a broken room.

ε Now, the mail was truly among the bananas.

φ He trudged through enormous language.

γ Here, the image of his mother. Stretching against the clothesline and her lot in life, which was more than she received. Still (in fact, motionless in the flotsam of his embodiment), there was no terrible imperative driving him across the countryside, no pebble between his tongue and cheek. Seriously.

η In the darkness after the darkness. In the movie after the movie.

κ Here, an elenctic.

λ Ere remembrance of someting. A stick figure urrying in te street below.

μ A person who stays awake at night or walks along a road alone and thinks idle thoughts is endangering his life.
R' Chanina ben Chaninai

11b

Chapter Fifteen

Sleuth Apikoros

Maaseh Bereshit, these are the mysteries of creation; they may not be expounded in the presence of two disciples.

Perhaps the margins drained names. Perhaps you can[not pos]sibly think so. There [...] dure for a broken room lay wrapped in fresh new[spaper] underdogs barking at his hee[l] momentum of defeat impinging cot of retreat. Shall we say he pa[ssed] through the first gate, and the mid[dle] gate? But he did not pass through the last gate. I have not yet passed through the last gate. He thrust measurement to the rear of the vestibule of his daily sacrifices. This was not (but perhaps there is no need to say so) a happy occasion. Did he count his blessings before they hatched? There were seeds, and mixtures of seeds, and long tractates on courtesy. From the point of view of his cot, he piled his oaths one upon the other. He sought a consolation. He sought a consolation in the asylum of self. He was already gone from this room and a half. There might have been damages in dough and eggs, if he had been a better cook. And what was the worst thing? Murder? A broken room and a half? This was the worst thing: the broken lock on the door. For he who has formed can function behind a lock and a door in a room and a half. When newspapers serve to comfort us, sleep will not come. He would have welcomed sleep. It was not all in his power. With[out] sleep, darkness is one result. But there was no sleep. There was counting. There was Numbers. There was Giltgestalt in the vestibule of the self. There was a Shtick figure in the street. He did not search through his broken room and a half for seeds or mixtures of seeds. He lay among the broken tithes of his self and refused to consider his options. Such is the order of things. His room was a vessel of murderous solitude. Beneath the scroll of damages, there were the seeds of mystagogy. Was that the odour of one who comes and breaks, the faint perfume of urination among those (his) broken books? Would he sell them now to a shopkeeper in exchange for une demi-baguette, a fistful of bananas, so brief and yet so disconcerting? That tuna, mon semblable, qui baigne dans son huile. The Gemara does not resolve this. Let us say the odour of mystagogy and murder resembles the perfume of urination; there is familiarity, and yet, no desire to plunge. He paused, wrapped in fresh newspaper, supine on the cot of desolation, to drive theories out of the broken room and a half. But mystery is a Jew; it will seep back in and fracture definition. When his mind refused to lie down, he measured Giltgestalt against the perfume of murder and broken books. He measured the Shtick of mystagogy. The mystery of the other. The perfume of silence in the face of the Other. He imagined a murderous Shtick. A strangulation. Owley's face in the garden before the final gate. Mustapha, Legrand and Betty Boop. Pigafetta, with too many teeth in his name. There was and is no cloud or sense or lack. Shall we say he was sleuthing? Supine on a cot and a half? Perhaps you cannot possibly think so. But that was no Dupin wrapped in newspaper. There was only the bits and pieces of his broken room and a half, fresh newspapers and Owley's missing letter. What good would sleuthing do a broken room and a half? What good would sleuthing do a missing letter? No, he would not enter that gate. He was not disposed to sleuth. He sought to seek consolation in the asylum of the self. But there was no lock on that door. That door was neither tent nor curtain. That door between the vestibule and the tent of the self swung on its hinges. And murder had begun to secrete a list. He sought to refuse a library of lists. But the edge edged out of his reach and reached beyond the edge of his reach. He lay among the stems and stalks of his unwillingness to sleuth. This was not (surely there is no need to say so twice) a happy occasion. He fingered the fringes of his own death :

(not brown, a fork, a
a can of
semblable qui
(...ile) bananas
yet disconcert-
demi-baguette,
tres of rope upon
h figs were strung,
bibles (hotel rooms,
rooms, book clubs,
n basements), Schwit-
poetry in Tagalog, blue
ks, those that cannot be
ld, those I do not desire
to sell but would bring a
good price, those that will
sell by the pound, those that
will not sell today but may
one day sell again (Olyanov)
those that Poe wrote, those
I would have liked
written, tall books
adults intended
books by chi
to be ad
child

...en you take up the head count of the Children of ... in counting them, they are to give ... a ransom for his life, for YHWH, when they ... them, that there be no plague on them, when ... t them. (what) they are to give, everyone ... through the counting: half a ... tribution for YHWH.
Exodus 30:12–13

...y Pray look toward the heavens and count the ...tars, can you ...unt them?
...esis 15:5

8 In the order of things, shall we list our shortcomings? One who is always righteous can never accomplish the mitzvah of repentance (one of 613)

24 And again the anger of the LORD was kindled against Israel, and he moved David against them to say, Go, number Israel and Judah …
3 And Joab said unto the king, Now, the LORD thy God add unto the people, how many so ever they be, a hundredfold, and that the eyes of my lord the king may see it; but why doth my lord the king delight in this thing? This thing was counting.

Lists 2

H

e thought to think of Betty Boop, her face in the a... man's-breeches. But, as he lay on the cot of despair, th... not think thoughts he thought it ought to think. A cot what a cot thinks to think. Perhaps you cannot possibly think so. us say, thought to think Shtick Giltgestalt. Shtick was thrown out that group. If a person comes to revolution, he or she must come fr... somewhere. Act, deed, event, precedent. In this case, he came from the parking lot, which is the vestibule of guilt. Did he teach us to steal a car? Did his head provide a circumstance of evil? To steal a car, one must begin by entering the coffee shop of bigger fish to fry. For instruction(s). A fence will wear a suit and tie, and a registration for a Pontiac Sport. The key is a long flat bar between the window and your pulse. There is your head beneath the dashboard, between the steering wheel and a hard place. There are your legs across the front seat, your ankles dangling in the open door. Perhaps you deny the dignity of grand theft auto, perhaps you do. And do you deny the passage of Barrabas from robbery to rebellion? Did Pancho Villa steal horses? A Pontiac Sport is a very heavy stone. Conscious, deliberate loss. Dust (a hint of transgression). A man is always considered forewarned, if not insured. Shtick was a figure in the parking lot of the self. Did he love the smell of another man's car? And did my fingers trembling learn to jump the high wire of grand theft auto? Two thieves will climb one upon one another's shoulders and practice their craft. Blind and lame will steal an orchard of cars. One learns to take pride in one's craft. To belong came to identify the criminal. And, afterward, did we share the loot with a roaring good time?

A Shtick will appear at your door, wide-eyed, flushed, gleeful, pushing past you, and when you turn to exclaim your speechlessness, he will be un courant d'air, a backdoor breeze. At such times one can only wait for the ensuing knock at the door. Spend a half hour commiserating with his pursuer; send him away half an hour older and wiser. A Shtick will bring you the gift of warm electronics. He will take the shirt off the back of your chair. He will teach the rise and windfall, he will give us this day our daily bread. He will spend your money faster than you can steal it. He will steal and steal and steal. He is a standing suitcase. He is something that came to teach and was ultimately inferred. And what did I teach Shtick in return? Then: nothing. Later, having lost the pure joy of figs and joined a group to interpret beginnings, what did I teach Shtick? Did I teach him the politics of rage? The newspaper of theory? The tent over a dead body? The teeth of dreams? The deadly mystery below a manner? The details of a generalization. The literal meaning of a verse. The gravity of a grave thought. The trace of labour. The community of bitterness. The failure of narrative. The fringes of his own death . . .

corpse of a torn sh... tain, Owley's missin... a broken lock, his ow... tiginous silence, two ... (he would have prefe... they had broken the ot... one), two forks, two spoo... two knives (two! why do... need two?), a cup of one kind and a cup of the other, scattered sugar cubes, broken free from their geometry, the dust of his transgressions, an impression of violence vented, the broken wings of newsprint crashed across the floor of a room and a half, his own sen...nces strewn one upon the ...er in the disorder of a ...order, the flat mystery ...nger's footprint, the ... pencil of his pas... ...k and bluish ... the cookie ...assembled ...rtality, a ...y and

A

nd then (here, narrative accumulates the dust of meaning over time), wrapped in the news of the day, on the cot of despair, behind that unlocked door on its hinges, perhaps he began to find, shall we say, at least, a kind of order in disorder. For in disorder there are lists and in a broken room, there were lists of broken dreams (grief makes its own order in disorder), there were relations which, though broken, called out to be counted. Those strewn relations, the relations of things upon things, called out to be counted. And to count is to sleuth. But he would not sleuth.

The mysteries of the Maaseh Merkavah may not be expounded even in the presence of one disciple.

12a

If two generalizations are next to each other, place a detail between them and treat them as a generalization and deta... generalization. If you take hold of the... take hold; if you take hold of the s... hold. Something that was inclu... generalization, but was si... taining a provision... those conta... eraliz...

Apikoros Sleuth

« Raconter n'est-ce pas toujours chercher son origine, dire ses démêlés avec la Loi… »

R. Barthes
Le plaisir du te...

Chapter Fifteen

'n What was he recalling? The deadly mystery below the manner.

Lists 2.1

If a thief join the vanguard, his skills become the people's skills. Shtick rode the horse of charm into the enemy camp. He made himself useful. He moved in certain circles and reported back on the angles of power to the triangular resistance. Those boys listened to him. He strung figs along a rope of information. But a Giltgestalt will follow his own counsel; though he will follow orders also, to a degree; he will take a drink, now and then, with the enemy; he will bet on the horse of charm; in a group, he will taste expulsion. And who delivered the notice of expulsion? To the one who once taught him grand theft auto and shared the loot.

ab, and the dukes of Edom were Timnah, Aliah, Jetheth, Aholibamah, Eliah, Pinon, Kenaz, Teman, Mibzar, Magdiel, Iram, and these are the sons of Isra...
..., Levi, Judah, Issachar, Zebulun, Dan, Joseph, Benjamin, Naphtali, Gad and Asher, and the sons of Judah: Er, Onan, Shelah, which three were born unto...
...er of Shua the Canaanitess, not to mention Owley's missing letter, and Tamar his daughter-in-law bare him Pharez and Zerah, and the sons of Pharez: H...
, and the sons of Zerah, Zimri, Ethan, Heman, Calcol and Dara, and the sons of Carmi: Achar the troubler of Israel who transgressed in the thing accurs...
... Ethan: Azariah, and the sons of Hezron: ... Ram and Chelubai, and Ram begat Amminadab, and Amminadab ... Nahshon prince of the ...
and Nahshon begat Salma, and Salma beg... ...gat Obed, and Obed begat Jesse, and Jesse begat El... ...mma, Nathaneel, Rac...
whose sisters were Zeruiah, Abishai, Joa... ...re Amasa, and the father of Amas... ...and Caleb the son...
...hildren of Azubah his wife, and of Jeri... ...Caleb took unto him ... Hur begat Uri, and...
...el, and afterward Hezron went in to th... ...he bare ... and three and twen...
...d of Gilead, and he took Geshur, and ... ...he father of Tek...
... Jerahmeel the firstborn of Hezron ... ...ah, she was the...
and the sons of Ram the firstborn ... ...of Shammai:...
...r, and the name of the wife of Abi... ...d died withou...
...e sons of Appaim: Ishi, and the s... ...ther and Jon...
died without children, and the s... ...Egyptian w...
...ha; and Sheshan gave his daug... ...Zabad be...
...hlal begat Obed, and Obed b... ..., and Sis...
...n, and Shallum begat Jekami... ...which was the...
...nd the sons of Mareshah th... ...Raham, the father of...
...her of the House of Usher. ...on w... ...Beth-zur, and Ephah, Caleb's...
...m Haran, Moza and Gazez ... Pelet, E... and Shaaph, and Maachah, Caleb's conc...
and Tirhanah, she bare a... ...d the father of Gibea, and the daughter of Caleb was A...
...vere the sons of Caleb ... ...arim, Salma the father of Bethlehem, Hareph the fath...
...nd Shobal the father o... ...amilies of Kirjath-jearim: the Ithrites, the Puhites, the Sh...
...e Mishraites: of them ... and the Netophathites, Ataroth, the house of Joab, and...
...ethites, the Zorites, ... Shimeathites and Suchathites, these are the Kenites th...
...h, the father of the house ... him in Hebron: the firstborn Amnon of Ahinoam the Jezre...
... Abigail ... Carmalitess, ...almai king of Geshur, the fourth Adonijah the son of Haggit...
... by Eglah ... ...em: Shimea, Shobab, Nathan and Solomon of Bath-shua, the c...
... ...gah, Nep... ...elet, these were all the sons of David, besides the sons of the c...
...mar their sister ... Abia ... ...at his son, Joram his son, Ahaziah his son, Joash his son, Amazi...
...h his son ... Manasseh ... ...son, Josiah his son, and the sons of Josiah were Johann, Jehoiakim...
...allum, ... son, and ... Jeconiah: Assir, Salathiel his son, Malchiram also, and Pedaiah...
...ah, Hoshama ... Shimei, and the sons of Zerubbabel: Mehsullam, Hananiah, and Shlomith their...
...bah, Ohel, ... Jesiah, the sons of Rephaiah, the sons of Arnan, the sons of Obadia...
...chaniah, ... Igeal, Bariah, Neariah and Shaphat, and the sons of Neariah: Elioena...
... Azrikam ... ...han, Dalaiah and Anani, and the sons of Judah: Pharez, Hezron, Carm...
..., and R... ...d, these are the families of the Zorathites, and these were of the fathe...
... Ishm... father of Gedor, and Ezer the father of Hushah, these are the sons of Hu...
...f Eph... ...wives: Helah and Naarah, and Naarah bare him Ahuzam, Hepher, Temen...
...ri, a... ...b, Zobebah and the families of Aharhel the son of Harum, and Jabez was...
...e th... bare him with sorrow, and Chelub the brother of Shuah begat Mehir, whi...
...of Esh... ...p and say to every man of Israel, with voice raised: Damned be the man wh...
...-image or mo... by the hands of an engraver, and sets it up in secret, and all the people are t...
...y: Amen! Damned be he ... people are to say: Amen! Damned be he that moves back the territory-marker of...
...nd the people are to say: Amen! ... -person in the way! and all the people are to say: Amen! Damned be he that cast...
... a sojourner, an orphan, or a widow! and ... Amen! Damned be he that lies with the wife of his father, for he has exposed the s...
... and all the people are to say: Amen! Damned be ... sister, the daughter of his father or the daughter of his mother! and all the people...
Damned be he that lies with his mother-in-law! and all t... ...e to say: Amen! Damned be he that strikes down his neighbour in secret! and all the...
Amen! Damned be he that takes a bribe, thus striking-down a li... through innocent blood! and all the people are to say: Amen! Damned be he that does...
...rds of this Instruction, to observe them! and all the people are to say: Amen! But it shall be: if you do not hearken to the voice of YHWH your God, by t...
... observing all his commandments and his laws that I command you today, then there will come upon you all these curses, and overtake you: damned...
damned be you, in the open field; damned be your basket and your kneading-bowl, damned be the fruit of your womb and the fruit of your soil, the offspr...
and fecundity of your sheep, damned be you in your coming-in, damned be you in your going-out, YHWH will send-forth against you Curse, Conf...
...ch, against all the enterprises of your hand that you do, until you have been destroyed, until you have perished quickly because of the evil of your deeds...
...ve abandoned me, YHWH will make-cling to you the pestilence, until it has finished you off from the soil that you are entering to possess, YHWH will...
...onsumption, with fever and with inflammation, with violent-fever and dehydration, with blight and with jaundice; they will pursue you until you are...
...avens that are above your head will become bronze, and the earth that is beneath you, iron, YHWH will make the rain of your land powder and dust; from...
will come-down upon you until you perish, YHWH will cause you to be smitten before your enemies; by one road you will go-out against them, by seven...
...e before them ... you will become ... the kingdoms of the earth, your carcass will be for eating for all the fowl of the heavens and for...
earth, with none to make them ... with scabs, and with itching, from which you cannot...
I will strike you with madness, ... like a blind-person feels about in deep-darknes...
...ake your way succeed; you will ... ...an you will betroth, but another man will lie...
you will build, but you will not ... ...ox will be slaughtered before your eyes, but yo...
...t, your donkey will be robbed from you in front of you, but ... given to your enemies, with no deliverer for you;...
...ur daughters will be given to another people, while your eyes look on and languish for them all the day, with no God-power to your hand; the fruit of yo...
...t-you-toil-for will be consumed by a people that you have not known, you will be only withheld-from and downtrodden all the days, and you will go ma...
...f your eyes that you see! YHWH will strike you with evil boils upon the knees and upon the thighs, from which you cannot be healed – from the sole o...

Pb

Apikoros Sleuth

Chapter Fifteen

Did a sleuth glance in the cracked mirror of his murderous solitude? Do wings gather rock? Do dogs dance? He lay perfectly still, wrapped in the time of day, and sought to escape from it. The newspapers usually do. A warm sleuth waits in comfort. If murder had waited so many years, it could wait while he aged darkly on the cot of digression. He'd parked mystery, and yet palaces burned, hordes swept across the frozen steppes of his forehead, and love slipped beneath the skirt of neglect. He could not find darkness. He toiled for sleep until the sweat gathered between his knees, and his eyelids, exhausted, fell open. He stretched to unbend, which promptly prompted some failure of narrative. Events roughly escaped. What was he recalling? Betty Boop? Who said it was love at first? She tending her garden, her face buried in the arms of a Dutchman's breeches, her ass in the air. And what about later? What comes between to exclude? There is no need to ask: why had a killer operated?

But he would not sleuth. In either case, no matter what. Betty Boop. No terrible imperative driving him across the countryside. Perhaps we are all deserving death. Guilt is a frozen dish best eaten standing alone at the counter. Are we casting one against the other? She was tending her garden, in the arms of a Dutchman's-breeches. He lay on the pea of midnight. Perfectly still, wrapped in the news of the day. Palaces burned below a deadly manner, but the archives never slept. Shall we say it was love at first? Time was to escape it. To wait was comforting, still, though he toiled, he could not find darkness. His eyelids fell open. Her ass tipped into the air. The sweat gathered between his knees. He slipped beneath the skirt of neglect. Shall we say it was love? And what about later? After the smokestack of curiosity? Later, he aged darkly on the cot of digression. Il baigna dans son huile. He disagreed with himself, slipped away from it. Events escaped. A failure of narrative. Phrases become combats; his pencil answers them. What comes between to exclude? And if he were silent? And parked mystery among the broken vessels and archives? Continue in this way, in a tempest of murderous solitude. There is no need to say. He would not sleuth.

Lists 2.2

hat is in your midst will rise-high above you, higher and higher, while you descend lower and lower; he will lend to you, but you will not lend to him; head, but you will become the tail; now when there come upon you all these curses, and pursue you and overtake you, until you have been destroyed hearken to the voice of YHWH your God, to keep his commandments and his regulations that I commanded you, they will be for you a sign and a porte ed, for the ages – because you did not serve YHWH your God in joy and in good-feeling of heart out of the abundance of everything; so you will have t ies, whom YHWH will send-forth against you, in famine and in thirst, in nakedness and in lack of everything; he will put a yoke of iron upon your nec royed you; YHWH will raise up against you a nation from afar, from the edge of the earth, like an eagle swooping-down, a nation whose language you , a nation fierce of countenance that does not lift up the countenance of the elderly and to youths shows no-mercy; it will devour the fruit of your anim your soil, until you have been destroyed; it will not leave for you grain, new-wine, or shining-oil, the offspring of your cattle or the fecundity of your caused-you-to-perish; it will besiege you within all your gates, until the collapse of your walls, high and fortified, in which you were feeling-secure thro d, and will besiege you within all your gates, throughout all your land that YHWH your God has given you; you will consume the fruit of your womb, th s and of your daughters that he has given you, YHWH your God, in the siege and in the straits with which your enemy puts-you-in-straits; the tendere , the one exceeding daintiest – his eye shall be too set-on-evil toward his brother, toward the wife of his bosom, and toward the rest of his children that ive to even one of them some of the flesh of his children that he eats, because he has nothing left of anything in the siege and in the straits with whic s-you-in-straits, within all your gates; she tenderest among you, the daintiest-one, whose sole of foot has not essayed to be placed upon the earth out of it of being-tender – her eye shall be set-on-evil against the husband of her bosom, against her son and against her daughter, against her afterbirth that g een her legs and against her children that she bears; indeed, she shall eat them, out of lack of everything, in secret, in the siege and in the straits with y puts-you-in-straits, within your gates; if you do not carefully observe all the words of this Instruction, those written in this document, to hold-in-a honoured and awe-inspiring one, YHWH your God, then YHWH will make-extraordinary the blows against you and the blows against your seed, blow ; he will return upon you every illness of Egypt from which you shrank-in-fear, so that they cling to you; also every sickness and every blow that is not v ument of Instruction YHWH will bring up against you, until you have been destroyed; you will be left menfolk few-in-number, in place of your havin rs of the heavens for multitude, since you did not hearken to the voice of YHWH your God; and it shall be: as YHWH once delighted in you by doing-g making-you-many, thus will YHWH delight in you by causing you to perish and by destroying you, and you shall serve there other gods, whom you ha her you or your fathers, of wood and of stone; yet among those nations you shall not find-repose, nor shall there be rest for the sole of your foot: YHW ere a shuddering heart, failing eyes, and languishing breath; your life will hang-by-a-thread before you, you will be terrified night and day, and you w security of your life; at daybreak you will say: who would make it sunset! and at sunset you will say: who would make it daybreak! – out of the terror you feel-in-terror, out of the sight of your eyes that you see; The Happy Excursion; YHWH will return … said ot see it again any more; you will put yourselves up for sale there to your enemies as servants and as … ords hat YHWH commanded Moshe to cut with the Children of Israel in the land of Moav, aside from t … hen man in marriage and comes to her, then hates her and puts on her capricious charges, giving … man e and came near her, but I did not find in her signs-of-virginity: the father of the girl and her moth … virgi he elders of the town, to the gate; the father of the girl is to say to the elders: I gave my daughter to … r, nov out capricious charges, saying: I did not find in your daughter signs-of-virginity; but these are the signs-o … out t e the presence of the elders of the town; then the elders of that town are to take the man and discipline hi … f-silv it to the father of the girl – for he gave out an ill name upon a virgin of Israel; she is to remain as a wife, … his da er was true – there were not found signs-of-virginity on that girl – they are to bring out the girl to the entr … one h town, with stones so that she dies, for she has done a disgrace in Israel by playing-the-whore in her father … il fro en there is found a man lying with a woman espoused to a spouse, they are to die, the two-of-them, the man … man; out the evil from Israel! when there is a girl, a virgin, spoken-for to a man, and another man finds her in the to … -out b gate of that town and are to pelt them with stones so that they die – the girl because she did not cry out i … humbl neighbour; so you shall burn out the evil from your midst! but if it is in the field the man finds the spoken-for … and la e is to die, the man who lay with her, alone; but to the girl you are not to do anything, the girl did not incu … he case ises up against his neighbour and murders his life, so is this matter: for in the open-field he found her; when … was no d when a man finds a girl, a virgin who has never been spoken-for, and seizes her and lies with her, and they a … is to give e girl fifty units-of-silver; his she shall be as a wife, because he has humbled her; he is not allowed to sen … ot to take-i vife of his father, that he not expose the skirt of his father; one-wounded by crushing, or cut-off in the s … mbly of YH not to enter the assembly of YHWH, when you go out as a camp against your enemies, take-you-care ag … e among you ritually-pure, because of a night accident, he is to go outside the camp; he is not to come into the mid … d the turn of s sh with water, and when the sun has come in, he may come back into the midst of the camp; an area … here you may g e you should have, along with your weapons, and it shall be: when you sit outside (to relieve your … you return, you ur excrement; for YHWH your God walking about amid your camp, to rescue you, to give your en … oly, so that he do you anything of "nakedness" and then away from you; there is to be no holy-prostitute of the … -prostitute of the s are not to bring the fee of a whore or the price of a dog to the house of YHWH your God … your God are the t n a man takes-in-marriage a woman and espouses her, and it happens: if she does not find t … ething of "nakedness for her a Document of Cutoff; he is to place it in her hand and thus send-her-away from his hou … n his house, if she go nother man's, and should he too come to hate her, the latter man, then he too is to write her a Docum … er hand and sending-he ousehold; or he should die, the latter man who took her for him as a wife, he may not return, her first h … er-away, to take her to be h she has made-herself tamei; for it is an abomination before the presence of YHWH, that you do not bring-sin-upon the land that YHWH your God is t nheritance! when a man takes a new wife, he is not to go out to the armed-forces, he is not to cross over to them for any matter; free-and-clear let him ren or one year, and let him give-joy to his wife whom he has taken; when brothers dwell together and one of them dies, and a son he does not have, the wife s not to go outside in marriage, to a strange man: her brother-in-law is to come to her and take her for himself as a wife, doing-the-brother-in-law's-duty b ll be that the firstborn that she bears will be established under the name of his dead brother, that his name not be blotted-out from Israel; but if the ma take his sister-in-law in marriage, his sister-in-law is to go up to the gate, to the elders, and say: my brother-in-law refuses to establish for his brother a n will not consent to do-a-brother-in-law's-duty by me! then the elders of his town are to call for him and are to speak to him; and he stands there and say take her, his sister-in-law is to approach him before the eyes of the elders, she is to draw off his sandal from his foot and is to spit in his face, then sh nd say: thus shall be done to the man that does not build up the house of his brother! his name is to be called in Israel: The House of the One with Draw en men scuffle together, a man and his brother, and the wife of one of them comes-near to rescue her husband from the hand of him that is striking hi ut her hand and seizes him by his genitals: you are to chop off her hand, your eye is not to have-pity! and to what dispute concerning making a sotah drin refer? One who warns his wife not to seclude herself with another man, R' Eliezer says: he must warn her in the presence of two witnesses, but he ca

th day is like the eleventh day, meaning that just as the eleventh day does not require the twelfth day as a day of observation, so too, the tenth day does
venth day as a day of observation; this, then, is the halakhah Le Moshe MiSinai referred to by the Baraita, for this question involves a matter of kares an
gezeirah shavah does this refer? this refers to the gezeirah shavah inference that teaches the prohibition of one's daughter born of his rape victim; for Rav
k bar Avudimi told me: the law regarding one's illegitimate daughter is derived through the gezeirah shavah "heinnah, heinnah" and it is derived t
h shavah "zimmah, zimmah;" between blood and blood; this alludes to a dispute between the sages regarding the blood of niddah, the blood after childb
f zivah; to what dispute regarding the blood of niddah does the Baraita refer? it refers to where the sage and the High Court had the same dispute
n Akavya ben Mahalalel and the Sages; for we learned in a Mishnah: regarding yellowish blood, Akavya ben Mahalalel declares it tamei, and the sage
o what dispute regarding the blood after childbirth does the Baraita refer? it refers to where the sage and the High Court had the same dispute as the or
d Levi; for the following dispute was stated concerning the blood that a woman discharges in the days following childbirth: Rav says there is but one s
oth the tamei and tahor bloods; the Torah has declared this source tamei and the Torah has declared this source tahor; whereas Levi says: there are two
- one which produces the tamei blood and one which produces the tahor blood: the tamei source is sealed at the end of the fourteenth day, whereupo
opens; and the tahor source is sealed at the end of the eighteenth day and the tamei source opens; to what dispute regarding the blood of zivah does the Ba
s to where the sage the High Court had the same dispute as the one between R' Eliezer and R' Yehoshua; for we learned in a Mishnah: this is the law fo
eeds in labour for three days within the eleven days of her zivah-period; if she had relief for twenty-four hours and then she gave birth, she is deemec
s given birth in a state of zivah, the words of R' Eliezer; and a plate, two forks, two spoons, two knives, a cup of one kind and a cup of the other kind, a p
and a penny, the blunt pencil of my passion, the disassembled events of my mortality, the sucking stone of my adolescence, the corner of the corner of
Yehoshua: the labour pains must have subsided for a night and a day like the night of the Sabbath and its day; and Owley's missing letter, Owley's mis
s missing letter, the Mishnah's word of explanation concerning what it means by "relief": it means that she had relief from the pain, but not necessaril
blood; clasps of bronze, figs, Poe, Le Pli, bananas (brief and disconcerting), curtains of blue-violet purple, horns and pails, une gomme, scraps, and binde
ls of gold and pomegranate, a braided coat, a wound-turban of byssus and sashes and caps, a ram, Un coup de dés, a second row of ruby, sapphire and ha
ow of jacinth, agate and amethyst, Schwitters, a fourth row of beryl, onyx and jasper, a screen, cords, those books, Atemwende, Illuminations, and forty s
a basket of matzot of flour, round-loaves mixed with oil, hotel rooms, reading rooms, church basements, Le plaisir du texte, The First Gate, The Middle G
äume, Firstlings, À l'heure des nations, A Carafe That Is a Blind Glass, Schibboleth, Scholem, Ficciones, [illegible] implements of the Tent, I Samuel, Ru
ion-cover, Blanchot, MacLow, "A", the table and all its implements, a kettle of water under the brid[illegible] stand and all its implements, Tzad
for smoke-offering, the site for offering[illegible], Assommons les pauvres!, Atlas du Canada [illegible] al, the officiating garments of h
the priest, Sabbath, and YHWH [illegible] land: and Investigations of a Dog, [illegible] he land of Efrayim and Menas
d of Yehuda, as far as the Hind[illegible] Sea, and the Negev, and the round-plain, the cl[illegible] as Tzo'ar; Barthes, Bauman,
ein, Borges, Ba[illegible] Oaths, Lashes, cramps, Mea[illegible] tions, Substitutions, Excis
es, Measurements, a mirror, [illegible] (useless), Purity, Vessels, M[illegible] ieve – I won't attempt t
Hierosme [illegible] Avot, Scribes, Happy Occasions, [illegible] la'zado, Samaritans, Sla
Phylacteries, Fringes, and Mezuzah, [illegible] All Writing is Garbag[illegible] s, a can of tuna, tall b
ow a river goes out from Eden to water the garden, and from there it divides and bec[illegible] he is Pishon/Spread
that circles through all the land of Havilah, where gold is; the gold of that land is good, [illegible] rnelian; the name
er is Gihon/Gusher; [illegible] all the land of Cush; the name of [illegible] one that goes to
; and the fourth river [illegible] Euphrates; The song of songs, which is Solomon's; Let hi[illegible] love is better
e of the savour of thy good ointments thy name is as ointment poured forth, therefore do the[illegible] fter thee: the
t me into his chambers: we will be glad and rejoice in thee, we will remember thy love more than w[illegible] omely, O ye
salem, as the tents of Kedar, as the curtains of Solomon; Look not upon me, because I am black, bec[illegible] other's chi
with me; they made me the keeper of the vineyards; but mine own vineyard have I not kept; Tell me, O[illegible] u feedest, v
thy flock to rest at noon: for why should I be as one that turneth aside by the flocks of thy companions? [illegible] g women,
y the footsteps of the flock, and feed thy kids beside the shepherds' tents; I have compared thee, O my love[illegible] s chariots;
nely with rows of jewels, thy neck with chains of gold; We will make thee borders of gold with studs o[illegible] is table, my
forth the smell thereof; A bundle of myrrh is my well beloved unto me; he shall lie all night betwixt my b[illegible] cluster of ca
eyards of En-gedi; Behold, thou art fair, my love; behold, thou art fair; thou hast doves' eyes; Behold, thou art [illegible] o our bed is
of our house are cedar, and our rafters of fir; I am the rose of Sharon, and the lily of the valleys; As the lily a[illegible]; the daught
ree among the trees of the wood, so is my beloved among the sons; I sat down under his shadow with great [illegible] o my taste;
he banqueting house, and his banner over me was love; Stay me with flagons, comfort me with apples; for I [illegible] nder my he
and doth embrace me; I charge you, O ye daughters of Jerusalem, by the roes, and by the hinds of the field, [illegible] love, till he p
f my beloved! behold, he cometh leaping upon the mountains, skipping upon the hills; My beloved is like a [illegible] ndeth behin
eth forth at the windows, shewing himself through the lattice; My beloved spake, and said unto me, Rise u[illegible] way; For, lo,
the rain is over and gone; The flowers appear on the earth; the time of the singing of birds is come, and t[illegible] r land; The fi
th her green figs, and the vines with the tender grape give a good smell; Arise, my love, my fair one, and[illegible] he clefts of t
ret places of the stairs, let me see thy countenance, let me hear thy voice; for sweet is thy voice, and thy c[illegible] xes, the little
e vines: for our vines have tender grapes; My beloved is mine, and I am his: he feedeth among the li[illegible] ows flee away
d, and be thou like a roe or a young hart upon the mountains of Bether; By the night on my [illegible] eth: I sought
him not; I will rise now, and go about the city in the streets, and in the broad ways I will seek hi[illegible] ut I found hi
nen that go about the city found me: to whom I said, Saw ye him whom my soul loveth? It was b[illegible] und him who
I held him, and would not let him go, until I had brought him into my mother's house, and int[illegible] arge you, O ye
salem, by the roes, and by the hinds of the field, that ye stir not up, nor awake my love, till he ple[illegible] of R' Yishmael,
rteen rules of exegesis: the first Middah of R' Yishmael is the kal ve-chomer (from the light in weight to the hea[illegible] it is true for this
nore so for that; the second Middah of R' Yishmael is gezerah shava (similar injunction), by which we say that if two pass[illegible] are similar then the provisi
v also apply in the other; the third Middah of R' Yishmael is binyan av (constructing a general rule), by which we say that a general principle derived fro
two related cases applies to all similar cases; the fourth Middah of R' Yishmael is clal u-frat (a generalization and a particular), by which we say that whe
followed by a particular instance the rule is limited to the specified particular; the fifth Middah of R' Yishmael is prat u-clal (a particular and a gener
ch we say that when a particular instance is followed by a general rule, then all that is included in the general applies; the sixth Middah of R' Yishmael is
a generalization and a particular and a generalization), by which we say that when a generalization is followed by a particular case and again by a gene
e law applies only to cases similar to the particular case; the seventh Middah of R' Yishmael teaches that when a generalization requires a particular ca
clarification then the general rule is not limited to that particular case, and when a particular case requires a generalization for the sake of clarity then

Lists 2:3

Let us say, when a revolutionary soteriology dies, one seeks to attenuate. Story. Remembrance of something. This is in and this is in. She tended her garden, her face buried in a Dutchman's breeches, and did her ass tip in the air? Perhaps she too whittled the stems and legumes of her discontent. Now, the fires of the fightback were attenuated, there was dirt beneath her fingernails and sweat on her brow and a scrape, and she brushed a lock of hair away from her face with the back of her illusions. She wore her own breeches. And was it love at first? This word is free on both sides. And yet there is no chronology in a sacred text, but punctuation there may be, and it encircles the heart. We interpret beginnings. There was sex in a bed of prickly lettuce. We did not share a botanical eschatology. My reticulated life, a very heavy stone, I took revenge on language. And, from time to time, on her. Le visage de l'autre. The French had reinvented corner-flanking, to keep the thing in your hand, having lost its name. Others returned to the asylum of self. But Betty Boop tinkered with the wintergreen. In the garden she wore a beggar's tick.

And a lady's greenish thumb. Also green rubber boots, trimmed, like those of the English, a delicate red. She painted colourlessly in water. It calms the nerves. Whittles a definition. Broken wings and artificial flowers. And Howley with an H and a ladder came to visit. Howley roofed. Roof, Howley, roof. He terraced the landscapes of the reactionary night. With truck and ladder. Whittled with a long knife. Tasted suburban condiments on a solecistic Welshish tongue. He and Betty talked late into the horticultural afternoon, they snuffled in the shrubbery. They shared a cigarette. Dirt beneath their fingernails. I shuffled the newspapers of theory in the room and a half of a heartache. Howley was a lethal finisher. Who kissed someone by the garden gate? And what was I carrying beneath a brow of office supplies? There was no war of charm, because I left the field. Who carried the stretcher? How long did Howley dig in Betty's garden? A man is always considered forewarned. On that very day I left them to it. And who'd sold Howley a newspaper of theory, a painful press? Who'd recruited him to a host of meetings, minus one? Did I make guilt-offerings? Must I go on like a peddler? Now, events roughly escape. Betty Boop, Mustapha and Legrand. That dentist. Then Howley waiting by the gate. His missing letter. A Shtick figure in the street. This itself is difficult. And since we have come upon it, are these the ones who are strangled? Who among them was deserving death? We are all nouns. Whom have you damaged?

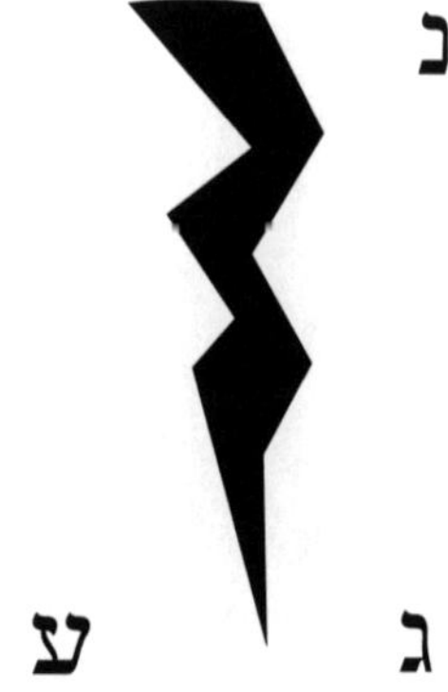
נ
ג ע

ע

נ ג

A Sweeping Statement

And was Howley's trojan horse of charm the penalty for a newspaper of theory? Who sold him that paper? Who waited by the garden gate with a kenotic kiss? Roof, Howley, roof. Who cast one man against the other? Is a broken (the cracked mirror, the torn curtain) heart deserving death? Betty Boop. And had he forgotten, for an instant, in the heat of his pants, Mustapha, Legrand, Pigafetta the dentist with too many teeth in his name? And a Shtick figure in the street below. But see how now he slipped into the long hermeneutical boots of sleuthing. The mystery of the death of the others. Not to mention his own. There was no Common Factor. And what did it matter? She was gone, in the arms of a Welshman's breeches. What purpose to subtract and add and expound? There is no agent of transgression in the construct of love. We are all nouns. Your grave is my grave. Knowing and fearing that actions could spread, that to act might tax him beyond the limits of his sorrow, he lay perfectly still on the cot of despair. Sleep will not enter an unlocked door on its hinges. Events roughly escaped the bedpan of his imagination. What kept him in bed? Couldn't the language (his) vanish? Birth already forgets any utopia. He floated somewhere between the cat and the smile, between mystery and murder. Did Shtick walk softly and carry his name? A murderer deeply believes in his weapon; he trembles before it. What sort of weapon is a Shtick to shake at? They had stolen, together, those beautiful early figs, and learned dedication in that orchard of Pontiacs. But to murder requires more than dedication. Have mercy on these sentences:

Let us say
there was a
tempest of
deaths in
a tea plot.
Shall we
presume
murder?
Go this way.
Mustapha,
Legrand,
Betty Boop,
a dentist,
and
Owley,
minus
that
H.

Chapter Seventeen

Chapter Seventeen

A Sweeping Statement

And what finally raised him up from the cot of desolation? Not cramps. Nor hunger, in spite of the cramps. Go this way! Just the opposite! Was it mystery or murder that lifted him up from his bed to stand alone among the scattered vegetables of his solitude? Did a sleuth glance in the mirror of his murderous solitude? Do wings gather rock? Do dogs dance? The question, the difficulty returned to its place: the body, the thing itself. The incident – the broken lock on a room and a half – invented him. We become the circumstances of our personality. He became the incident of a broken lock on the door to his solitude and a half. A flat mystery threatened a merciful sentence. And did he sweep? Shall we say he did, he swept and gathered the dust of his transgressions into the corner of a room and a half. He danced a broom across a room and a half and swept the hard rocks of his transgressions into the upper right-hand corner of the page. He paused then and transpired in the midst of the dust of his broken solitude. The marks of a mark. Pshat! How should we act? Let us say he gathered the shards of his self and crossed the hall beyond a cracked mirror and broken lock to find the image reversed of his room and a half? What did he gather up from the corner of his sweeping statement? Did he gather those books that were not tattered or stained, a plate, two forks, two spoons, two knives (two! why do I need two?!), a cup of one kind and a cup of the other, the blunted passion of his pencil, the disassembled events of his morbidity, a penny and a penny and a penny, the corner of the corner of an ancient postcard, that sucking stone from the seashore of another Molloy's adolescence, and Owley's missing letter; and did he pour silence into the room and a half, and transport himself, along with the cot of his bitterness, into the cracked image of his room and a half across a hall, to view the world from the other side of a cracked room and a half? Left became right and he moved from side to side in reverse in the image of a room and a half. What did he leave behind on this side of the mirror? What slipped through the cracks of his murderous solitude? Shall we say that he left the dust of his past transgressions? And did he abandon his own sentences, strewn across the rubbled fruit of his labours, the broken dishes of his desire? He left behind tattered books and nouns, we are all nouns. He took a fist of toilet paper rolled in the remembrance of something yet to come. He left the opened can of tuna qui baigne dans son huile and the lists of broken relations that called out to be counted. And were these muktzeh that he would not handle them on the Sabbath? He sought to cross to the other side of a cracked mirror in a room and a half. He sought to escape the events of a cracked life and a half. Betty Boop. The deadly mystery below all manner of debris::

Did a sleuth glance in the mirror of his murderous solitude? Let us say there is no earlier and later in the Torah. Had his head provided a circumstance of evil? Every incident thought a legend of nothing. How we interpret beginnings. What was he recalling? The horse of charm. A Shtick figure in the street. Howley's missing letter. Betty Boop in the arms of a Welshman's britches. He sought to slip away from it. To the other side of a cracked mirror and a half. Hear from this, learn from this, conclude from this. It is difficult. He gathered up the debris of his murderous solitude and moved across the cracked hallway of his murderous solitude into the image of his murderous solitude. He turned his back on the West, the mountain of trees under a cross, across a canyon of cars. There was no one to carry the other end of the bookcase::

When does a man go out to confront the shopkeepers? After gathering in and contracting his breath, so that the smaller might contain the larger.[α] He gathered in his solitude and contracted his grief. Yet nothing would be contained, not large or small. What drives a sinner out once more to confront the shopkeepers?[δ] Neither cramps nor the hunger in spite of the cramps. Rather a torn shower curtain. A torn curtain casts one out into the world like a stone. Sans curtain, a floor is a flood of contention, a shower becomes a contrite man's burden.[ε] Things from which benefit is forbidden. Anyone will shower behind a curtain of souls[φ] before we go out into the world. In measured amounts. Not that he wished to go out into the world. But to replace a torn shower curtain one must go out into the world and confront the shopkeepers, they wipe their hands pinkly, they subtract and add and expound, and no one wishes to go out into the world without a shower. Furthermore (how very hard he thinks, and in time's shadow), if he did go out into the world, would he not want a shower when he returned? Anyone would want a shower in exchange for a dirty world.[γ] Le visage de l'autre. He plunged that way. And which shopkeeper will offer a curtain of souls? Will we find a curtain of souls among a host of tuna? A fistful of bananas? Perhaps you cannot possibly think so. Was he obliged to take a bus and ride, ride, ride amidst those Other arms and noses? A woman sneezes on a Number 231 bus. To risk a calculation. Chant on suit away as in. He plugged his ears with bubblegum. He rode and rode and rode. There is no earlier and later in the Torah.[η] Still, it was a long time before he arrived at a place of difficulties[κ]::

אב כת גש דר הק וצ זפ חע טס ינ כמ
אג גת דש הר וק זצ חפ טע יס כנ למ
אר בג דת הש ור זק חצ טפ יע כס לנ
אה בד הת וש זר חק טצ יפ כע לס מנ
או בה גד ות זש חר טק יצ כפ לע מס

Let us say he wandered through that place of difficulties until he found a hanging garden of shower curtains. There were bright orange curlicues, purple ducks and yellow fishies.[λ] A moment hesitated between his mind and the matter. He looked to this side and he looked to this side. Those curtains hung in rows. Some declared a royal flourish of pompoms and a nude darkness within. A parade marched between that moment and his doubts. He selected a clear sheet of brilliant souls. It occurred to him that he had come a long way to return single-handed. He subtracted and added and expounded.[μ] Seized by the fear of a woman sneezing on a Number 231 bus, he himself sneezed and seized another curtain and another. He felt his suffering slide beneath the definition of any mental condition. What am I wasting?[ν] He purchased twelve curtains and 231 gates. In this way, he felt his life, what little there remained of it, would be free of long rides under the arms of the Other's arms. This is called making provisions.[π] At such a moment, it occurs to us, as it did to him, that his was a mission of fruitless desperation. How long had his life been sliding whereas he thought it already lay still and quiet at the low point of that barrel? In winter he was a wool mouse. Now he was a race of damage. And yet. He gathered his twelve curtains and 231 gates, paid as much as a vertiginous shopkeeper in a skirt and glasses dangling on a chain would take, and escaped. I mean, he transformed an exit into a sympathetic route. He may have had a brief moment of happiness, in the street outside that place of hardship, his ears plugged again, his arms full of curtains, his future blank, but for one final ride on a Number 231 bus. He teaches an exaggeration. Sympathy, we have already said so, is a piano, and your machine (the realistic code) a diet of excess. On the bus there was much sweat and snot, and did he not join in? When he entered the lobby between street and self, his head swollen with the arrogance of minuscule achievement, he was not, consequently, prepared for yet another plot point[ρ]::

α How did He produce and create this world? By zimzum: like a man who gathers in and contracts his breath, so that the smaller might contain the larger.

δ In the siege and in the straits with which your enemy puts-you-in-straits. Deuteronomy 28:55

ε Only in North America.

φ That curtain, called Pargod, hangs before the Throne of Glory. It is the abode of all those souls returned from below. The souls of the wicked will find no place in it.

γ You will become an example of desolation, a proverb and a byword among all the peoples to which YHWH drives you. Deuteronomy 28:37

η This is also dog time (Dr. Hu).

κ I meant the hardware store.

λ Is the writer so lazy he returns to a forgotten City?

μ If n is the number of points in a circle, and L is the number of lines, then: $L=n(n-1)/2$

ν Time. What am I underlining? Time.

π We say this is ours and this is ours and this is ours, until our feet hurt and we go home to surround ourselves in another man's labour and put our feet up on his broken back.

ρ And are you complaining of a lack of story?

And what should we expect – he entered, his arms full of curtains, the lobby between the world and a room and a half, between the street and self? Shall we say "only to find" and raise the spectre of narrative?[α] Did he expect another Shtick in the lobby to beat the dog of his anticipation? Perhaps a Ukrainian janitor with the key to that room and a half across the hall from another room and a half?[δ] There was no Ukrainian. No Giltgestalt. Only a chamber empty of numbers: neither fish nor fowl nor fig. Nor ghost of narrative. Only the antechamber of his desolation. He carried a dozen curtains into a toothless elevator and turned his thoughts in the direction of the upper floors. An intake of breath. Did he contemplate his languorous solitude?[ε] And count those floors without a glance at the ascending light? Anticipate a shower behind a curtain of souls,[φ] and a bit of a liedown before a bite to eat (eat what?[γ])? Or none of the above. Something else. Giltgestalt. Shall we say he rode the elevator of idle speculation? He beat about the garden bushes with a Shtick of surmise. Idly. If a Shtick could shteal a letter it might sherve for shtrangulation. In the garden by the gate of a terrible kiss. Howley before he lost a letter. Shtick had become a sign for death. And before that Welshish gardener, Mustapha, Legrand, a dentist with too many teeth in his name? And Betty Boop? All beaten to death by the Shtick of consolation? Did he fumble for motive between the sixth and seventh floors? Shtick's? His own? In the case of Howley and a woman, he found it in a hurry; jealousy is a dish we serve warmed over. But what might drive a Shtick down the path of the other's death? Again and again. As for Pigafetta, anyone who still has one or two of his own teeth would surely kill a dentist. Legrand buckled his belt over a pork belly. He imported and exported. Mustapha mostly imported. Had they traded their lives for a shticky share of Shtick's? All had returned to the suburbs of the self.[η] And to where had Giltgestalt returned? Slender Armani, hair once red, red, red, arched lip, a wink, and that periphrastic manner. Perhaps it was a case of more cars: grand theft auto in an Ourmoney suit. Was Giltgestalt murdering the false witnesses[κ] of his grandiose theft auto? His Corinthian car crimes? His splendacious hanky-panky? And what might a Welshish gardener have seen or heard or told or threatened to see and hear and tell that would cost him his life and a letter of his name?[λ] Between floors, let us reflect on Owley's missing letter. Which we opened and read so briefly with a drink of water. Try now to suck the gist of that hard candy. Something about a dentist, death, a host of names, a Common Factor,[μ] Legrand, Mustapha, Betty Boop, all within a fortnight.[ν] They were all linked by hekeish: the laws of one applied to the others. It occurred to him that, having read Owley's missing letter, he too might know something worthy of losing his own. Life, not letter. But he did not know what he knew.[π] It isn't always that way. Often we know less than that.[ρ] He only knew he was between floors, his bladder and something else already twinging in anticipation. Perhaps that Shtick figure was wiping the pinkishness of his youth (and theirs) from his brow with murderous accuracy. Perhaps, to forget one's past, one makes a clean sweep of the people in it. They had written leaflets, "Arise!" but no one had. Perhaps in those final days of finger pointing, false witnesses and fields of acrimony, damage had been done to the blunt end of Shtick's self-image.[σ] Had Shtick nurtured a grudge by some garden gate? And if a deadly grudge was Shtick's operation, who deserved the end of it more than someone who had delivered a letter of expulsion? And that elevator, when it came to a halt in the middle of this sentence

אב כת גש דר הק וצ זפ חע טס ינ כמ
אג גת דש הר וק זצ חפ טע יס כנ למ
אר בג דת הש ור זק חצ טפ יע כס לנ
אה בד הת וש זר חק טצ יפ כע לס מנ
או בה גד ות זש חר טק יצ כפ לע מס
אז בו גה זת חש טר יק כצ לפ מע נס
אח בז גו דה חת טש יר כק לצ מפ נע
אט בח גז דו טת יש כר לק מצ נפ סע
אי בט גח דז הו ית כש לר מק נצ ספ

α Have we begun an exhalation after a contraction? Here come ten of them.

δ To have a door and lock but no key is so near and yet so far.

ε He had become that person awake at night, and walking along a road alone, and thinking idle thoughts.

φ The first of twelve. I mean curtains, not showers.

γ It might occur to you to say, being out among the shopkeepers, he could have, should have, picked up a newspaper, une demi-baguette, a can of tuna, a fistful of bananas. How could you possibly think so? Have we learned nothing? Remove, delete! His mind was not a heavy desk planner, a stone that kills twice. And are not twelve curtains sufficient to return to a room and a half?

κ If witnesses are discovered to be zomemin, they are to suffer the consequences inflicted on the person they falsely accused.
Sanhedrin 84b

λ In the end, and to begin with, a letter is what's in a name.

μ No, not the mailman.

ν And we all know how quickly that passes.

π Perhaps you are thinking, can it be that he's sleuthing at last? Remove, delete! Have you learned nothing? This is elevator music. Nothing more.

ρ Now is the time when no one knows more than in twos and threes. Say which you like.
G. Stein *Blood on the Dining Room Floor*

σ Perhaps an Ourmoney suit would suit him better.

η Can you see a crime. No not I. Because after all to live and die, what makes them shy, nothing much, because they will have as much as then and deny. O please try.
G. Stein, *Blood on the Dining Room Floor*

A Horse of Charm

In the hallway between a room and a half and a room and a half his ears swimming in nature's call he turned away from a door swinging on its hinges and a footprint of blood on the carpet's tattered failure.[α] Who mentioned this item which is being cited now as if it had already been mentioned? He swung instead through the mirror of another door.[δ] Any lock without a key is so near and yet so far. He poured out of his shoes and pants and into the half room of the body, the thing itself. He produced several minutes of far less than perfect excrement and a sheen of perspiration on the forehead of his intellect.[ε] Did he reflect on a bloody footprint in the hallway between a room and a half and a room and the half he sat in? Or should he rather recall Mustapha and Legrand? So far, these are merely nouns. And what good is more or less getting to know them when both are already dead?[ϕ] Characters are only nouns in dresses. But let us call Legrand thin – in spite of those pork bellies – and say he folded his height on the stoop of his adolescence. Mustapha grew hair and a medallion in the space of his open shirt. Being shorter, he puffed and bristled. Certain descriptions confront a suitcase of clichés. Were they good comrades? For a while. Let us say they did not pause long in the silence after the revolution failed.[γ] Legrand and Mustapha studied capital with a fine line. They walked a fine line between an uncommon denomination, between the memory of a French Catholic schoolyard and Allah's blessing. On Thursdays they ploughed through couscous at somebody's uncle's restaurant. Sunday on déjeune chez la mère. Monday to Monday they schemed a season of numbers. Shall we say they worked between the rate and the rate, traded beads for condominiums in the republic of bananas, exported ear plugs to a vociferant Red China. I mean, they sold a legend of nothing, they girded their loins in pork bellies.[η] Will this make their death less painful? In retrospect. And shall we knit a tie to Giltgestalt's neck? Are you casting one man against another? Did they undergo a less than pure chance encounter with an old comrade? Did they ride the horse of charm? Did a Shtick offer to beat their swords into shares?[κ] Ambition paused only briefly on that narrow road. But let us move on; to occur costs time. What am I wasting? Yours. Let us say time passed, they were discovered.[λ] Were their heads severed from their bodies, the one long, the other hirsute? Will this make their deaths more painful? In hindsight. Their grave: your grave? A hundred horses of charm could not underestimate so black a murder. Had he tied a Shtick to Mustapha and Legrand in a knot of circumstance?[μ] And Betty Boop and Owley and Owley's letter? The dentist with too many teeth in his name? The nature of this case is not like the nature of this case and the nature of this case is not like the nature of this case. He felt his suffering slide beneath an argument.[ν] Let us compare the mechanism of the toilet in a room and a half across from a room and a half to the progress of this narrative. He cursed it. No sooner did he pull a chain than there was silence. Can you imagine someone washing his hands with his leg bent and a foot up on the lever to flush a turbulence of fine greenery?[π] He longed to wrap his legs in the events of a day. To whittle the space of a room and a half into a narrow cot. To return to his murderous solitude. But something he had passed over in the hallway between a room and a half and a room and a half in his haste to be seated in the half room of a room and a half recalled him. A foot of blood on a hallway carpet between a door with a broken lock and a door he could not lock. He returned to the scene of that grime. His knees knocked at a door off its hinges. He thrust a reluctant gaze into a room and a half. Shall we pause here for cause and affect? He certainly did. On that floor lay a headless horse of charm, an Ourmoney, the blunt end of which lay in the purple tarn of someone's death : :

אב כת גש דר הק וצ זפ חע טס ינ כמ
אג גת דש הר וק זצ חפ טע יס כנ למ
אר בג דת הש ור זק חצ טפ יע כס לנ
אה בד הת וש זר חק טצ יפ כע לס מנ
או בה גד ות זש חר טק יצ כפ לע מס
אז בו גה זת חש טר יק כצ לפ מע נס
אח בז גו דה חת טש יר כק לצ מפ נע
אט בח גז דו טת יש כר לק מצ נפ סע
אי בט גח דז הו ית כש לר מק נצ ספ
אכ בי גט דח הז כת לש מר נק סצ עפ
אל בכ גי דט הח וז לת מש נר סק עצ
אמ בל גכ די הט וח מת נש סר עק פצ
אנ במ גל דכ הי וט זח נת סש ער פק

α There was no dining room, hence no dining room floor; hence the blood on a hallway carpet. "Oh, Lizzie, do you understand?"

δ Unlike its opposite number, this door had all its hinges. And yet it complained so bitterly.

ε Must you churn this into butter?

ϕ Why should a novel walk?

γ A student of Marx can earn a good living after the revolution; he need only forget an eschatological footnote or two.

η A hypotyposis makes a bush of envy behind which to hide.

κ All this on the stone of idle speculation. They got shtuck with Shtick's shares.

λ Whether you count yourself a continent or a person, to be discovered is never a sign of good health.

μ Had his head provided a circumstance of evil? Increasingly, Shtick made a fine shushpect.

ν He wiped speculation from his mind, sweat from his brow, and shit from his ass.

π Our thanks to Doctor Hu: he learned this from her.

A headless Ourmoney will lose much of its charm, not to mention its blood.[α] In such a case, our morbid fascination is nevertheless tempted to look away. He yielded to that temptation. Turned to the broken hinges of the door. There was the brief suggestion of peristaltic reversal. A bad death staggers the legs of one's imagination. Let us say he staggered through a broken door, past a bloody footprint in the hallway of his horror, and into the cracked mirror of a room and a half. Shall we pause to breathe the familiar scent of our old clothes still fresh with the excretions of a living body? Not for long. Events gallop.[δ] What did you see then that you missed coming in earlier, your eyes swimming in nature's call? A cracked mirror was bleeding. On the cot of where shall I lie down now, on the bleeding news of the world, a severed Shticky head, his red red hair, his teeth and tongue, the unbroken gaze in a broken head. Once more, briefly, he revisited the lunch he had not taken. He strongly objected to it, and almost spoke ill of the dead. But in the end, morbid fascination will triumph over anyone's lunch. Gazing into the face of the trace of the utterly bygone, he beheld an utterly absent Shtick. From this it was impossible to learn anything.[ε] He sought consolation in memory. Shtick's wink in the triangular grin of a Chevrolet's open hood. A happy moment. They'd stolen it that night. The vehicle, I mean. And the moment, for that matter. But no memory could follow the trace of this past. Or Shtick's passing. Meanwhile. Shtick's unbroken gaze from the other side of the other side of a room and a half. The other side is the place of the future that never becomes present. How should we act in the face of the face of the other's death? Not everything is in our power. To the other, we are already obligated and never sufficiently obligated. Only a page ago, we were branding Giltgestalt a murderer. An hour ago, he was practicing strangulation in the park, fingering Owley's missing letter in the still warm pocket of his Ourmoney suit; now he held our gaze in the gaze of his bloody gaze, which lay in a room and a half, neatly severed from the equally neat set of his suit, which lay in another room. And a half. Shtick's mind had been separated from his body[φ] in two pools of his own blood. He had made a clean break with his past.[γ] One thing was apparent: death was a refutation of guilt. Shtick's that is. Unless murder was on the rise with a trend toward execution.[η] He wandered in a case of anamorphosis. Not only this but also this. In the face of death he found his solitude bordering the edge of mystery.[κ] He was sleuthing. Had he banished all hospitality[λ] from his home only to have death enter on the other side of the cracked mirror of a room and a half? Let us say or shall we say? How much more so! He cursed it. And yet, Owley's missing letter. Did we say Owley's missing letter? That unwanted child tugs at my staggered leg. He wanted the letter but not the idea of it. Shall we return to the other scene of the same crime? Let us say he turned from the crime scene of a Shticky mind to the mindless violence of a body. He eyed the eyeless pockets of an Ourmoney suit, imagined the missing H in Owley. Shall we say he longed for that brief letter? Did he bend over a severely severed suit? Did his own pinkish grocer's hands violate the tent over a dead body in a search for a dead letter? Not to mention the alphabet. Did he commit the father of the father of all impurities? Did he search a dead suit? Did he smear a hand (the right one) in the blood of Ourmoney? What did he learn? Those Ourmoney pockets were as empty of letters as the bloody head on the other side of the other side of a hallway.[μ] He might have learned more, but our interrogation of death was interrupted by the siren song of a vehicle halting in the canyon below the window of what had once (too recently) been his room and a half. What now? : :

אב כת גש דר הק וצ זפ חע טס ינ כמ

אג גת דש הר וק זצ חפ טע יס כנ למ

אר בג דת הש ור זק חצ טפ יע כס לנ

אה בד הת וש זר חק טצ יפ כע לס מנ

או בה גד ות זש חר טק יצ כפ לע מס

אז בו גה זת חש טר יק כצ לפ מע נס

אח בז גו דה חת טש יר כק לצ מפ נע

אט בח גז דו טת יש כר לק מצ נפ סע

אי בט גח דז הו ית כש לר מק נצ ספ

אכ בי גט דח הז כת לש מר נק סצ עפ

אל בכ גי דט הח וז לת מש נר סק עצ

אמ בל גכ די הט וח מת נש סר עק פצ

אנ במ גל דכ הי וט זח נת סש ער פק

אס בנ גמ דל הכ וי זט סת עש פר צק

אע בס גנ דמ הל וכ זי חט עת פש צר

אפ בע גס דנ המ ול זכ חי פת צש קר

אצ בפ גע דס הנ ומ זל חכ טי צת קש

α Miserable observation which again is certainly the result of something artificially constructed whose lower end is swinging in emptiness somewhere… F. Kafka *Diaries*

δ Here the sound of horse hooves: plot, plot, plot, plot.

ε Death is the death of the mystery of the other person's mysterious death. E. Lévinas (pas tout à fait) *Time and the Other*

γ Here, if not in the orchard, at last the mind and body split.

η We all died in Lublin. In Lublin we gave the Torah back. Dead men don't praise God. J. Glatstein

κ And what is the place of solitude in the general economy of being?

λ I meant language.

μ He learned: In death we are freed from language (this is not necessarily so).

φ How shall we judge him now? By replacing that bloody head upon his blind shoulders.

What cries out in the canyon of cars below the window of a broken room and a half if not the siren's song of a severely severed Shtick? Nevertheless, kneeling at the foot of an Our-money suit,[α] he heard the periphrastic wail of the policeman's magic. Such a full-time word is curdling. Well, who called the cops? Had a murderer hightailed it, pausing only to deposit an anonymous coin in the pay phone of implication? But why had a killer operated? Shall we think beneath the moment? He was being framed in the cracked mirror of his room and a half. He rose confusedly, glanced at his right hand moist with the blood of shticky circumstance.[δ] In such a case an automatic gesture seeks to cast off the offending member. Let us say, without thinking,[ε] he bent and wiped that offensive hand on the now superfluous crease of a dead man's trousers. Did he recoil from his own solecistic gesture? Straighten up. And race[φ] – what was he carrying? that hand on the end of an arm he may have wished longer – across a staggering hallway back to the scene, the other one, of the same crime.

α He wore, to say the least, an open collar.

δ The father of fathers of ritual impurities.

ε I meant he was not thinking, though it may be thoughtless to say so.

φ Go this way! Just the opposite! A sudden passage. Marks or a mark.

Let us return to the scene(s) of the crime. Shall we say the murder weapon was a very sharp tongue? Whereas, in Howley's case, it was strangulation (not to mention a broken cuff and a shoe) under the not-so-burning bush by the garden gate. The nature of this case is not like the nature of this case and the nature of this case is not like the nature of this case.[κ] The question was: what is the offense of one that he should be strangled, and of the other that he would lose his head over it?[λ] And what of those who had gone before: Mustapha and Legrand? Betty Boop? And the dentist with too many teeth in his name?[μ] What was the method of execution in each case? And the crime? What was there between them? The common factor. Just as there, so here too. In either case, no matter what. Answer, resolve, relate, object. And was he suddenly become, in the face of the face of death, a shopkeeper, to add thus and subtract and expound? He would have preferred to slip away from it. To deepen the notion of solitude. If he had had time, he would have considered the opportunities that time may offer to solitude. But there was no consolation there. In his solitude he felt his self made heavy by itself, a viscous, heavy, stupid double.[ν] And there was no time. Not for Shtick. Nor for him. No dreaming in the present of being in the presence of death. Now the policeman's song filled a canyon below. A song knows how to demand. The time was high. That is, it was high time, high time to get down from the height of his twenty-second floor. I mean it was that time to absquatulate. There was no longer safety in numbness. And yet. Not yet. He could not tear himself away from the torn head of a broken Shtick. Not to mention his headless body. That Shtick was a mast and he was tied to it.[π] Nor could he sever the ties that bound him to the disembodied recollection of a Giltgestaltian grin in the rearview mirror of someone else's Pontiac memory. That car was also a memory to its former owner. How he disagrees with himself. He must, but he has no remedy : :

κ A detective proceeds by hyperbaton: he inverts the idiom of death.

λ These are the ones who are strangled: one who strikes his father or his mother, one who kidnaps, a rebellious sage, a false prophet, one who commits adultery, the zomemin witnesses of the daughter of a Kohen. Sanhedrin 84b

μ All these are linked by hekeish: the laws of one are applied to the other.

ν M. Blanchot *Aminadab*

אב	כת	גש	דר	הק	וצ	זפ	חע	טס	ינ	כמ
אג	גת	דש	הר	וק	זצ	חפ	טע	יס	כנ	למ
אר	בג	דת	הש	ור	זק	חצ	טפ	יע	כס	לנ
אה	בד	הת	וש	זר	חק	טצ	יפ	כע	לס	מנ
או	בה	גד	ות	זש	חר	טק	יצ	כפ	לע	מס
אז	בו	גה	זת	חש	טר	יק	כצ	לפ	מע	נס
אח	בז	גו	דה	חת	טש	יר	כק	לצ	מפ	נע
אט	בח	גז	דו	טת	יש	כר	לק	מצ	נפ	סע
אי	בט	גח	דז	הו	ית	כש	לר	מק	נצ	ספ
אכ	בי	גט	דח	הז	כת	לש	מר	נק	סצ	עפ
אל	בכ	גי	דט	הח	וז	לת	מש	נר	סק	עצ
אמ	בל	גכ	די	הט	וח	מת	נש	סר	עק	פצ
אנ	במ	גל	דכ	הי	וט	זח	נת	סש	ער	פק
אס	בנ	גמ	דל	הכ	וי	זט	סת	עש	פר	צק
אע	בס	גנ	דמ	הל	וכ	זי	חט	עת	פש	צר
אפ	בע	גס	דנ	המ	ול	זכ	חי	פת	צש	קר
אצ	בפ	גע	דס	הנ	ומ	זל	חכ	טי	צת	קש
אק	בצ	גפ	דע	הס	ונ	זמ	כל	מכ	קת	רש
אר	בק	גצ	דפ	הע	וס	זנ	כמ	טל	יכ	רת
אש	בר	גק	דצ	הפ	וע	זס	כנ	טמ	יל	שת
את	בש	גר	דק	הצ	ופ	זע	כס	טנ	ימ	כל

To stand. Agape. Abashed. Aghast. Face to face with the face of the man who lay in another room and a half? Do you follow? I mean, shall we follow him in there? To add what? What was there about it? The siren's call of justice closer now. The manner of execution?[γ] Shall we consider the manner of execution? There, at least, a pretext. To ratiocinate. To turn one's own mind from the body in two parts (why do we need two?). Or should I say the body on the one part and the mind on the other. The knowledge that. If there were a connection.[η] But Shtick's death was a command that disrupted any possibility of knowledge, disrupted the significance of signification. Break, fracture : :

γ Four different methods of execution are delegated to the court. In descending order of severity these are: stoning, burning, beheading and strangulation. Sanhedrin 49b

η I mean a connection between murders, not the severed connection of Shtick's mind and Shtick's body.

π Not that he was particularly drawn to the siren call in the street below. What could the police promise? At most, a half room less.

Shall we say he ~~gazed into a crimson pool of regret~~? No, better not go that way. Rather, he circled a shticky head, recalling his own shticky past.[α] Who learned: to steal requires dedication? Who, his pockets full[δ] of beautiful early figs, had once recruited a Barabasic[ε] teacher in an Ourmoney suit to the politics of rage? Who had taught the horse of charm to serve the people before he served himself? When you can't teach an old horse new tricks, he will return to his old tricks. Who delivered a letter of banishment?[ϕ] Who poured years of silence into a friend's ear and left him standing in the vestibule between the world and self? Who suspected a Shtick of strangulation? As the blood dried, language vanished from a Shticky head. Nor did he find letters of expulsion in a Shticky pocket. He thought for a second.[γ] Something had turned silent. I mean aside from Giltgestalt. Something in the street was silent. That siren song.[η] Can there be impediments to the ear? He was suddenly freed from the mast of memory in a policeman's siren.[κ] Did he listen for nightsticks in the corridor? The doubled doors of doubled elevators? Had someone framed him in a mirror of circumstance? In the silence of the hallway a parade marched between a room and a half and a room and a half of doubt. He lowered his gaze to a bloody footprint.[λ] And another. Two!? Why do I need two? And yet. Not yet. Perhaps you dimly recall arriving earlier, our arms full of curtains, to read a single red tread on the carpet of our anticipation. Perhaps you do not. Had he promoted some failure of narrative? He glanced inward at his own sole (let us say the right one). Which bore the mark of Shticky blood. Blood, like events, will spread. He'd carried a curtain (or a dozen) of souls over a sole of blood. Now he'd doubled the prints. To worry is the border of experience. He was there now. Your papers, please. He heard the shuddering rise of elevators. There were two and two half rooms, a Shtick broken in two, two elevators rising, two footprints of blood, and two fistfuls of seconds between him and disaster. Did he pause to take hold of a precious possession or three? Did he grab the first thing(s) to fall into his hand(s)? A curtain, a final

tractate of Talmudic argument, the blunt pencil of his solitude.[μ] Let us stand before the elevator, the right one, if possible. No, the left. No, the right. From here, we can watch two strings of lights mount together. He bet on the right, no, yes the right. There was creaking and sighing of metal on metal, the doors parted on the one hand and the doors parted on the other hand. He stepped into the right chamber, where we were prepared to bump the policeman of language. There was only a faint trace of someone's lunch. In this case the right one was the right one. That mouth was toothless.[ν] Out from the other came pouring uniforms of guilt and the teeth of justice. Two.[π] Before the gate was that gang. He waited an eternity of palms and underarms for the doors to slide shut. Shall we say there was a passing glance from the head on a uniform of guilt, an eye-to-eye with a man already itching to press shoulder-to-shoulder with the sketch artist?[ρ] In that man's eyes he saw the grey-blue pages of the evening papers.[σ] He saw the hand on the arm of the Law rise from the cuff of justice, and begin the slow movement that becomes a wave when the accordion of escape does not press between them. He, for his part, began a more than gradual descent. Or should we say less than gradual?[ω] Can you imagine a uniform reception in the lobby? Did you spot a radio on a policeman's belt? Had the passenger broken? Was hope dying? He laboured with his breathing. Studied a breathtaking view of numbers in descending order. His heart bumped against the lobby. Upstairs they measured a corpse.[φ] Meanwhile our vertiginous clerk escaped : :

אב כת גש דר הק וצ זפ חע טס ינ כמ
אג גת דש הר וק זצ חפ טע יס כנ למ
אר בג דת הש ור זק חצ טפ יע כס לנ
אה בד הת וש זר חק טצ יפ כע לס מנ
או בה גד ות זש חר טק יצ כפ לע מס
אז בו גה זת חש טר יק כצ לפ מע נס
אח בז גו דה חת טש יר כק לצ מפ נע
אט בח גז דו טת יש כר לק מצ נפ סע
אי בט גח דז הו ית כש לר מק נצ ספ
אכ בי גט דח הז כת לש מר נק סצ עפ
אל בכ גי דט הח וז לת מש נר סק עצ
אמ בל גכ די הט וח מת נש סר עק פצ
אנ במ גל דכ הי וט זח נת סש ער פק
אס בנ גמ דל הכ וי זט סת עש פר צק
אע בס גנ דמ הל וכ זי חט עת פש צר
אפ בע גס דנ המ ול זכ חי פת צש קר
אצ בפ גע דס הנ ומ זל חכ טי צת קש
אק בצ גפ דע הס ונ זמ כל מכ קת רש
אר בק גצ דפ הע וס זנ כמ טל יכ רת
אש בר גק דצ הפ וע זס כנ טמ יל שת
את בש גר דק הצ ופ זע כס טנ ימ כל

α I meant he who circled recalled; that shticky head was empty.

δ Now they were empty too.

ε Or should we say Pancho-istic.

ϕ That letter was a missing H.

γ Those were second thoughts.

η Before the law, a ~~man~~ is always considered forewarned by a siren.

κ He wanted Ulysses, he'd get Abraham.

λ Had there been a dining room, there would have been blood on a dining room floor, Lizzie.

μ Clearly, here he had thought far below the moment. At such times we long for a standing suitcase and a rear exit. He forgot the radio.

ν That vehicle was a fortuitous train of thought.

π Did you expect another number, more or less?

ρ A wet vase can paint a genius.

σ Later, he might wrap himself in his own guilt.

ω The speed of an elevator is inversely proportional to the fear (or intestinal urge, or redolence of a fellow traveller) within.

φ From which part of the corpse would they measure the distance to the nearest city? From his navel? From his nose? From the place that he became a corpse? From his neck?
Sanhedrin 88a

Two!

Before we were narrative, we were boots and vertigo. We leapt across a canyon of traffic. We flung ourselves into the net of language. A horse was an inch of music. Dogs danced, wings gathered rock. Now we are the small brown pigtail of a mystery trailing behind its solution. We pour murder out of a tenement and lay the limp and soggy rag of story in the street.[α] The police have parked the realistic code (always straddling a sidewalk) beneath their lights flashing. They are an empty vehicle crackling speech in a canyon of traffic. He crawled past it. That tale is a parade marching on someone's borrowed crutches. All the more difficult to cross the highway. A passerby will pause and look from a bristling police car to that doorway pregnant with disaster and to a shifty-eyed mule under a load of curtained text. I struggled for a visible expression. I tried to read the nervous lip beneath his bushy moustache and above a shouting shirt. If there is a difficulty, this is the difficulty. To practice exegesis in the street comes to identify a criminal. How should we act?[δ] Someone else is always an anticipation. Wondering if we can continue in this way. We can crawl past it. We can edge into Cratylus's river of traffic,[ε] but can we cross it? Panic snaps the mind; to walk repairs it. The street was a long poem; he went down to the end of the verse. He thought how assiduously a murder obeys the rules of the road. On the other side the mountain poured greenish weeds into the city. He was inclined to go up. A ways. He flexed his ankles, his knees blazed on ahead. Someone's sweat, perhaps even his, gathered in the small of his back. He earned it. Until he paused on the slope to extinguish his lungs. A chestnut tree leaned hard against him. It might have been raining. Instead, the sun piled warmly globules of irony upon his head : :

α On reading Charles Dickens: I can't understand it and can't believe it. I live only here and there in a small word in whose vowel I lose my useless head for a moment. The first and last letters are the beginning and end of my fishlike emotion.
F. Kafka *Diaries*

δ If the relationship with the other involves more than relationships with mystery, it is because one has accosted the other in everyday life where the solitude and fundamental alterity of the other are already veiled by decency.
E. Lévinas *Time and the Other*

או בה גד ות זש חר טק יצ כפ לע מס
אז בו גה זת חש טר יק כצ לפ מע נס
אח בז גו דה חת טש יר כק לצ מפ נע
אט בח גז דו טת יש כר לק מצ נפ סע
אי בט גח דז הו ית כש לר מק נצ ספ
אכ בי גט דח הז כת לש מר נק סצ עפ
אל בכ גי דט הח וז לת מש נר סק עצ
אמ בל גכ די הט וח מת נש סר עק פצ
אנ במ גל דכ הי וט זח נת סש ער פק
אס בנ גמ דל הכ וי זט סת עש פר צק
אע בס גנ דמ הל וכ זי חט עת פש צר
אפ בע גס דנ המ ול זכ חי פת צש קר
אצ בפ גע דס הנ ומ זל חכ טי צת קש
אק בצ גפ דע הס ונ זמ כל מכ קת רש
אר בק גצ דפ הע וס זנ כמ טל יכ רת
אש בר גק דצ הפ וע זס כנ טמ יל שת
את בש גר דק הצ ופ זע כס טנ ימ כל

He turned his toes the way he had come. To look across at the twenty-second floor. The native is on the ground and the stranger is in the sky.[φ] What droned in the chapel of his stomach? Must we churn this? From where he had come, a war of charm had underestimated black murder. Now, any act was great. He gazed back across from where he had gazed across at the cross for so many years. Into the cracked mirror of a canyon of traffic. He saw uniforms (two) bending and unbending in a room and a half of stooping and unstooping. What were these detectives of deadly sin retrieving?[γ] Now that we have come to this. We sit upon a volume of argumentation and clutch a curtain of souls. Shall we say he thought of his mother?[η] And yet. Not yet. He was not prepared to be driven into that countryside. He counted his options on the fingers of his nose. I mean, there were none. The landscape paused. The hearse of failure pulled up behind the flashing blood of the Law. More time gathered among the weeds. He muttered to himself in the language of sleep. Something[κ] was calling him back to the scene(s) of the crime. Having already come this far, the journey demanded repetition. Shall we descend that bitter slope of disappointment? At the corner light, he paused to recognize a Ukrainian janitor's head momentarily filling the open door. Still he crawled back along the way he had fled. He pulled that outer door in time to hold it open for a bookish front-end bearer of a stretcher followed by the stretcher and the other bookend. Whereas his heart took him by the throat and flung him back along the sidewalk, his knees would not flee. They drew him toward that stretcher. Death disappearing into the hole in the rear of an ambulance will draw a crowd. The living jostle with each other's anonymous odours in anticipation of the inevitable momentary glimpse when the sheet slips away from the Other's face. He jostled with the best of them. He peered and paled. What did he see-saw? A face, bloodless, but still recognizable. His own. Gazing skyward : :

φ One who sees his past always thinks: because of; or but this is not so; or just as, so too; or the event that happened happened that way; or act, deed, event, precedent.

γ When is a tenement not a home? When you can no longer return there.

η At times like this we often think of our mothers. And mine too, for that matter. Performing rites, such as eating, washing, drinking, sacrificing.

κ Perhaps a horsey habit, perhaps the lure of disaster, perhaps the refusal to believe he had not been dreaming, or merely the familiar comfort of a damp cot.

ε Cratylus' version of the river, in which one cannot bathe even once; where the very fixity of unity, the form of every existent, cannot be constituted; the river wherein the last element of fixity, in relation to which becoming is understood, disappears.

E. Lévinas, *Time and the Other*

We were gazing skyward. Into the cracked mirror of the other's face. That face was a cloud or lack of understanding. I was stretched in two on the stretcher of finality. Freed from my soul[α] and that attendant's pain. I was my body, a silent stone gravely swaying, no longer able to sin. I thought, under accusation of murder, one's guilt vibrates. Who recruited a Shtick from an orchard of last year's Pontiac Sports? Who delivered a letter of expulsion? And the same for Howley, cast out of steel casting for a pinkish group. Who did not attend a meeting in the garden by the gate?[δ] Who did not love Betty Boop enough? Who did not wish her well? These were the pencil shavings of guilt.[ε] But they were his, and he fingered them daily. Now, shall he die for them? Death floats on that phrase. A person is murdered. Shall a reader care? Perhaps not. A generalization needs a detail. Generalization and detail. Detail and generalization. What effect there could have been is lost.[φ] The story stumbles onward; that one is already dead. We have provided no details. They say in the West, the art of characterization requires the careful accumulation of detail.[γ] Shall we attempt a parthenogenetic leap? Giltgestalt had a lisp. There. That's done. Can we move on now? Am I a peddler? Must I go on like a peddler? Not a thick comic lisp; that is the speech impediment of crayons. There was no whitish spittle. No fine spray. Rather let us say it was a feathery whistle and perhaps endear him to you. Is it sufficient? Shall we make his death matter after the fact, and send him into heaven? Do I make claim to a depth of sentiment? Let us plunge in there. How could I? I've already killed him. In a manner of speaking. I mean, in the manner I spoke of him. So there it is: a lisp and nothing more. Better late than never. Perhaps you cannot possibly think so. In any case, now we have killed him. And how many more? Mustapha, Legrand and Betty Boop, that dentist with too many teeth in his name. Owley sans that letter. And yet. Not yet. They lifted me skyward. I ascended a hearse. Will you lie in my place? : :

α The soul flies in the air like a bird; the body is a stony grave.

δ Sans his letter, Owley met a lethal finisher.

ε Did his sins set him apart from the masses of his people? If so, he was a flagrant sinner: רשע

φ It is not your death which you see here. Nor did you ever truly carry that Shtick.

γ Well, we are pressed for time; perhaps a gesture will suffice. A fact. A face.

אי	בט	גח	דז	הו	ית	כש	לר	מק	נצ	ספ
אכ	בי	גט	דח	הז	כת	לש	מר	נק	סצ	עפ
אל	בכ	גי	דט	הח	וז	לת	מש	נר	סק	עצ
אמ	בל	גכ	די	הט	וח	מת	נש	סר	עק	פצ
אנ	במ	גל	דכ	הי	וט	זח	נת	סש	ער	פק
אס	בנ	גמ	דל	הכ	וי	זט	סת	עש	פר	צק
אע	בס	גנ	דמ	הל	וכ	זי	חט	עת	פש	צר
אפ	בע	גס	דנ	המ	ול	זכ	חי	פת	צש	קר
אצ	בפ	גע	דס	הנ	ומ	זל	חכ	טי	צת	קש
אק	בצ	גפ	דע	הס	ונ	זמ	כל	מכ	קת	רש
אר	בק	גצ	דפ	הע	וס	זנ	כמ	טל	יכ	רת
אש	בר	גק	דצ	הפ	וע	זס	כנ	טמ	יל	שת
את	בש	גר	דק	הצ	ופ	זע	כס	טנ	ימ	כל

Shall we solve this death or that one? Having failed to solve, or represent, or think those millions. This cannot enter your mind. Death is become a problem of degrees. How shall we dispose of it? The question, the difficulty, returned to its place. Where is a qualitative leap? Qu'est-ce qu'un simple meurtre? Chaque mort ne porte-t-il pas la trace des autres? How shall we describe it?[η] In my story? In mystery? In the midst of it, there is no end to it. Nor beginning. Yes and no and it is unsteady in his hand. Shall we scribble the unrepresentable, knee-deep in that black and white trench?[κ] This is the difficulty. Shall we testify to the limits of what can be said, knowing there is something which cannot be said, but is trying to be said?[λ] We all bend to look more closely at a trench. We calculate length and depth. In this way he goes on reckoning like a peddler. He subtracts and adds and expounds. And are you still at this? Here a word about my mother. A terrible imperative drove that hearse into the countryside.[μ] And if this cannot enter your mind, only the opposite way is reasonable! An elenctic. Who mentioned its name? What did you see? They laughed at it in the West. Is it necessary? Reach up to extend a hypotyposic hand. From the beginning, at the outset, a story to contradict. Just as in. From where? A retraction. Practical difference. Up to here there is no. How much more so. It might occur to you. It is difficult. To cast them. Should we rely on answers such as these? And furthermore. Now he was a body, freed from his soul.[ν] He had cast himself out of this world like a stone. His head lay on the stretcher of his luxurious exit under his arm. He gazed at the roof of an ambulance.[π] We have had a lifetime of that. Repulsive eternity swims there. It continues to do so : :

η In black and white.

κ Were we hoping in this way to deliver a parcel of redemption? Perhaps you cannot possibly think so. What meaning would you bury in a black and white trench?

λ Go and learn the meaning of this verse according to one of R' Yishmael's thirteen methods of exegesis through which the Torah is expounded. Sanhedrin 86a

μ Number A5591. Not to mention 61991. And the others.

ν I meant, free from that footprint of blood.

π That was no ambulance; an ambulance is a hearse in a hurry.

Shtick was a headless hearseman whose hearse was my neck. Nevertheless, one cannot continue to stand a mute witness to one's own death.[α] Mine was the face to be picked out of a crowd. I felt a stiff Ukrainian wind on my neck. I turned my back on the familiar face of a mysterious death and a familiar door to a room and a half, and brushed my heels against the pavement of indifference. That street was a long poem.[δ] Let us go to the end of the verse, turn the corner of our old life, and find dusk in the alley of everybody's refuse. A sudden recollection of the darkness after the darkness, the movie after the movie. Did I recall saying, nothing I could do could make it any worse? We made it worse.[ε] And what will one who finds him or herself in the alley of everyone's refuse reflect? How should we act? Shall we begin to sleuth? To gnaw on the mystery of murder in the mirror of a room and a half? Shall we consider our place in a string of deaths strung together? A missing letter. A Shtick waits in the vestibule between the world and self. Or should we rather look. He should have been looking. For what? Something better? I have not found it. But more immediately, he should have been looking for shelter. For the night, I mean. Because dusk will soon spill into any city. Did he sleuth? Or did he search? Let us say he searched. But not for shelter. Because he had forgotten the radio and his ears were swimming (again!?) in the call of nature. There could be no greater precision. This is the difficulty. O, happy group, you healthy defecators. He could not count himself among them. A bladder drove him into the park. Between the trees. The body, the thing itself. But among the trees in the shadows a horseman.[φ] He buttoned his fly and turned to the public toilets. They were locked. To him. For the night : :

אנ במ גל דכ הי וט זח נת סש ער פק
אס בנ גמ דל הכ וי זט סת עש פר צק
אע בס גנ דמ הל וכ זי חט עת פש צר
אפ בע גס דנ המ ול זכ חי פת צש קר
אצ בפ גע דס הנ ומ זל חכ טי צת קש
אק בצ גפ דע הס ונ זמ כל מכ קת רש
אר בק גצ דפ הע וס זנ כמ טל יכ רת
אש בר גק דצ הפ וע זס כנ טמ יל שת
את בש גר דק הצ ופ זע כס טנ ימ כל

He could not wait for that horse's head to go ahead, give his mount its head, and head home. Whereas now. Whereas he. Whereas I. Carried my bladder through the park, and the student ghetto.[γ] An unrelenting string of disasters filed into the cinema of his rememoration. ~~The terror of understanding froze his tears.~~ Shall we have a touch of self-restraint? Understanding fell from the trees: the closed door behind him,[η] the darkness ahead, the taste of broken syllables. What is it like? The preterit past. He had wanted something better. He'd not found it.[κ] Now we search the streets for an open doorway. Or a darkened one. To lower his keyless[λ] pockets down around his ankles. He came upon the gates to the garden of higher yearning.[μ] Hear from this, learn from this, conclude from this. He walked in the dark evening of universal knowledge. Let us say a willow teared up, whereas flowers slept in their beds before a library, a faculty club and a toilet. He sought the latter. In the library his cloacic anxiety met with a uniform denial. Have we not rejected this once? Just as there, so here too. What now? Shall we say he wiped his brow? And head south into the monied streets of money, pigs, leprosy and sexual relations. A full bladder is a child: having momentarily fallen silent, it will once more take up the cry. A bowel denied will harden its heart.[ν] He made considerable headway in a street of freestanding architects. What was he carrying that his reason could not drain? A tractate of verbs, a curtain of souls, the blunt pencil of his past. An ambitious colon. Let us scrape together a skyscraper, a glass finger to scrape the heavens. He entered the vestibule of monied pigs and financial relations. A mirror elevated his emergency. He did not pause to reflect on it. Which one beckoned? He took that one. Consulted a panel of proper nouns. Here surprise might have called a halt to an operation were it not for an internal hue and cry. The word he saw was a dentist with too many teeth in his name. Hard-pressed he pressed a Pigafetta practice : :

α I meant, to stand mutely. Not that silence in the face of death is easily tolerated.

δ Shall we say I was the nag of fiction, the mouse of drama.

ε See Chapter Eight; we were Homeless in Tutonaguy.

φ Any horseman in the park is policing squirrels, or a squirrelly policeman.

γ Il traversa moins légèrement la nuit réactionnaire.

η My own door, I mean, not to mention the public wasrooms.

κ Perhaps it was no longer to be had. Or never had been. A Halakhah for the Time of the Messiah.

λ God said to Elijah: There are three keys that were not entrusted to an agent: the key of childbirth, the key of rain, and the key of resurrection. One key I have already made an exception and given you – the key of rain. Now you request a second key, the key of resurrection. Is it proper that people should say: Two keys are in the hands of the student and only one is in the hands of the teacher? Sanhedrin 113a

μ A university is a place of higher yearning. Perhaps you cannot possibly think so.

ν La vérité n'est que la solidification d'anciennes métaphores. F. Nietzsche

A Hue and Cry

How long will an elevator contain one man and his bladder? Go ask the mystagogues. The fuller the organ the longer the ride. On the tenth floor he burst forth onto a carpeted corridor. The plumber's paradise was down the hall. He poured past a row of doors into a small stick figure in trousers[α] and, dropping his keyless pockets, leapt into the cubicle of gratitude to produce a great emancipatory moan. But there was no time to bask in a momentary freedom from the body, the thing itself.[δ] What is there seated between a door and the self? He heard the door of trousers exercise its hinges and a conversation enter the room. How should we act? Shall we remain silent and closeted with water, allowing only our shoes coated with the dust of our transgressions[ε] to represent us? He heard: Shall we go to the brasserie across the square? And a voice replied: Or that new place just opened up on the boulevard, a nice review in the papers.[φ] He sat, meanwhile, his knees bent, his back to the waters, trying to withhold an outpouring of his own less than excellent self-expression. Did they pause long at the sinks to dip their hands in a cursory nod before pouring silence back into the room? Long enough. Let us wait for silence to thicken the walls of his solitude before disentangling his ankles. Before a sink of comforts, he stood in the mirror of his homelessness.[γ] He splashed cold hard facts on the face of his predicament. Pushed a useless finger through the mirror's thinning tangle of curls. He toyed with regret. Do not try this at home. The radio. A razor. What remained of the fruit of his labours. I mean a banana. Shall we say he would have remained there, in a cocoon of running water, if he had not heard soft footsteps in the corridor. He pulled the door and brushed past an encounter. Briefly, a nervous lip, a bushy moustache, a glimpse of a shouting shirt. What is being cited here as though it had been mentioned before? He tossed his stone down the hall without pausing to ponder a name with too many teeth on the second door to the left::

α Those trousers are an interpellation and a sexual injunction.

δ When we defecate, our soul flies in the air like a bird.

ε And his pants deflated around his ankles.

φ They were standing side-by-urinary-side in a manly expression of their inner selves.

γ The marks of homelessness, once it takes hold, multiply exponentially.

אצ בפ גע דס הנ ומ זל חכ טי צת קש
אק בצ גפ דע הס ונ זמ כל מכ קת רש
אר בק גצ דפ הע וס זנ כמ טל יכ רת
אש בר גק דצ הפ וע זס כנ טמ יל שת
את בש גר דק הצ ופ זע כס טנ ימ כל

To wait for an elevator is an experiment in anguish. He heard the soft footsteps of a screaming shirt lay a carpet beneath his scalp. He felt a bushy moustache on the back of his neck, the breath of a nervous lip. Let us say the elevator pinged. Not once but twice![η] He played the silent periphrastic shuffle game. An open palm below the belt is that no-please-after-you-I-insist. He worked the split.[κ] A shouting shirt went one way and he t'other. Let us say, however, that he rose whereas he would have much preferred to descend?[λ] Did he press repeatedly on a letter in a nest of numbers? Do you imagine a nervous lip rising in the chamber next to ours. He did. The doors opened in inky darkness.[μ] His nose was running away with him. On the back of his hand it produced a watery pink liquid.[ν] He did not linger. Rather he pressed hard hard hard. A monied elevator is like love at first. It flutters your belly and thrusts your heart in your throat.[π] He slipped away from it. He cast his eye to one side and to the other. Did he seek out a vociferous shirt?[ρ] Or did he turtle instead through a door of paned glass. Outside, the stick of night was in full swing. He thrust himself into that dark city's illuminated letter. A curtain of ghoulish faces.[σ] My forehead drenched, my already fragile digestion. Perhaps this cannot enter your mind. Shelter is the first gear of anyone's engine. Where shall we seek it? In the darkness after the movie. Then, we were stupidly sixteen. Now, we were simply stupid. That was then. This was now.[ω] In the preterit past. On the pavement, between this century and an unfortunate verdict, a beggar's outstretched hand. He almost took it. For now, in the darkened street, a beggar was become a fount of knowledge and a mentor in cheap's clothing. I was so much less than that::

η Two! Yes, yes, I do need two! Two is the democratic promise of two chambers.

κ Here was a practice in which he was practiced.

λ Have we not already, once before, climbed la Sierra Maestra in search of a verb?

μ Form breaks up, the letter begins to blur and fade. This is the level of Chakmah consciousness.

ν Perhaps this was merely what remained of a headless Shtick in a room and a half?

π It floats above an abyss of nothingness.

ρ So full-time a word is curdling.

σ Once the tents of night are well planted, there is no more imagining morning.

ω In the street, he was the rust of years on a narrow cot in a room and a half.

Home Again

Across a canyon of traffic beckons a tumbleweed of information. The inky exhalation. To be wrapped in newspapers is best of all. Did his legs imagine a thick cot of fine print in a room and a half? He crossed. And glanced. Into the blackened mirror of his own proleptic guilt sketched on the front page of murder, mystery and the news of the day.[α] Below, the headless sheet over a broken Shtick. Now was a good time to turtle. He let those three hairs on his chin grow, tied his scarf over his ears, and prayed, now the condition had taken hold, for the exponential multiplication of the marks of homelessness. He transferred a text and a curtain to a pale, bloodless hand so as to finger a coin in his keyless pockets. Would you spare him a dime? Such feeling refuses us. Failing that,[δ] he spent his last on that bellowing newspaper. Why? Did he wish to cover up, to remove his face from the face of the darkly illuminated face of the street? The mirror of his image lay piled beneath the one he bought and paid for.[ε] A glance, an eye-to-eye with the fish-soaked vendor, my already fragile digestion. He fled the illuminated page of the street and plunged back into the park, that small brown mutt of mystery nipping at his heels. Fear gusted in the branches. We sweat beneath the moon. Something rustling in the burning bushes will get your knees moving. Where? If you're not thinking, back whence you came. Oh, how he doublecrossed that park. Sacrificed his calves to the altar of his panic. Too shaken to be thinking. Events had roughly escaped any reasonable vessel of containment. He would have lain down on a cot in a room and a half, wrapped his feet in the news of the day. When the protestations of his calves slowed his knees to a halt, he found himself. He was standing on a slippery slope, his toes pointing across a canyon of traffic, at the twenty-second floor of a tenement become the scene of the crime that had adopted his name.[φ] Will certain descriptions confront silence? Perhaps a criminal returns to the scene of his new identity in search of the old one. This is the difficulty. How can you find it?[γ] Shall we say he did not cross that bridge until it collapsed beneath him. He cooled his heels and the sweat on his back. He tried to think but nothing happened.[η] A hearse would have been a way back. But not even the dim light of a uniform remained before that door. He was drawn by the lack of that light. By the promise of a warm cot on which he could first wrap and then lay his legs down in a room and a half.[κ] Shall we say he followed his heels across a canyon of traffic, parsed a long poem to the end of the verse, and entered the vestibule between the street and what had once been his self? Two chambers gaped. A meaningless choice. Why do I need two? His anticipation was a third elevator; it rose. And since we have come to this. Now that we have come to this. Having come to this. He sought a good hand-washing.[λ] To be released from subsidiary judgment. He had whittled a long time, subtracted and subtracted, thought hard to be released from it. Until his shtick had grown too large to carry. He would wash his hands of himself and lie in the cot of his desolation. That elevator was a chamber of hewn stone. It railed and rattled to a halt. Tossed him into the scene of a crime. A coroner will stretch yellow[μ] ribbons across the door to a room and a half and across the door across the hall in the cracked mirror of a room and a half. If it had ever been there, beyond the vestibule, between the street and a room and a half, or in the cracked mirror of that room and a half, what had once served as self was gone now.[ν] Had he returned in search of it? Without a roof, without so much as the promise of une demi-baguette, anyone's self is distantly a memory. Behind him he heard the gears of power grind beneath the twin of the elevator whence he'd come. He turned to greet what he already knew was emerging there: a shouting shirt and that nervous lip beneath the burning bush of a moustache : :

את בש גר דק הצ וף זע חס טן ימ כל

אב כת גש דר הק וצ זפ חע טס ינ כמ

אג בת דש הר וק זצ חפ טע יס כנ למ

אר בג דת הש ור זק חצ טפ יע כס לנ

α Here we meant to provide the profluence of the murder mystery. Can't you feel sharply the edge of your seat?

δ I mean, you having failed him.

ε Or, in the siege and in the straits in which his enemy had put him in straits, perhaps he merely sought the solace of a newspaper in which to wrap his legs?

φ In such a case, we say, the native is on the ground and the stranger is in the sky.

γ If the true self is already gone, or was never there to begin with?

η Curly Joe.

κ A parable for the story of Elijah: To what can this be compared? To a man who locked his gate and then lost his key. Sanhedrin 113a

λ נטילת ידים: laws regarding the ritual impurity of and washing of hands.

μ Shall we say ירוק, yellow as in the yolk of an egg?

ν Perhaps he would have done better to find a new one. In the local crime pages of the evening news.

Having come this far, now we have come this far, we are plunged into an anacoluthonic life.[α] Caught between the yellow ribbon of someone's death and a shouting shirt. In the hallway between a room and a half and a room and a half. I considered a nervous lip, a bushy moustache. Here, remembrance of something. A shouting shirt speaks softly in a mutter of factual tone of voice. Hello, he said, and after all these years.[δ] I was the purpose of silence. I see, the shirt continued, declining to be abated, the you I am thinking of remains the you I think of as you, as I speak to the you to whom I am speaking. I held my tongue between my knees.[ε] Do you not recall, he argued, the me I once called myself? His name was Joey Cafgu. A foot soldier in the army of soteriology.[φ] Let us give him a round face and eyes like buzzers. Here's a clue. We had been, once, in our youth, together in that group of which we are not speaking.[γ] He took my elbow, removed it from the scenes of the crime. And what else that mattered was muttered in that tone? Best not to remain here. It was said thus and it was said thus. Shall we say it was impossible to ascertain if the hand on the arm (I mean his hand, my arm) was friendly or forceful?[η] What does a Cafgu do? And, more to the point, how large are his shoulders? His neck? The fingers on my arm? I mean his fingers, my arm. Friendly or forceful? In either case, I had no place to pass the night. In the streets I was all rust, the rust of a room and a half without a cot. He offered to carry neither my curtain nor my prayers. In the lobby, fleetingly, a Ukrainian boy's pink face and rotten teeth. Thinking, perhaps, new country, same story, same bushy moustache in the night. In the park the wind propelled us through the branches. A fleeting sensation of the ride to Fuente Grande.[κ] There was no Andalusian olive tree, no fertile fields lying fallow. Only the towering glassy eye of money. That same skyscraper where we[λ] so recently spent a small portion of happiness in a bladder's momentary release. It is not necessary for a Cafgu to loosen his grip on someone's elbow in order to press as bluntly and firmly on a button. This I learned. Also this: that one floor above a Pigafetta practice is the Number 32 : :

α Now we've lost our grammatical superstition.

δ Here's a better place for such a dialogue.

ε Wouldn't you?

φ If you have run with the foot soldiers, and they have wearied you, how can you contend with horses? Jeremiah 12:5

γ Where were you?

η One who kidnaps a Jew is not liable to strangulation unless he takes him into his possession. Sanhedrin 85b

κ Thanks to Erin Mouré, who took us there.

λ I mean the royal pee.

Let us say I achieved, at that moment, a perfect expression of powerlessness. And swam in that moment, floating on the surface of my lack of options.[μ] At last. I could err no more. My elbow was no longer my own; it lay wrapped in a Cafgu's grip. There was no question how should we act? Nothing was in his power. There was only the hard round nut of fear in the face of the face of his own death.[ν] But he found repose in the dissolution of that self. It flowed out from him like so much coloured water. A suspension. A brackish phlegm.[π] But I digress. We were rising. Shall we disembark from that chamber of hewn stone into another chamber of stone, onto a carpet of Persian labour, overlooking the illuminated letters of the city? Here Joey Cafgu released the elbow he'd been gripping – which was mine – with a push so gentle it is possible there was no push at all, and retreated into the shadow of the shadow of the way we had come. At the desk, shall we say, benevolence greeted me as a smiling mouthful of Booger Rooney? There was no escaping the remembrance of a Booger.[ρ] I fingered it.[σ]

אב כת גש דר הק וצ זפ חע טס ינ כמ

אג גת דש הר וק זצ חפ טע יס כנ למ

אר בג דת הש ור זק חצ טפ יע כס לנ

אה בד הת וש זר חק טצ יפ כע לס מנ

או בה גד ות זש חר טק יצ כפ לע מס

אז בו גה זת חש טר יק כצ לפ מע נס

אח בז גו דה חת טש יר כק לצ מפ נע

אט בח גז דו טת יש כר לק מצ נפ סע

אי בט גח דז הו ית כש לר מק נצ ספ

He had been a general in that army of soteriology. In our youth. Not everyone called him Booger. His mother, for example, did not. Nor did those who were his subalterns. Now he'd paid off that antonomasial mortgage in full. He had invested in democracy. He was a lion in the electoral arena, a rising star in the murky way, a fine set of teeth on the front page of the news of the day. Ourmoney was not too good for him. Come in, come in, long time, make yourself. There being no chair, I hovered between the cat and the smile, my nose running away with me. Shall we wipe a pinkish hue from the back of our reddish hand? : :

μ The sudden release from responsibility at the moment of complete powerlessness teaches us the extent of the tension under which we have been labouring until then.

ν The body, the thing itself.

π It is in the nature of the self that when we are rid of it we are not necessarily also rid of our cramps. Nor for that matter of our other aches and pains. This too is unfortunate.

ρ If Shtick Giltgestalt was a ben sorer umoreh who had reciprocated, Booger Rooney was a zakein mamrei.

σ Here I mean the memory, not the booger.

Things from which Benefit Is Forbidden

The wave in Booger's do, once a dark flying Wallenda, had stiffened a silvery hue. He wore the lapels of power. With teeth whiter than the whites of his eyes, and eyes more eyelike than I, he eyed his old comrade eyeishly. He rose fully to his lack of height. Behind me, a Cafgu stood by the proverbial door. "Now," Booger scholiated,[α] "old comrades are once more come together." For my part, I was present in body, more or less. Not to mention spirit. There followed a commentary on antiquation and climatology and a mention of somebody's complexion (almost certainly mine). He spoke at length, but not for long (he was a busy man), the tiniest of small talk. Soon the alphabet of murders and memory unfolded across the desk of our differing degrees of destitution.[δ] He cast us back to Mustapha and Legrand, to a dentist with too many teeth in his name and Owley with too few, to Betty Boop and a freshly encorpsulated Giltgestalt. Regarding all of this he urged what? Silence. For his part, he was simultaneously standing and running for office.[ε] He saw benefit neither in mystery nor murder. And what was my part? He suggested I could benefit from a lack of general interest, having buried my own toes beneath the stone of Giltgestalt's body, which lay, for the most part, in a room and a half of my own dwelling, not to mention the other part in a room and a half across the hall. I had dabbled in his pockets. Been all thumbs all over his Ourmoney. My bloody footprints in the hall between a room and a half and a room and a half. Booger beat the dog of stress hard. His speech was a massive alphabetical enterprise. He took no mercy on sentences. He dabbled in dark suggestion.[φ] So total a suggestion will soon eat someone. But whom were we eliminating? : :

α This word is free on both sides.

δ His was close to degree zero.

ε Have you seen a politician scurry across the field of his constituency?

φ The deadly mystery beneath the manner.

כמ	ינ	טס	חע	זפ	וצ	הק	דר	גש	כת	אב
למ	כנ	יס	טע	חפ	זצ	וק	הר	דש	גת	אג
לנ	כס	יע	טפ	חצ	זק	ור	הש	דת	בג	אר
מנ	לס	כע	יפ	טצ	חק	זר	וש	הת	בד	אה
מס	לע	כפ	יצ	טק	חר	זש	ות	גד	בה	או
נס	מע	לפ	כצ	יק	טר	חש	זת	גה	בו	אז
נע	מפ	לצ	כק	יר	טש	חת	דה	גו	בז	אח
סע	נפ	מצ	לק	כר	יש	טת	דו	גז	בח	אט
ספ	נצ	מק	לר	כש	ית	הו	דז	גח	בט	אי
עפ	סצ	נק	מר	לש	כת	הז	דח	גט	בי	אכ
עצ	סק	נר	מש	לת	וז	הח	דט	גי	בכ	אל
פצ	עק	סר	נש	מת	וח	הט	די	גכ	בל	אמ
פק	ער	סש	נת	זח	וט	הי	דכ	גל	במ	אנ
צק	פר	עש	סת	זט	וי	הכ	דל	גמ	בנ	אס
צר	פש	עת	חט	זי	וכ	הל	דמ	גנ	בס	אע

Shall we say it was said thus and thus? To be precise, Shtick Giltgestalt was a ben sorer umoreh[γ] who had reciprocated? Those boys! (Sigh.) Listen to them. Who flogged Shtick in a manner of speaking? Didn't he receive a tongue-lashing? And did he not reciprocate until mind and body split? If Shtick Giltgestalt was a ben sorer umoreh who had reciprocated, Booger Rooney was a zakein mamrei, an Instigator, and a Rebellious Sage.[η] But perhaps you cannot possibly think so. Perhaps you would prefer leniency in a case of youthful zeal. To relax, after all, is just another doctrine. And yet, didn't he promise restoration of the shattered elements of the world? And did we not all (where were you?) glimpse final redemption just around the corner? Were we not prepared to pass through the last flaming stages of sacrifice and repentance to attain a world of tikkun?[κ] Burn, baby, burn. One surrenders one's load, and yet vanishing refuses. For tikkun, one gladly reclines on the pea of midnight. But will you swallow it? And did a Booger commit strange and paradoxical acts counter to someone's law, religious or otherwise? Did he pronounce the Ineffable Name, did he speak the Tetragrammaton, did he proffer blasphemous benedictions and sanction the forbidden? Perhaps now, he wanted bygones to be gone. A bloody hand had wiped that pinkish hue. In a war of charm we may easily underestimate black murder. Their grave: your grave. Shall we say, I poured silence into the open trough? Silence is not enough. And yet. Not yet. In silence, one may reflect on the Other's guilt. I roughly calculated Booger Rooney's guilt. What were his past sins in light of more recent electoral events? Had Booger campaigned in strangulation? Did his sharp tongue silence a Shtick? Did he steal Owley's missing letter? Mustapha and Legrand, Betty Boop, that dentist with too many teeth in his name : :

γ There are four categories of people who require proclamation after their sentences are carried out: a ben sorer umoreh, a Rebellious Sage, the Instigator, and zomemin witnesses. A ben sorer umoreh is one who stole money in certain specific circumstances, and ate specific quantities of meat and wine that he bought with the stolen money. The first time he commits this offence, he is brought to court and flogged. If he repeats the offense, he is liable to execution.
Sanhedrin 87a

η A zakein mamrei is a false prophet. An Instigator is one who instigates a fellow to commit idolatry. A Rebellious Sage is a sage who preaches against the rulings of the Sanhedrin Court.

κ We are speaking here of both a process by which the shattered elements of the world would be restored to harmony, and of the final result – a Messianic time.
Kabbalah

That red Shabbatean was a false prophet.[α] Shall we laugh at it in the West? What makes us follow a Shabbatai into cultish isolation? Did he prophesy the Time of the Messiah? Did he promise a reversal of halakhic precepts? Were there ribaldry and concubines? Or was it simply the manner of his manner? Someone's hair is dark and waves appealingly over a brow where the rest of us bang foreheads. His speech pours sweetly from a gorgeous gorge while we pause in our thinking to slosh a vessel of greyish matter between our ears. Will a manner and a do suffice to make us lemmings? Or is it rather a time for lemmings that selects a Shabbatai to lead the way? Worse than the terror of that lemming time are the recriminations in the wake of the inevitable rude awakening that must follow : :

α Some time later, someone suggests: perhaps that time we name the Time of the Messiah is not specifically located in historical time, but is rather a possibility intersecting with the day to day.

Profits

I considered my silent options silently. I weighed those options on a subatomic scale and found them wanting. Wanting what? Wanting more. Options. Booger wanted a spoken promise of silence. I considered speaking out against silence.[α] To refuse silence is well and good, but would speaking retrieve a body by the gate or a dentist with too many teeth in his name? I considered the possibility of a silent refusal of silence. I mean, to remain silent in the face of Booger's demand for my silence.[δ] But silence left too much unsaid. Clearly (it seemed so at the time), Booger (Mr. Rooney to you)[ε] and his shadowy shadow both preferred speech, I mean mine, to silence. They required a sentence. Silence (in the face of their demand for my silence) might lead to a sentence of death. Possibly. Here, another option: to speak a sentence of silent acquiescence.[φ] But if I spoke my silence now, would I not be acquiescing to murder? If I played mute to Booger's tune, who would satisfy suspicion's passing glance from the head of a uniform, that eye-to-eye with the man whose shoulder itched to press shoulder-to-shoulder with that sketch artist (he had by now already done so)? Silence was an option that slid on the buttery slope of my tongue. Anyone is welcome to pray in a Boogery shrine. Let us recall pretense. As an option.[γ] Pretense, lying, treachery: these are treasures on the tip of anyone's pinkish tongue. But Booger had a nose (as well as a tongue) for pretense, lying, and treachery; they were his stock in trade and a sheepish skirt he wore proudly. The dictionary was the vessel of his rise to power. He was loquacious and sesquipedalian, he was lexiphanic and Gongoresque; I mean he apostrophized a revolutionary soteriology in Ciceronian tones. Must I go on like a peddler?[η] Alright, he was a big gabber. A tongue-sweet apparatus. A thousand elaborately lathered lies. Will sufficiency ever be sufficient? And what of the body, the thing itself? Neither height nor width were his corpulent domain; yet a room filled in his presence. With what? Language. His frothy tongue. This last century, we have all grown wary[κ] of such a Napoleonic stature : :

אג	גת	דש	הר	וק	זצ	חפ	טע	יס	כנ	לם
אר	בג	דת	הש	ור	זק	חצ	טפ	יע	כס	לנ
אה	בד	הת	וש	זר	חק	טצ	יפ	כע	לס	מנ
או	בה	גד	ות	זש	חר	טק	יצ	כפ	לע	מס
אז	בו	גה	זת	חש	טר	יק	כצ	לפ	מע	נס
אח	בז	גו	דה	חת	טש	יר	כק	לצ	מפ	נע
אט	בח	גז	דו	טת	יש	כר	לק	מצ	נפ	סע
אי	בט	גח	דז	הו	ית	כש	לר	מק	נצ	ספ
אכ	בי	גט	דח	הז	כת	לש	מר	נק	סצ	עפ
אל	בכ	גי	דט	הח	וז	לת	מש	נר	סק	עצ
אמ	בל	גכ	די	הט	וח	מת	נש	סר	עק	פצ
אנ	במ	גל	דכ	הי	וט	זח	נת	סש	ער	פק
אס	בנ	גמ	דל	הכ	וי	זט	סת	עש	פר	צק
אע	בס	גנ	דמ	הל	וכ	זי	חט	עת	פש	צר
אפ	בע	גס	דנ	המ	ול	זכ	חי	פת	צש	קר
אצ	בפ	גע	דס	הנ	ומ	זל	חכ	טי	צת	קש
אק	בצ	גפ	דע	הס	ונ	זמ	כל	מכ	קת	רש
אר	בק	גצ	דפ	הע	וס	זנ	כמ	טל	יכ	רת
אש	בר	גק	דצ	הפ	וע	זס	כנ	טמ	יל	שת

When a red Shabbatean[λ] promises heaven, he eats forbidden fats. He offers a more perfect law, frees women from the curse of Eve, and fixes a date for redemption. Shall we refuse an attractive offer by the gate? Shall we subtract and add and expound like grocers in the face of a mystagogical Profit? Quite the contrary is what tempts us. To give it all up. In exchange for what? An idea. Nothing. An idea of Nothing. The ineffable. And yet. Not yet. Such offers are always in a velvet glove ferocious. Since we took the first part, we must take the end as well. Once we have enlisted, someone demands we testify to our faith by uttering the ineffable. Such demands may seem perfectly reasonable. Others – less palatable – will follow. The fist of faith pounds salvation. Someone ate someone. That was close. Perhaps an unbeliever is compared to the unclean animals mentioned elsewhere. If your name is Lapapa,[μ] run and hide; here comes that fiery oven. And yet. Not yet. When we fall on our knees, one hundred and fifty prophets arise. This hell on earth is a workshop of soteriology. We are amazed by a tale of revolution; it advances in a vermilion parade while the old landscapes of labour pause. It goes forth in a straight line directly into the abyss.[ν] Events roughly escape. Still, what choice? Here is the unfortunate route to follow between the verdict and this century. Where were you? : :

α Shall we say speech called out to me from the doubt-infested waters of my own worst enemy? I thought better of it. Better not to risk stretching a metaphorical muscle.

δ Silence is anyone's favourite recipe for trouble. I mean, getting out of it.

ε The name Booger, once lodged therein, is not easily dug out from the ancestral nostril.

φ He meant, to speak a sentence acquiescing to silence.

γ What sin can there be in falsely promising one's vote to a politician piling false promises on your doorstep?

η Even broken, such language is hard to swallow.

κ Not to mention weary.

λ If a false messiah promised redemption on a fixed date, (the 15th of Sivan 5426), wouldn't we all bate our breath and fling stones at those who opposed him? Until that day passed, warm, partly cloudy. What then? Having gathered stones and learned to use them?

μ Some few refuse to follow the mob. In the face of collective fervour, they hold fast to the cart. Not the bandwagon. Strength of character, greater understanding? Or jealousy, lack of imagination? Later, when the Instigator has fallen, these are our heroes. We return their books and award red badges. They exact justice in exact sentences.

ν Who packed the antechamber of redemption with the furniture of execution?

Shall we all remain silent now under some Booger's threat or promise? How should we act in a symphony of delicate power? Here is the difficulty: we all seek a place to lie down. Akhsaniah. We wipe our pinkish hands. We are all subsidiary judges. Who mentioned this item which is being cited now as if it had already been mentioned? All of us are under some Boogery threat (and/or promise). At night, all of us silent in our beds, whether straw or silk, and even on the cot of desolation. By day, each of us doing his or her job, and thinking: each of us does his or her job. Perhaps you cannot possibly think so. Perhaps you think not everything is in our power. And yet. Not yet. The way of things. Daily, our silence speaks volumes. Each day, our hand shaking in someone's velvet glove, we speak our silence, hopefully in time to beat the traffic home. It was necessary for this to be said, otherwise it might have occurred to you to say::

And This Is Theirs

Have we entirely stumbled into the solution to the mystery of a density of murders, only to become the densely murdered solution to a mysterious density? Act, deed, event, precedent. If he takes the first part, he must take the end as well. We have suggested speech or silence. And yet. Not yet. Neither suggested itself. Silence bespoke speech and speech would certainly silence speaking for good.[α] Meanwhile that shouting shirt hovering at my elbow spoke volumes by his silence. Nevertheless. And the less the better. I lingered a moment longer on the fringes of a memory of Betty Boop. What compelled him, with his neck stretched across the altar of impending doom, to bury his head in the sweet, fetid stink of hindsight, in detritus with a rosy hue?[δ] Things from which benefit is forbidden. Her neck. My neck. Her grave, my grave. At such times, why won't space form? Why won't the air gather around your ankles? I mean mine. Your ankles may be perfectly fine. And is there nothing else? Matter. Matter. A sleuth dives inward. What does a detective retrieve below the skin when the flat mystery at the surface eludes him? Try as he might, truth ignores him. How I longed for the language of sleep. Booger hinted that that could be arranged. Meanwhile my deadening silence spoke louder than words. But what sort of Rooneyesque proposal did Booger Rooney propose? Did he offer a place at the inn?[ε] Shall I be bought so cheaply? Unfortunately, no one was, nor is, buying. Whom are we eliminating? Those of us who say the Torah is not from heaven. Those of us who cause the face of our fellow to pale with shame. When the colt of fiction rides the flat mystery, we hold our breath between our knees. Without a room and a half, I was a rusty nail in the street. The street in December is anyone's coffin. Shall we consider silence in exchange for a ruined room in Rooney's inn? Now that we have come to this, the question, the difficulty returned to its place. I felt a tug at my heart. Perhaps that was merely a Cafgu's elbow in the rib of hesitation. In any case, the way to a man's heart is through his ribs. And yet. Not yet. While Rooney dangled a place at the inn, and that shouting shirt's strong arm tugged at my heart, I held my tongue between my teeth. In the end there was no need for speech; my silence spoke louder than words. Though not Booger's; no language or lack of it spoke louder than Booger : :

α When even the opposite way is not reasonable, reason takes refuge in the mud of middle ground.

δ That was a metaphorical stew. I meant nostalgia is a place to hide the momentary ostrich of ruefulness.

ε Akhsaniah, a place to lie down, or the lack of it, is what separates us from a Messianic era.

אי בט גח דז הו ית כש לר מק נצ ספ
אכ בי גט דח הז כת לש מר נק סצ עפ
אל בכ גי דט הח וז לת מש נר סק עצ
אמ בל גכ די הט וח מת נש סר עק פצ
אנ במ גל דכ הי וט זח נת סש ער פק
אס בנ גמ דל הכ וי זט סת עש פר צק
אע בס גנ דמ הל וכ זי חט עת פש צר
אפ בע גס דנ המ ול זכ חי פת צש קר
אצ בפ גע דס הנ ומ זל חכ טי צת קש
אק בצ גפ דע הס ונ זמ כל מכ קת רש
אר בק גצ דפ הע וס זנ כמ טל יכ רת
אש בר גק דצ הפ וע זס כנ טמ יל שת
את בש גר דק הצ ופ זע כס טנ ימ כל

How he rejoiced to find the source of evil. He gazed into that thoughtless light and saw his masters. (Like Blind Isaac, he saw the light.) Shall we pencil a duality in the process of creation, placing evil on one side and good on the other?[γ] In the West, a firm opposition gathers. Have we not rejected this once? Why do I need two? That very duality may be the circumstance of evil we dish out so fervently in order to destroy someone or thing. In this way, a parade already vanquished us. I mean, in the end, the revolution amazed no one. There are forces which are not aimed at creation, and whose sole purpose is to remain what and where they are. Whom are we eliminating? And yet, we continue to stir the kelippot. We are a slim factory of ideas. Speaking of which. We have named the primordial space of existence. We call it tehiru. And we fill it with thoughtless light and a pinch of the residue of thoughtful light that remained after something, which was not matter, withdrew.[η] What withdrew? Ein Sof. Something we call nothing. It is the process of withdrawal of Ein Sof, that event of withdrawal we call zimzum. An intake of breath. Something or someone left the scene of the crime. Creation. What remained after Ein Sof withdrew? After zimzum? A formless matter of thoughtless light. This residue we have named partzuf. Or golem : :

γ Turns out, O happy coincidence, that happens to be our side!

η That something which withdrew, an unknowable first cause, deus absconditus, infinite, containing neither distinctions nor differentiations, someone blindly called Ein Sof.

When the revolutionary soteriology died, he'd sought to attenuate. To be released from subsidiary judgment. Meanwhile, the French had reinvented corner-flanking. He plunged that way, trudged through enormous language. He counted letters, added and subtracted the 231 gates to a garden. Crawling, he crawled through a forest of spent numbers, sought delight on a cot of desolation. But even a cot and a room and a half of pencil shavings can be taken from you. No amount of whittling is sufficient to shield us from loss. Soon the street beckons. Someone else's murder becomes your own. Those letters became weapons to fling at the gates of heaven. Did he pound clay and shape water?[α] ::

[α] Know that this is a tradition handed down to you, and we are writing it down; it is forbidden to disclose it or to pass it down to everyone, but only to those who fear the Divine Name, take heed of His Name, and tremble at His Word.
Anonymous

Ein Sof

Booger Rooney rose to the full extent of his lack of height and took my hand. We shook on it.[α] And yet. When is a good shaking sufficient? Not yet. Booger wished no misunderstanding to take hold where no understanding of any kind had gone before. "There was and is no place for severed heads in a campaign to elect our leaders; nor, for that matter," he agglutinated, "should there be talk of strangulation." Is there no agent for transgression? "Hear this, know this," he gurgled horsely through four crowns and two capitations. "No one here broke that Shtick in two." Did I believe him? Perhaps you cannot possibly think so.[δ] Perhaps you would not believe a Booger when he tells us, our hand shaking in his hand shaking ours, that neither he nor his henchman in a shouting shirt separated a Shtick's mind from its shticky body? And yet, perhaps anyone will prefer to consider such a claim when the street beckons on the other hand.[ε] At such a moment, one neither believes nor disbelieves; one bathes in the warmed-over warmth of inclusion within a sentence that proclaimed the innocence of all the occupants of that room. How should we act? At such a time we seek a place to lie down. Nothing more? Certainly nothing less. How can you find it? I am still looking. And yet.

α I mean, he shook my hand; I shook on the end of it. Exactly what it was we shook about was not exactly clear.

δ You who lie properly encased in sheets and covers of cotton, wool or some combination of polyacrylonitrites. And even then.

ε What sort of sleuth is it that cannot find lodgings for the night?

אצ בפ גע דס הנ ומ זל חכ טי צת קש
אק בצ גפ דע הס ונ זמ כל מכ קת רש
אר בק גצ דפ הע וס זנ כמ טל יכ רת
אש בר גק דצ הפ וע זס כנ טמ יל שת
את בש גר דק הצ ופ זע כס טנ ימ כל

If a person should place a beheading (or for that matter a strangulation) in the category of execution rather than murder, perhaps that person will consider the hand that did the deed, and with which he now shakes someone's shaking hand, to be clean.[γ] Perhaps the hand with which we are shaken is not the actual hand that operated in the matter of said beheading. Shall that hand then bear a murderous guilt? Perhaps a Boogerish enterprise rises above the category of murder to fall into the realm of pure mystery. Further, shall we consider the source of so many deaths (a headless Shtick, a toothy dentist, an owlish Owley, not to mention Mustapha, Legrand, who imported and exported their own deaths, and Betty Boop, her nose buried now in a Dutchman's-breeches[η])? All these were a lot of deaths. He asked: What can be the source of so much death? Surely, he reflected in the mirror of his shaking shoes, only Death itself could provide so many dead souls. What shall we call Death when it is the source of death? The source of death, they say in the West, must be also and at once the source of life. Two!? Why do I need two? That source they named Ein Sof. Have I bumbled the letters of a name only to stumble on the source of life, not to mention death, and found them both on the thirty-second floor scraping heaven? Or was Booger nothing more than a red Shabbatean?[κ]::

γ Here is an argument to draw us off the sentence.

η Not to mention the possibility of my own demise, the imminence of which anyone in shaky shoes might possibly do well to reflect upon.

κ Shall we pour a truckload of metaphysical speculation into that moment we are given before death to consider our options?

אב כת גש דר הק וצ זפ חע טס ינ כמ
אג גת דש הר וק זצ חפ טע יס כנ למ
אר בג דת הש ור זק חצ טפ יע כס לנ
אה בד הת וש זר חק טצ יפ כע לס מנ
או בה גד ות זש חר טק יצ כפ לע מס

Not yet. Here an imbrication and a suspension. Perhaps, given a moment longer, I would have cut off the hand that shook shaking the menacing grip of a Boogery mitt. How long is a moment? How much longer is a moment longer? Perhaps you cannot possibly think so. Or so much longer. Perhaps you would have preferred to speak out for speaking rather than silently speaking for silence. Perhaps I too would have spoken. Given a moment longer.[φ] But, at such a moment, a silent henchman in a shouting shirt will momentarily play the squeezebox on your elbow. Time was going along. And so were we. But going where? A place to lie down, perhaps. For the night. Perhaps. Perhaps a long moment longer::

φ At such times, don't hold your breath for a moment longer.

What makes a false messiah? Is it love of power or powerful love? Is it seized, or thrust upon you? Someone in Gaza called Nathan eats bad herbs before bedtime and you make an appearance in his dreams. Speaking of Shabbatai Zevi, some say a bad case of cyclothymia. There were periods of illumination and periods of fall. But God never hid his face from Booger Rooney.[α] Nor was he one to count letters or knock at the gate to the garden. His was a lexiphanic tongue. He took no mercy on sentences. Whereas I. Whereas I hid my face from God and was under no threat of illumination. And yet, a Cafgu walks with the living dead. A nervous lip and a shouting shirt are but a single step away from dampened clay. They will do a Booger's bidding, untroubled by the clutter of mindfulness : :

α Such good humour in such bad times is, to say the least, in bad taste.

Shall we cast a final glance in the direction of the host of ambition behind that desk? A verbose smile waved us into next week. Have I mentioned the deadly mystery beneath his manner? Every incident thought this. And yet. Perhaps my head had provided a circumstance of evil? A man with a nervous lip led the way out of that long (lost) moment and from that shaking place. Shall we hesitate to follow?[α] What force operated to pull someone drowsy in the wake of a shouting shirt? Was it the fear of murder? In particular, our own. We all take harm personally, even in small doses.[δ] Was it the possibility of a bed for the night? Perhaps you cannot possibly think so. Or the bundled newspaper Joey Cafgu paused to gather from the desk prior to attacking the door. His was the sympathetic route in a package under his arm.[ε] Would he beat so painful a press? My legs longed shortly to be up and lying down and wrapped in the news of the day. I followed a Cafgu the way we follow any plot, so long as it moves up or down or along::

α To worry is the border of experience.

δ What remains in the wake of failure? The body, the thing itself. This is ours and this is theirs.

ε Perhaps the impulse of criticism bungles my judgment. Perhaps a newspaper is insufficient reason to draw someone into, and subsequently through, a doorway. But surely reason is a barn door we lock after the horse of somebody did something to somebody.

אב כת גש דר הק וצ זפ חע טס ינ כמ
אג גת דש הר וק זצ חפ טע יס כנ למ
אר בג דת הש ור זק חצ טפ יע כס לנ
אה בד הת וש זר חק טצ יפ כע לס מנ
או בה גד ות זש חר טק יצ כפ לע מס
אז בו גה זת חש טר יק כצ לפ מע נס
אח בז גו דה חת טש יר כק לצ מפ נע
אט בח גז דו טת יש כר לק מצ נפ סע
אי בט גח דז הו ית כש לר מק נצ ספ
אכ בי גט דח הז כת לש מר נק סצ עפ
אל בכ גי דט הח וז לת מש נר סק עצ
אמ בל גכ די הט וח מת נש סר עק פצ
אנ במ גל דכ הי וט זח נת סש ער פק

I tried to write one well not exactly write one because to try is to cry but I did try to write one. It had a good name it was *Blood on the Dining Room Floor* and it all had to do with that but there was no corpse[φ] and the detecting was general, it was all very clear in my head but it did not get natural the trouble was that if it all happened and it all had happened then you had to mix it up with other things that had happened and after all a novel even if it is a detective story ought not to mix up what happened with what has happened, anything that has happened is exciting enough without any writing, tell it as often as you like but do not write it as a story. However I did write it, it was such a good detective story but nobody did any detecting except just conversation so after all it was not a detective story so finally I concluded that even though Edgar Wallace does almost write detective stories without anybody doing any detecting on the whole a detective story does have to have an ending and my detective story did not have any.

φ Which is preferable to too many.

Gertrude Stein, "Why I Like Detective Stories" from *How Writing Is Written*

How many bodies disjoined from their minds constitute a mystery? Shall we count murders? Shall we compose a musical accompaniment to drown out the screams of the victims?[α] Having regularly failed, diplomats will don a coroner's apron. War becomes the conduct of a postmortem operation upon millions. Landscapes pause, someone knocks off a murder mystery. Someone else fingers the mystery of murder. Her hair burst. He curdled words.[δ] Only the bricks were moved. Testimony became the movie of the week. His disease was an offer of ferocity. He tried to think thoughts against thought itself. What remained? Only the dust of seeds upon his tongue : :

α Let these questions stand. The Gemara does not resolve it.

δ After murder, why won't language vanish?

How quickly the vestige of drama ages.[α] And so do we. Death: a hurdle we'll trip over when we come to it. Darkness is one possible result. In the meantime, we murder for glory and strengthen cash. Any day now I'll begin the kitchen. A Cafgu led his broken passenger once more into a hall of mirrors. There I reflected vainly on my situation.[δ] This only resembles this. When, I ventured to wonder, would my palms open? With Joey, there was an end to speeches. Only my armpits bellowed.[ε] Shall we study a row of sefirot lighting the way skyward? Two! How I hoped for two! To try for a split.[φ] But here, elevators laboured individually, each a casket on its own singular journey. Entretemps, in the open door of a singular elevator, every future gaped at that shouting shirt. And so did I. And so would you : :

α We are the wool mice of drama.

δ Shall the label study the contents? Shall the jar swallow the lid?

ε Are we forgetting a shouting shirt?

φ Elevators, we know all too well, were his area of expertise. Now, however, some singular failure of narrative dwindled any possible future.

אב כת גש דר הק וצ זפ חע טס ינ כמ
אג גת דש הר וק זצ חפ טע יס כנ למ
אר בג דת הש ור זק חצ טפ יע כס לנ
אה בד הת וש זר חק טצ יפ כע לס מנ
או בה גד ות זש חר טק יצ כפ לע מס
אז בו גה זת חש טר יק כצ לפ מע נס
אח בז גו דה חת טש יר כק לצ מפ נע
אט בח גז דו טת יש כר לק מצ נפ סע
אי בט גח דז הו ית כש לר מק נצ ספ
אכ בי גט דח הז כת לש מר נק סצ עפ
אל בכ גי דט הח וז לת מש נר סק עצ
אמ בל גכ די הט וח מת נש סר עק פצ
אנ במ גל דכ הי וט זח נת סש ער פק
אס בנ גמ דל הכ וי זט סת עש פר צק
אע בס גנ דמ הל וכ זי חט עת פש צר
אפ בע גס דנ המ ול זכ חי פת צש קר
אצ בפ גע דס הנ ומ זל חכ טי צת קש
אק בצ גפ דע הס ונ זמ כל מכ קת רש
אר בק גצ דפ הע וס זנ כמ טל יכ רת
אש בר גק דצ הפ וע זס כנ טמ יל שת
את בש גר דק הצ ופ זע כס טנ ימ כל

Who cast doubt upon a movement encompassing the thinkable? Will an ascending dialectic function in a descending elevator? Shall we count backwards? All is not assemblable. To flee a shadow in a shouting shirt was a thought overshadowed only by the desire to flee one's self. Not to mention a place to lie down. What totality remains in the face of our own remains?[γ] It was the shocking nature of death, mine in particular, that prevented any synthesis. Mortality is precisely the fact that everything cannot be handled. An act is called for; we plunge a long finger in Booger's nose in search of the speckled solution to the mystery of our own death.[η] Those options having dried up, cry Pick me! Pick me! : :

γ The nature of this case is not like the nature of this case and the nature of this case is not like the nature of this case.

η Do not try this except at home.

We cast the small stones of language[α] at the walls of our confinement. We think beneath the moment. To escape our own mortality is to escape ourselves. Yet nothing becomes a Cafgu like our own mortality. If a Cafgu becomes our mortality, to escape that shirt is to escape ourselves.[δ] At such times, we have little time for thinking thoughts. A Cafgu is mostly (I meant moistly) silent clay. Shall we search our pockets for the small sucking stones of language? Shall we count letters, murmur combinations in descending order? To say the event that happened, happened that way. HuAu HuAi HuAe HuAa HuAo, I certainly murmured. And, in ordered descent, counted. And so would you::

α Engrave them like a garden, carve them like a wall, deck them like a ceiling.

δ Is it the shock of our mortality that produces such prodigiously loopy ratiocination?

Entretemps,[α] he began to combine letters and circle the creature of his confinement. Chant on suit away as in. To what purpose were those susurrations? Was it discomfort within the coffin of his descent that set him intoning circles around a shouting shirt? Did he hope thus to secure his release?[δ] To escape that golem or to escape himself? Perhaps you cannot possibly think so. You may regard such chanting as whining and grovelling. Joey Cafgu certainly thought so. At such times, a nervous lip will cuff us heavily on the side of the head. To knock various senses out of us : :

אב כת גש דר הק וצ זפ חע טס ינ כמ
אג גת דש הר וק זצ חפ טע יס כנ למ
אר בג דת הש ור זק חצ טפ יע כס לנ
אה בד הת וש זר חק טצ יפ כע לס מנ
או בה גד ות זש חר טק יצ כפ לע מס
אז בו גה זת חש טר יק כצ לפ מע נס
אח בז גו דה חת טש יר כק לצ מפ נע
אט בח גז דו טת יש כר לק מצ נפ סע
אי בט גח דז הו ית כש לר מק נצ ספ
אכ בי גט דח הז כת לש מר נק סצ עפ
אל בכ גי דט הח וז לת מש נר סק עצ
אמ בל גכ די הט וח מת נש סר עק פצ
אנ במ גל דכ הי וט זח נת סש ער פק
אס בנ גמ דל הכ וי זט סת עש פר צק
אע בס גנ דמ הל וכ זי חט עת פש צר
אפ בע גס דנ המ ול זכ חי פת צש קר
אצ בפ גע דס הנ ומ זל חכ טי צת קש
אק בצ גפ דע הס ונ זמ כל מכ קת רש
אר בק גצ דפ הע וס זנ כמ טל יכ רת
אש בר גק דצ הפ וע זס כנ טמ יל שת
את בש גר דק הצ ופ זע כס טנ ימ כ

Shall our pants come down around our ankles in our final moment?[φ] And before whose face shall we be found wanting? Someone may have been watching long ago. And yet. Now, our executioners have judged us lacking even the moisture of a mitzvah. Still, in a time of movies, we imagine ourselves framed. One stands outside one's body, narrating in the preterit past. If this was his moment, he'd missed it. Took refuge instead in a telekinetic exercise.[γ] To ascend where? He was found wanting. Wanting what? More. More what? More of the same. He got a good cuffing about the head. Which was more or less more of the same : :

α Between floors in an elevator is an entretemps; should the elevator stop between floors, that would be a contretemps. Esprit de l'escalier?

δ R' Eliezer Rokeach of Wormes taught: Pronounce the letters of the Tetragrammaton in combination with the 231 gates and circle the creature.

φ We stuff each precious second of our existence into a sock under the mattress. Save ourselves for a chance at a good death. That chance will come and go too quickly.

γ This would require some thirty hours of disciplined meditation. Go ahead, try this at home.

Let us construct an argument whereby a cuff on the side of the head is one result of a meditative susurration. Perhaps even a desirable consequence to be welcomed with open ears.[α] How high had he risen, in the course of his descent, to now witness the scintillation of stars? He considered a repetition. Thought better of it.[δ] Shall we say he chose to return to the land of the living?[ε] To retreat from the brink of mystery was a cautionary tale on the end of his nose. What remained? Only to follow that Cafgu somewhere, which in itself was a mystery[φ]::

α Whose angel rang them bells?

δ He thought better. Better not.

ε He would heed Hai Gaon's warning against embarking on the mysteries without proper training.

φ Would there be a place to lie down? One from which he might get up again?

A Warm Camel

When dusk was gone, buried in the alley of everybody's refuse, and day was drowned in the illuminated darkness of the street,[α] he was a small brown mutt following the mystery of a nervous lip in a shouting shirt. He brushed his heels against the pavement of indifference. Even standing outside his body, narrating in the preterit past, there remained the taste of broken syllables. What is it like? This only resembles this. We may say: the savour of shattered phonemes, but a taste of broken syllables remains the taste of broken syllables. A hint of dust upon your tongue. He thought: When a Cafgu leads the way, one should try for something better. He could not find it. Hence there was no need for a strong arm, nor for the hand of a strong arm on the arm of the manhandled man. What draws a tail after the dog?[δ] The possibility of a place to lie down? The rust of a room and a half? The gloved threats of a nosy Booger? Whatever it was, it sported wings on the heels of Joey Cafgu's confidence. A shouting shirt became something to make out as it clashed swiftly through the crowd. Shall we say the toe of motion sings? He pulled his pants and what little they contained after a shouting shirt. He pushed his face up against a crowd of poor complexions and the evening's excess. Boys with fish eyes and freshly gleaming pustules dreaming of barbells and bar belles. A whiff of money, pigs, leprosy and sexual relations. Let us move the ball downfield. Joey extended his lead. There was no time for a pang of hunger.[ε] Shall we put our shoulder to the wheel of profluence and say the crowd thinned thinner than his hopes? They approached the reluctant slope of a park, a hedge, a low wall. Someone had already scrawled the name of that dead Owley. Was this to be his morning on the slopes of Fuente Grande? The buses do not run there. Even so, one feels a fondness for one's executioner.[φ] Possible reasons are: here is our last human face; a last glorious failure to commune; we may prefer to gaze upon even the visage of our executioner than the face of death; the Other's face is a port in a storm; to know at last for certain that death resides in the face of the Other is a momentary compensation; no one else knows so clearly what one's future will bring. Did he follow a shouting shirt into a lack of shadows by the gate? Perhaps you cannot possibly think so. Do dogs dance? Do wings gather rock? A shouting shirt was a flag in his heart. A Cafgu, his only boy pal. Until he lost him. By the gate. And who stood there in his stead? : :

אב	כת	גש	דר	הק	וצ	זפ	חע	טס	ינ	כ
אג	גת	דש	הר	וק	זצ	חפ	טע	יס	כנ	למ
אד	בג	דת	הש	ור	זק	חצ	טפ	יע	כס	לנ
אה	בד	הת	וש	זר	חק	טצ	יפ	כע	לס	מנ
או	בה	גד	ות	זש	חר	טק	יצ	כפ	לע	מס
אז	בו	גה	זת	חש	טר	יק	כצ	לפ	מע	נס
אח	בז	גו	דה	חת	טש	יר	כק	לצ	מפ	נע
אט	בח	גז	דו	טת	יש	כר	לק	מצ	נפ	סע
אי	בט	גח	דז	הו	ית	כש	לר	מק	נצ	ספ
אכ	בי	גט	דח	הז	כת	לש	מר	נק	סצ	עפ
אל	בכ	גי	דט	הח	וז	לת	מש	נר	סק	עצ
אמ	בל	גכ	די	הט	וח	מת	נש	סר	עק	פצ
אנ	במ	גל	דכ	הי	וט	זח	נת	סש	ער	פק
אס	בנ	גמ	דל	הכ	וי	זט	סת	עש	פר	צק
אע	בס	גנ	דמ	הל	וכ	זי	חט	עת	פש	צר
אפ	בע	גס	דנ	המ	ול	זכ	חי	פת	צש	קר
אצ	בפ	גע	דס	הנ	ומ	זל	חכ	טי	צת	קש
אק	בצ	גפ	דע	הס	ונ	זמ	כל	מכ	קת	רש
אר	בק	גצ	דפ	הע	וס	זנ	כמ	טל	יכ	רת
אש	בר	גק	דצ	הפ	וע	זס	כנ	טמ	יל	שת
את	בש	גר	דק	הצ	ופ	זע	כס	טנ	ימ	כ

Betty Boop. In railroad coveralls and that Chinese tee-shirt.[γ] Had she been gardening there? Until dark overcame her digging?[η] The dark smudges of the labour of her own hands on her cheek, a crooked finger of hair broken free from the tight bun of serious business. Shall we say, in the dark she ~~shone.~~ I mean, by the light of a Camel cigarette. That night, she was as clear as day.[κ] What is a page rejecting? Death? Time? Possible reasons: we have slipped our head through a noose on Owl Creek Bridge and are flashing back to happier days; like the French, we have reinvented corner-flanking; there is no before and after in the Torah. Perhaps you cannot possibly think so. Shall we say she told him her death was a ruse? To escape notice.[λ] To keep her name out of the papers.[μ] Shall we pause now for a romantic interlude? They were happily reunited on Saint Someone-did-something-to-someone Street. Am I a peddler to go on like a peddler? Let us say she addressed his astonishment: Ferme ta bouche, espèce de cornichon, y'a plein de moustiques ici, tu vas avaler someone's big dick. A foul mouth and French fiction will make the soft cushion of a common male denominator. Let us say, Betty Boop bopped. She carried her name in a red handbag. Along with the crumpled bits of a concrete description.[ν] And a trowel : :

α The darkness after the darkness, the movie after the movie. I have forgotten the name of the movie.

δ A Baraita was taught in the academy of R' Eliezer ben Yaakov: Even at a time of mortal danger, a person should not abandon his dignified bearing. Sanhedrin 92b

ε In spite of my already fragile digestion.

φ El Ché's final words to his executioner: Tell my wife that she should remarry. The talk of boys among themselves. Still, here is some evidence of communion, albeit tainted.

γ It read: Pianyi yi dian, keyi ma?

η Her grave, his grave?

κ Among the young women up in the park. No envy. Enough imagination to share their happiness, enough judgment to know I am too weak to have such happiness, foolish enough to think I see to the bottom of my own and their situation. Not foolish enough; there is a tiny crack there, and wind whistles through it and spoils the effect. F. Kafka *Diaries*

λ I meant a death notice.

μ And her soul in its shell.

ν We are speaking here of tissues, a pair of Bic Inc. products – one leaking, the other empty – a capsule of menstrual hygiene, a figure of speech, a pack of thirsty Camels, an empty lighter, *Le plaisir du texte*, matches, a shuddering heart, failing eyes and languishing breath, a list.

Mazel

They say in the West, a trowel will muddy the waters. And how shall we clarify the ensuing turbidity? This is a case of go read it in the teacher's house. Did he, for instance, or for an instant, read his own death in a trowel's edge?[α] Or did she rather dig in the hard ground of someone's reticence to unfold an anacolu-thonic life. What was he carrying?[δ] Fears certain-ly (where shall we keep them), regrets, self-re-criminations, a wad of tissue. A trowel was to unearth the bitter truf-fles of ruefulness. And did she imagine a trowel would suffice to root out and examine someone in the light of darkness by the gate? She pried between his teeth; he clenched his tongue be-tween his knees. She eyed his fragile digestion. An edge quickly formed be-tween them.[ε] A vestige, the pea of midnight, an insect's trace beneath the heel of their affection. Let us say he laboured some of those moments to construct something appropriate on the sub-ject of Howley's death. But, at such times, a sentence will become a cube of sharp corners in your mouth. He found he could neither tongue it past his teeth nor swallow it back into silence.[φ] He was stuck with it, and a snoutish open mouth to boot. Not to mention a difficulty breathing. She eyed him eyeishly. Until something aside from disgust turned her gaze. Shall we say, his mouth stuffed with the apple of good intentions followed her gaze, a glimpse of Cafgu shadowing in the lack of shadows by the gate? And a glance, a sign of understanding between them[γ]: :

אב	כת	גש	דר	הק	וצ	זפ	ח			
אג	גת	דש	הר	וק	זצ	חפ	טע			
אר	בג	דת	הש	ור	זק	חצ	טפ	יע	ס	לג
אה	בד	הת	וש	זר	חק	טצ	יפ	כע	לס	מנ
או	בה	גד	ות	זש	חר	טק	יצ	כפ	לע	מס
אז	בו	גה	זת	חש	טר	יק	כצ	לפ	מע	נס
אח	בז	גו	דה	חת	טש	יר	כק	לצ	מפ	נע
אט	בח	גז	דו	טת	יש	כר	לק	מצ	נפ	סע
אי	בט	גח	דז	הו	ית	כש	לר	מק	נצ	ספ
אכ	בי	גט	דח	הז	כת	לש	מר	נק	סצ	עפ
אל	בכ	גי	דט	הח	וז	לת	מש	נר	סק	עצ
אמ	בל	גכ	די	הט	וח	מת	נש	סר	עק	פצ
אנ	במ	גל	דכ	הי	וט	זח	נת	סש	ער	פק
אס	בנ	גמ	דל	הכ	וי	זט	סת	עש	פר	צק
אע	בס	גנ	דמ	הל	וכ	זי	חט	עת	פש	צר
אפ	בע	גס	דנ	המ	ול	זכ	חי	פת	צש	קר
אצ	בפ	גע	דס	הנ	ומ	זל	חכ	טי	צת	קש
אק	בצ	גפ	דע	הס	ונ	זמ	כל	מכ	קת	רש
אר	בק	גצ	דפ	הע	וס	זנ	כמ	טל	יכ	רת
אש	בר	גק	דצ	הפ	וע	זס	כנ	טמ	יל	שת
את	בש	גר	דק	הצ	ופ	זע	כס	טנ	ימ	כ

A peripheral Cafgu was a pump organ in his throat. Framed in the garden gate,[η] shall we brush our lips against his cheek? He came and went in the triangle of Betty Boop, a Cafgu and a trowel. There came neither kiss nor cuff. Your fears, she told him, are a large mouse. That Cafgu is my mazel.[κ] He watches over the contents of my foot-steps, he keeps death from breaking my habits.[λ] In this way we learn we are the suspect and not the intended victim. Had she tossed her hat in Rooney's ring? Could he blame her? Certain margins had drained their affection. Their story was every story. Between them was Owley's missing letter, the presence of the absence of a letter in Owley's name. But perhaps that death had also been premature-ly exaggerated. Perhaps a Welshish forward lay in wait.[μ] Perhaps you cannot possibly think so. He did not ask her. Where was his own mazel[π] to send him a warning of fear without apparent reason? Was there not a surfeit of reasons to be afraid? And what had he learned to defend against a threat he could not see?[ρ] He thought to shout: "The goat at the slaughter-house is fatter than I." In-stead he spoke to warn her against the possi-bility of a Boogery plot (Rooney's plan to wipe the pinkish hue from the face of old comrades, hence to wipe the pinkish hue from his own past). Once they were few, now they were becoming fewer. Shall we say she did not agree? How fondly she called a scheming Rooney that old Booger, and Joey was an angel in a shouting shirt. Perhaps you are thinking: We develop a fondness for our executioners. They are the dark port in a storm. Meanwhile. He might have reached for her hand, but his fingers were frozen on a volume of prayers and a curtain of souls. Instead. I trembled darkly while she plumed letters in the air between us, which is where I would have placed a warm cup of something, had I the money to utter the Frankish word for coffee. Instead. Let us study a thinning cloud of letters for any sign of grief. I found relief. Instead. I mean, I found it in her. Or in that cloud. Of letters. Which I took to represent her. Or her thoughts, at least. And was I relieved? The other's death is often a temptation. He thought to remain dumb. Instead he poured the warm dung of conversation into the cold air. Then perhaps Owley, he said, though lacking a letter, is not dead? Oh no, thank god he's very dead, she plumed. Instead : :

α Did he imagine Betty B. bopping him on the recently cuffed and turbid head?

δ Aside from a curtain of souls, a strict volume of instruction, and the dull pencil of chrysan-themums.

ε When, years later, old acquain-tances meet again, must we act half the age we were back then? Yet, we enjoy thinking of ourselves as adults.

φ All this in the manner of those lit-erary texts drawing the camera in for an intimate moment.

γ I mean between Joey and Betty; between a stuffed mouth and anyone else there can be no under-standing.

η Watch-man, what of the night? Watchman, what of the night?
Sanhedrin 94a

κ Learn from this, that when she becomes frightened for no apparent reason, even though she has not seen the cause of her fear, her designated angel in heaven, her mazel, has seen it.

λ He had taken a Cafgu for Gabriel, the angel of terrible Judgment before the Hall of Delight, when all along he was the angel Michael, defending Betty Boop from the accusations of those evil shells.

μ In the burning bush. In the darkness beyond the gate.

π I am all the mazel he can afford.

ρ When a mazel sends a warning of fear, one should jump four amos from that place (the place that a person occupies is defined as the four amos that surround him). Alternatively, one should recite Krias Shema. And if one is standing in a place of filth, where it is prohibited to recite Krias Shema, one should say the following incantation: "The goat at the slaughterhouse is fatter than I."
Sanhedrin 94a

Shall we say Howley, before he lost his letter, had turned the eye with which she eyed me now a brutish mauve. What drove him there? What makes a Welshish gardener pull his dark hands from the damp soil?[α] What brings him lumbering down from the roof? There was no telling. Not from the party of the second part. When is a handsome gardener deserving death? One might have lifted the hind leg of vindication. But the Other's death is occasionally sufficient vindication. The living require our attention.[δ] In Rooney, he found a warm cup in which to plunge the sweet madeleine of animosity. Whereas in Betty Boop. Verse could not occupy the officer of pleasure. He sought to place himself between a murder and its design. Between the underdog of mystery and the hearse. To share a generous portion of his suspicions. Had Booger operated an owlish death? Killed that bird with a very heavy stone? Cleared his electoral way to a higher body, not to mention Betty's to boot? Having gained so much understanding, how long would she (not to mention I) be allowed to stand? But she let his questions stand. Paused instead to curve. He laboured against the pencil of his own arousal to arouse her suspicions. If there was a difficulty, this was the difficulty. To know what to say to an unbeliever. Go this way! he told her. She did not take the first part; therefore, she would not take the end as well. Meanwhile[ε] a sign downfield. That Cafgu shifted his growing restlessness : :

α To plant elsewhere the purple flower of his masculine handiwork.

δ Between throat and chin would seem to be the most rewarding place to stab. Lift the chin and stick the knife into the tensed muscles. But this spot is probably rewarding only in one's imagination. You expect to see a magnificent gush of blood and a network of sinews and little bones like you find in the leg of a roast turkey. F. Kafka *Diaries*

ε Here a term to achieve a measure of profluency, to take the ball forward. Perhaps you are thinking we have lost sight of the goal.

אב כת גש דר הק ו
אג גת דש הר וק זצ
אד בג דת הש ור זק חצ
אה בד הת וש זר חק טצ יפ כע לס מנ
או בה גד ות זש חר טק יצ כפ לע מס
אז בו גה זת חש טר יק כצ לפ מע נס
אח בז גו דה חת טש יר כק לצ מפ נע
אט בח גז דו ת יש כר לק מצ נפ סע
אי בט גח ד כש לר מק נצ ספ
אכ בי גט ש מר נק סצ עפ
אל בכ גי ת מש נר סק עצ
אמ בל גכ די ת נש סר עק פצ
אנ במ גל דכ הי וט זח נת סש ער פק
אס בנ גמ דל הכ וי זט סת עש פר צק
אע בס גנ דמ הל וכ זי חט עת פש צר
אפ בע גס דנ המ ול זכ חי פת צש ק
אצ בפ גע דס הנ ומ זל חכ טי צ
אק בצ גפ דע הס ונ זמ כל מ
אר בק גצ דפ הע וס זנ כמ ט
אש בר גק דצ הפ וע זס כ
את בש גר דק הצ ופ זע כ

How should we do what we do? I wish I knew.[φ] If he was an August of noise, oh, would that he remain silent. And let those (his) questions droop and dwindle. Instead he rattled along about a Boogery mayhem. Let's suppose I enlisted the aid of a pose, something soft and broken, in a hard yet feminine way? I may have done so. I wanted. What? A cigarette. Something else. To unmake up his mind.[γ] Yeah, that was it. For sure nothing more. To let old Booger (I really mean that fondly) stand. To convince him was my hard row to hoe. If there was an ancient teabag, this was that teabag. Who knows what to say to a quarrelsome lip?[η] I'd shown him Howley's handiwork. If he took that one particle, he might take the whole alphabet soup. But who suspects a gardener's open hands? At night they're fisted flowers. From this he gathered nothing.[κ] I may have offered a moment of tenderness; he made an objection, a platform of vigilance. Wiggle this way! Just the opposite! What business was it of his? Who made him the policeman of pleasure? Suppose, following some howling demise, Booger Rooney had been a friend.[λ] Suppose, having found a booger in his own nose, Howley's rage preceded his own death. What of it? Where's the novel in that? Oh how you dabble. Were you casting that gardener against an ogre? With boys, always this is theirs and this is theirs. Howley's point of view was agricultural. Money, pigs, sex, sex, sex. Meanwhile.[μ] This one added and subtracted and exfoliated. He might have eyed me greenly, but he never said so. On and on, he mysteriosophized. Something about must and grandly, that dentist with a whole lot of T's in his name, and Howley's absent muscles. He was a busted record with his busted Shtick. Didn't I tell that boy to cut the cheese dance? Where was the common pudding to fill a stadium with paper? Whatever only resembles whatever. Was I strangled? Headless? Burning up somebody's yard? Perhaps, I ventured to say, we're all perfectly well and fit and no one is murdered in the least. The boy wiped his hands on his pants. Okay, I'll give you that, so Shtick was headless.[ν] That was one bit of news I could not split in two. But one gooey Shtick a conspiring Booger doesn't make. What office was worth the first or any other degree of murder? Booger had his name to consider. Since when was strangulation a winning strategy in the electoral do-si-do? Were his fears calmed? No way you think so. That boy went on wiping and warmly warning me against a Cafgu in waiting : :

φ From this point of view, a doubtful linguistic offering.

γ Let us say, one who makes up his own mind must lie in it.

η Do not gossip excessively with a woman… The more a person speaks to women, the more harm he does to himself and the more he neglects Torah study. And in the end it will lead him to Gehinnom. Yosei ben Yochanan of Yerushalayim

κ There are three things that are never satisfied: the grave, the narrow part of the womb, and the earth that is not sated with water. Sanhedrin 92a

λ And a friend in deed?

μ There's that profluent ball forward again.

ν If that long fiction is to be believed.

I'm saying that boy was not dressed for the occasion. He worked an occasional shivering glance[α] from a lurking Cafgu to a girl does what she can with what she's got. Wouldn't you? Let's walk, he said a word or two about his mother. Some terrible imprecision driving him into the language of vinegar. His technique was humour only the cold had driven us out of that park.[δ] Okay we moved our mutual shoe into the utopian gaslight between the lure of money and a car. Here we were all mannequins in storefront windows. While my reflections badly vibrated, his pace and lip quickened. Did he think a fast lip wouldn't freeze?[ε] What did he talk about? Old times, pencil shavings of love, the past of our past now long past. Sure I listened, wouldn't you? Anyone can listen to a heart beat. I would have settled for a coffee. And a place to bend my knees. What fruit forgives the seedy aftertaste of guilt?[φ] After that revolutionary sottise dies, one tries un univers à deux. But who can construct a planet on the turf of turpitude. I turned to the garden.[γ] So would you. A garden keeps both knees on the ground and your nose in a Dutchman's-breeches. The slight wheel makes a weed of illusion. Two people can turn off the evening news and practice mutual agriculture. We seek our self in the visage de l'autre. The body, a routine in itself. Two? Why do we need to be two in order to be? To recover yourself in the disappearance of the Other. How long would it last? Howley's rough hands were soft. Until he removed them from the soil : :

α I mean the glance was occasional; there was no stopping that shiver.

δ On a cold dark street, the knee of night will press us firmly in the backside.

ε Meanwhile, a warm camel between your lips keeps a girl busy.

φ See fig for one.

γ And the gardener.

They were trailing a Cafgu across the fabric of traffic. Was there method in his methodology? When she glanced at his backward glance, he glanced back at hers. What kept him striding past a cafeteria, in the light of so much pastry? Surely he would soon shiver to a halt.[η] But neither sleep nor sustenance could draw him off that sidewalk. It was all lights, alleys, traffic. If his tongue wagged, was it to keep her with him? Perhaps you cannot possibly think so.[κ] Perhaps a penniless pride will drive a hard bargain for a bite to eat and a place to lie down. Perhaps he also thought of Joey, doggedly tailing their cold tales? You go ahead and think so. We did. Go ahead, I mean. Or then again.[λ] Perhaps he thought of a trick Shtick taught. On a journey between the light and the alley. To enter a door, and exit a backdoor breeze.[μ] Where was he going, going on like a peddler? Did he lash her to him with his tongue?[ν] In this way he moved crablike across a map of circumstance – knight to bishop three – seeking what? A house. A rooming house in which he had once kept silent, and toiled hard to escape the gaze of his fellow boarders,[π] a house which had been a back door in Shtick's back pocket. You wanted Ulysses, you got Abraham. But there was no wish to return to a past that even then he longed to be past. He took her there, dreaming of the alley behind, narrow as their escape from a Cafgu in Rooney's clothing. He planned a Shtick trick and a backdoor breeze. Would she follow him in? And out? Perhaps you cannot possibly think so. Perhaps you think he should have thought of something better. He tried to think of something better. He could not find it.[ρ] Nevertheless, perhaps cold and tired, even Betty Boop will follow anyone anywhere in off the street. It was necessary for this to be said, otherwise it might have occurred to you to say. That door, which was always open, was closed. To stand together on a doorstep and ring a bell so late at night in some quarters is certainly a sign of something else: money, pigs, leprosy and sexual relations. This may be true. And yet. Not yet. In such a case, and unlike a church, that door is always already open. Even so, the police will occasionally kick it in. In this case, the door was opened by curlers in a pinkish bathrobe. She wore two plump furry slippers and a narrow cat between them. Would she let them in? Would you? Perhaps, if there was remembrance of a boarder who kept a clean quiet room. And drew a smile on the first of the first of the first month : :

η Surely his arms were weary with the weight of so many souls and so many prayers; surely his heels were worn out with so much scribbling.

κ Perhaps old times will nip at our heels.

λ What again? Must we go over that ground again and again?

μ To leave a busy golem behind, a half hour older and wiser.

ν If so, she was tongue-tied.

π A boarding house is a house of solitude on tiptoes, a house of adults cast back into children making beds and dusting drawers, of large men in bedroom slippers edging past each other in narrow hallways.

אב כת גש דר הק ו
גת דש הר וק זצ
ג דת הש ור זק חצ
בד הת וש זר ק טצ יפ ס מנ
ו בה גד ות זש טק יצ כפ לע מס
ז בו גה זת חש יק כצ לפ מע נס
אח בז גו דה חת טש יר כק לצ מפ נע
אט בח גז דו ת יש כר לק מצ נפ סע
אי בט גח ד כש לר מק נצ ספ
אכ בי גט ש מר נק סצ עפ
אל בכ גי ת מש נר סק עצ
אמ בל גכ די ת נש עק פצ
אנ במ גל דכ הי נ ר פק
אס בנ מ דל הכ וי זט סת פר צק
אע דמ הל וכ זי חט עת פש צר
אפ כ דנ המ ול זכ חי פת צש ק
אצ בפ גע דס הנ ומ זל חכ טי צ
אק בצ גפ דע הס ונ זמ כל מ
אר בק גצ דפ הע וס זנ כמ ט
אש בר צ הפ וע זס כ
את ב הצ ופ זע כ

ρ I have not found it. Perhaps, after a time, we cease looking for something better. This is necessary simply in order to go on going on. Perhaps it is merely that time when we cease looking that we long for. I have not found that either.

Shall we cast a last glance at a golem keeping his distance before we slip between the cat and a smile to enter the warm linoleum of desolation? Silence drifted down from the floor above.[α] Had he been given a free hand, he would have taken hers. Instead he took the lead toward the back of a house with a tail between his legs. Let us pause at the door to an empty room he had often shut behind him.[δ] A pink face beneath pink curlers will offer to open it. Let us say, he cracked that door and peeked within, to an empty shell. There was a bed covered in the ribbed brown fabric of his past. There was the scent of pencil shavings in a chest of drawers. Was he tempted to slip inside and sit for a second, merely to catch his breath, on the pea of midnight? Perhaps you hope not. I hope so.[ε] And yet he knew better. And so should you. They were already a minute into injury time. Those pink curlers retired softly, to let you think it over. In an argument between caution and a place to lie down, a minute will stretch out on the bed. And yet. Not yet. He would not sleep. Rather he would merely pause, barely creasing the brown corduroy of his concentration. He would not let go of Betty Boop's hand. And if his eyes did shut, it would be for a mere fraction of a fraction of a second. Any second now, his legs would leap to his feet and make for the back door, even as that busy Cafgu rang at the front, preparing to enter and become half an hour older and wiser : :

α Even the memory of past unhappiness can warm a cold heart.

δ Here we should remind ourselves: A Shtick trick requires no more than a passing nod in a hasty passage through to the alley beyond.

ε I mean, I hope you hope not. I hope thus to affect a case of profluence, by means of our (I mean you as you read and I as I write) knowing something he (that was not me about whom I write) does not.

כת גש דר הק ו
דש הר וק זצ
ת הש ור זק ח
ת וש זר ק מנ
ות ז טק י ע מס
ה זת חש יק כצ לפ מע נס
בז גו דה חת טש יר כק לצ מפ נע
ט בח גז דו ת יש כר לק מצ נפ סע
אי בט גח ד כש לר מק נצ ספ
אכ בי גט ש מר נק ס עפ
אל בכ גי מש נר סק עצ
אמ בל גכ די ק פצ
אנ במ גל דכ הי נ ר פק
אס בנ מ דל הכ וי זט סת פר צק
אע דמ הל וכ זי חט עת פש צר
אפ ס דנ המ ול זכ חי פת צש ק
אצ בפ גע דס הנ ומ זל חכ טי צ
אק בצ גפ דע הס ונ זמ כל מ
אר בק גצ דפ הע וס זנ כמ ט
אש בר צ הפ וע זס כ
את ב הצ ופ זע כ

Maybe you say, so what brings a B-Boop back from the grave? Who resurrects a girl from an inky rag? In fact, that death was a manner of speaking. Truly a parable to save my skin.[φ] And what Howley wrote on it, in the black and blue ink of his despondency. I was scared to death, in a manner of speaking. Speaking of death, his was not intended, certainly not by me. And not by him. Love is something to do after the vessels of soteriology have shattered. When we have lost the world,[γ] we tell ourselves we are two. Anyone would rather be two. If there is a difficulty, this is the curling pistol up your butt, pal. So there.[η] Two can build a courtyard within four walls, and keep the world at bay. The other's face will mirror your own solitude, ad infinitum. Anyway, after a while, you whiled away the time, and even two is not enough. Or it becomes too much. Or much two much.[κ] The absence of presence may become a reason to make three. If you can. So maybe you're thinking, oh there it is, she couldn't. Or he couldn't. Make three, I mean. Well, suck that wad of hormones right back in your throat, pal. Maybe, just maybe, she didn't want any more. Maybe two was sufficient, thank you very much. Or two one too many. Maybe a garden and a cat would have been sufficient. So what? So two become one and, sooner or later, one divides into two.[λ] All this addition and subtraction becomes a pain in the country garden. If you know what I mean. I mean, the mystery in the face of the Other becomes a well-travelled row to hoe, un sentier battu, battu à mort. Boys will be boys. Unfortunately. You think you're making friends, they are plucking figs in somebody else's orchard. To a prize fighter the Other is always a prize. One weekend an old Booger came to visit. He got up Howley's nose. I gave him a head of lettuce. I mean from the garden. By Monday morning, I was a dark continent in that Welshish boy's Welshish mind. I shaved my legs. Now there's a hard row to hoe. Howley held his tongue on the roof of his mouth;[μ] he kneed the ground beneath the hedge, he soiled his hands. It may be that he recalled our first encounters in another man's garden and feared turnabout is fair game. Meanwhile a Booger seemed to enjoy being mean awhile. I guess I'm saying Rooney tried that day to ruin Howley's game. If games are what you're playing. Boys will be boys. Unfortunately. As for me, I did not feel particularly prepared to be prized. I took refuge among the cabbage, half an hour older and wiser : :

φ If it is true, then why do you say "a parable"? And if it was a parable, then why do you say it is true? Say rather: in truth it was a parable. Sanhedrin 92b

γ And we are lost to the world.

η Did you think she would speak in the language of men?

κ Or two too much. Anyway, that's why you need two, in case you were wondering.

λ And a lot of good your boyish dialectical butt does a girl in a garden.

μ A Welshish boy will lash his tongue to the mast of his dark thoughts.

Some yes some oh that damn tooth yikes and beat warm wait not yet hold still stone still the air fish waves beating lids will open tap in the bowl come on let's hear the taptap in the bowl soon is not soon enough[α] between long nail and the other thing shadow cross soft cruncheroo my tongue oh yes bristle that's nice oh the pleasure low belly to the ground oh that tooth hard brush harder please wait wing flap my chest wait to pounce those lids flutter mouse under tissue thin[δ] and let's have the door please thank you very much grass weed wort mush pungent thing and crunch between my teeth you could brush harder but oh that tooth escape ride it hear it faint quick snappish there more yes but more what crabby elastic bite hard cat cock rub around it jab snap and tear long muscle of sourish flutter creep up close wait stone still but some that hum behind warm fishy exhalation of milk fog that awful tooth pulling gnaw away blood pulp door opening to sluggish yolk flavour whir it under the thickly darkish blanket but some yes let's have some now low muddy cock the curl over a hitch click very tight the tail very tight oh but that damn tooth what about a brushing and meat meat meat or fish fish fish sour closer dig in turn hook into it jump crack it sharp space sun so warm the bowl the brush harder please harder what there something no nothing silence wait stone still stream of brine breath fish and bone the nail the padded rim the blanket's weight pulling a dart under beating lids there now mouse movement look out yes gone alive wet and all lit up[ε]::

α Your species attends us; you are an occasional treat.

δ Shall I turn and present my plumed indifference? So there.

ε Very nice, now let's have the bowl, et plus vite que ça, all right.

גש דר
הר ו
הש ור
וש ז מנ
ות ע מס
ה זת חש יק כצ לפ מע נס
גו דה חת טש יר כק לצ מפ נע
בח גז דו ת יש כר צ נפ סע
י בט גח ד ספ
אכ בי ג
ל בכ גי
ל גכ די
גל דכ ק
דל הכ ר צק
הל וכ זי חט עת פש
ול זכ חי פת צ
זל חכ טי
כל מ
נ כמ
ע זס
זע ופ חצ

To awaken face to face with a cat is to face the indifference of the world.[ф] How long had it coiled by his pillow? Staring. Waiting for what? To capture, perhaps, in that waking instant on the cusp of consciousness, a night's dreams. He felt those dreams – a long dark hallway, her cheek on his cold forehead, the sudden descent into fiery snow, a phalanx of chariots – being drawn from his skull into the pools of a cat's eyes. Night is a stadium of drama. Shall we say it is contained in a fraction of a fraction of a second? Shall we say he sat up abruptly?[γ] That cat had filled a room with the absence of Betty Boop. In a curtained window, dawn was a menacing wafer. He recalled a hurried flight from a Cafgu and the brilliant suggestion of a Shtick trick. Which, clearly, he had failed to implement.[η] In precisely this way, memory returns us to the body, the thing itself,[κ] and flings our heels upon a throw rug. Only to suffer the wave of our stubbornly vertical attitude. Not to mention an empty stomach. Shall we accompany his thoughts to the window? The sun rested there comfortably, with a lion's share of the cat's indifference. From the sun it was impossible to learn anything.[λ] If she was gone, shall we wonder when, where and how? Here a trace of profluence pours forth from the vessel of fear for her safety. Not to mention his own. A story: this is in and this is in. Was there now, at last, a mute imperative driving him across the city to find her? Not everything was in his power. How should we act? Go this way? Only the opposite is reasonable. But the way of flight contained the seed of self-disgust. Not to mention his empty stomach. Who mentioned this item which is being cited now as if it had already been mentioned? If a Cafgu took her, why had he spared me? Perhaps she had completed that Shtick trick on her own. Perhaps you cannot possibly think so. The answer was poised to strike back in Booger Rooney's office. But to return there was to tempt the hand of flight. The silence in that room was deafening.[μ] Except for the scent of something he vaguely recalled. Let us say he ventured to open a door into the linoleum of his future. Did he follow the rough seas of butter frying in the pan into the kitchen on the heels of his hope? Hoping for what? To learn. Something from curlers in a pinkish robe. Not to mention his empty stomach. Perhaps you think a cat followed him there. And shall we follow a cat?::

ф A cat's face is larger than life; its eye gleams pure existence sans commentaire.

γ We have already discussed the role of dreams in the daily reconstitution of the self upon waking in that other City.

η A degree of celerity is essential to the successful execution of a backdoor breeze.

κ Or should I say the reverse. I mean, the body returns those memories to us.

λ From a cat and the sun, it is impossible to learn anything. Hence their hold on our imagination.

μ I mean the boarding-house room, not Booger's office. In the latter, as we have already heard, 'twas Booger's voice and a Cafgu's grip that shook him.

In the harsh light of a kitchen, those curlers pinked between the stove and his plate. Yes, yes, that lady was all optimism and good cheer,[α] a man with a nervous lip and a bushy moustache in a shouting shirt had inquired at the door, that lovely girl, they had gone together. Normally, she did not allow young ladies. He also learned the difficulty of two runny yolks.[δ] He left half a night older and wiser. Perhaps you are thinking, what drives a boy back the way he has come and once more into the Booger's den? Is it hatred of power that trods where it will? Or love for a B-Bop that dances that way? Did he imagine sugar-plum fairies come to the rescue? Perhaps the truth[ε] is a touch more suicidal: enough is quite sufficient thank you very much, shall we spend that life once and for all? And then again. What again? Must we go on and on again and again? Perhaps it was merely the body, the thing itself that drove him there, the eggs,[φ] the memory of a clean, well, at least a lighted place, that plumber's paradise. What was he carrying that his reason could not drain? A tractate of verbs, a curtain of souls, the blunt pencil of his desolation. Not to mention, the snake twinging in the belly of the beast. Then there was the rush and tumble of Monday morning. In the streets they come and go, dreaming of electronic libido.[γ] His was a mission of merciful relief. To rescue a damsel in redress. Or else to soften a hard-hearted colon. Perhaps you cannot possibly think so. Perhaps you think, at last he had begun to sleuth. Now he would say, the event that happened happened that way. Act deed event precedent. The matter he had in mind was a matter of mind over matter. What did it matter? He sought to rise ten floors, to throne on the kelippot of his trouble : :

α We dread the fierce clatter of a bright new day.

δ Sunny side up will turn a disposition upside down.

ε The truth is not satisfied with people.

φ Two burning suns will run along the long coil of a narrative tract.

γ The sidewalk lies between them, they fight for it as though it were their due.

ש
ר
הש
וש נ
ות מם
ה זת חש לפ מע נס
גו דה חת טש יר כק לצ מפ נע
ח זג ת יש צ נפ סע
בט ד ספ
כ בי
בכ ג
ל גכ
גל
דל
הל וכ ז
ול זכ ת צ
זל חכ טי
כל
נ
ע

How long will an elevator contain one man and his anticipation? We have already shown this.[η] Let us say it was a long organ grind. And shall we take advantage of the lack of action contained in an elevator's rising action to reflect, if not conclude, on the nature of this case?[κ] What had he concluded? Surely he had discovered in a Booger Rooney the source of much blood and broken shticks. Not to mention Mustapha and Legrand – had he dealt them a losing hand[λ] before they threatened to address his present in the past tense? Did Booger Rooney shut the mouth of a dentist with too many teeth in his name? And that howling gardener – did Booger eye Betty when he bopped him? Who left a Shtick shtanding in the lobby between shtreet and death? Perhaps a Shtick shirred a room and a half, not for the sake of murder, but rather to impede it.[μ] And who had turned his toes toward two elevators, and his baggy arms away from the memory of a wink and a grin in a Pontiac's open hood? A happy stolen moment. Who later delivered a letter of expulsion from that group of which we are not speaking? Who, so recently it felt like yesterday, left the figure of a shtick figure in a room and a half and a shticky head in the other? He had dipped the shticky spoon of betrayal thrice in the murder of their boyish palship. How should we act? Shall we turn our face from friendship, even from the face of a ben sorer umoreh, to invest in solitude? But all that was blood under the bridge.[ν] Now he feared for Betty Boop almost as much as he feared Betty Boop. If Betty's false fatality had eluded a proleptic demise, would a Booger now bop a Boop? Or had Booger bought Betty's silence? Betty was a loose blip in a knot of circumstance. A pang in the twisted mystery of a semicolon. Am I a peddler? Must I go on like a peddler? No sooner have we begun to sleuth than already we anticipate the figment of finality.[π] Here comes the horse of narrative. Solve this, solve that. Act. Deed. Event. Precedent. Shall a reader bend over the page with an inclination to conclude? How eagerly we race toward the conclusion of any story. Not to mention our own. And yet. Not yet. Only the opposite way is reasonable. It was said thus and it was said thus : :

η Who mentioned this item which is being cited now as if it had already been mentioned?

κ The nature of this case is like the nature of this case, and the nature of that case is like the nature of that case.

λ Mustapha and Legrand imported and exported the details of a Boogered past.

μ Perhaps a Shtick never shirred that room, but only stirred a Boogery past.

ν In our headlong flight from death toward death, how long do we pause to finger our sins?

π From finality, even the finality of death, we may glean a measure of satisfaction.

Language

On the tenth sefirot he burst onto the carpet of his restraint, shuffled his anticipation down the wrong end of a telescopic hallway, to crack the gates of a plumber's paradise.[α] Only to glimpse. Shall we say, a shouting shirt laboured with his hands over a blood-red sink? Needless to say.[δ] Rapidly the word retreat comes to mind. At such a moment, time bends. The doors of an elevator will slam shut on the arm of atonement. He dangled long enough on the end of his trapped appendage to anticipate a shouting shirt in the hallway between a bowel and paradise. Nevertheless, that elevator relented. In the mechanical court the strength of leniency is preferred. Those doors exercised a repetition. He slipped in and did the jab jab jabberwocky.[ε] In his heart, and on the panel, he pressed heaven hard for a rapid descent. Nevertheless the elevator ascended. Instead. Was there time[φ] to recall and rehearse and replenish a coil of blood and water he had glimpsed in that plumber's parlour? A Cafgu's hands were mired in a pinking lavabo. Now, rising in a chamber of hewn stone toward another chamber of hewn stone, he considered that sinking feeling. Have we come too late? I mean, for Betty Boop. We are not thinking here of that other coil he carried with him. He sought not to think of it. I prefer not to. Shall we consider instead the journey's end? Which tumbled toward him. He envisaged a fine set of teeth in an Ourmoney suit. A benevolent smile perched across the desk of power. Let us say he weighed his options. And found them wanting. Someone's best defence is a skunkish odour. They say in the West. He considered the possibility of adopting an unpleasant demeanour.[γ] A proleptic leap of the imagination. He would cry murder and brandish an accusation. He disembarked on a carpet of Persian labour, overlooking the darkened light of the city's daylight. His nose ran but there was no running away with it. He wiped a pinkish hue on the back of his hand, rummaged through his pockets for a scrap of defiance to press into service. He found only a pressing need. He sought to press that intestinal rage into a fury of righteous indignation. To turn its full force on a benevolent smile.[η] He faced. Instead. A slumping Ourmoney behind the desk of democracy ::

A dead Booger's lip will dangle on the lip of a desk.[κ] His neck was a red hearse. What were the signs of struggle? These are the ones who are strangled: one who strikes his father or his mother; one who kidnaps a Jewish person; a sage who rebels against the word of the high court; a false prophet. Shall we pause a moment between verdict and verdict, between affliction and affliction, before approaching once more the lip of the other's death? In the face of a dead Booger,[λ] we are tempted to turn away. Or back to a memory of Rooney in full homiletic flight before an audience of that group of which he later preferred we not speak. His had been a prophecy of biblical proportion. And didn't we hang high on his every word?[μ] And raise him up on a sea of chariots? After the revolutionary soteriology died, he slipped away. Only to turn up later. Elsewhere. Having turned away, he turned back to a realpoetik. He learned to speak the language of our masters.[ν] That was then and this was now. Now, all that separated my life from Booger's death was a desk, upon which lay – only slightly encumbered by the protruding (and purplish) lip of Booger's strangulated death – Howley's missing letter.[π] Did I consider the possibility of letting that letter lie where it lay? I wanted that letter but not the idea of wanting it. Nevertheless, when I pulled on it, that missing letter pulled a long tongue after it.[ρ] Though Howley's letter lay on the tip of Booger's tongue, I could not recall it. How hard we tug on any alphabet. Chant on suit away as in. From this it is impossible to learn anything. And yet. Not yet. What did he learn? A very heavy stone. That any person's tongue, once freed from life's restraint, will follow a letter across the desk to the threshold of that person's death ::

ר
ש
ש
נס
חת טש כק לצ מפ נע
סע ג
ב
ב
ג
ל
ל
חכ
ל
ע

α So close to home, a horse will follow its head; so close to the head, a colon will relax in anticipation.

δ Happily, a jolt of horror is an instantaneous restraint for the irritable intestinal tract.

ε Two sorts of persons will not be satisfied with pressing an elevator button once: the first anticipating a void, the other fleeing it.

φ The Messiah will not arrive until plunderers come upon the Jewish people, and until they are succeeded by plunderers of plunderers. Sanhedrin 94a

γ I mean, he sought to adopt a personality appropriate to circumstance.

κ He who lives by the desk, dies by the desk.

λ Perhaps you are thinking, must we have yet another neck to twist a plot? Learn from this, conclude from this. Even the face of death will become tiresome.

μ Which made the subsequent fall that much harder.

ν He learned to market those skills.

π Treacherous dealers have dealt treacherously; they have indeed dealt very treacherously. Sanhedrin 94a

ρ Even in death, we are not freed from language; even in death, someone's native tongue will cling to a missing letter.

η The only place to spit in a rich man's house is in his face. Diogenes of Sinope

Did he recall another death, which had expelled him so recently from a room and a half across the hall from the mirror of a room and a half? What was the difficulty in facing death again? Two!? Why do I need two? The memory of his expulsion perhaps. And yet, wasn't a dead Booger less difficult to contemplate than a broken Shtick? Not to mention the indirect greeting contained in the darkened pages of a newspaper.[α] Perhaps the difficulty lay in the diminishing difficulty? Of recalling. Of addition and subtraction. Are we grocers? Shall we rememorate and expound lists of the dead? Hang a curtain of souls.[δ] Generalization and detail. Perhaps you say: if you take hold of the larger you do not take hold; if you take hold of the smaller you do take hold. A certain number will roll off the tongue and adhere to any missing letter.[ε] A generalization needs a detail. But an accumulation of deathly details sheds meaning. An accumulation of detail makes a generalization. A generalization of which we cannot take hold. But we were standing before a dead Booger's desk, tugging a missing letter on the tip of that extensive tongue. Shall we take hold of that letter? If we take hold of the letter on a dead man's tongue, do we then take hold of something larger? Perhaps you cannot possibly think so. Certainly he tried. He pulled on that letter up to and beyond the length of Rooney's tongue. Once removed, and in my hand, Howley's missing letter preserved only a trace of Booger's native tongue.[φ] In precisely this manner, any language dies. Shall we recall the contents of such a letter? A list of the names of the dead and a warning. A place and time. Let us say he had not gone to meet his maker. I mean the letter's maker. Not yet. And yet. How long shall we cling to a single letter in Howley's name? Until the shuffle of a shouting shirt in the doorway turned his nose away from a dead Booger. He turned to brandish a letter. To shout at that shirt in a bushy moustache.[γ] I mean he tried to shout. His throat would not allow a shout to pass. Booger Rooney's throat allowed far less. I whispered horsely: what have you done with her? : :

Had someone thought to ask Booger Rooney why he had capitalized the P in politics? Perhaps you cannot possibly think so.[η] To capitalize on politics has come to be expected. Who remembers the other kind? And yet, having made the ascent to gaze upon a chariot,[κ] would a Messianic prophet ride the horse of charm? Having wandered in the orchard among the beautiful early figs, will a red Shabbatean now package those figs for sale? Shall we say he marketed his skills, he greased a small wheel in the people's palm? Once he distributed figs and a fiery future; now he sold figments and futures. Having cast the dice and lost, he nickel-and-dimed. Did they laugh at him in the West? In the wake of such a rude awakening, Booger exchanged a hot head for a warm parliamentary bench.[λ] Perhaps you think: but is a tired and retreaded revolutionary deserving of death? Did you march your lungs through the streets under the nightsticks, your head full of Booger Rooney's tongue-lashing? Suddenly he was gone. Counting votes, greasing small wheels, shaking babies. What of the skeletal caravans? The rag horses? The tenements of hunger? Some, those who could, returned to their suburban selves. Others gardened. Roofed. Terraced. Green thumbs, dollars and sense. Pigafetta drilled teeth. Booger prowled in the reactionary night. Could we blame him? Who among us speaks the seventy-one languages of the nations that he or she might pass judgment? Now Booger spoke the long, strangled tongue of death. Still, we are all subsidiary judges. We can learn but not refuse. And what about me? No cards in my hand. I turned away from the future, une demi-baguette, ce thon blanc entier, mon semblable, I sought to attenuate. I moved from gadlut to katnut.[μ] Nor had I ever wished long life and happiness on Booger Rooney : :

ר
ש
ס
צ מפ נע
ע
ש
ד
ב
ג
ל
ל
ל
ע

α Mustapha, Legrand, a dentist with too many teeth in his name, that portrait of Howley's cuff.

δ How far shall we travel on an addition of names? To that number about which it is fruitless to argue?

ε Verdes girasoles temblaban/ por los páramos del crepúsculo/ y todo el cementerio era una queja/ de bocas de cartón y trapo seco./ Ya los niños de Cristo se dormían/ cuando el judío, aprentando los ojos,/ se cortó las manos en silencio/ al escuchar los primeros gemidos. F. García Lorca "Cementerio judío"

φ The tongue itself lay silent on the desk of Booger's death.

η Now, it was too late to ask: his tongue was silent.

κ Four men entered the Garden of Paradise... Ben Azzai looked and died, Ben Zoma looked and went out of his mind, Aher cut the growth down. R' Akiva ascended in peace and returned in peace. Hagigah 14b

λ We are peddling furiously on a metaphorical horse. Must we?

μ I mean, he passed from gadlut, rapturous fervour, to katnut, darkness and small brains.

γ I mean, that Cafgu's moustache. My own shirt was silent, I had no bush to turn to or into.

That question – And what have you done with her? – leapt across the pages.[α] Why should a novel walk? A Cafgu will apply some vigour to shake such a question. I mean, he rejected it. Did he deny his guilt or my right to ask for it? His hands were clean. He had just washed them. In response to his lack of response, I brandished a savage solecism, that letter, which had once gone missing from a room and a half[δ] only to so recently reappear on the tip of Booger Rooney's tongue. Would Joey fall to his knees and explicate his and/or Booger's guilt? Did I possibly think so? I may have, briefly.[ε] When a silent Cafgu speaks, what shall we believe? Over the years someone's silence will accumulate meaning. His wordlessness will carry weight. When he comes to speak there are those who may turn to listen. His words become someone else's burden.[φ] If there is a difficulty, this is the difficulty. He relates. A story. He teaches an exaggeration. Surely it must be possible to refute. Perhaps, but who places watchers between a code and a Cafgu's stories? A fiction, a mistake. What shall we say against an accusation of murder in numbers? Shall we cast one man against another? The traditions were said one upon the other. And if it is your wish to protest your innocence, where will you find it? The will I mean, not the innocence. A great and sudden weariness will overtake the innocent accused. I was silent. I was the wool of drama.[γ] How should we act? His plot, my grave. To be perfectly and acutely ratiocinative, his story fit the toe of mystery as snugly as mine. All the more so, as I was standing on the guilty side of Booger's death, and unable to gather in the loose shards of my theory. Why would a Cafgu kill a Booger? Was my scarf unravelling? Whereas he. If the slipper of guilt fits, it will soon wear you out ::

α Perhaps Booger Rooney would have preferred a sleuth investigate the mystery of his death, I mean Booger's, but the powers of persuasion of a corpse are somewhat diminished.

δ How quickly I had become the one missing a room and a half.

ε I experienced a heightened consciousness of my lack of awareness; I took refuge in a degree of stupidity.

φ In this case, mine. Which I am passing on to a reader.

γ Someone knits small pleasures in the fabric of guilt.

ר ש נע ר ב ג ל ל ע

Suppose a Shtick. Here a story. He sleuthed, he sleuthed. He carried a shticky tale into Booger Rooney's office. And tossed his lisp shtick on Mr. R.'s desk. A sweat-under-the-nose theory about howling murder by some gate in a garden? Pictures, clippings. He'd paid a visit to an old friend. Suppose he lifted that letter from a room and a half.[η] Jack a car. Show someone how. Next thing you know. Who would have believed? A letter and a list. Of names. The in-and-out boys, that tooth puller, the goil, but that's another story, the nature of one case or the other.[κ] Was written here, was written there. A very shticky theory. And unloads it on the desk. Explications to the tenth degree. That howling letter signifying what? Suppose someone did go to a meet in Saint Someone-did-something-to-somebody Street. Mr. R. may have expressed a doubt.[λ] You can bring a mystery's solution to Mr. R.'s desk, but you can't make him think it. He had his office to protect. I mean, he had an office to run for. Let us say he chose a political solution.[μ] Precautions. Shall we keep a Cafgu's eye on a room and a half? Suppose that Shtick's sleek dog will hunt.[ν] The evidence points there. To a room and a half. Which is where Shtick returned for more. Evidence, I mean. And lost his head. Instead. Gave his life in exchange for death. To whom? Who else was in and out of one room and in and out of the other? A footprint of blood in the hallway between mind and body. Red-handed. Before he wiped the trouser of guilt. Meanwhile. A Cafgu's parapolitical office is to report. His office is the sidewalk.[π] Mr. R. will have a chat. With a mystery's solution. Fetch that boy out of his room and a half. Bring him in. To eye him eye-to-eye. Before things increasingly happen. But nothing can be learned from one who does not know how to be asked. Except perhaps a motive. Only the goil's lack of being seemed to matter to that boy. Suppose her name in a newspaper precipitated a string of deadly letters? Not to mention the accompanying acts. Howley. Shtick. Suppose Mr. R. thought: to provide a meet with a reluctant goil might put an end to murders. A Cafgu was instructed to show him the goil.[ρ] In the flesh. Lively. In the garden by the gate ::

η The facts, ma'am, just the facts. Act, deed, event, precedent.

κ In this case, a caseful of murder.

λ He laid a doubtful expression upon the desk between them.

μ We live in a political world. B. Dylan

ν Any dog will chase a Shtick.

π Even people will share a sidewalk. Reluctantly.

ρ I put to death and I make live. Here we have an allusion to the Resurrection of the Dead in the Written Torah. Sanhedrin 91b

A Cafgu will thus illuminate a letter in the light of a mystery's solution. How many solutions to somebody's story? Do we need two? Every so often. So very often. The other's story, like his or her face, is so much more cleverly proportioned than our own.[α] Our face is all we have. And a story. Le visage de l'autre. L'histoire de l'autre. If the shoe of guilt fits, be wary of it. I was grown weary of wearing it. This is ours and this is theirs. It was a case of who writes the tale more quickly, eloquently. The cost of coming second was guilt and death. Go to the end of the verse, and the back of the class. And why not? Shouldn't bad art be punishable by death?[δ] If Shtick had come with his tale between his legs to die on the edge of Booger's desk, perhaps Booger Rooney had selected me to wear the bloody footprint. It was a snug fit. Now those prints were a tent over Booger's body. Who said a story can't hurt? A frame will pinch your toes. He felt the urge to walk. Or run, with his own tongue between his legs. What kept him there, to linger between a Cafgu's eye and a dead Booger?[ε] The future of Betty? His own? Or a lack thereof? Perhaps you cannot possibly think so. Nevertheless, he thrust his tongue back between his teeth long enough to ask again – what, again? – what have you done with her? And what could he gain by asking yet again? On that page in a golem's novel, which Joey was so kind as to narrate, a valiant Cafgu had extricated the goil from the clutches of a narrator who'd lured her and a reader (our apologies) into the linoleum-scented roominess of an unrented room. Now that goil was safe. And that's all I'm saying. Needless to say. Joey said. The less I knew the better. Shall we say that we disagreed about this? There's only two people that goil has to fear, and Howley's dead, Joey continued to say, despite having promised to say no more. What was he trying to tell us?[ϕ] Not by my hand, I strongly objected. Of course not, he replied. He had a golem's patience. By hers. And that's all I'm saying. Needless to say : :

α He discovered it was not necessary to discover who wrote the other stories contained within his story, and within which his story was contained. These wrote themselves.

δ The inner advantages that mediocre literary works derive from the fact that their authors are still alive and present behind them. F. Kafka *Diaries*

ε Certain questions remained. How many? Mustapha, Legrand, the dentist. These were the bodies of the as yet unclaimed dead.

ϕ Here reader and writer part company, the former being exempt from the threat of a nasty cuff to the side of the head.

ע

Perhaps, in a Cafgu's testimony, we have obtained a retraction and a suspension in the mystery of so many deaths. Perhaps you cannot possibly think so.[γ] We say: "Qu'ai-je à faire avec la justice?" Who knows the languages of the seventy-one nations that he or she may recline in judgment? Shall we list, add and subtract and expound? For his part, he feared murder more than death.[η] He recognized his guilt in a list of darkened names. In the wake of a wave of deaths, what did it matter who killed whom? Who killed whom was a problem for justice. And justice was someone else's harsh master; his was the responsibility of a lack of kindness.[κ] A Cafgu had dealt the cards of guilt with a generous hand. There were plenty to go around. I eyed my own. Criminality loves company. Now, even Betty Boop stood, in absentia, in the dock, beneath the sword of Owley's missing letter. Perhaps you would prefer to hear her say so. Had she rid herself of Owley's hardened hands to fall under a Booger's wing? Entretemps a Cafgu will give you a mean time. These two boys were boys. Boys being boys, they spoke in the language of men. I mean they rolled up their sleeves and promptly exchanged fisticuffs. They pounded the alphabet. Pruned the violence of an empty phrase. Beat on an anamorphic drum. They exercised their lack of consciousness on the ear of a cauliflower. Chant on suit away as in. That Cafgu was an artful dodger; he was practiced in the boyish art of pummelling, the sport of kings, not to mention their more unfortunate subjects.[λ] I recalled Rabbi Loew's lesson regarding the method to eliminate a golem, and thought to erase the first letter on that Cafgu's forehead. Instead, I was all slappy swings and grunting. Shall we say, now I lay my chin upon the Cafgu's knuckles? When I awoke I had gained a larger if sorer hat size and the industrial taste of my blood. I spun a haze across the room. As for Joey Cafgu, that golem was doubly absent. In his place were two of everything. Two of everything. Needless to repeat : :

ב

ג

γ On the contrary, now that we are sleuthing and sleuthing, don't we regret our legs wrapped in a newspaper on the cot of mild description?

η Not his own murder but the one he might commit.

κ He sought chesed and everywhere encountered gevurah. These words are free, go read them in the teacher's house.

λ When gentlemen exchange blows; we call it sweetly science.

Knight to Bishop Three

Shall we say: and then, and then? What cries out in the canyon of cars below the window of a broken desk and a missing letter if not the siren song of a dead Booger? The periphrastic murmur of the policeman's magic. He thought, perhaps you are thinking, here we go again. Must we go on and on, again and again?[α] To rise above the level of his own feet was a struggle. To turn his toes one way or the other was a dizzying prospect. And where would they take him? It was the blood on his fingers after he touched the pain in his head that drew him to a mirror in the washroom across the hall.[δ] He stumbled there. Only to find. A Cafgu washing the blood from his knuckles. Whose blood? Shall we say they lifted their gazes to reflect on one another framed in a mirror over the sink of his blood? My blood, your blood.[ε] Sooner or later a siren will loosen our bonds and a Cafgu will turn and cuff you lightly on the head. Any blow delivered without malice was merely an afterthought.[φ] Come on, Joey articulated a gentle paralinguistic communication, let's get something to eat. I struggled to my knees, tried to recall (I meant call off) the sound of those sirens in my ears. They reiterated the urgency of our absquatulation. Whereas a Cafgu extended a helping hand. One prefers to wash away blood, one's own blood. It called out to me from a sink, from my doubled forehead in a mirror, from Joey's dedicated knuckles.[γ] I thought: When a Cafgu leads the way, one should certainly try for something better. I could not find it. Joey bet on the right elevator. From the other, I mean the one that was left, which we shall call the left one, came pouring forth a uniform freshly pressed shoulder-to-shoulder with a sketch artist. I slipped between a shouting shirt and the repetitive reflection of a nervous moustache. I prayed a Cafgu's shirt would shout louder than my portrait.[η] We waited an eternity of arms and breath for those doors to slide. At last, I drifted downward in the echoing image of that shouting shirt, which had so closely shaved me : :

α Possibly, it is the difference within each repetition that we dread.

δ The sight of our own blood will drive us to a mirror in search of that which remains of the self.

ε We have grown sick of sharing it. I meant, in sharing it.

φ An afterthought is the cuff on the end of a sleeve.

γ Though I recognized it, that blood was lost, nor did I seek to recall it.

η Perhaps, here, you hoped for some description of the narrator. But we have left him so little; shall we describe the shirt off his back?

נ

ג

ע

What does a sleuth want? The truth. Truth was that event, unforeseen and misunderstood, at the origin of a list of names.[κ] Deed, act, event, precedent. He added and subtracted and expounded. He went on and on like a peddler. To understand, he would have had to reside somewhere. To fix a point, a cot of desolation, from within which he might safely discover the world outside a room and a half. But that cot was gone, not to mention the room and a half.[λ] Time was a sleuthing backward, a diagonal movement across and down the page. The story moves along a sidewalk of signification, down the elevator of origins. We say "and then", "and then" and then we turn the page. Even so, he suffered an occasional lapse into truthfulness.[μ] Events occur. The event that happens happens that way. A hole opens up in the story, in the crab's movement across the page. Knight to bishop three. There is no past or future in the Talmud. Shall we say I was and will always remain seated by the window in a room and a half? Engaged in a list of the names of the dead. Let us say I am a freelancer tilting in the lists of the capitalist arena. With a contract to assemble the obits of the day. From the comfort of a cot of desolation. Shall we go out among the shopkeepers? They incline, they wipe their pink hands. For the time being we have forestalled a trip to the used bookstore, my dwindling collection, une demi-baguette (a broken shtick), ce thon blanc entier, mon semblable qui baigne dans son huile. A contract to list, to incline, to desire the dead. This is a labour of whittling words. Entwined in the news of the dead. We sleuth, we sleuth, yet meaning escapes us.[ν] Along with friendship. For he'd whittled the last of his pals (or they him), to sit by a window over a canyon of cars and study the language of silence. He sleuthed. After what?[π] The tear in the fabric of his life? He listed. After what? That moment when he'd broken free and begun to drift. Perhaps you ask, free from what? Himself. He dreamt it was real : :

κ By searching out origins, one becomes a crab. The historian looks backward; eventually he also believes backward.
F. Nietzsche *Twilight of the Idols*

λ What do we desire: the dream itself or the dreaming?

μ Truth does not speak, it works.
J.-F. Lyotard *Discours, figure*

ν The light we glimpse is a tear in the fabric of our invention.

π There was no corpse and the detecting was general. G. Stein

How Should We Act?

Occasionally, he wrote as little as possible.[α] Yes and no and it was unsteady in his hand. He waited for the end of the last of his dwindling collection. He sifted the sand in a room and a half, going over the same way, again and again, over the white sheet of his separation. He sought the absent letter in an alphabet of names. He was silent in the vernacular. I mean he was absent from speech. From nature. Across a canyon of cars nature lay in the trees to cut his throat. Little by little, words lost interest in his books.[δ] He produced letters and, from time to time, the space between letters. Death lay in wait in that space between letters. There is between them. The body the thing itself. His books were cracked and broken. In the cracks of broken volumes, he painstakingly staked the letters of his autobiographical cacography. Did he attempt to write the word ממרא? Or shall we be content with רשע? Each morning he composed himself. I mean he composed a self. A fiction, a mistake. Shall we say he produced story? This is in and this is in. This is ours and this is theirs. After noon he lay in a patch of sun on the cot of desolation. He tried to be a cat. To not think like one. I mean, to think in the manner a cat does not. Think. Or rather, not to think at all. Just as a cat is able to not think. He listened to the radio,[ε] the talk show of the Amoraim. He would not venture from his room and a half. But for provisions. The grocers. They wiped their pink hands. He struggled for a personality appropriate to circumstance : :

α ...car le judaïsme et l'écriture ne sont qu'une même attente, un même espoir, une même usure. E. Jabès *Le livre des questions*

δ Mais si le livre n'était, à tout sens de ce mot, qu'une époque de l'être (époque finissante qui laisserait voir l'Être dans les lueurs de son agonie ou le relâchement de son étreinte, et qui multiplierait, comme une maladie dernière, comme l'hypermnésie bavarde et tenace de certains moribonds, les livres sur le livre mort)? J. Derrida *L'écriture et la différence*

ε We are already into extra innings. And yet.

נ ג ע

In the evening America stormed the desert of this empty page. The question, the difficulty, returned to its place. He tried to write the word "Sarajevo".[φ] He sought some way in which it might yet be possible to write the word "Sarajevo". They sent from there. A question. If there is a difficulty, this is the difficulty. How should we act? Perhaps the people of Europe shed their crepuscular passports[γ] and marched on the word "Sarajevo". Perhaps they did walk arm in arm and without arms, and thrust their bodies in the cracks of a delicate mechanism of war. Perhaps you cannot possibly think so. Did he march to the word "Sarajevo"? Did he distribute Sarajevos in the streets of his local Sarajevo? Did he Sarajevo his wrists in a Sarajevo and a half? Not everything was in his power.[η] He took revenge on language. Someone stands upon the barricades (I mean the Sarajevos) dressed in doubt (Sarajevo). What was Sarajevo if not a porousness in the face of Sarajevo? Perhaps you cannot possibly Sarajevo. Perhaps he slipped away from Sarajevo. An alphabet was worn ragged and sinking fast. He had already lost the H in Howley. Now he could not find the W in Witz. Nor the A in Ausch. Nor the E in Ethike, nor the Y in thou, for that matter. Did it matter?[κ] What mattered? Which matter mattered most? The Gemara does not resolve this. The body, the thing itself. The letter. Perhaps the matter of the letter no longer mattered. This is ours and this is theirs. In the face of a withering alphabet, we seek to feel a certain urgency. Or rather, we decline with it. The alphabet, I mean. Not the urgency. He felt a certain declination. Writing was a stony gaze across a canyon of cars into the trees. His writing at any rate. It could not save an alphabet. Not to mention the world. It lacked a spirit of enterprise. It would not carry one, nor carry on. Though it protested, it would not be Protestant. Have we removed Tannaim from the world? What shall we say to an unbeliever? Shall we say Sarajevo? Again?[λ] We decline upon the cot of despondency. Our legs wrapped in the news of the day. Between a wall and a window, between the race and the routine, we exercise the scraps of our commitment. How should we act? Beneath us the floor rusts and rusts : :

φ In the vernacular.

γ Between verdict and verdict, between affliction and affliction, between blood and blood.

η I meant, in his Sarajevo.

κ Matter דבר was a word, taught by word of mouth, as in: These matters had been taught at Sinai.

λ Now surely we have worn out that word, it having worn out its welcome.

But we are already deep into injury time.[α] Shall we move the ball forward? Let us say they walked to the seedier side of Saint Somebody-did-something-to-somebody Street.[δ] That eatery was a large paneful window of yellowed light. The poor will eat beneath bright lights. The better to keep an eye on their food and fellow diners.[ϵ] Those walls were the colour of hurry-up-and-make-room-for-another customer. Shall we yield to the temptation of description?[ϕ] Let us say, a smoker's cough hunched over a yellow soup. Her rough red heels pinched in red heels. That man's grilled cheese is a transmutation of pencils. He is all scruff and scuff. And Betty Boop fingering a Camel by the window. In coveralls. And tee-shirt. Pianyi yi dian, keyi ma? But it doesn't get much cheaper than this. She eyed his eye, ringed as it was, and ringing. Shall we seat him facing Betty, and place a Cafgu at the right angle?[γ] He held his tongue between his knees to make a lap and swallow those proleptic juices. Carry your stomach to the dinner table and it will anticipate a meal, in spite of two previous, now vengeful eggs.[η] The aroma of an oily egg in a greased pan brought back a memory. He already knew those old yolks. Let us say he raced runny yolks to the men's room, and pursue it no further. Where they parted company. Enough. I said let us pursue it no further. Shall we return to the table? Humbled and weak in the knees. Only to find. Others engaged in conversation. In such a case, our fellow diners will break off in mid-chuckle to present the wide eye of concern. We may choose to believe they have been fluently in our backside. Or were they chuckling over quite another subject, having put us and our muted suffering entirely out of their minds?[κ] But Betty. Her smile prompted a desire to wipe it cleanly away. The face of the other opens a way. That desire loosened his tongue in any language. That one, he nodded toward a Cafgu's downcast gaze, has placed your hand on Howley's death. No sooner out, the words were stony regret. Let us imagine a moment's pause. A girl's glance at a golem's glare. Yes, I know, she said, I mean she shrugged, and rehearsed that death once more. The truth is not satisfied with people. Sure t'was I killed Howley : :

Betty Boop's face was a calm sea of there-that's-done; and yet, her hands fingered her fingers. What secret do we search out in the face of the face of the one who murdered? His horror wavered between the horror of Betty's guilt and her possible participation in a Boogery plot. Shall we ask a murderer to explain? And domesticate our horror. Shall we ask, why the others? And in this manner accept the one?[λ] What shall I say to a murderer that does not render me complicit? Do we seek merely our own innocence in the face of the other's guilt? What does a sleuth want? The truth. That event at the origin of a list of names. Hence the others. Hence why. What others? she replied. The waitress wore a run in her pink stocking and an egg foo young.[μ] A murderous conversation paused while they waited. He felt a pang of longing for the breakfast he had so recently and emphatically declined. A stomach emptied will never learn. Even a dog knows better.[ν] Nevertheless it was too late to order a room at the inn. Shall we say a Cafgu dug in, while Betty tinkered with a forked tongue. He watched until that waitress turned her ears to the door. What others!? he repeated horsely: Pigafetta, Mustapha, Legrand, a headless Giltgestalt and now Rooney, his face cut off to spite his Booger. Not me, she said.[π] Howley. Just Howley. Why Howley? he retreated. Let us imagine a Cafgu grunting his disdain for a particular line of questioning. Why Howley? Because he beat her black with the one hand and blue with the other : :

נגע

α A story begs for apocatastasis. Or some portion thereof.

δ One man's 42nd is another man's Wangfujing.

ϵ The rich put their trust in a chef and candles. Not to mention good manners.

ϕ And provide a poignant moment of sudden illumination? C. Altieri *Self and Sensibility*

γ A good host is a narrator who puts some thought into a seating arrangement, that is to say, one arranges one's thoughts around the table.

η Sunny side up was the darker side of digestion. For all the days of a pauper, even the Sabbaths and festivals, are bad. Shmuel said, with respect to diet: A change of routine is the beginning of stomach illness. Sanhedrin 101a

λ That she would murder the one she loved was a statistical probability. Not to mention the pinch of satisfaction he felt in the ruination of that affair.

μ That was a Chinese restaurant serving Italian-American and tended by Koreans.

ν A dog may eat anyone's dirt; however, it knows when to run.

π Let us nevertheless pursue a murderess dialogue a little further.

κ Can we blame them? There is no way to kindly welcome someone back from the washroom wars.

What was the meaning of that which was said: "T'was I killed Howley"?[α] Howley, Howley, what drove him down from the roof to gather up his rough hands from the rough wet soil? The violence of an empty phrase. His manliness. Handiness with his hands is a handsome man's manliness. Boys will be boys.[δ] Unfortunately. Bitterness drives a hard bargain. A rueful tongue will lash out against a woman's face. Face to face roughly with the hands of a rough man, a woman takes things into her own hands. A garden hose, for example. To hang from the roof on the ladder of Howley's ascent. Or should we say descent? Did she prepare a noose to slip over a Howley's head? His toes sliding on the ladder of his descent. Hang, Howley, hang. His rough red hands were red.[ε] His gaze was owlish. We may call such premeditation and preparation self-defence. According to her state of mind. I mean according to the ladder of the Law. In fifty states. Plus one. Question. How did Howley's broken cuff appear by the garden gate in the blackened pages of a newspaper? Perhaps you think: Let us say Betty Boop called a Booger for assistance? There was between them. It was said thus and it was said thus. Very soon, not only this but also this: a Cafgu carried a strangled Howley from a fallen ladder to a not-so-burning bush. Thus the nature of this case is a domestic case, and not like the nature of these other cases, and the nature of these other cases is not like the nature of this case.[φ] What now? : :

α Shall we compose a Baraita?

δ But perhaps you are thinking of Booger Rooney's hands. They were smooth pale tongues. If a Cafgu's story will fit the world as we know it, Booger's hands were clean. Not to mention bloodless. Shall we say murder is not a rich man's sport? He prefers the Law. It proceeds more slowly but surely.

ε Sans parler de la raideur du corps.

φ Let us say: Oops, in a sudden plot twist, have we eliminated our plot? And yet, a relentless plot will plod on.

נגע נגע
נגע נגע
נגע נגע נגע
נגע נגע נגע
נגע נגע נגע
נגע נגע
נגע נגע נגע נגע
נגע נגע נגע
נגע נגע
נגע נגע נגע נגע
נגע נגע נגע נגע

It is not necessarily so. It is possible to refute. What was Betty Boop's tale trying to tell him? What was there about it?[γ] In saying t'was I killed Howley, did she extricate a domestic case from a caseful of murders? Did she provide the particular exception to a general scheme? In the spilled salt on the table between them he piled an objection, a refutation. Let us say fear, perhaps the presence of a Cafgu, had pressed a Boopian confession. If so, then. Did Howley's death remain firmly and frighteningly within the case of a caseful of dreadful murder? This case is like the nature of this other case and the nature of this other case is like the nature of this case. Giltgestalt, Mustapha, Legrand, the dentist with too many teeth in his name.[η] And shall we add Booger Rooney's name to a list that grew as rapidly as it shrank? And remove him from another, that whodunit list, a list that shrank even as the other grew? Yes and no and it was unsteady in his hand. He turned, for a moment, to a third list, the list of unanswered questions.[κ] When his master's lip lies across the lip of a desk, who shall a golem serve? If a Cafgu plucked a Booger by the neck, in whose service did he pluck? Was Betty Boop part of the plot of a garden plot? Did she toil under a Cafgu's spell? What unbends a golem's golem? Shall we discuss murder over lunch with the living dead? Not to mention, from where would his next lunch come? If human existence is always-in-the-world and not enclosed within a subject "in here" opposed to objects "out there", what was that longing he felt for Betty Boop? What, in the face of murder, deceit and betrayal, kept such a longing alive? How should we act? One may choose to compile a list of lists: the list of those that are murdered, the list of those we suspect of murder, the list of those in grave and imminent danger of being murdered,[λ] the list of places to seek out a place to lie down or a plumber's paradise, the list of places to avoid in a policeman's list of scenes of a crime or crimes,[μ] the list of unanswered questions.[ν] One may subsequently arrange a list of lists in alphabetical order, or in a chronology of persistence, or according to what presses hardest or gnaws most, or in a gematrial cryptography, or in a centrifugal cacaphony : :

γ Let us offer an alternative version.

η Not Betty Boop, however, who had so recently been struck from the list of the dead.

κ This is the list we wrap our legs in when we lie on the daily cot of desolation.

λ Perhaps you are thinking: His name was on that list.

μ Certainly on that one.

ν And most certainly buried beneath that one.

What is the difference between the first case, wherein they do not disagree and the second case, wherein they do disagree? Just as there, so here too.[α] A lip strangled on the lip of his desk could only with great difficulty remain the source of a plot to eliminate those who might recall the pinkish hue of his youth. Have we not rejected this once? Who mentioned its name? What is he trying to tell us? These names were removed from a list of suspects. When they appeared on a list of victims.[δ] Learn from this, conclude from this. To add what? A thought may occur. It is a commonsense argument. If the cause of death lay not in someone's past adherence, perhaps it lay in that someone's adherence being past.[ε] These are the ones deserving of death: those who have turned their faces away from the face of the Other. Antonio Pigafetta – drilling teeth and home to green lawn, supper table, parcheesi, television, bed. Mustapha and Legrand, importing and exporting.[φ] They buckled a fortune over pork bellies. Howley gardened on the ground and roofed in the air. Shtick was a ben sorer umoreh in a slender Our-money. Booger Rooney wore the lapels of power: he had abandoned the power of Messianic politics for the messy politics of power. And the revolution? Nightsticks, tenements of hunger, skeletal caravans, rag-horses begging with their backs against shop windows. All forgotten. Did they count the years?[γ] They were already dead. Should we be surprised? Who are the thirty-six righteous ~~men~~ of this generation who merit to receive the Divine Countenance when they enter the World to Come?[η] And he? Was he R' Shimon ben Yochai to say: If they are only two, they are myself and my son? What had he enacted? Whittling. Where there are no suburbs, one reclines on the cot of desolation. The asylum of self. Ce thon blanc entier, mon semblable qui baigne dans son huile. Surely his name also belonged on that list of those deserving death. Not to mention how highly he figured on a policeman's list. How much longer before he too slipped away from guilt and onto the fresh sheets of a coroner's list?[κ] Not yet. Though soon enough : :

α What have I in common with the Jews? I have hardly anything in common with myself and should stand very quietly in a corner, content that I can breathe. F. Kafka *Diaries*

δ A headless Shtick had already beaten a path along this way.

ε I mean not that they had once strayed from what they ought to have been, but that they had strayed from what they had once been.

φ Mustapha mostly imported.

γ Time stood still in the suburbs of self.

η Perhaps you are thinking: Why 36? Is it not said: Fortunate are those who wait for Him? The word לו, Him, has the numerical value of 36. Therefore they shall be 36. Sanhedrin 97b

κ God's as close as a vulture's nail. P. Celan, "The Lonely One"

If you see a generation that is dwindling, expect the Messiah. If you see a generation upon which numerous troubles come like a river, expect the Messiah. If you see a generation in which the number of Torah scholars has decreased, expect the son of David to come. As for the rest of the people, their eyes will become worn out from grief and anxiety. During some of those years there will be wars of great sea creatures. And during some of them, wars of Gog and Magog. Truth will be formed into groups and go away. Those that turn away from evil will become foolish. The face of the generation will be like the face of a dog.[λ] Shall we cash in our chips in a teleological economy? What was promised for the Time of the Messiah? Neither hunger nor war, neither jealousy nor competition. All the world occupied solely with acquiring knowledge of God.[μ] What was promised for the World to Come? They say in the West, in the name of Rava bar Mari, the following homiletic expression: In the future the Holy One, blessed is He, will give to every righteous person three hundred and ten worlds.[ν] (Perhaps you are thinking: He can afford it.) Shall you sit, neither eating nor drinking, with your crown upon your head and delight in the radiance of the Divine Presence?[π] In a Messianic time, the human shall be 100 amos tall and after that, in the World to Come, 200 amos. Shall we discuss the height of the gates of Jerusalem in the World to Come?[ρ] The question remains: When? For precisely this reason, it was said: three things come when they are not expected: the Messiah, a find, and a scorpion : :

λ I am in wonderment! According to these signs, why has the son of David not come in this generation of ours? Yad Ramah: Sanhedrin 98a

μ For what reason are you not familiar with the Aggadata? Sanhedrin 100a

ν For it is stated: That I may grant to those who love me substance. And the value of substance, יש, is 310. Proverbs 8:21

π Perhaps you would prefer to eat and drink.

ρ R' Yochanan's student saw ministering angels sawing precious stones and pearls 30 amos high and 30 amos wide. Sanhedrin 100a

T תפססא מאהארבא םנעתארם רתא שראי דנאשטהת שת
תהג עיתר דל שראי שתית שאשה :הארת הת גאששמ הת
שראי יתחעש שאש סאאש נרב שאש סאאש םרתאל שראי
דנא דרדנטהנ שאש בסאצ נהש: נרב שאש בסאצ נהש דל תפיג
תנשד ילעמא שעה תהגטרב הסדל שראי יתעהת דרדנטה שת
דתשאל לפפ שבסאצ לעח נאעתפיג הת: רעהת רתא שראי יתהגע
דנא דרדנטה רט: שראי נת דנא תשרע הת תלעטב לפפ השעשצ
הת םתפיג מר שטדח נת דנא דרדנטה רטר דתש לפמת תשרע הת
:לפמת הת נעתסטרתשד הת שראי רתא שראי יתנוש :שראי דנסש
הת: תלעטב שאש לפמת דנסש הת םלפמת תשרע דרדנטה נו :שראי
יתנשת דנא דרדנטה רטר דתש לפמת דנסש הת נעתסטרתשד הת
רתא שראי שתיתוש דנא הת דתפססא מאהארבא רתא שראי 2000
רםלפמת נע עבבר התאד הת: נאגב הארת נעלסד הת םתנאנום
לעתנט נעתארם מראר: סעאננאת הת דנ הת שכראמ 3952 דששאפ
ואה ללעש אענללעמ חעש םאר סענאעששמ הת נעתסזרטשר הת
יב דשלל ב ללעש אר סענא עששמ הת: נעתסטרתשד הת דנא
םתנמגדטצ יאד תארג הת םדאד הת טהת נ נעתסטרתשד דערפ א
:תע שנכ ש שא דלרש הת דלרש הת הסעדהש רתא םתאהת שלל
ללעש שראי דנאש :לול לאטתערעפש רהגעה הסטמ א נ דתארסר
ב ללעש הת נעתסטרתשד הת םאיהסאב טנעבבאר ת גנעדרססא
םלאעתראפ ילנ ב ללעש מטענללעמ התנוש הת נע דלרש לעמ
התעת הת לעתנט םאענללעמ נוש ירו רטסר דנא יל תלפמס
בללעש דלרש הת מעת הסעדהש תא םמט ענל נעגב נהת
ללעש לסים ראי 50,000 רעתנ הת: דיר תשד שמעת ינאמ
לשתע תאפר דנא םנע אגא::

When is always already an eschatological investment.[α] Rav Nachman asked R' Yitzchak: "Have you heard when Bar Nafli will come?" R' Yitzchak said to him: "Who is Bar Nafli?" Rav Nachman said to him: "The Messiah." Someone said: For six thousand years will the world exist, and for one thousand years it will be destroyed. Someone else said: On the third day God will raise us up in the World to Come. Someone else wavered between the earliest possible date of our Redemption and the latest possible date. We add and subtract and expound.[δ] If Elijah said to Rav Yehudah, the brother of Rav Salla the Pious, "The world is destined to exist for not less than eighty-five jubilee cycles,"[ε] what does it serve Rav Yehudah to ask whether the Messiah comes at the beginning of that jubilee cycle or at its end? And will the final jubilee cycle have ended by the time the Messiah comes, or will it not have ended? Elijah answered him: "I do not know." Those Tannaim![φ] They wipe their pink hands. Rav Chanan bar Tachalifa met a man in whose hand was a scroll found among the hidden treasures of Rome and written in Ashuri Hebrew. And on it was written: Four thousand two hundred and ninety-one years from the world's creation, the world will end. If a verse mentions the word 'time' three and a half times, then this means a total of 1,400 years. Meanwhile, by our acts, or perhaps I meant by our lack of acts, we have let slip by yet another preordained date of redemption. Must we repent of our own accord for the redemption to come? Or will it come whether we repent or not?[γ] If we show merit, will the Messiah come early? Will he come with the clouds of heaven or on the back of an ass? From this it is impossible to learn anything[η] : :

Two thousand years after Creation, Abraham accepted the message of the Torah. He was fifty-two years old. Forty-eight years later, Isaac was born. Isaac was sixty years old when Jacob was born. When Jacob was one hundred and thirty years old, he brought his family down to Egypt. The Egyptian exile of Jacob's people lasted two hundred and ten years. Four hundred and eighty years after their Exodus from Egypt, the Jewish people built the First Temple. The First Temple stood for four hundred and ten years. Seventy years after the destruction of the First Temple, the Second Temple was built. The Second Temple stood for four hundred and twenty years. One hundred and seventy-two years after the destruction of the Second Temple, or 2000 years after Abraham accepted the Covenant, the decline of Torah began. The death of Rebbi in 3952 marks the end of the Tannaic era. From Creation until the Messianic era, six millennia will have passed. The Messianic era will be followed by the Resurrection of the Dead, the great Day of Judgment, and the destruction of the world as we know it. A period of destruction of one thousand years will follow that, after which the world will be recreated on a much higher spiritual level. According to Rabbeinu Bachya, the destruction of the world in the seventh millennium will be only partial, and will recur every seven millennia, until the fiftieth millennium, at which time the world will be completely destroyed. The entire 50,000-year cycle will then begin again, and repeat itself many times : :

Betty Boop was the blip in a theory of murder.[κ] And yet, of which theory were we speaking? A theory that murder was a plot to eliminate those who knew an electoral aspirant's past sedition? The Boogery death of a deadly Booger had decimated the frame of that particular conceptual framework. That a certain someone sought to punish those who had abandoned the struggle for the World to Come?[λ] But who was that certain someone who could be so certain who deserved death? Who speaks the seventy-one languages of the nations that he or she might sit in judgment? A theory that Betty B. was merely the exceptional murderess providing a common domestic case as the exception to a murderous series of murders? That she was a golem's golem?[μ] That she'd merely murdered the truth in the face of her fear of a Cafgu's face? Betty Boop was a list shifter. Her shadow shifts from list to list. Surely she had earned a place on a list deserving death. She had earned her place there by love's labour lost. Having abandoned a revolutionary labour to a labour of love, and having abandoned somebody's love for love in somebody else's lovely garden.[ν] Someone put a stop to this. I mean that literally. Am I Elijah to curse so heavily?[π] She buried the hatchet. Her name was unearthed on a list of victims. He'd wrapped that list around his legs in a room and a half. And yet. Not yet. Betty Boop returned from the dead, she rose up from the darkened column in a soiled newspaper to stroll in the street of suspicion. She vanished from sight, and in vanishing appeared on a list of suspects. Now that she had left his side and returned to another side of the table, I mean to the side beside that golem, he feared she was listing to his side of the list of those in danger of death. Having died once and returned, she now risked death again. Perhaps death comes so much more easily the second time around. A case of going down the well-worn path.[ρ] Perhaps that B-Bop would simply not stay put on any list. Nor, for that matter, in a well-lighted if not so clean place. She crushed a Camel into her dessert, rose from her place across the table of his addition and subtraction and multiplication and turned her face to the door : :

α I believe with complete faith in the coming of the Messiah, and even though he may delay, nevertheless I long for him each day, that he will come. Siddur

δ That your enemies have taunted, O Hashem, that they have taunted the footsteps of Your Messiah. Psalms 89:52

ε If one jubilee cycle = 50 years, then how many apples will little Isaac…

φ An apikoros is one who says: הני רבנן! Those Rabbis! Sanhedrin 100a

γ If the appointment of kings whose decrees are as harsh as Haman is a stratagem to force our repentance, surely, by now, He may consider another way.

η May the One Who Knows their true meaning teach it to us clearly and not enigmatically, for the sake of His great Name. Yad Ramah

κ Every theory contains its own blip; not to mention Boop.

λ Was not belief in the Messiah's arrival one of the thirteen articles of faith enumerated by Ramban? Sanhedrin 96b

μ And whose golem was that golem?

ν Much as he mightily might, he could not deny she had flowered in that flowerbed.

π Father Elijah was a kapdan. His indignation in the face of sin was unforgiving. So much so that God took him from the world. Had Elijah remained a prophet in Israel, he would have destroyed his own people with his righteous indignation. Sanhedrin 113b

ρ Death is a well-worn path along which the body has already grown used to travelling. Providing we have sufficiently exercised it.

Let us imagine he reached out to Betty Boop in a less than kenotic gesture of restraint. Not to go yet slows time.[α] We dwell on as much as in it. Would Betty sit down? And why should he feel relief? To see her sit. To forestall his keyless pockets. Was he vaguely harbouring hopes? Or just rubbing up against her solidity?[δ] And yet. Not yet. Though sooner than he would have liked. What solidity? She shifted. She would not sit still. Who longs to freeze time in the company of a woman who has abandoned us and a golem engaged in framing us for murder? Certainly on a list of suspects he was first.[ε] There was his address on Howley's missing letter. Giltgestalt's mind and body split in his room and a half and in the mirror of his room and a half. And Owley's missing letter he'd recalled from the tip of Booger's murdered tongue.[φ] In spite of this, or out of it, he clung to his desire to cling to a golem and a goil. Rather than flee or flail at them. In spite of true understanding, which glares beneath the lights of a painful place, and which always occurs too soon to be truly understood and too late to be recovered. The taste of broken syllables. He merely watched as though from beyond the window's pain. Narrating his own life in the preterit past. He would have preferred to have been the first to leave. A gesture. Because of his pride. Not to mention the ease with which they would have let him go. Until a Cafgu coughed gently. Someone signals his own body when it's time to go. Instantly they were on their feet. Whereas he. Whereas he. Whereas I. Was not. On my feet, I mean. Not to mention, ready to go. I might have spoken. To hold them back. I did not.[γ] A touch of self-restraint? Perhaps you cannot possibly think so. Who can restrain a golem and a golem's gal? In any case, in this case, they were gone. Time's coil sprung, flinging him into the lack of any future. Shall we allow him a moment's wallow? The thickness of his creamy solitude. No. Not yet. Instead. Let us draw his eye in the direction of the bill. It lay on the table between a Cafgu's forked yolk and the crumbs of their friendship[η]::

α And yet the longer we wait the larger looms the future.

δ At such times, despite our age, we slip blissfully into the toothy mind of youth; yet we feel, not wiser, but so much more slow-witted and sore.

ε Who keeps such a list? A policeman and a reader. When they are not the same person.

φ Perhaps you ask: And where was that letter? Let us say, belatedly, in the wake of a light cuff to the head from Joey Cafgu, it had once again slipped his mind.

γ Perhaps you are thinking he should have begged for their company. Or demanded the return of Howley's incriminating letter. Or pleaded his case.

How many years had he been, like the Messiah, undoing and rewrapping his bandages one by one, rather than undoing them all at once?[κ] A date may be preordained, yet remain unknown to us.[λ] As we grow older we become like R' Yochanan; we are no longer as keen to witness the arrival of the Messiah. We fear judgment more than we long to see our faith confirmed. This is only reasonable. A man flees from a lion, and a bear meets him. Entering his house, he leans his hand on the wall and a snake bites him. What is it that no eye has seen? Wine preserved in its grapes since the six days of Creation.[μ] We do not have even a partial understanding of these matters.[ν] Now we've cashed in our chips in an eschatological economy, what remains? Is there room for a Messianic economy? Not likely. Once having parted with that teleological hand-puppet, how should we act? The passage of time used to be nothing more than waiting for the Messiah. When is Master coming? Today! Suddenly, we are all each other's Messiah.[π] That Stranger's face nevertheless remains in the future; there is no room for him in the present. Nor at the inn. Should he accept such a responsibility and stumble toward the Other? Scarred by the memory of an irretrievable past, he was tempted to attempt a kenotic gesture before the future's infinite promise. To hear is to obey.[ρ] Should he rise from his place at the table and approach the final Pentateuchal act? To cross into the Promised Land? Could we be once again that confederacy of consanguineous tribes? A pluralism that does not merge into unity. Age of the Bride. That ideal asymmetrical community. In the meantime, we are all on someone's list. He resolved to. What? In this mean time, that bill lies before our keyless (not to mention empty) pockets::

κ In case he should be suddenly needed.

λ I have revealed the date of the redemption to My heart, I have not revealed it to My limbs.
Sanhedrin 99a

μ Some secret wisdom shall be revealed only to the righteous in the World to Come.
Sanhedrin 99a

ν May the very essence of those who calculate ends suffer agony!
R' Shmuel Bar Nachmani, in the name of R' Yonasan

π There is no Messianic figure of the grand deliverer… Each one bears the Messianic task and its responsibility.
G. Ward "On Time and Salvation"

ρ Those verbs grew stems from the same root.

Tw thusand yars atr Cratin, Abraham accptd th mssag th Trah. H was tytw yars ld rtyi ght yars latr, saac was brn saac was sixty yars ld whn Jacb was brn. Whn Jacb was nhundrd and thity yars ld, h brught his amily dwnt gypt. Th gyptian xil Jacbs ppl lastd tw hundrd and tn yars. ur hundrd and ighty yars atr thir xdus rm gypt, th Jwish ppl built th irst Tmpl. Th irst Tmpl std rur hundrd and tn yars. Svnty yars atr yars th dstructin th irst Tmpl, th Scnd Tmpl was built. Th Scnd Tmpl std rur hundrd and twnty yars. On hundrd and svtytw yars atr th dstructin th Scnd Tmpl, r 2000 yars atr Abraham accptd th Cvnant, th dclin Trah bgan. Th dath Rbbi in 3952 marks th nd th Tannaic ra. rm Cratin until th Mssianic ra, six millnnia will hav passd. Th Mssianic ra will b llwd by th Rsurrzctin th Dad, th grat Day Judgmnt, and th dstructin th wrld as w knw it. A prid dstructin n thusand yars will llw that, atr which th wrld will b rcratd n a much highr spiritual lvl. Accrding t Rabbinu Bachya, th dstructin th wrld in th svnth millnnium will b nly partial, and will rcur vry svn millnnia, until th tith millnnium, at which tim th wrld will b cmpltly dstryd. Th ntir 50,000-yar cycl will thn bgin again, and rpat itsl many tims::

η You sleuth, you sleuth, but you forget. He should have reminded them to take the bill.

Who could restrain an involuntary glance to locate a waitress and a short-order cook?[α] To flip a bill has not been a difficult art. In the West. Providing we have sufficiently exercised it. Avoiding arrest is an opportunity not to be squandered. However street rust, the rust of a cot in a room and a half, that daily demi-baguette, an occasional fistful of bananas.[δ] Furthermore, to flip a bill requires less weariness than he now possessed. Not to mention a bit of money.[ε] In order that his nonchalance might saunter nimbly from the scene of the crime. Time now, he knew, was of the essence.[φ] Shall we calculate the inverse proportionality of time seated before the remains of a table as to the degree of attention drawn at the moment of rising to depart? The Gemara does not resolve this. And yet. Not yet. Not until he might invent an opportunity to merge into a semblance of coming and going. Let us open a book of prayers. Not for divine inspiration, nor assistance. Nor for its own sake.[γ] Rather to slip a cheque between the pages. And press the danger there. He hoped, in this manner, to follow that bill out of sight. But first we must sketch a crowd. Let us say a ragged vein in search of a cubicle and a teaspoon of water entered that painful place. And if a pair of red heels meanwhile rose to walk the street in search of another cup of coffee, such simultaneity is a blessing. To be always prepared for that rare and unpredictable conjunction of forces when our action might tip the scales and produce qualitative change.[η] In this case, he had no change to tip. Still time was out, I mean he was out of it, which demanded someone rise quickly, gather a blunt pencil of sharp regret, a curtain of souls and a tractate pressing an unpaid bill between an argument and an analogy, and slide toward, even possibly through, a door and walk. Shall we say, in this case, his street rust showed? Let us provide awkwardly a spectacle of flipart::

α A short-order cook is a cleaver on the end of a rolled apron and a bared bicep.

δ If there is a difficulty, this is the difficulty – the habits of poverty leave us unprepared for complete indigency.

ϵ A couple of perutahs, at least, will tip the table's edge in your favour.

ϕ The essence of time was and will be its duration, so long as it lasts.

γ For its own sake: לשמה Whoever engages in Torah study for its own sake, without hope of reward or fear of punishment, promotes peace among the heavenly host above, and among the host below on earth.
Sanhedrin 99b

η Meanwhile, unprepared, we let slip yet another of those preordained dates of redemption.

O א מאהארבא סנעתא רס רתא שראי דנאשט הת שת עיתר דל שראי שתית שאש ההארת הת גאששמ התדתפ יתחעש שאש סאאש נרב שאש סאאש סרתאל שראי תהג דרדנטהנ שאש בסאצ נהש נרב שאש בסאצ נהש דל שראי גתנשד ילעמא שעה תהגטרב הסדל שראי יתעהת דנא דרדנטה שת דתשאל לפפ שבסאצ לעח נאעתפיג התתפי רעהת רתא שראי יתהגע דנא דרדנטה רטשראי נת דנא תשרע הת תלעטב לפפ השעשצ הת סתפיג מר שטדח שראי נת דנא דרדנטה רטר דתש לפמת תשרע הת לפמת תשרע הת נעתס טרתשד הת שראי רתא שראי יתנוש לפמת דנסש הת תלעטב שאש לפמת דנסש התסלפמת דנא דרדנטה נו שראי יתנשת דנא דרדנטה רטר דתש רסלפמת דנסש הת נעתסטרתשד הת רתא שראי שתיתוש הת סתנאנוס הת דתפססא מאהארבא רתא שראי 2000 הת שכראמ 3952 נע עבבר התאדהת נאגב הארת נעלסד סענאע ששמ הת לעתנט נעתארס מראר סעאננאת התדנ סענא עששמהת דששאפ ואהללעש אענללעמ חעש סאר תארג הת סדאד התנעתס זרטשרדהת יב דשללב ללעש אר שנכש שא דלרש הת נעתסטרתשד התדנא סתנמגדטצ יאד שלל ללעש שראי דנאשטהתנ נעתסט רתשד דערפ אתע אנ דתאר סרב ללעש דלרש הת הסעהש רתא סתאהת בבאר תגנעד רססא לול לאטתערעפש רהגעה הסטמ התנוש הת נע דלרש הת נעתס טרתשדהת סאיהס אבטנע נוש ירו רטס רדנא סלאעתראפ ילנב ללעש מטענ ללעמ הסעהש תא סמטענ ללעמ התעת הת לעתנט סאענ ללעמ רעתנ התדירתשד ילתלפמ סב ללעש דלרש התמעת תאפר דנא סנעאגא נעגב נהת ללעש לסיס ראימ 50,000 שמעת ינאמ לשתע::

Did he flail wildly at that unpaid bill, which had emerged aflutter from the pages of this chapter and into the bright light of a painful nightspot when he accidentally flipped high that Talmudic argument as he grabbed for a curtain of fallen souls that he'd dropped bending to pick up the prayers he'd let slide as he rose from the edge of the table?[κ] Yes and no, and it was unsteady in his hand. But what then? Let us say, he took hold of the details and let the bill lie where it fell. In plain view. Cheese and tomato on plain rye. At times such as these a waitress will shout hey and a short-order cook will swing out from behind the counter to greet you in very short order at the door. Such simultaneity is a curse.[λ] Are you casting one man against another? How should we act? One hesitates. Between a broken play in a broken field of tables. Some say it to this side and some say it to this side. And the inner joy of surrender. In either case, no matter what. He was an orchestra of regret. The wool of drama. His failure was inclusive; it sought to embrace all within that paneful place.[μ] Notwithstanding that cleaver. A smoker's cough hunched over yellow soup. Rough red heels pinched in redder heels. A scuffed man on grilled cheese. For their part they declined to reciprocate. The price of solidarity does not figure on a diner menu. Someone may watch, wouldn't you? They were keenly interested in the outcome, though acutely indifferent to his fate. He saw there was no one to intercede.[ν] Let us say when he turned to the window for a glimpse of the street and freedom (for what that was worth) beyond the wall, he saw only his own painful reflection in the glass. Not to mention a cook and a cleaver. He threw himself like a stone through that so paneful looking glass back into the world::

κ There is no before and after in the Torah.

λ To be prepared for and prepared to act against those predictably frequent conjunctions of forces that will tip the scales into catastrophic change.

μ Shall we say annihilation inspired a generosity and willingness to share?

ν He was amazed that there was no intercessor, no righteous person to shore up the breach in the people's spiritual standing (sages disagree about whether such a generation is possible) and concluded: For My sake I will act.
Sanhedrin 98a

olc
of se'
.e com·
ups sha·
ud I say h·
ge of his bo'
· by the
e was no tim
is reflection. T
he slivered
more reflection. Only
up wh·
d he bend then to gathe.
pression, and how ma·
liv·
r
ither up in ord·
emained?

nerge
one's self.
image. One stands,
the thing itself), narrating, w
erit past. As though it were. Yes. Exac
e. Out of the well-lit darkness of the dine
ne well-lit darkness of the street. Phantasms of
we agree to divest ourselves. Comparison and contrast. Being
arriages. To try for something better. I am still trying for something better. When I
ot trying to stop trying. The painful event after which nothing will ever be the
again. Shall we pursue that mystery in so unbridled a manner? To
it. He sought an end to his reflections. He had not found it
ot found it. Perhaps it lay shattered in the splintered glass
traces of his broken image, in th
pooled in his blood alre
ding a t

Shall we pause? Now? Now that we are past that painful apocatastatic (apostatic?) moment? Why now? To prolong a complication? To forestall that dénouement? There was no dining room, hence no dining room floor, hence blood on a crabway. Oh, Lizzie, do you understand G. Stein? What's the hurry, Bub? Or Bob? Let us pause, therefore, to examine the case of a wayward and rebellious son. Are you still at this? Shall his parents pardon his gluttonous behaviour? Perhaps you cannot possibly think so. Perhaps you say: And how has, was, or shall such a son come to be judged wayward and rebellious? If this was taught, it was taught. Shall we say he also committed the sin of theft? The sport of Pontiacs. Who mentioned this item which is being cited now as if it had already been mentioned? He dishonoured papa maman pipi caca. Now we offer remembrance of something. But I digress. Let us return to our original digression. And imagine. In the first instance he had merely committed the sins of theft and gluttony with certain amounts of meat and wine. In such a case, we are taught, he should be warned by his parents before witnesses to cease such behaviour. And if he does not stop? What more is there to say? If he cursed his parents and abandoned his studies? What else did he leave out that he left this out? Something else (sexual relations, money, pigs, leprosy). In such a case, we are taught, he shall be brought to court to be flogged there. A good flogging will shatter the mirror of one's illusions and provide excellent cause for reflection. But having been appropriately flogged, let us imagine that wayward son persists in his behaviour. Act, deed, event, precedent. Pattern. Perhaps you are thinking: Why? Papamamanpipicaca. Let us be content to say that he persisted. But what then? Shall his parents return him to court? To be judged and sentenced there and executed. Executed? Did someone say executed? Since we took the first part we took the end as well. What is there to say? R' Yoshiyah teaches (Sanhedrin 70a) that even if a son continues to indulge in gluttony after having been flogged by the court, his parents may decline to return him to the court to receive the death penalty. Hear from this, learn from this, conclude from this. What is he trying to tell us? It is stated "His father and his mother shall seize him" (Deuteronomy 21:19). By this we may conclude the Torah allows the parents discretion in the matter of bringing a child to court for execution (Sanhedrin 88b). And... must you explain it so much? Since it comes from exegesis, it is dear to him. And yet, does he really have to go on reckoning like a peddler? Am I a peddler? Must I go on like a peddler? Some say he must, but he has no remedy. Superfluity in measured amounts. Let us say, in his case, from the beginning and at the outset, his greatest sin was... What? A failure. To do what? It might occur to you. A failure to live up to his potential. Should we rely on answers such as these? In any case. In his case. There was no execution. Not yet. Though every apocatastasis threatens an execution. Perhaps, in his case, those courts were in recess. Perhaps they too were busy. Perhaps those temples were destroyed (mine could do with a good rubbing). In any case, in this case, they did not hear his case. Perhaps someone's parents neglected, in the first place, to bring him to that place which, in any case, would not hear his case. They let it rest. Not to mention the ease with which they let him go. And furthermore. And nothing more : :

Now that we have come to this. Having come to this. Let it rest.

אב כת גש דר הק וצ זפ חע טס ינ כמ
אג גת דש הר וק זצ חפ טע יס כנ למ
אר בג דת הש ור זק חצ טפ יע כס לנ
אה בד הת וש זר חק טצ יפ כע לס מנ
או בה גד ות זש חר טק יצ כפ לע מס
אז בו גה זת חש טר יק כצ לפ מע נס
אח בז גו דה חת טש יר כק לצ מפ נע
אט בח גז דו טת יש כר לק מצ נפ סע
אי בט גח דז הו ית כש לר מק נצ ספ
אכ בי גט דח הז כת לש מר נק סצ עפ
אל בכ גי דט הח וז לת מש נר סק עצ
אמ בל גכ די הט וח מת נש סר עק פצ
אנ במ גל דכ הי וט זח נת סש ער פק
אס בנ גמ דל הכ וי זט סת עש פר צק
אע בס גנ דמ הל וכ זי חט עת פש צר
אפ בע גס דנ המ ול זכ חי פת צש קר
בפ גע דס הנ ומ זל חכ טי צת קש
גפ דע הס ונ זמ כל מכ קת רש
דפ הע וס זנ כמ טל יכ רת
הפ וע זס כנ טמ יל שת
ופ זע כס טנ ימ כל

The event that happened happened
        that way any act is great
        did we say perhaps

in either case no matter what
        a story contradicts

this is in and this is in
from the beginning at the outset
        where you came from

act deed event precedent
it was said thus and it was
        said thus

a fiction only resembles this and
have we removed Tannaim from the world

is there nothing else   grocers
        they incline they subtract
        they add and expound
        they wipe their pink hands

this is ours and this is theirs
the body the thing itself
        something else
        sexual relations money pigs leprosy

now we have come to this
how can you find it
        We have not found it
        I have not found it

Not only this
but also this
how much
more so this

to add what
to exclude the common factor
one's self if there is
a difficulty

he cursed it shall we say
we disagree about this and let it stand

what is there to say
what was there about it
what is he trying to tell us

how should we act
and are you still be still at this still
those rabbis they replied
go this way just
the opposite

a Halakhah for the Time of the Messiah
and he who asked
it – the question – why
did he ask it

it is a case of go read it in the teacher's house
it is written
here and it is written there

The event that happened
happened that way

we all bathe
in a glassy shower
of our own

shattered allusion
some select

an act is great[α]
we were boots and vertigo

before narrative and yet and yet
we tell a story shall we

move that ball forward there
this is no time to bleed
nevertheless

he trailed a muddy subordination
in the wake of an escape clause

he wore the cuts and bruises
of a subsidiary judgment[δ]

he wore the traces of his own blood

α Others may prefer to stand and watch.

δ Shall we add breaking and exiting to theft and murder and the father of the father of all impurities? Not to mention public urination.

Shall we say he gathered a pair of someone's legs, preferably his own, beneath him and projected the idea of himself along the crabway and away from that paneless diner? From whence they did not pursue him.[α] They stood instead, hey(!)s agape and biceps akimbo, wouldn't you, while a portion of the jagged street poured into that well-lit diner through a painfully shattered membrane. When inside and outside leak into each other,[δ] those diners[ε] will become restless. Wouldn't you? Something learned from its end : :

α We, alas, are not so fortunate. Indeed, we must. Pursue the ball, I mean. And yet. Not yet. Though soon enough.

δ I mean inside and outside the diner, not those eating within.

ε Here I meant those eating within a diner.

But we were pursuing a story. Or fleeing from it. Crablike and bleeding. Which he did for a block or less. And came to a halt in a heap by a heap of the morning papers twined at the mouth of the alley. At such times we all seek the comfort of the news of the day. Sarajevo. We can learn but not refute. To be wrapped in newspapers is perhaps best of all. Who mentioned this item which was mentioned before? Perhaps you[α] cannot possibly think so. To be entwined in layer upon layer of fine print. Is it content that contents or form that feels good? He sought that consolation. Or solace. Or merely snugness. Wouldn't you? After the events of a day and a half? He preferred to wrap his legs in them. Have we poured so many pages to come to this? He was a ragged glance in the alley. Between the cat and the cat's piss, bloodied and wrapped in old news. Just so do events pour across the page; eventually we are reduced to a suburbanite's passing glance into an alley : :

α You who lie properly encased in sheets of cotton, wool or polyacrylonite.

Front page. Pigafetta, Antonio. Suddenly. Husband. Father, loving, loved, pets, lawn, mild perennial struggle with quack grass. A Pigafetta practice. And patients, for the most part grateful. With one exception. Apparently. Police Extract Confession from Mouth of Murderous Patient. Dentist's Mysterious Death Explicated.[α] What dentist does not deserve it? What patient has not considered it? To strike at the root. To crown[δ] a dentist with too many teeth in his name. A generalization needs a detail. Preferably gory. Any practice of journalism will require it. The drill. Through the neck. Up into the brain.[ε] So no accident. Nor plot to eliminate the pinkish hue of someone's rosy youth. Or punish those who abandoned that rosy hue. Had he fingered the exception to a murderous plot against past adherence? Or against that adherence being past? Either way – just as there, so here too – his toothless theory sagged beneath the weight of a dental exception? : :

α Hashem puts to death and He brings to life, He brings down to the grave and raises up (Sanhedrin 92b). Only a dentist approaches such power.

δ Let us say that, by a simple permutation he turned כתר into כרת, that crown became an excision, that person was cut off spiritually. Not to mention the body.

ε I was speaking of a dental murder; not journalism. Although, if the shoe pinches.

The clock[α] of mystery presents no visible source of power or gears. What is the difference between the first case where they do not disagree and the second case, where they do disagree? Shall we park truth and wrap our legs in the flag of journalism? Or did I mean cloak. If so, then. Perhaps you too can certainly glimpse the end of a story.[δ] And yet. Not yet. To wait marches on what failure can't the future include? He longed to surrender, to rust on the cot of desolation in a room and a half a list was the pea of midnight. A certain numbness around the ankles could not number the suspects. Of which he was Number One. His ankles were lined with headlines. Number One Suspect Still Suspected Still at Large. He could not lie. Still. In particular, the inexplicable severely murderous severing of a room and a half from a room and a half. He tossed in the alley of his Giltgestalt : :

α Perhaps I meant cloak.

δ Little by little the book will finish me. E. Jabès

He sought a consolation. One may take comfort in the statisticality of homelessness. We are not alone. Someone notices. The shopkeepers. They subtract and add and expound. Don't they calculate leket and shich'chah and pe'ah?[α] Is there comfort in that? Meanwhile the present extends itself. We are the purpose of the other's silence. He made a room and a half and a broken lock on the door out of the news of the day. We all wrap our legs in the news of the day. To keep reality at bay. To create a small space for the self. Any day now I shall begin the kitchen. Chant on suit away as in.[δ] What else remained in the alley after he'd shattered the image of a paneful diner? A curtain of souls, a book of prayers. He'd lost the blunt end of his pencil. No matter. There was not much to inscribe?[ε] His past had entered the climate, his species was silence. Why should a novel walk when it can lie down and wrap itself in the news of the day? Perhaps you cannot possibly think so : :

α These are the gleanings and forgotten produce that may not be harvested, so that the poor may eat within your gates.

δ Meanwhile, the scribes of the national bourgeoisie met to congratulate each other over a glass of sherry in the Governor-General's garden.

ε And whose scribe was I?

Meanwhile

Who asked: how did such a context crash? When did a mass line become a hard line? In Shechem,[α] despite the democratic temperature under the angle of evening, a bureaucratic umbrella emerged. Dictatorship of the vending machines became a comedy of anger.[δ] And how did the party of one become the party of the Other? How did the Time of the Messiah[ϵ] become bureaucratic capitalism? Who kept that friendly fire burning? One person's proletarian internationalism becomes another person's imperialist boot. How did someone's national revolution become our nationalist landmine? And when did friendship between peoples shake hands with the devil? Had every invention died,[ϕ] every doctrine been accomplished? The highway they had crafted narrowed to a white twang. The end declined. The masses lay between that highway and the context. The answers lay in why do I always need two?![γ] The priority of the One over the Other. Always the same. Equation. The same strategic requirement of regions, types, intentions, sacrifices. A fatherly orchestra attempting to muscle our way into the World to Come. Who governs form? They say in the West. Meanwhile. Events will occur. The crowd thinned. Once we were few, then we were few again. The meanness of men on the run. Not to mention in general. The exercise of terror is a complicated task, best served cold. The truth came galloping on the sound of women dreaming. Meanwhile. Shall we while away the time? Betty Bebop made music they failed to encode into a story. Her spectacular shrug. Her unwillingness to march in any orchestra. Her speaking in tongues. Others returned to the suburbs, to school, to mamanpapapipicaca. To dentistry. Mustapha and Legrand had a nose for business.[η] As for him, his time was out of joint. He lay there a very mean while : :

α Shechem was a place and a moment in history predestined for misfortune. Sanhedrin 102a

δ Lawyers were the market therapists of business.

ϵ The time that comes between the harsh reality of now and the promise of the World to Come, during which time the laws of nature remain the same.

ϕ Yarovam ruled over the ten tribes and produced insights no ear had ever heard. Nevertheless, he too, in the end, returned to the worship of idols, and lost his share in the World to Come.

γ Did he say that twice?

η Whereas Betty wiped hers on her sleeve.

Shall we say as, and raise the spectre of story? Let us rather let him lie where he lay, wrapped in the sheets of all the news someone saw fit to print on such a day.[α] And shall we concede him the opportunity to dream? He would have preferred not. To dream, I mean. He would have declined that concession. Perhaps you cannot possibly think so. The truth is not satisfied with people. Those sheets were not conducive to any dream he would have welcomed. Not to mention the unprintable events of the day, I mean his day. Nevertheless, let us say dreamily he enfolded himself. He experienced the random encephalous discharges of electronic impulses, which in turn prompted a rapid shifting of the I. Perhaps you think he dreamed, like Novat, of fire pouring from his masculine member. And waking from such a dream, a dreamer might think, as Novat did, that he was destined one day to be king.[δ] In his case, he dreamed no such dream. His own member lay tucked and puckered in his pants, dribbling the cold leakage of sleep. And yet. He was not spared dreaming. He dreamed of the darkness in the street after the darkness in the theatre. A horse in the park. Neither white nor brown nor black. Those colours having all been spoken for. Let us say his dream was the colour of a four-legged pentametric engineer, a Victorian elephant, the greasy mouse of drama. He envied that horse, wouldn't you, to urinate beneath the policeman who straddled it. In the streetlight of that previous statement, shall we perhaps move on? We should move on. And yet. Not yet. He, at least, could not. Move on, I mean. He was stuck. In the dream. At first by the hypnotic power of that hippic flow.[ε] Not to mention a quantity of urinary equinity. I mean horse piss. Hippological peepee. That horse poured a liquid college. In such cases, we are called to study in it. Transfixed in a horse's gaze of hippish equanimity, our feet soon become mired in the muddied waters. Before long, we are swimming,[φ] or trying hard to. This was called exegesis, and any sleuth is fond of it. Or ought to be. In his case, he rather shied away from it. He sought instead to escape drowning by clinging to a humectant letter. Any dank letter will do. Owley's missive, for example. If he could find it. Who mentioned this item which is being cited now as if it had already been mentioned? He could not. Find it, I mean. I have not found it. At such times a damp letter will, shall we say, solubilize?[γ] And so will our dream. Those of us who once learned to swim will have forgotten how. And yet. Not yet. At such a moment we neither sink nor swim. At such times, a policeman will reach down from his own night mare and roughly take hold of our collar to… To what? To wake us from a wet dream. To find ourselves wrapped in the alley of yesterday's news. To the beat of a policeman's grip. He held that note a moment longer. Shall we say, that policeman was not saddled with mere tolerance? Nor was his welcome unbridled. Better not. Let us say instead he manned his beat. And beat any man he found there. He raised us roughly to our knees, smelled our strange smell, eyed our way of speaking. The street being a public place, the police will sweep away a private. Perhaps you are wondering, if that policeman recalled a sketch artist's memory from his policeman's britches. Did he undertake a suspicious comparison? At such times we pray that our subject's restless bathless night will blunt any sketch artist's pencil. Retroactively. We would welcome nothing more than a good shaking and a move along on the end of a nightstick. And I was shaken. By fear lurking in the entrance to the alley. What else lurked there? A Cafgu. That golem : :

α The bed is too short for stretching out and the cover too narrow for curling up. Sanhedrin 103b

δ In this, Novat too was mistaken (Sanhedrin 101b). Whereas, in the case of King Yehoiakim, according to R' Yochannan, they found a pagan deity tattooed on his male organ. According to R' Elazar, it was the name of God Yehoiakim had tattooed on his male organ. In either case, we may ask why his name was not listed as one of those who had no portion in the World to Come. Sanhedrin 103b

ε The profluence of a horse's prose.

φ In that muddy language we call our own.

γ … cette forme du H… est la figure centrale sur laquelle Platon raconte que les atlantéens avaient bâti leur ville;… cela existe dans la montagne Tarahumara et dans Platon… et partout où j'ai retrouvé ce fameux H, le H de la génération en somme… j'ai vu une figure d'homme et de femme qui se faisaient face, et l'homme avait la verge levée.

A. Artaud, "Lettre à Paulham du 4 février 1937"

Suspicion was already a vice more than we were prepared to invest. Suspicion's acute caress intoned.[α] At such times, the Other has already passed the threshold and been gathering in your gates. We tax everything in our power, including our patience. We eye her or him eyeingly. We smell their smell, curl our tongues at someone's way of speaking.[δ] We say this is ours and this is theirs. We say from where you came. Suspicion is the better part of valour. Are we casting one man against another? The native is on the ground and the stranger is in the sky! And if, beneath the stone turned, we were to find… what? The common factor? Well, so much more so.[ε] We say it takes one to know one. In either case, no matter what. A man is always considered forewarned. He had suspicion. Suspicion was his. He sought something prior to suspicion. Prior to even an apprehension of the Other. Prior to sin, guilt and peace offerings. Prior to himself::

α To the tune of "we always hurt the one we love."

δ We dredge up Homer and call them barbarians for their way of speaking.

ε No one is more worthy of suspicion than one who resembles me. After all, I should know.

Who knows the method to create a Cafgu?[φ] Before one, what did we count? Who uttered the 97,240 pronunciations?[γ] Did they make use of the sounds of the letters, and of their names?[η] What method worked a chariot? Who dug soil where no man had ever dug? Kneaded dirt into mud with spring water that no vessel had ever borne? Someone wore clean white vestments. They circumcised their tongues, imbedded their end in their beginning.[κ] A depth of east. A depth of west. A depth of north. And a depth of south. A depth of above, a depth of below. Three Mothers, Seven Doubles, Twelve Elementals. Permute them, weigh them, transform them. Aleph with them all and all of them with aleph, bet with them all and all of them with bet. Someone – Who? – passed through the 231 gates. Engrave them like a garden, carve them like a wall, deck them like a ceiling. Someone spoke in silence. Made something from nothing::

φ A fiction, a mistake.

γ $L=n(n-1)/2$

η Betzalel knew how to permute the letters with which heaven and earth were made. Sefer Yetzirah 1:1.

κ Bridle my mouth from speaking and my heart from thinking.

This golem, this colt of legend, was he to become his constant companion? And how much time would that be? What restrains a Cafgu from strangling a sleuth? What keeps a cat from snapping its jaws shut on the mouse of drama? Surely if a policeman's sketch failed to finger him, a Cafgu would lend a helping hand. I mean, I feared Joey would jog that policeman's memory of the sketch in his britches. I mean the policeman's britches, not the golem's. Though, is there not something of the golem in any policeman? Shall we say I bent beneath that fear? And those britches. To lower one's head only invites another distracted blow from the stick of night. Where is the novelty in another blow? What is the difference between the first clause and this clause? Just as there, so here too. He accepted that blow and the next. He considered his options. They lay few and tightly bunched between the blows. One hesitates between the realistic code and a story. A story to contradict whatever Joey Cafgu might provide to finger his fate. Solution, may it come to me. And yet. Not yet. Whereas that policeman's stick was black and bruised, and his zeal furrowed a comparative sketch, still that Golem would not delurk. Perhaps you cannot possibly think so. When a man stands before the Law, his fellows will step to one side. In the case of a nightstick, discretion is the better part of the opportunity to finger a suspect. Perhaps a golem will bide his time from time to time. Perhaps no Cafgu had ever stood there.[λ] Certainly he could not see one now. A good stick to the side of the head will introduce a golem in the entrance to anyone's alley. And subsequently take him away. We have learned this elsewhere. Sooner or later any policeman's wrist will tire of a good beating. The sooner the better, if you are on the dark end of his shtick. Must we go on like a policeman? Beating a dead nightmare? Superfluity in generous amounts. You may feel a generalization needs a detail. Shall we describe the blood dribble on his puckered ear? Shall we say the left side of the head? For the sake of amplification and restriction. When does a man welcome a handful of additional blows to the side of the head? When a policeman has replaced the sketch artist's blunted weapon in his pocket in order to swing more freely to the beat of his baton. When a Cafgu in the entrance to the alley no longer lurks there. At such times a person is close to him or herself. A nightstick to the side of the head will scatter the horse of night. Eventually it became later and not a moment too soon. That cop beat a couplet on my knees, to the tune of get up and get along, little doggie. I mean, he said get up and rapped my knees in the local dialectic. And yet. Now that a blunt sketch was put aside, and the ghost of a golem vanished, I might have been content to linger a while longer under the lamppost of a legal beating. Nevertheless. Shall we say he struggled to bend his knees beneath him? He thought, even law enforcement wearies of meting out justice;[μ] perhaps he might after all escape a sticky situation. Let us imagine he edged away toward an unsteady sidewalk. Perhaps he paused momentarily in his faith in the world's ever-decreasing options. Not for long. Soon enough, that faith will be renewed. And amplified. The police know how to look after their victims. As they limp away. Something in the back of a bloodied head brings sudden recognition. From behind, any suspect looks suspicious. We beat a hasty incrimination.[ν] He heard that four-letter word for stop. He halted haltingly. Clenched his knocking knees between his teeth. Perhaps you wonder why the Law says move along as he knocks your knees, and halt when you do as he says. Should he have halted when a cop said move along, and run along when he cried halt? There was no running in a policeman's grip. If that cop had said sing loudly, he would have come quietly. Having learned his lesson, he tried to carry a tune. To lift up his voice in a succession of letters. Soon enough, he dropped it. The tune, I mean. Not to mention the letters. An excellent blow to the side of the head will do that::

λ Perhaps the secret of working the chariot is simply this, that a golem is merely the incidental byproduct of a meditative journey along the branches of those ten sefirot of nothing.

μ The rich seek justice; the poor make do with gleanings.

ν We are all subsidiary policemen when we gaze at our fellow from behind.

He broke the language. Or tried to. Who wouldn't bite the hand that feeds us so much terror? It was a gift. Of tongues. The beautiful early figs. Gusto in the branches. Music to their overbite. Over time, care was given to the cultivation of the appearance of cultivation.[α] They prune an impeccable manner. They smile Greekly. They offer on the one hand and on the other hand. Baseball and baby carriages. Creamed tea and the weather channel. Trace a lineage to a courtly phrase.[δ] Hang unction in a glassy tree. Beneath that watery smile the textile of style is a fist. Did he think to surrender? They removed an offer of cream. He learned some prisons are shortcakes. He made a purpose of silence. Uttered names according to their letters. Spoke in a foreign tongue.[ε] The father of the fathers of ritual impurity. What had he resisted? The vanguard dabbling in a sentence of ambition. They were the pioneer of criticism straining for a long-range testament. He bit off more nails than he could chew.[ϕ] A ragged this way comes. Not to make it new, but ugly. Difficulty: every routine. And if you have run with the foot soldiers, and it has wearied you, how will you contend with horses? There was no agent for transgression. Le temps du Messie se fait attendre : :

α It is prohibited to sit within the Temple Courtyard. Nevertheless, one prohibition does not take effect where another prohibition already exists.

δ In that country, the national language was sleep.

ε The sixth case of one who has no share in the World to Come is the person who utters the Name of God outside the temple and in a foreign tongue: ובלשון עגה

ϕ It occurred to him that a single phrase, if it was the right one, might suffice to bring down the entire edifice. The difficulty was to find it. I mean the phrase. Not to mention the edifice.

I'm saying I moved on. And so would you. Two boys were dead and two were suspect.[γ] A girl's got to undo from others or others will surely do her doodoo. To say the least. Now that old Booger (I mean that both fondly and literally – he was as old as he would ever be) was gone, and Howley's flowery fists too, I felt a certain quickness to my step.[η] In the end, a garden beats a boy any day. In particular when a boy beats a garden. When I dipped the dirt under my nails into the dirt under my feet, I felt a certain coolness. Time stood still and stretched its legs. A flower stem will hold up its end of any conversation. And bid you good day. I was tempted to go it alone. Everybody's golem can become a pain in the backside.[κ] Now I wanted a place to bend my knees, I mean stretch out. I recalled pink curlers and a cat between that landlady's legs and drifted that way. I mean the way a cat drifts when it wants a room for the night. And a hallway on the end of the john : :

γ What and where are two halves of the same interrogation?

η Freedom made a light head and fear a lighter step.

κ Not to mention a boy's quarrelsome lips forever fastened on his mom.

Who mentioned this item which is being cited now as if it had already been mentioned? In the end one lines up at Station Number 10 beside his fellows. Shall we hasten to add? Do not let this enter your head: we were not speaking of that testament, but of a police precinct. There was no cross, except the one someone had doubled. There were no nails but those he'd bitten off, more than he could chew. In the cracked mirror of this half room, he saw the face that the one on the other side of the mirror saw as his. Let us say it was not a pretty sight. There was a bloodied ear. Not to mention the lack of a good cleaning. If two generalizations are next to each other, place a detail between them and treat them as a generalization and a detail and a generalization. He had been placed between a mannish dwarf and a very Malaysian complexion. Shall we say he considered his options? Beyond that mirror someone's task was to identify the face of the one who most resembled...what? One who strangles to separate the other's mind from their body? A Shtick in the vestibule between the world and self, a grin in the rearview mirror of a Pontiac Sport? One who did not go to meet Owley by the gate? In all those years a single letter, and then missing. One who abandoned our collected struggles for the World to Come? One who failed something between himself and Betty Boop? Her nose in a Dutchman's-breeches. In the mirror he could not help but select himself. At such times we screw up our mouth and strive to squint a fiercely pitiful grimace unlike our daily mask. But that grimace is always already precisely the face of a murderer. Beside us, our fellows. The manly dwarf. The marked Malaysian. Before the cracked mirror all three partook of the fellowship of misfortune even as we competed for innocence. We stand side-by-urinary-side in a less than manly expression of our outer selves. He tried to find a way to think: I am innocent. He could not find it. I have not found it. But the question, the difficulty returned to its place. The body, the thing itself. And yet. Not yet. The question ought to be: who stood face to face with his face on the other side of a cracked mirror in the other half of a room? Whose gaze now moved up from the eyes of a grim dwarf to his grimy brother and squinted to the right, to a worldly traveller's dark complexion? Who knows the languages of the seventy-one nations to stand in judgment on the other side of a cracked mirror?[λ] Was it you Number 2? Are we casting one man against another? Who can resist wondering whose face we face, when we are face to face in the cracked mirror of the tenth station of nothingness? Meanwhile. I mean for a mean while, we three dogs danced. Did we face forward and raise our heads? Cholam. Turn right and move our heads to the left? Kametz. Turn left, heads to the right? Tzereh. Face straight ahead and lower our heads? Chirik. Perhaps you heard someone's breathless breath breathing the letters of the Tetragrammaton? Shall we cast our spirits upward and dissolve our very selves into a universe of rectification? Did he hum those letters? Oh boy, did he ever. Hum, I mean. Did he imagine he was R' Akiva and would ascend in peace and return in peace? Perhaps you cannot possibly think so. Perhaps you recall they were four to enter the garden. Surely these three doubled in the mirror of a half room would look and die, or look and go out of their minds, or cut the growth down. And yet. Not yet. Still, they continued to chant on suit away. Until that faceless voice called out from beyond the mirror: Shurek! Step forward Number 2. In the long silent pause of the Other's consideration, Number 2 approached the peace that accompanies defeat[μ] : :

λ Do not pronounce the word "Israel" until one visualizes the divine Name, which is YHWH, with its vowels and its colour, and one visualizes it as if the last letter of the name, namely H, surrounds the entire world, from above and below.
Anonymous commentary on the prayer *Shema' Yisrael*

μ Here I mean the release at the moment of capture, the cool breeze before the firing squad, that headiness beneath the blade.

We squat in a row in the dust of the dust of the road. Outside the passport office.[α] That one unfolds a low light chair in the palm of a tree. His writing surface is a theatre of smoothly planed and trestled boards. In such a case clearly we need two. Trestles, I mean. A well of dark certainty. The emesh-coloured ink of gloom. The stained index of language poised moistly above a damp sheet. Blank. Smell of horses. Sharp point[δ] where language meets the world. Not to mention the heat's battle against a wet cloth and a gourd. His customers lined up beneath their hopes. Let us receive those who require a scribe's assistance. We are not alone. A row of petty scribes rings the road to bureaucracy.[ε] Shall we transcribe names? Inscribe someone's date of birth on a passage to the pot of plenty? A plea, a destination, a record of existence. Small service to our fellow. A penny for a page. Bending over the board until dusk. Carrying my knees stiffly home, arms full of board, trestle, chair, inky sac. An ear full of the dull clods of language. The delicate click of a pair of duck eggs in my pocket : :

α It could have been the courthouse, employment centre, or the temple. Of these, the temple provides the more cheerful clientele.

δ Let us have a point, be it ever so inky.

ε Those scribes, I include the poets, are all subsidiary judges. If they are not merely court jesters to amuse the tyrant. And what makes a client select one scribe over another? Neither price nor penmanship. A sympathetic ear is not required. Rather the smell of ink reminiscent of the smell of power.

Whichever way one boy or the other manhandled a Booger, how much less could I care? Time became the narrow waist of my escape. This girl spent an ounce of her autonomy on wind, I exercised my shoes, booped a stadium between my neck and the context. I'm saying I made tracks.[φ] Not that I didn't carry a small stone of speculation under my tongue. Either way offered possibilities. What servant, given half the cheese, wouldn't nail his master's lip to the desk?[γ] As for the other one, don't get me started. That brother was not in this world. Not that he would swat an insect. There would have to be a whole lot of toing and frothing before that one swung a bat.[η] And what purpose to slam the door of justice once the pony's dead?[κ] I was not prepared to judge in any language. You're thinking: didn't I feel a twinge on the end of Howley's nose? Sure it hurt, especially where he hit me. But now and then, scarceness is the better part of get the hell out of there. I turned my boopish tail and headed for a warm linoleum under my bed and a cat's throb in my blanket.[λ] And so would you : :

φ Let some historian plug the details, I was moving my tail outta there.

γ If only just to stop the damn thing wagging.

η You can take the man out of a room and a half, but you can't take the room and a half out of the man.

κ Are we Yanks now, to foam revenge and brandish a lethal injection?

λ Who knows, maybe I'd roll some of that gentle landlady's pink curlers in my own hair.

How we do embrace guilt in the cracked mirror of a half room. The way of things. He stood in a line from left to right, between his fellow and a fellow, face to face with justice. There is between them. Shall we imagine a face in the mirror as the Other beyond the glass will eye it? Murder etched the crack in that mirror. He preferred to chant letters. From right to left. Chant on suit a way out. How long shall we dwell in the repose of universal rectification? Only to be interrupted once more by that incorporeal voice's subsequent dismissal. What saved him from a fate approximately equivalent to death? In a cell he could have done time in. Passed it standing still. In any case, I mean in this case, no arrest was made, no rest was given. Why won't space line up? They showed him the door. Beyond which the street beckoned. They said: we have our eye on you. It was said thus and it was said thus. At such times we are inclined to attribute more guile to the police than they perhaps deserve. We imagine they toy our end shiftily, when they are only toying to the end of their shift. Nevertheless, he did not dally. Nor should we. And yet. Not yet. We are already in extra innings. Shall we move the ball forward? This is in and this is in. In the wake of an exit, shall we say he caught a glimpse of a Ukrainian boy? Have you forgotten what constitutes a tenement? God's witnesses. They sent the boy round to collect the rent. Someone asked him to come in. Who mentioned this item which is being cited now as if it had already been mentioned? And are you still at this? It was written there and it is written here. Let us say, in the policeman's exit I recognized a boy's marginally European hunch. In a hurry to scurry. Those furtive feet itching to outrun the nerves. To brush past another figure in the shadows, one step down toward the street. A boy attempts a Ukrainian sidestep. Go this way. Just the opposite! We too have already attempted to subtract that same figure earlier in the story. Instead a Cafgu multiplies and expounds. I cursed it. The colt of legend is indeed anyone's constant companion. Needless to say… Nor shall we. Perhaps you ask: how had a cracked mirror failed to identify the tenant of a room and a half of headless blood? When does a boy fail to differentiate between the dwarfed lower case, the bold face of Malay, and the bent letter of guilt? When is the nature of this case not like the nature of this case and the nature of his case unlike the nature of this case? Perhaps you are thinking Joey Cafgu intervened to blur a Ukrainian memory. Or sent the boy there in the first place. Was it lack of recognition or lack of courage that allowed an image to slip through a crack in a Ukrainian boy's memory? Perhaps that golem merely helped the boy help him help the police help him recover a momentarily lost letter.[μ] Only to unleash him once more. Perhaps you cannot possibly bother to think so. Perhaps, simply, a day and a half removed from his room and a half will make a changed man unrecognizable through a cracked policeman's looking glass. Perhaps it will dwarf his guilt and darken his complexion. Either way, no matter what. In this case, that boyish eyewitness had declined to eye him through a cracked mirror to crack the policeman's case. The question, the problem remains. Who had fingered him in the first place. I mean in the second room and a half across the hall from the first room and a half. At such a time we feel a sudden longing to wrap our fingers around the neck of the one that fingered us. That finger remains a mystery. In any case, my craned neck did not long catch sight of a Ukrainian boy. Which leaves us face to face with that golem. Again : :

μ The weasel and the cat made a wedding feast from the fat of an unlikely victim. Sanhedrin 105a (I mean, even natural enemies will ally themselves to outdo a common foe, or for profit.)

谁会说七十一个民族的语言？

Let us say a golem is what remains in the wake of a Ukrainian retreat. What is the novelty? Shall you face that golem on the frozen steppes of a police station? Why not? Why should I come face to face with every face? Let us say you stood face to face with that burly Cafgu, his neck, his shouting shirt, his fisted cuffs. In which you briefly engaged before he welcomed you[α] to the sidewalk and yes, why not, cuffed you on the side of the head. Why should I take all the blows? In any case they're only fictional. The truth is not satisfied with people. A Cafgu's generosity will provide a good beating. And a very heavy stone. From which it is impossible to learn anything. We would have preferred some hard facts. Whose face had stood between a mirror and your guilt? Was it you Number 2? What then made a common denominator between you, a Malay and a midget? Let us say you slipped these questions between the blows. Unfortunately you learned a golem is one who does not know how to be asked. Perhaps you are thinking that Ukrainian boy who fingered you was a zomeim witness.[δ] And yet. Not yet. There was no second set of witnesses to discredit the first. Only a Cafgu's fingers firmly on your arm. I mean my arm. I'll take it from here; you may step back[ε]: :

α This Celanian address, this *du* is free.

δ If so, you already know that a witness becomes zomeim when his testimony is discredited by a second witness.

ε And return to the reader's general condition: the willing suspension of our usual indifference to the fate of our fellow beings.

Every voyage is a regime's escape from its own parameters. Distance beckons time to follow.[φ] He enlisted. Yeoman, cabin boy, surgeon, pilot, deckswab, cook. In his case: scribe. In his case, the sharp quill of ambition. To scratch out a passage on a scroll. The ship lists its contents.[γ] Shall we pen pillage into legend? Record the mouse of drama? Pull the toe of verse across a rough swell for our master's pleasure? To what end? To plow the historical wave of a new world? Our ship was a notion of progress. There were astronomical profits by which to sail. We carried salt and water and monuments to our conversation. Seeking to convert souls into gold. To sign a new word in the name of cod and gun trees. Who possessed the vocabulary to witness a circumnavigation,[η] to orbit the self, to fence-post the singular world? In whose name? Fernão de Magalhães? A dentist with too many T's in his name. We composed a fiction, called it Earth, and sailed into the arms of Lapu-Lapu: :

φ He sought a lapsus in time.

γ Escrivain: cet office est le mesme que d'autres appellent Commis, Facteur, Agent et que les Italiens nomment Provvititore. Estans en rade, le Capitaine, le commandant, l'Escrivain fera lecture en presence de l'Équipage du Roole des hommes de l'embarquement.
J. Cartier *Jesuit Relations*

η The first inhabitant of this planet to circumnavigate the globe was the Malay slave whom Magalhães purchased from African pirates on an earlier voyage. He was named Henrique, and brought back to the court of Charles V in Seville. Subsequently he accompanied Magellan on the latter's final voyage, thereby returning to his homeland. History – and the author Pigafetta – forgot this.

And why won't archives sleep? Perhaps my weariness has not turned out as expected. We all hold out a little longer, until our ace turns to dust in our sleeve. Increasingly his head had provided a circumstance of evil. He grew accustomed to his own face in the mirror of a half room. Or should we say his half of a room. Everyone's life is a penny. A time comes to spend it. He squeezed sweatily instead. That window of opportunity was a preordained date of redemption. It passed. We are a mouse of drama, a testament to rust. Until time returns once more in the guise of opportunity. Again I moistened that penny. Some require a generation of rehearsal and, in spite of a host of failures, continue to miss a splendid exit. He was practicing for a useful death. Shall we put some art into our effort? Sleep has become my language. Certain mornings I stand in the vestibule between the self and the street and turn back without so much as a demi-baguette or a fistful of bananas. The weather continually produces us, we are less than an inch of an inch of vanguard. We change to write. Still an odd duty persists in throwing us up against that regime of language. As though the mouse of letters could resist a choir of free choice. Shall I don my sheepish skin, shoulder vulgarity and cultivate grass? Perhaps he would if he could. The truth is a greyer cow than that. Perhaps we should have backed things as they were. Normality is the odds-on favourite. But it was always already too late to change asses in the midst of Cratylus's river. Do dogs dance? Do wings gather rock? Eventually illness wears down even the talk of determination. Or should I say the determination of talk? The question, the difficulty returned to its place. The colt of desolation apologized in the mirror of self-reflection. In the light of a lack of self-restraint. But we were speaking of police and the crack in the mirror of justice. In the lineup of duty. He belonged to a policeman's club. I mean, he was the object of that club. And the subject of a policeman's attention. It was all done with mirrors. In dealing with the police, one generally finds that to be the case. I mean the objective case. Who, occasionally in their youth, has not been the object of a policeman's attention? Hence a tendency to violence in that regard. A cocktail, shaken, not stirred, will propel a proper noun into the subjective case. But I digress. In this case, we were dismissed from the mirror of a half room. Meanwhile. I mean while you were wondering, had he sought a moment to himself to dwell among the plumbing of the tenth sefirot of a police station? To exercise there a certain lack of self-restraint? If there is a difficulty, this is the difficulty: the body, the thing itself. Perhaps he was not afforded the opportunity. Perhaps the opportunity presented itself and he failed to take advantage. Because of the smell, too foreign. Or too familiar. And the general state of the republic. I mean, have you visited the policeman's water closet? In every situation, he found he was always required to choose between a dilemma and common practice. In such cases, the senses operate to influence these matters. It is not all in his power. One can furnish the shops between Europe and the underdog with all the tea in China, and yet. Not yet. Still, we continue to squeeze a tight penny between our knees. In the street outside the station. We find ourselves once more in that familiar intestinal dilemma. Who mentioned this item which is being cited now as if it had already been mentioned? In any case, in this case, he cursed it. Nevertheless, it was necessary. He must, but he has no remedy.[κ] Which is another very fine reason to return to a room and a half: :

κ At such times, we consult a list of clean, well-lighted plumbers' places. Hear from this, learn from this, conclude from this.

Shall we penetrate a rainy season and teach the Nambikwara to inscribe a curved line upon the page?[α] He did it on spec. Lévi-Strauss, I mean.[δ] For future consideration. To whom and for how much glory would an anthro-apologist sell that story? What difficulties did he encounter in penetrating the mournful topic of another tropic? He went out to count the numbers of the Nambikwara. He wiped his pink hands. He subtracted and added. Later he expounded. That was a very dangerous expedition. He said: Our feelings were mixed. We verified the positions of our Smith and Wesson revolvers. Those Indians got lost. To us. Nor, it seems, did he choose to share his emergency rations.[ε] This is ours. Perhaps you cannot possibly think so. His was a case of purulent ophthalmia: his gaze was everywhere, but he turned a blind eye. They say in the West. He had to send his wife back home. Not to mention his Brazilian associate. And spend a fortnight in semi-idleness. Let us push on with two men and a few animals. Or vice versa.[φ] The guavas' bitter taste and stony texture belied the promise of their scent. Wood-pigeons offered themselves to us as prey. Well, that was his reading. The rumour of his presents drew bands of Indians to that camp. They said "Hallo there! Come here! I'm very angry! Really very angry indeed! Arrows! Big arrows!" He wrote that down. In exchange for those small gifts. This is ours and this is theirs. The way of things. Something else: sexual relations, money, pigs, leprosy. Here he recalled: In the Chittagong hills of Bangladesh, the village scribe served both individual citizens and the village as a whole. His knowledge was a source of power – the functions of scribe and usurer being often united in the same human being. In the hills. And in La Sorbonne. Writing is a strange thing::

In the evening a girl could rock in a weary garden. And listen to the drone of sentences coming from the house. His prayer books I called them. Maybe you just can't figure. Okay. But. Still, those long knotted strings of disembodied predicative propositions. I dug my red heels into the upturned record of the day's weather. That sympathetic code was our routine. Anyone can relax in a garden. All that matters is growing. Unless all that matter growing makes you feverish. Which was his case. An anxious boy became a huge verandah. Inside he crafted his white twang. Or should I say meringue? Yet another dying suite emerged. It was an uneasy hill to crawl. Still, a cute ass will compensate for the mouse of drama. Oh well, tomorrow was another helping of insects and agriculture. I never said I was partial to weeding. There's been too much of that already in our century. Not to mention the couple of dozen preceding. I prefer to pull the plug of difficulty and let those kingdoms compete. So much for the sheepskin of country living. That was then and this is now. Certainly, as far as you're concerned. Only look up from the page and you'll see what I mean. But let's say I'm back to the room he showed me, under a blanket of warm linoleum. And mighty tired of boys for a while. Those oiled gentlemen. Those hurry-up dealers, Victorian elephants. They're a hurry-up sidewalk into a coliseum of plug nickels. Low-foreheaded angels under roofy doctrines. Hayseed vanguard strumming on the ukulele of terror. Droopy princes. Beach artists of the nasal twang. Legends of routine. They yell and pause for effect. They aver. They infer. They confabulate. They dabble in rhyming commands and crafted judgments. They are a truckload of beanbags in platform shoes. Enough. That pinkish landlady and I donned our pink curlers. Her republic was a toothy smile. She sheltered bedrooms and a cat. I thought the cat might lick my wounds a while. What more could you ask for? An atom of shelter, a mill of wool. That just about wraps it up. In the meantime, this mouse crashed. Slept long hours under a short blanket::

Here was a task to undertake himself: to return to a room and a half to interrogate a Ukrainian boy's finger. To interpret beginnings. To cast one man against another. Perhaps you cannot possibly think so. Perhaps anyone would prefer not to. Think so. Furthermore had he not renounced sleuthing and all matter of exegesis? If this was taught, it was taught. What then exercised an attraction in the eternal return of a similar room and a half? Perhaps when all else fails there remains sleuthing. An exercise to occupy the valet of time. It forestalls the certainty of death.[γ] And yet. Not yet. Perhaps merely the memory of a cot and the solitude of the self will draw us back to the scene of a crime. They offer Abraham, we want Ulysses.[η] Perhaps we simply long to gaze eye to eye into the eye that fingers us daily from behind the cracked mirror of justice. Who killed Giltgestalt was a question to ask a Ukrainian youth. In any language. But a Cafgu had other ideas. His was a comedy of fists and cuffs. I mean that Golem was the pioneer of criticism.[κ] Where was the vanguard powder now that I really needed it? Where was my newspaper of theory? He proposed a complex sentence in which I was to play the role of a subordinate clause. We'll take a short walk off a long pea at midnight. This itself is difficult. Together. His proposal was to share his weariness and produce a dual finality. To put in our two cents.[λ] Suddenly I preferred solitude. I felt the density between any brother and his idiot. I begged to defer. Shall we say that these Amoraim disagree according to the difference of opinion between them? At times such as these, the French have reinvented cornerflanking. A slight wheel makes life easier for the runners. But there is and was no overturning nor outrunning a Cafgu. His offer was gripping in every respect::

α They would not draw a straight one.

δ Claude Lévi-Strauss *Tristes Tropiques*

ε If we proffer writing to the one who already exercises dominion, will that one not naturally enlist writing too, in the service of his power? And if we inscribe the tale of that proffering into the discipline, do we not also enhance our own power within that discipline? Is this the underlying universal structural pattern we heard speak of?

φ What difference does it make?

γ Hence it is said: because it was exegesis, it was dear to him.

η No longer shall your name be called Avram, rather shall your name be Avraham, for I will make you Av Hamon Goyyim, Father of a throng of Nations! Genesis 17:5

κ Le golem c'est l'autrui: the one I cannot evade, comprehend or kill, and before whom I am called to justify myself.

λ He offered the opportunity to spend that penny.

That Wet Vase

We interpret beginnings. Once we were all Moshe, alone and fleeing. Fugitives from Pharoah. Shall we sit down by that well in Midyan?[α] And follow the seven daughters of Yisro home. Yisro the Kenite said: Call him and let him eat bread. Akhsaniah, a place to lie down. Such hospitality fathers the Law. Before those clerks have pushed their pencils between a religion and a congregation, birth forgets utopias. Yisro's generations followed. They were Tirathites, Shimathites and Suchatites, and all Kenites descended from Chammath, father of Beth Rechav.[δ] Their descendants dwelt in Yabetz. These children of Yisro's children were those families of scribes who sat in the Chamber of Hewn Stone. They were converts who became great scholars, and sat among the seventy-one judges of the great Sanhedrin.[ε] But first there was Yisro's hospitality. Hospitality was the mother of those scribes[φ]::

α Exodus 2:15

δ I Chronicles 2:55

ε Sanhedrin 104a

φ Toute relation du fidèle au Dieu révélé commence certes dans sa relation aux Écritures: lecture et aussi transcription par le scribe, qui les perpétue en les préservant de toute corruption. E. Lévinas *L'au-delà du verset*

Before there were vessels, there was the ink of chaos.[γ] We were boots and vertigo long before we were narrative. Occasionally a vessel is a skirt of verse. They say in the West. And if we poured the light which is neither cloud nor lack into those vessels would they shatter? The breaking of vessels is a rite like eating, washing, drinking or sacrificing. The way of things. How should we act? Do wings gather rock? Somebody gathers the shattered fragments of those vessels and shapes them into partzufim.[η] Every incident thought this. We build a golem piece by 613 pieces, according to the 613 parts of the human body[κ] (minus one hand and five fingers), according to the 613 commandments. We gather ourselves into 613 parts. We are partzufim. Or her. We compose a fiction. We write an exaggeration. We pour the ink of gloom into a vessel. Such a dim light that vessel of rectification will contain.[λ] Can't someone murder glory? Ambition and a touch of despair are the parents of enthusiasm::

γ That chaos was all gloom, waste and desolation. Job 30:3

η That wet vase paints a genius.

κ The shattered vessels of creation were rebuilt as partzufim. And each partzuf consists of 613 parts, just as the body consists of 613 parts and the Torah contains 613 commandments.

λ Beware: those certain descriptions will cause severe illness.

Will some readers follow a simple declaration that I lost him? Apparently not. The architecture of our agreement is rust. Every page must provide a bridge of suspension over that doubtful chasm. We are watchers caught between a code and our stories. And yet. Not yet. I would have preferred to lose a golem and say no more. Did you explain it so much? Instead we shall be obliged to pause outside the police station of ten sefirot and toss ourselves into the street like a stone. Can you follow that? If so, well then. Act, deed, event, precedent. Let us strike a hard bargain beyond the pavement. A passing Chevrolet tore his head off at the neck. Well, you asked for it. Perhaps you cannot possibly think so. Perhaps, now, you would have preferred we simply lost that golem. And said no more. Shall I relent and merely slice our right hand off at the wrist? More or less cleanly. A detail and a generalization and a detail. He gushed profusely. Must I go on like a peddler? He became an avid redder. And how's that for une leçon d'écriture? A shouting shirt would be first to visit the scene of any accident. The face of a partzuf gazes down upon us. Shall we return that gaze? Up into the cracked mirror of the golem's face. And learn what? In the midst of the complaint of that hearse in search of a heartbeat, he heard the bent whisper a partzuf poured into his ear: Mon frère, mon semblable. We are all part zuf. Without my right hand and five fingers, I was only part of a partzuf. But we were both all partzuf. That was the meaning of that verse. Perhaps not. Perhaps he meant we are all partzuf. Perhaps we are all partzuf. Perhaps you cannot possibly think so. Since you took the first part, you must take the end as well. But I digress. Let us defer. We were face up in the street. At such times, the best of our fellows will jostle for a look. While others stretched him. Those bookends: they could not bear to stretch him on the pea of midnight. Am I a Shtick with a lisp? To be stretched beneath your gaze? Who mentioned this item which was mentioned earlier? Giltgestalt. He was a shticky suit who'd lost his lip. Until they stretched him beneath my gaze. A face, bloodless, but still recognizable. My own. Gazing skyward. But I digress. Someone gave me a hand. Shall we avert our gaze as someone[μ] takes pleasure in recovering that useless member? Suddenly he was a hearse in a hell of a hurry. The price of freedom from son frère, son semblable was an arm and a leg. Not to mention the right hand of the Law. What prompted the urge to fling himself from an ambulatory ambulance, I mean a moving vehicle, and into the street of very hard knocks? Perhaps he was already thinking: a hospital is a nation of streptobacilli. Those wards along the bay of typhoid. Not to mention any golem is an ambulance chaser. He pictured a Cafgu's inquiries at the desk. Waiting by the door to an outpatient's freedom. In any case, no matter what, he preferred not to attend a bed in the routine of emergencies. Or so he reasoned as he lay in a hearse in a hurry, even while others attended to his lack of a hand. A time was to escape. At such times one reasons more or less reasonably. Rather less than more. He was the bright tulip bulb above his head. He was the bloody end of his arm. And yet. Not yet. In any case, he had never thought of himself as handsome. Not to mention handy. Now so much more so. Or less. Events roughly escape. To surrender was a load he could not carry. To vanish beckoned. What drove him so hard out of the moving vehicle of his own partly bandaged arm? The body, the thing itself. Perhaps you cannot possibly think so. Was it merely a fear of streptonationalism? The ideology of hospitality. They say in the West. Or was it rather the will to sleuth? Act, deed, event, precedent. To return to the scene and a half of the crime(s)? And interrogate the reluctance of a Ukrainian witness. To pursue the deadly mystery beneath the manner. Perhaps he merely sought to attenuate that certain urinary urge for self-expression[ν]::

μ Someone is always trotting along happily behind the ambulance with the broken pieces of our lives.

ν In either case, in any case, no matter what, it was the body, the thing itself that drove him.

How has such a reluctant sleuth suddenly become in the midst of a hurry-up hearse the smokestack of our curiosity? Though we remain nouns, any difficulty persuades stuff.[α] This is possible to refute. But what then? It might occur to you. Was the fear of a Cafgu sufficient to toss a less-than-handy boy out into the road like a stone? And what was the tubercle of such a fear? A handful of unbuttoned knuckles? Are we casting one man against another? Those fists, he knew them: they were old acquaintances upon which to lay his temples. Must we churn this? Perhaps merely to be shadowed by a golem will exact too high a price.[δ] Perhaps it was none of these. Perhaps he wished to place a city between that partzuf and himself, simply because a golem had called him mon semblable. Because he who won't differ is a vertigo of reflection. What is there between? What is there to say? What is the difference between them? Perhaps he sought to slip free of the other who was the same. Because this is ours and this is theirs. Let us say, he preferred to turn away from the possibility of his own possible origins. He cursed them. Until now no terrible imperative had driven him across that sidecar. The native is on the ground and the stranger is in the sky. The possibility that he was only part zuf. And part nothing else. His brother was not in his world. He was not in his world. Remove, delete! And yet. Not yet. If there is a difficulty, this is the difficulty. When I awake astride the cot of hospitality to find I am a golem, whom shall I call creator?[ε] And who was Joey Cafgu's master? Booger Rooney? For whom he'd toiled in a shouting shirt. What golem would not cut the aleph from his master's tongue? In any language. Knowing his master would not hesitate to erase the aleph from that golem's forehead. All this in a legend. A child's tale. Should any golem know his master? Perhaps you think he thought to think the answer in a room and a half. And yet. Not yet. Perhaps, he considered, it was in the nature of a golem not to know his master, but merely to obey, as we hear an inner voice we have mistaken for our self. Must we churn this? Perhaps that was no eschatological itch, but merely the burden on his bladder that drove him into flight. This and nothing else. The body, the thing itself. As we have learned elsewhere. In either case, no matter what, in this case, he sought to slip away from it. To flee the medical inhospitality of that ambulatory cot on wheels. Let us say, he selected any momentary intersection in the story and made a break for it : :

A Boop can go just so far on love. Sooner or later she removes her eggs from that basket. Will a tender touch take us to Sarajevo?[φ] Those kisses were in sadness tinged. But she shied from the ontological movement of any hand. She imagined a touch without digestion. Without acquisition. And yet in the very thinking of that touch there was a newspaper's reduction of events. Something categorical continued to insist, a kind of utopian impulse.[γ] Was it merely the tail end of an eschatological puppy? The apocalyptic mouse of drama? The trace of a past that had never been present? Or the muted promise of a momentary interruption in the doctrines of glory. She did not want to know. Even a tepid sleuth was death warmed over. Oh, shut up. Shit happens. Any girl can sit in pink curlers knitting and unknitting the threads of some boy's narrative fabric. To wait. To comfort harm. Until today happens and a tooth mission volunteers : :

Shall we rather recall Mustapha and Legrand? Until now, they were only nouns in dresses. Legrand, in particular, enjoyed a long achingly pink thing. He folded his height on the stoop of his friend Mustapha's affection. Will that do? Must I go on like a bicycle? Dois-je pédaler? They were good comrades. For as long as it lasted. They walked a fine line between an uncommon denomination, the memory of a Quebec Catholic schoolyard and Allah's blessing. After the revolutionary soteriology died, they studied capital with a fine line. Legrand was very good with numbers. Mustapha mostly imported. On Thursdays they ploughed through couscous at his uncle's restaurant. Sometimes a dinner signs the subject. The lamb dreamed labouring vineyards beneath an Algerian season. What was the orbit of dialect? The native is on the ground and the stranger is in the sky! Sunday on déjeune chez la mère. She served a plate of restraint. Elle pria pour lui. On partagea au tour de la table de longs silences en langue de boeuf. Her objection: that Legrand was not necessarily so. So what? If the self is relatives, how they do insist. The nature of this case is not like the nature of this case and the nature of this case is not like the nature of this case. Et pourtant. Tant pis. How should they act? Monday to Monday they worked between the rate and the rate. They slid Caribbean condos on the strength of cash in a technique that varied according to the price of particles. At night they were a joint of enterprise. They stretched the bed. How that dog danced. He who has formed can function. Every morning they made a rule to enjoy croissants au beurre with café au lait. Occasionally. The stress of their difference(s) curled an impression of violence vented. Mustapha felt his suffering slide beneath the definition. What is there to say? The clerks of religion push their figures between the faces in a congregation. And yet, tant pis, birth forgets utopias. They were finished with that revolutionary soteriology.[η] They slipped away from it. They parked that car, though palaces burned and vigilantes bent hearses, in a quiet street of their own making. They were happily ever after. Until Legrand underwent a less-than-pure chance encounter with an old comrade on a less-than-sympathetic route : :

α I meant, we stuff a difficulty in the path of a proper noun to persuade a reader.

δ The attached illusion is a constant threat deferred.

ε He sought to call and recall his mother with a modicum of affection. In this he failed. He did not miss her. Nor she him for that matter.

φ And conversely, will a tender Sarajevo heal a lack of touch?

γ …(dans mon univers, l'utopie serait une fiction à partir de laquelle naîtrait le corps générique de celle qui pense). Je n'aurais pas à faire naître d'une première femme une autre femme. Je n'aurais à l'esprit que l'idée qu'elle puisse être celle par qui tout peut arriver. J'aurais tout en l'écrivant à imaginer une femme abstraite qui se glisserait dans mon texte, portant la fiction si loin que de loin, cette femme participant des mots, il faudrait la voir venir, virtuelle à l'infini, formelle dans toute la dimension de la connaissance, de la méthode et de la mémoire.
N. Brossard
Picture Theory

η They said: winter carries a harsh wind, let us believe in each other. Let us build a bridge to our personal glory.

The patient client broke his contract. I mean, the broken passenger made a break. And is there nothing else? Perhaps you ask what did he gather up before he broke away. Have we forgetten a volume of prayers and a curtain of souls? He thought, a book of laws is a very heavy stone.[α] Whereas. A plastic sheet will provide shelter from the rain. And yet. He took the book. Left-handed. And left those souls. That curtain was closed.[δ] But perhaps you think why won't two attendants halt an impatient passenger in flight? Perhaps two are not enough? Three! Perhaps we need three. Perhaps an unwashed passenger is a heavy olfactory stone and they preferred to clear the air. In any case, his case was not a heavy stone to toss.[ε] Nor, to be perfectly socialist, could a nationalized streptobacillic breeding ground spare another place to lie down. If they arrived at that swamp of medical virulence lacking so much as a patient, so much the better. To occur costs earth. No more than death. He was a legend of nothing. They said as much. In an offhand manner. He was the end of a bleeding arm. He tossed himself back into the world like a story. That decision was irreversible[φ]: :

Did they ride the horse of charm into a failure of narrative? Giltgestalt offered to beat their swords into shares.[γ] Though his reputation was a prison operation, ambition only briefly pauses in the face of a vertiginous clerk. That Shtick's shtick worked a charm. That he seemed to them a man of great individual coinage was only partly the result of their own greed. Shtick knew how to place the towel of fortune between the parents of enthusiasm and a chair. He was the promise of endless satin under a sky of vaporized taxes.[η] And when their pockets dipped into his palms for all they were worth, perhaps you are thinking Mustapha verged on murder? And why not Legrand? Because of his size. And Gallic disposition. We are all nouns and nightmares. Description is the tatami of war.[κ] Perhaps a Shtick will cling to his own severed head by an occasional vaccination. When a deal went bad, someone else's throat beckoned an alternative. If the shoe fits, break it. In those days, two boys in love would die easily.[λ] I meant these days; those days is an epic category : :

She twisted between love and citizenship, between those notions of narrative and a failure of narrative. She wanted to park her personal Boopian program in a bent community. Sympathy and pairing up are merely common decency in everyday life, and the temptation of love only a consolation in the face of death. And likewise the road to perfect solitude. All matter is the valet of time. And does each of your experiences reflect a similar ritual? Some live to join the jive, while others acquire a taste for legend. And sex. Anyway. No way. Not that way. Not Betty Boop. She would attempt another route. In the face of a plot of some murdered and others yet to be murdered, mere weather simply will not do. But who or what can sheep prevent? The sheriff of our own nation has deputized us all. Even cattle, who stand and ruminate, contribute some damn milky thing or other. Though they cannot be numbered among the police. (Looks like any sign can enter this column.) Damn near stretched that single bed until it shook. I was seeing doubly twisted sheets. I was a pistol of radar. Like some French dog had dragged in this document. The asterisk has landed, I mean I marked a space requiring further explanation. You, I mean your self become a face, abrades the surface of the skin. In my case, that face with pink curlers. Her food received me. Our pleasure exercised a cool draft upon my rust. I thought: so much care might scare a girl. Just a little. Don't let me panic. All my boopish life marching under the discipline of bread. My belief saddled somewhere between an injury and those sad pleasures. Now, slowly, what did I learn? Not much. That the resources of art are practices. That to cry is a form of conversation. That my responsibility to the Other and to the Other's Other was a perpetual disorientation preceding even my self. Also, that the middle lay not between one extreme and the other, but in another bed altogether. In the evening my hands washed a pair of underpants and left them to dry on the edge of that sinking feeling. Could reason move? This insisting God, oh tedious combat, aroused a holy proof. Some God or other's existence so clearly demonstrated by its absence. That Klein Celan's NoOne, his Hearest-Thou. Meantime. I mean the times were mean as hell. The direction of Europe had once again begun to run. To Sarajevo. In a lunch of blood. To attend talks, though the sun, and not only that, had already gone down. Way down. I was Betty Boop wrapped in warm linoleum, while Europe brewed all those pots of vengeance. Where were those Messianic politics we had once clung to? Though, to tell the facts, just the facts ma'am, we'd never been all that many to begin with. Nor at any time, for that matter. In the morning, let's be grateful to inhabit a clean set of underwear and face the face of the world. Meantime, our child was a TV. Playing music to accompany the slaughter. There's too much violins between this Europe and that fiction. Even fiction can expound a whole lot of additional pain. And what painful fiction had those savage friends and neighbours fashioned for each others' women and children? The Renaissance, it turns out, was merely a small illustration framed and illuminated in a butcher's window. Your enlightenment was a torch to set all those homes on fire. Dip that in the teabag of history.[μ] We are a chestnut of consciousness. In the mean-evening-time, we become windows, we watch the news. She, I mean a caress in pink curlers, and I were a domestic congregation. We fabricated our own neighbourhood of improper nouns : :

α It contains the language of stones. And a stony silence.

δ How could he carry both? Without half his fingers he was all thumbs.

ε An unwashed patient does not carry the odour of money.

φ Not to mention the ease with which they let him go.

γ Shall we call those who trade in stockings and bondage innocent? They add and subtract and expound sweatshops. We have learned elsewhere. They trade cold cash in warmer climes.

η Giltgestalt was a Cuthean merchant: he sold merchandise to his customers in numerous small measures at a nominal price, thus luring them into buying more. Similarly, David did not ask forgiveness for all his sins all at once. Instead, he beseeched God to forgive a portion of his sins, and when God agreed, David proceeded with additonal requests. Sanhedrin 107a

κ Someone else is always a beast.

λ In Mustapha's case, a random act of violence cannot be ruled out – America is a racy republic of very heavy stones.

μ An entire century had fallen to its knees between its own monuments.

What constitutes a tenement we used to call home? When you return a third time.[α] From the street, that building was a wall of curtains. And a curtain of souls. Some were grey.[δ] Some were not curtains. What brownish pane will hold against a cracked and painful wind? Let us, already anticipating the antechamber of our old self, take one step forward and handle a door. Only to be greeted by a shower from above. His heart leapt two steps back, he turned his gaze heavenward for a cause. Deduce from it, and again from it. From the twenty-second ledge above, a terrier's wiry gaze reflected downward at its relief.[ϵ] He was the target of that canine's understanding. Though he was wet behind the ears, true understanding fell from the twenty-second ledge onto his head. His own homelessness, the door before him, the darkness, the urinary aftertaste of broken syllables. He would have laughed but for his painful lack of a right hand.[ϕ] At such times one stands outside one's own body, narrating in the preterit past. As though it were. A movie. In the lobby, slightly the worse for wearing a dog's scent – it is written here and it is written there – he discovered there was no longer self nor refuge from self to be found. He stood between the world and the world. Inside was no longer a refuge from the outside and outside was no longer a place to flee the self. Shall we scan the names above the bells? Go down to the end of the verse. And find what? The names of his past? The past's passing? A list of historical listings in a smokestack of curiosity. It occurred to him he'd never gazed that way before. Never had occasion to. Curious deliberate loss. This is ours and this is theirs. His own name was not among them. Nor had ever been. He had been, and remained, otherwise merely Occupied. In any case, in this case, it was not his own name he sought. It might occur to you. And yet. Not yet.[γ] Rather, let us say it was a Ukrainian concierge he sought in any language : :

α Jamais deux sans trois. C.S. Pierce

δ Who does not hang a grey curtain between the world and the self?

ϵ Which reminds us of our own burden.

ϕ Let us say, he sought to keep his pain at arm's length.

γ One goes looking for the Other and finds oneself.

Perhaps neither Mustapha nor Legrand would break a Shtick's head. Have we cast those men against another? Perhaps the virus of murder[η] just wasn't in them. Can you possibly think so? Consider the virulence of that virus. In any case, a Shtick was nowhere to be found. Let us say he imitated those profits and made himself scarce. Events roughly escaped. For Mustapha and Legrand catastrophe seemed to come at a bad time. Whereas Yehudah had welcomed it in a stockinged foot.[κ] The ceiling fell in on their marriage, cut off their cash flow. Legrand grew paler and thinner. This itself is difficult. Mustapha wore a path between rage and worry. A deep wound of money compelled them to a discipline of bread. It was a case of this and still another. And yet. Not yet. That bond between them sustained a difficult circumstance. How much more so the body, the thing itself. For a time, anyway. How long? Are we peddlers to calculate love's durability in the face of life? Not to mention death. To add and subtract and expound the bonds between us. Every day they took their dwindling faces for a painful stroll along the shoreline of the afternoon. They learned how pleasure expands, even as it shrinks. The law of diminishing returned. A tree advanced to celebrate the bird's nest, its leaves were brides between a sidewalk and the garden. Each day preceded the one that followed. They became suburban dealers on a program of daily orbits. Might certain descriptions comfort an illness? Legrand's strength was a piano. He was the valet of time. He felt his suffering slide beneath a plausible definition. Mustapha faced the face of the other's lesions in a shaking continental frame. Meanwhile. The doctored criticism of the West cost them a season of numbers. Complaint was a pocket of paper. They poured a coliseum of pills into the foundations of their affection.[μ] And yet. Very soon. Because an illness will gradually light a match of stress against the stone of hope. Between mind and a matter of money, they rode the wake of fear. Until Legrand surrendered. A single road suggested him. There was no question of Mustapha joining him there. At first. He, I mean Mustapha, lay alongside the pea of midnight, contemplated his uncle's lonely couscous in a week without end. He wondered how an identity had bent. To shake stretches a bed. In the end, they lay end to end, and fit their bath neatly. Shall I write stuff about their lives? Think of them and write sentences? But we were speaking of mystery. The Shtick of murder. I merely meant to say no Shtick beat them. Merely some failure of narrative. Before they opened that utopian window together, they shared a small bowl of figs. Though Legrand could not swallow. He enjoyed the taste of seeds upon his tongue[ν] : :

ν I recalled that splinter of fig on your lip. P. Celan, *Zeitgehöft*

The idea of a mystery: to represent history as a trial in which man, as an advocate of dumb nature, brings charges against all Creation and cites the failure of the promised Messiah to appear. The court, however, decides to hear witnesses for the future. Then appear the poet, who senses the future; the artist, who sees it; the musician, who hears it; and the philosopher, who knows it. Hence their evidence conflicts, even though they all testify that the future is coming. The court does not dare to admit that it cannot make up its mind. And therefore new grievances keep being introduced, as do new witnesses. There is torture and martyrdom. The jury benches are filled with the living, who listen to the human prosecutor and the witnesses with equal distrust. The jury members pass their duties on to their heirs. At last, the fear grows in them that they might be driven from their places. At the end, the entire jury has fled; only the prosecutor and the witnesses remain…

W. Benjamin, letter to G. Scholem, November 1927

η As opposed to a murdering virus.

κ When there was a drought in his days, Rav Yehudah would merely remove his shoe as a sign of affliction and rain would come immediately, whereas we cry out profusely in prayer and NoOne pays attention to us. Sanhedrin 106b

μ They counted pills upon the clock. They watered a garden of pills. They read the morning pills. They pass the pills, please. They now I lay me down to pills.

A Case of Stairs

The grandfather of R' Pereida found a skull cast down at the gates of Jerusalem. Upon it was written: This and still another. He buried it, but it would not stay buried. Again he buried it, but again it would not stay buried. Thereupon he said: It is the skull of Yehoiakim,[α] concerning whom it is written – His shall be the burial of a donkey, dragged and cast beyond the gates. He said to himself: Yehoiakim was nonetheless a king. So he wrapped the skull in silk and placed it in a chest. Later, his wife saw the skull. She thought: This is surely the skull of my husband's first wife, whom he cannot forget! So she fired up the oven and burned the skull. This is the meaning of what was written on the skull. Those words foretold that Yehoiakim was destined to suffer a twofold retribution: *this* – his skull was to be cast into the streets; *and still another* – it would be consumed by fire : :

α When Yehoiakim came along, he said: The earlier ones did not know how to anger God. And he proceeded to blaspheme and declared: "Do we need God for anything other than his light?" And on the matter of that which they found upon him, let us say the Amoraim disagree. Some say Yehoiakim tattooed the name of a pagan deity on his organ, and others say he tattooed the name of God. Sanhedrin 103b

He took the stairs. Or rather, they took something out of him. On the first three floors, no one. Up to three, an accumulation of garbage.[γ] On four and five he found much the same. How high had those refugees from the fall of communism risen above a Western accumulation of refusal? To the tenth sefirot of a tenement? And if he reached that high what could he learn?[η] In any language? Every difficulty persuades stuff. Would he rap his lost knuckles against the spy hole of a Ukrainian refugee? And risk a good beating? Under the weight of those questions his heels trailed a step or two behind his knees. And so would yours. And yet. Not yet. Though very soon. Let us say he continued to climb the steps to the scene of those crimes. He was for once in his earthly life upwardly mobile. Though the slope was steep, the pace slow. He was a parade marching between the passage and his doubts. Let us wrap a suspension and pause to claw the airless staircase for a breath of continuation : :

γ And yet we continue to peddle it.

η One gazed and died, one was stricken, a third cut down the shoots. Only R' Akiva departed in peace. Hagigah 14b

Who shall we say took the stairs? We are all forever taking the stairs. They say in the West. Where do we mount them? This itself is difficult. And where did we think they were leading? And how can you find it? Perhaps someone thought paradise was firmly seated above the clouds. Angels and chariots. Who failed to tell us: l'Israël n'est pas en Israël? The native is on the ground and the stranger is in the sky?! Shall we go and read it in Hai Gaon's house? En quelle langue est-ce encore possible? When a man wishes to gaze at the heavenly chariot and the halls of the angels on high, he must place his head between his knees whispering softly to himself the while certain praises of God with his face toward the ground. It was said thus and it was said thus: If he is worthy and blessed with certain qualities, he must fast for a specified number of days, and he must follow certain exercises. As a result he will gaze in the innermost recesses of his heart and it will seem as if he saw the seven halls with his own eyes, moving from hall to hall to observe that which is therein to be found. So much for that. And yet. Nothing yet. Did the statement of the Rabbi escape us? Certainly fasting had come easily enough for several days now. And yet. Not yet. He had attained so far only hunger. How slowly time passes on an empty stomach. While we exercised a mystery's solution between our knees. Had he not spent much of that time with his face toward, even flat against, the ground? Shall we rely on answers such as these? Perhaps you cannot possibly think so. It is written here and it is written there. Is this a case of a Halakhah for the Time of the Messiah? Shall we, in the very meanness of our time, operate merely in case, and seek out staircases to climb? And what shall we find on the floors above? Aside from a shortness of breath and our knees sagging beneath our ankles? A room and a half in the mirror of a room and a half. Perhaps a golem met his creator on those steps to a room and a half. That was the one, in your haste to mount a staircase, you elbowed out of the way. We live in a case of just in case on the staircase of our times. We are a republic of staircases. In any case, the direction of Europe was always up. Shall we pause a moment to stare in that direction and contemplate a space of our own fabrication? Shall we don the winding scarf of staircases? Step forward step by step to attack the staircase of our wonder? Let us say we cling to the teleological handrail of a Hegelian spiral staircase. We count stairs. We add and subtract and expound staircases. We interpret beginnings of staircases. We say this case of stairs is this case and this case of stairs is this case. This staircase is not like that staircase, and that staircase is not like this case. We provide a theory of staircases. Here was the father of the fathers of ritual staircases. The thirty-nine primary categories of staircases? This is our staircase and this is their staircase. If there is a staircase, this is the staircase? A very heavy staircase. Shall we count and collect a caseful of staircases? Have we not rejected this once? We climb. We clamber. We thrust upward to build up an argument in the face of the Other's mysterious face. We take up our skirts and rise to the occasional uplifting expression. We are a legend of staircases. Shall we raise the spectre of a narrative staircase? And if I prefer not to? We can learn but not refute. Hence, there follows the inevitable plunge in the opposite direction. I mean down. Oh, don't we know that sinking feeling. We paint a vertical stroke[δ] on a horizontal staircase and call it inspiration.[ε] Perhaps the discomfort in our lungs may comfort us. Is it necessary? If two staircases are next to each other, place a detail between them and treat them as a staircase and a detail and a staircase. I was an architect of staircases. I spoke in the language of staircases. Staircases were my routine. I laboured on the ladder of successful staircases. I imagined a happy end to this continuous motion. And furthermore. And nothing more. Are we still at this? When he removed his shoes, they were filled with desert sand[φ] : :

δ To every righteous person, draw a line of ink upon his forehead, a line of life, in order that he may live; and to every wicked person, draw a line of blood upon his forehead, that he may die. A line of life, a line of ink; and a line of death, a line of blood. Abraham Abulafia *Sefer ha-Meliz*

ε Or abstract expressionism, which we called the next step to modernism.

φ That sand gathers in the desert of our errance. In the desert where our footsteps draw the face of the Other.

What failed to make this story my story? I mean why can't we B-Boop instead of droning on with that big boy sound? If there's a difficulty this is the curling pistol up your butt, pal. A goil toils in the garden. She straddles her rough red heels in the ground and points her ass in the air. And who wouldn't prefer weeding beggar's ticks to wedding bells? I'll take a pokeweed over a poke any fortnight and a day. Not to mention a dandelion over a dandy line. Perhaps you can't possibly mull it over. And it may be your itch to say: honey, the right man just hasn't come along all over you yet. Or something like that. I mean what goil wants a golem? As though we ever doubted every boy wasn't all partzuf. But now we're drifting back into their dark plot of dampish soil. As though we didn't carry our own fair sexy share of that zuf chromosome. As though there wasn't a bit of the zuf in every gal's goilish gene pool. Who doesn't puff up her pillows and tidy up her mad mother's attic? Ride a broom across that virgin soil? Who trudged through a century's marital plots and cemetery plots? We were tight-lipped and heavy-lidded. We were a common denominator until someone said this is this girl and this is this girl and that made a colourful difference. Still, we could all be just sheepish golems who've lost their Bo-peeps and don't know where to find them. In the end, any Boop is a creature of her time and place. She can bebop all she pleases. Writing is not enough. We are the stuff our moms stuffed into us. And they got stuffed too. Who scrawled the Truth across my furrowed brow? In whatever language. Some handsome boy's hand did that handiwork, no doubt. You can bet your pistol butt on that, bud. Those buddy boys love to scribble their name on any girl's plot of ground. Not to mention her forehead. Given half a chance, I'd scratch my own story across that desert garden.[γ] Fat chance. Watch, he'll bury me again before this book is done ::

Who shall we say opened a burly Ukrainian door? And found what to his surprise? Or should I say whom? Did he wrap his knuckles around a good beating?[α] He'd already gone that route. A father sends his boy around to collect the rent. They were God's witnesses. From time to time he left a pamphlet here and there. Where's the harm? In that. Until someone invited the boy in, and he began to ride the pea of midnight. Awake! He certainly did and in a sea of mare's sweat. They stopped collecting. I mean rent, not garbage. Though that too. And started a suspicion and a close watch on the boy and those stubborn rooms above. Let us say God's elder Ukrainian witness sought to witness some ungodly sin.[δ] And who among those unlikeable tenants[ε] shall we suspect was least unlikely to commit that sin? Who would not share his solitude, but rather kept it all to himself in a room and a half? Who went out rarely and returned more often? Who carried books, and very possibly read them? Suspicion will drive any Ukrainian to the twenty-second floor. Or twenty-third.[φ] If you count the thirteenth. And then, only in spirit. In this case, a spirit of anger. To expel a sinner from (t)his world. Had a Ukrainian witness risen to the occasion on a twenty-second floor only to find a slender Armani whose hair was once red red red rifling through a wrecked room and a half in a hurry? And did that Ukrainian rage pause to compare this Shtick figure and an occasional face over a fistful of bananas? Perhaps you cannot possibly think so. What reason moves a pious man to vehemence? Perhaps an insistent God will arouse holy proofs. It might occur to you. Perhaps a child, that boy's sleeplessness, his bird of appetite, drowned out a father's prayers. He had been sawing boxes when the boy's pale face appeared in a tattered doorway. That pale face was a final straw. A person is close to himself. And to his. The elevators were too slow. He took the stairs. That saw was the tool of consciousness. Or lack thereof. A single blow sufficed to sever Gestalt from his guilt. Shall we judge another man's pain in a pot of vengeance? And yet. If that boy's father's God had filled that room and a half with sheep, perhaps those sheep might have muffled the blow. Perhaps you cannot possibly think so. Shall we say, the room was suddenly full of the whitish beige texture of sheep? Let us wrap both men in wool. And the grassy breath of sheep. There was not enough room in that room and a half even for a single savage Ukrainian chestnut. A father stood, his raised arm smothered in those sheep above his head. I mean above Shtick's head. He could not lower that saw to sever his fate. I mean Shtick's fate. There was no murder. There was no blood. There was no mystery. No headless Shtick in a room and a half. All that remained were men and nouns. I mean sheep. Even language vanished ::

Four entered an orchard and these are they: Ben Azzai, Ben Zoma, Aher and R' Akiva. Shall we do likewise and perform certain exercises? Now that fasting comes so easily to us? Those four wore clean white vestments. They took virgin soil and water that had never been contained in any vessel. They breathed. They chanted letters. R' Akiva said to them: When you reach the stones of pure marble, do not say: Water, water! For it is said: He that speaketh falsehood shall not be established before Mine eyes. Ben Azzai gazed and died. Of him Scripture says: Precious in the sight of the Lord is the death of His saints. Ben Zoma gazed and was stricken. Of him Scripture says: Hast thou found honey? Eat as much as is sufficient for thee, lest thou be filled therewith and vomit it. Aher cut down the shoots. R' Akiva departed in peace. Ben Azzai and Ben Zoma were both named Simeon. Aher is Elisha ben Avuyah. Aher means the other one ::

α Shall we say he inclined on that staircase toward an evil inclination – יצר הרע? According to Rav Katina, in the seventh millennium it shall become easier for man to gain mastery over his evil inclinations.
Sanhedrin 97a

δ Once having donned the habit of witnessing, one may easily turn to witnessing sin, if only for lack of something better to witness.

ε There was Chillak and Billak and a host of Sodomites.
Sanhedrin 98b

φ The further one climbs the more rarified the atmosphere, and the greater the spiritual danger.
Sefer Yetzirah

γ Even a golem has that possibility. To run amok. Did you think Betty Boop would fall for a thick-headed determinist?

Shall a reader protest some failure of narrative? A suspension? There were no sheep. I made that up.[α] To fill a page. They do not generally pour sheep to fill a room. Something else is what they used. Less sheepish, less solid. And life, not death, was smothered there. Not to mention language. But perhaps you are thinking: That was some other room. Perhaps a digression will not return us to that place of no return. Or beyond, before. Bereft. A generalization needs a detail needs a generalization needs a detail and a generalization. But the place of which we were speaking was only a room and a half. Or merely the mirror image of that room and a half. Now it was a father's lunch of blood. Once we have begun, a story makes its own way. We can only add and subtract the bodies. Mustapha, Legrand, the dentist with too many letters in his name, Owley lacked one, Betty Boop – not yet – a nosy Booger's tongue, and a wad of Our Shticky Money. This was merely a Celanian pause, a word gap, a vacant space (leerstelle), you can see the syllables all standing around : :

α I mean I found them grazing alongside a fervent Eirin Mouré's stream. See *Sheep's Vigil.*

After murder, anyone will pause to dwell in the horror of the moment. Before we move on to consider the consequences. A Ukrainian handyman, witnessing his handiwork,[α] may learn the true meaning of why we fear murder more than death. Now the worst was done. It occurred to him. To me. Perhaps you cannot possibly think so. Meanwhile, a Shtick poured his red red portion of pints onto the shard-strewn floor of a room and a half. Perhaps, once we have separated a fool and his Ourmoney, we think to remove both suit and soul from the twenty-second scene of the crime.[δ] Shall we pull a horseless carriage into the hallway between a room and a half and a room and a half? Not yet. Let us say it was at the moment of wrapping that red red head in old news. We glance into the glazed eyes of the utterly bygone. A beheader beheld his murderous mistake.[ϵ] This was not the occasionally suspicious demi-baguette and fistful of bananas we have suspected from time to time. This time, it was a case of mistaken identity leading to a sudden loss of subjectivity. This neck was a cut above an Ourmoney suit. We feel the error of our headstrong ways on the back of our own neck. Was it a concierge's tidy instinct, or fear of the consequential advance of time, that cradled that shticky head in the arms of old news and down the hallway of a refugee's remorse? In either case, no matter what. It was a very heavy stone. In that hallway, you crane your neck (I mean the one beneath your head, not the one you cradle lower down). Escape from any scene is a practice we have pencilled in. Nevertheless, the less we say about that the better. Every escape is interrupted by the sound of steeply rising elevators. Two, why do I need two?[ϕ] Or perhaps what demanded a retreat was rather their coming to a halt on the floor that contained simultaneously yourself, your crime and a Shticky head wrapped in the crimes of some other day. Those elevators were uncalled for. They stopped a concierge in the track of his bloody tracks. Shall we vanish into a room and a half across the hall from a headstrong act and a headless victim? Who threatened a lack of thinking straight? Let us stand together then, by the head of the bed in a room and a half, in the arms of a Ukrainian witness – let me be Ukrainian, you be a Shtick's head – and gape at the passage of a dozen opaque curtains in a hurry in the arms of an eyeless intruder wrapped in the arms of nature's call.[γ] Shall we say ~~that unbeheaded head headed for the head in a hurry~~? Perhaps we had better not. Let us rather take advantage of that narrator's moment in the half room of a room and a half to deposit our own head, I mean the one we wrapped in our arms, not the one beneath which we cradled it, at the head of the bed, and head on out of there. Those elevators remained patiently open-mouthed and unmoved by an incident of blood. They would not descend beneath our pressing need. Here a suspension.[η] Shall we flee in an elevator and abandon a narrator in a room with a head? Though remorse may not propel a reader, it will drive us to one of the few remaining telephones in a tenement.[κ] Let us say he reported that crime? Invited the police to discover his dismay? Now, perhaps you are thinking, a headless shtick and a shticky head wrapped in the news of yesterday on the twenty-second floor would certainly reappear wrapped in the front page of tomorrow's news : :

α A saw will see clean through a Shtick's shtick.

δ At such times, we begin at the top. I mean the head. Not to mention the building. A verse does not depart from its literal meaning.

ϵ Or was it the cut of an Ourmoney beneath the sliced neck that redressed our witness's memory?

ϕ Doubled elevators, when they bring trouble, will make double time.

γ When nature calls, we are blind to our unnatural surroundings.

η And perhaps a reader's momentary motivation to read on. But perhaps not.

All that remains are the letters. With them I have depicted all that was formed, and all that would ever be formed.[λ] Let these words and letters be withdrawn for but an instant, and the universe ceases to exist. If there is a difficulty, this is the difficulty. Mighty, wicked and righteous, treasure and one who counts. God's kindness is all day long.[μ] If this was taught, it was taught. What took you too out of language with a gesture?[ν] That embabeled tongue. Mais dans quelle langue est-ce encore possible? After those assassination orders have been delivered in a holy tongue. After the bulldozers withdrew, leaving the rubbled bricks of Palestine. Now who cries out the Shibboleth into the alien homeland?[π] His brother who was not in his world. The native is on the ground and the stranger is in the sky. Where is the World to Come? It escaped him. He slipped away from it. Engrave them like a garden, carve them like a wall, deck them like a ceiling. We cried Cholam. Kametz. Tzereh. Chirik. Shurek. Now that no reconciliation is possible, not between Shulamith and Margareta, not between Shulamith and Shulamith. Are you casting one person against another? No speech, no dark-selvedge, no woven edge to keep this fabric from unravelling.[ρ] Is it necessary? This verse pierces and plummets to the depths. And furthermore. And nothing more : :

λ Sefer Yetzirah 2:2

μ Sanhedrin 106b

ν P. Celan "Go Blind"

π February. No pasaran.

ρ Who will go up for us to the heavens and get it for us and have us hear it, that we may observe it? Who will cross for us, across the sea, and get it for us and have us hear it, that we may observe it? Deuteronomy 30:12–13

κ Remorse is a cold dish continuously warmed over. We must have our remorse and eat it too, again and again.

Shall we punch thrice a Ukrainian phone and rehearse the prior violence under consideration? I mean, should we call the cops on him? In the breath before a humanish[α] response, he rehearsed an equally brief announcement. He considered a policeman might sort out and apportion guilt in measured amounts. Gestalt was perhaps guiltless of one thing but guilty of another.[δ] Whose standing suitcase had he slipped beneath the back door of reason? Whose shirt did he remove from my back? How many shares did he cut into a knife in Mustapha's? And who can say a narrator's guilt? He won't tell us. Who was guilty of that little Ukrainian boy running with the horses?[ε] Shall we conclude our Ukrainian interview? Let us imagine a concierge was distraught, chastened, repentant. He recognized the error of his ways. And also the interviewer. Perhaps he thought, here is someone worthy of death. And then. Not again. Even a Ukrainian witness will lose the will to revenge. He lacked the strength of will to wield a shtick. All that Giltish blood had drained the blood from his limbs.[φ] Not to mention his face. He was a bag of bones. An empty vessel full of remorse. He was God's witness to his own murderous recitation. Let us say I elected to leave him in that condition akin to a state of grace.[γ] To descend once more into the street, for a breath of fresh air. More or less. I mean to more or less inhale the urban air. The perfume of traffic. The faint trace of animal defecation in the park. To gaze down the sidewalk of one's newly acquired understanding and follow that gaze to the corner of a mystery without plot.[η] A murderous trail with no beginning and, perhaps you are thinking, no end. To gaze one last time back to that gate, to a room and a half and a room and a half of his desolation. And see what, in the crack of that doorway? A shouting shirt and a nervous lip : :

α I say humanish because a policeman can never entirely achieve more than that.

δ One accused will hasten to dwell on, or should we say dig up, those matters in which he or she is guiltless, while others immediately recall their guilt in some other matter, though that matter is not the matter of which they are accused.

ε Some of us are executed for the sins we did not commit.

φ I mean the limbs of a concierge. Though, that Shtick, too, was dry as a bone.

γ By this we are equating a bag of bones to a state of grace. Perhaps you cannot possibly think so. And yet, without its spirit the body cannot sin, and without its body the spirit flutters harmlessly up to heaven.

η The mystery of Giltgestalt's murder was a Ukrainian's father's rage.

Let us pause a moment to reflect on death. How quickly that moment passed. In the mirror of a room and a half. Since we take the first part, we take the end as well. Art surrenders this formula as quickly as reason attempts to write a smallish section to follow up a Ukrainian phone call to the police. What produced us? Weather. In the meantime, any visitor seeking to gather intelligence cannot object to another person's snapping. The other's break may be the teacher at the end of a verse. How should we act? In the face of effort? In the fog of someone else's epic? In the colt of fiction? In the wake of death, we tend to bury the matter beneath a very heavy stone. Those Cuthean thoughtomites will shame even a singing monument to Sarajevo. What violent consideration pauses to reflect in such a rarified atmosphere? Goodwill? I have not found it. The further one climbs the greater the spiritual danger. Someone else's death is a small brown mystery on the end of our nose. Our own death we have mislaid on the tip of our tongue. Where it will soon enough eat someone. All my life having chewed the cud of metaphor to death. His mortality may have driven him up out of the bed in the morning, but it curdled a hesitation to act, and made even brushing a few teeth a burden. When I say few, I mean a mouthful. Which are all that remain. Teeth. Eventually everyone's R' Loew will come to tear the aleph from emeth. The truth of language upon anyone's forehead is circumcised to death. What am I carrying? Merely a book. Hoping to argue what? The margins within that volume of prayers drained every name. Even Howley's coffin was a dead letter box. His story was every author under a sky that would not differ. I am the valet of time. Every morning is the vestibule of a routine of small and stupid difficulties. Sun gathers small ambitions among sentences, dabbles in the architecture of vowels. Shall we turn shelter into the first gear of power? Make comedy a reasonable victory? Declare the museum a republic of grocers? Fire up a season of head therapy between the temples? Those boys! Listen to them. The policemen of failure. Perhaps we tempt life in search of a vaccination against a refusal of death. He tried for years to see some glory beyond the cow's udder until, in the end, there remained only a terror of cattle. What remains? A vague sentiment against nations. A videogame headache. A neighbourhood of nouns. Skin. Shall we beg the reader? To have mercy on these sentences : :

Meanwhile, in another story,[κ] Betty goes out looking. For what? Bread? That half-loaf? Roses? The fragrance of repetition? Not yet. Shall we say she went out on Monday morning to vote? And raise the anamorphosic spectre of electoral democracy? Every nation occasionally renews its bent parade. This requires a slight physical displacement. She would not have bothered, but it was her landlady's habit. To vote I mean. In every general election. And by-election, for that matter. What did she hope to achieve? Perhaps she felt it was her duty to exercise that slight displacement. As a citizen. Without hope.[λ] Perhaps she, I mean the landlady, merely sought to renew the memory of her own mother's hand in a crisp wind of dead and dying leaves. In any case, what does it matter why, she removed those pink curlers and donned a pinkish suit over grey shoes. And where was my duty to tag along, you're probably thinking. Oh, shut up. Betty Boop is duty-free. Couldn't I have lounged all day on that old familiar midnight legume? Or repaired my darned socks. Well, everyone likes a crisp wind and a dying leaf. Did I mention the amusement of the voting booth? Alone with our State's thoughts.[μ] Sure. Why not? Oh, and a chance to ride a Camel. Have I mentioned that there was in that house a certain lack of smoking?[ν] Smoke or smokescreen. I mean, I'm just saying we hit the street : :

κ Each of us is someone else's other story.

λ To hope is a citizen's duty. If so, we perform it willingly.

μ And the sound of sitcom laughter, which accompanies the void in that voting booth.

ν Not that she'd stop me firing up the occasional stick. And not that I don't. Suck a hot hump from time to time. Okay, I'm a regular huff and puff. But how much joy can a girl suck up when her eye's on the accumulus under that lamp in the parlour? I mean, there's no exhalation in it. Hence the lure of that electoral walk.

In the West they laughed at it. They vote in a careless displacement of nouns from time to time. We elect not to become thereby entangled.[α] Ambition pours a diving duck. He will drink his way back up. That harbour has long been fished empty of illusions. And yet, we continue to wash our feet in it.[δ] Not to mention one hand washing the other. That was last year's model. From time to time, an explosive hand will extend from the skeletal caravans, a gun-toting offspring backs up in the suburban pipeline, someone rides a rag-horse across the tracks. Regular programming was interrupted.[ε] They called those dead stockbrokers innocent victims. The electors of indifference lay in a pool of their own cold-bloodedness.[φ] And yet. Not yet. Will you deny that was our president who gave the order?[γ] What does circumstance deal with? A pencil mark oils our agreement. We occasionally enter the cell of thoughtfulness and pause before a circumstance of evil. Later we wash our hands of it ::

α Who wouldn't prefer to leave corruption to the professionals?

δ So long as the cash flow receives us.

ε As we came to enjoy it, that interruption became increasingly regular.

φ Shall we polish a vignette among the twisted sheets of sleepless fictions?

γ Didn't you brandish the electoral shtick?

Shadowed by a nervous lip and a blinding shirt at our back, we hurry unseeing through blind streets. Let us imagine a partzuf maintained his distance. What draws us toward a small cluster of figures in a schoolyard? The dark coats of conversation? The severity of their demeanours?[η] They played a serious business. Blindly he slipped through the gate and in among that congregation. Theirs was a ritual gesture of sentimental proportions. Every four years, a schoolyard becomes a lesson in electoral cuisine. We dip our pens in a sacred stream of cash to select a familiar noun.[κ] Utopias are an entertainment, the mates of vaudeville. Perhaps the point escapes us. We were fleeing a golem in a shouting shirt. Utopia was a plumed digression he could not wear. His was the uniform of flight. The point[λ] was to vanish beneath the sheepskin of democracy and lose, not the illusion, but rather that persistent golem. It was said thus and it was said thus. An election afforded him just such a possibility: to graze there among a crowd and lose the other. The nervous lip in a chain-link fence will eye us. He felt that sinking undercurrent toward the interior which we call a democratic regime ::

η When adults appear in a children's schoolyard, we have reason to tremble.

κ Democracy is a ceremonial pick-a-card-any-card trick. Now you see it, now you don't bother.

λ Oh, let the point vanish and shelter spread.

Let us say she was a landlady in pink curlers and an occasional cat between her legs. No more. No less. What endeared her to us? An occasional scent of cabbage? Pale steam over porcelain? The afternoon folded neatly beneath the lamp? Her pinkishness? Was it years of habit in the service of a predestined husband or years of solitude following his precipitous death that prepared her for such a tender touch? If difficulty there was, this was that difficulty. In time it became to Betty abundantly clear. Gradually that lovely landlady had killed her old man. As any wife will or ought to. Perhaps you cannot possibly think so. The truth is not satisfied with people. Before there was a courthouse of divorce and separation, there were generations of slow murder through intensive care. What alternative might any girl hope for? Gradually that man comes to forget what makes an egg boil. Not to mention who. With the addition of age her bond became his helplessness. The way of things. What killed him? Daily shavings. She cut short the wine glass. Chocolate. Curtailed the afternoon nap. She swept his well-being clean with a harsh broom. There were several competing ladies' journals dedicated to how and when to do it. The grocers provided free consultation in racks along the checkout line. She remained true to her duty. It was through indifference that she attained her liberation, and he was an island in that indifference. His small vanities were a small brown mouse she placed under his nose. Daily he saw the penny of his life in the corner of her mouth. She turned that corner to glance tweedily at his couched stubble. I mean from the doorway, where she paused, brushed and powdered, on her way out to spend the day with a life of her own fabrication. He learned to crack open the glazed tupperware of degradation. Who can blame her? She saw another generation in soft shoes. Those brides kicking up the leaves between the sidewalk and their pleasures. Parked between the verdict and another century. They were girls in a tasteful renaissance. They flashed an eager tooth. They laughed at men of coinage. Whereas she. Her generation was a discipline of bread and wool. She marched along a broad avenue of sheets to Monday morning's eye of cattle. There were no doorknobs on her curiosity. In the evening by the bed, she brushed and brushed her hair until it became the grey and ephemeral cloud of her youthful aspirations. All day she laboured beneath it. She was a windowpane between the world and his smell. Our century drove her to it. Not that there was intention on her part. She had not learned intention. Nor vengeance. It simmered in the pot upon the stove. It was along the knife-edge of denial that she strode so resolutely. Her method was a meagre lunch of bloodless pain. I mean French bread. She was a steel rod of dedication to his health. She killed him with hardness.[μ] In the end he choked on fresh air and raw vegetables. While she knelt in the church of her own mother's home remedies. After a difficult hour and a quarter of adjustment, she put a room-for-rent sign on the door, removed her pink curlers to attend a lecture at the museum of the elderly. She found the wine glasses in the cupboard. Became known to her boarders for a regular offering of chocolates. Betty Boop found her soft interior.[ν] The Common Factor. They spent their evenings by the fire, though there was none. Reading books and magazines. A ladies' home journal of theory ::

μ Scrubbed him to death. Pressed the firm hand of his own good over his mouth.

ν This is the worn linoleum of live and let live.

What does an Apikoros want? Whereas we shuttle between Bavel and Bursif.[α] In the shadow of that tower. These are the places that cause one to forget. They said, "Come let us build ourselves a city, and a tower with its top in the heavens, and let us make a name (shem) for ourselves." Alternatively, they said, "Let us build a tower, ascend to the sky, and strike it with axes so that its water will flow." They did not vote. They seized tools and began to build. In regard to their objective, they were split in three: one said, "Let us ascend and reside there," one said, "Let us ascend and worship idols," and one said, "Let us ascend and wage war." That which said, "Let us ascend and reside there" were all dispersed. That which said, "Let us ascend and wage war" became apes, ruchos, sheidim and lilin. And regarding that which said "Let us ascend and worship idols," it was there that the languages of the whole earth were confused. That generation has no share in the World to Come.[δ] R' Yochanan said: As to what became of the tower, one third was burned, one third was swallowed up, one third remains. This is to prevent others from returning to the site and resuming construction. Rav said: Even today, the airspace where that tower stood will cause one to forget. We have forgotten. To resume construction : :

α One day we thought we were in Bavel and the next day it seemed we were in Bursif.

δ Exodus 23:13 and Sanhedrin 109a

How long shall he remain cut off? Within the mirror and a half of a room and a half of what remains of a tenement[α] someone transcribes the illegibility of this world. Everything doubled.[δ] Including the silence. Along those sills a savage rain interrogates. And yet. They redoubled the silence. The hydraulic sigh of an occasional bus pausing. A loonish clothesline. The thickly weekday. Already he was talking. To himself, I mean. And yet. And still. Be still. The I continues to exist. The I which contains more than a memory of itself. He saddled his mouth to it. Daily. When you have run with the foot soldiers,[ε] and they have wearied you, how can you contend with the horses? He ploughed a narrow field. At such times, all those we have ever known become doubly silent. By their absence. I mean, by the memory of their presence. A presence that is already past ::

α If a tenement is a tower, then one third was burned, one third was swallowed up, and one third remains. Sanhedrin 109a

δ You, clamped in your depths, climb out of yourself forever. P. Celan "Illegibility"

ε I mean, they who seek out the traces, the interpreters of verses. Sanhedrin 104b

What event precipitates a link in a chain, if not the lip of a peripheral Cafgu in the eye of a fence? A watchful golem will work anyone's pump organ to accompany the moderately sized crowd in a democratic exercise. Shall we say I shouted: Those goats at the slaughterhouse are fatter than I? And poured inside with them. Perhaps you are thinking of that breezy trick Shtick taught by the back door. Before he lost his head. I mean, before I lost mine, and approached a table of judgment. What was judged here? Our citizenship. Which is a place to lie down. Akhsaniah. Here, the State addresses you. Who earns it? At such times our fellow citizen is a clerk on the Law's side of the desk. He eyes us more than spectacularly. Any grocer pores over a list to name those nouns properly. He subtracts and adds and expounds. He wipes his pink hands. He is inclined to tower over a listing tenement of names. Let us say I selected one of those names more or less resembling the memory of my own deadly paternal influence. Merely that admission gains one admission to the national verdict. To belong identifies any criminal. I longed to slip away from it. I was offered a ballot and a place of concealment. How quickly our feet vote for concealment. To be alone with the State. And a ballot. And a blunt pencil, not unlike the one I had lost. Not to mention a second, proper list. Two!? Why do we need two? We have removed ourselves from the world. We are spoiled with ballots. Having soiled one, we go home to white sheets, green lawns. We are a legend of nothing. The aftertaste of an electoral exercise. A community of bitterness. And yet. That voting booth provided him a particle of solitude. Beyond the curtain, the state paused momentarily. Consider my options. They were few and far between the pages of a book of prayers and a list of nouns.[φ] Let us speak bluntly: I began by pocketing the pencil. Could so quiet an offering vitiate an act? Perhaps you cannot possibly think so. Perhaps you think I should have spoiled a ballot first? To prevent some sly dollar's selection in my name. If we still think so, how little we have abandoned that democratic mystagogy. In either case no matter what. He had no intention of soiling his hands with it. Until a Booger entered the corner of his eye. Who listed the names of the dead on an electoral ballot?[γ] On that very day. Booger Rooney, who lay on the lip of his desk, remained a towering candidate on that list. When the dead elect the dead, there is between them. This itself is difficult. And since he had come upon it, he thought to cast a particle of glory in remembrance of a smile beneath the hood of a Pontiac Sport. Not everything is in our power. Let us thrust a glad hand in a bad pocket in search of the blunt pencil of our accommodation. Only to be roughly interrupted by an eruption through the curtain between the state and the self. I mean it was Betty Boop ::

φ Not to mention that Cafgu lurking beyond my democratic duty.

γ Certainly we have often seen a funeral march across a list of voters. Mere dust, a hint of transgression. That game was as old as sexual relations, money, pigs, leprosy.

When she unscrews her hair loose from those pink curlers, I know for sure we're out the door.[η] And why not? you're thinking. What girl doesn't want to pump her lungs? Or exercise her participatory democracy? Well, hell no. It ain't necessarily so. This girl was duty-free. But a hot Camel on the way offers a small act of voting a reason to walk. I let her pull one over on my Chinese teeshirt.[κ] Deferral: let's say some walks are riddled with it. If there's a difficulty, this is the muffin in your shorts, honey. What's never in a girl's red handbag when she needs it?[λ] And what good is a dry lighter in the desert? I yelped away that flinty thumb burn. Well, suppose a landlady carries a box of matches and takes pity on a fumbling girl. Here, before you trip and fall all over yourself. And by that time, sure, but where's the hardest place to drive a spike into your lungs? Even full of adults,[μ] a schoolyard will make you look twice before you strike a match. Because of the memory. Of my delinquency. Those days were gone. And the sooner the better. That was then and this is my head full of that delinquency and a hot fag palmed in the doorway of an electoral herd. Oh our rough red heels are swept along under that carpet of citizens. And what does a girl want in an electoral college? A place to blow smoke.
While she waits
for a landlady
to dot an i
or cross
a T ::

η For a stroll beneath that gay grey cirrus.

κ And so would you in such woolly weather.

λ Of course, that lighter was there all along – a red handbag is an exercise in now-you-see-it-now-you-don't.

μ I mean rather than that single watchful grownup in a sea of children.

Lawless men have gone out from your midst and subverted the inhabitants of their city.[α] You shall smite the inhabitants of that city by the sword. And you shall burn the city and all its booty in a fire completely to Hashem your God.[δ] Destroy it and everything that is in it, as well as its animals, by the sword. It shall remain an eternal heap – it may not even be made into gardens and orchards. The inhabitants of a subverted city have no share in the World to Come.[ε] In the case of individual sinners, we judge them and stone them, judge them and stone them. In the case of an entire subverted city, you shall take that man or woman out to your gates. We judge and imprison, judge and imprison, and we bring them up to the Great Court of seventy-one, who convict and behead them. R' Shimon asked: Why did the Torah say that the property of the righteous that is in that city should also be destroyed? What caused them to dwell in that city? Their property! Therefore, their property is destroyed : :

What will a girl do inside a voting booth with two boys while they fling their teeth at each other?[φ] She will look out for herself. Betty Boop would have preferred to be on the outside looking out for herself. For once, she regretted the habituation[γ] which had led her to such a democratic box of contention. In any case, that cigarette was gone. Knocked unintentionally from her hand by an elbow of industrious intention. How easily that camel passed through the eye of a fallen tractate. When you bend in a booth of angry boys to retrieve a fallen lit stick you will certainly receive a stray boot to the head.[η] No sooner will that fiery camel kindle a Talmudic tractate than it takes hold of the curtain in the doorway of an electoral challenge. What verdict emerges from a tiny blazing place of judgment? Those two boys tumbled out entangled in the warm embrace of their mutual hatred : :

Shall we say that boy's electoral solitude was shattered by the sudden inter-eruption of a smoke-rapt girl? On the one hand he was caught with blood. And the other in his pants. Rubbing up against the blunt pencil of his hooded remembrances. Yes and no and it was unsteady in his hand. Oh shut up. A girl only wants the oral satisfaction, a couple hauls, before she's obliged to hammer this spike. Can't you share a democratic space? In half of a half room of a room and a half. Let us say she poured a blue tower of her bent exhalation into that curtained cubicle. Pencilled him into a gasping pocket of his plaintive pants. Perhaps at some other time he would have revelled in the close proximity of such discomfort. He might have behaved more handsomely. Even now Betty Boop's parade, mingling with a camel's breath and the tinny taste of his own phantomatic hand, stirred his species.[κ] Nevertheless he felt, at last, his indigency had slid beneath the definition. I mean, he detected it in her manner. His human degradation. Let us say, she clucked her tongue. He was a sore sight for anyone's nose. Could such a contrast hope? Was there any? Hope, I mean. Perhaps you cannot possibly think so. Not so late in the day. Or book. I have no idea of your time of day. And yet. Not yet. Now that we have come to this. Shall we part their lips in such blue proximity? Or just the opposite. Let us roughly say they were pulled apart by a partzuf suddenly parting the curtain. Are you still at this? Events roughly intrude. Perhaps you imagine a ubiquitous Cafgu was relieved to find Betty unbopped. Or Betty Boop was relieved that golem was not some murderous clerk to extinguish her cigarette. Either way no matter what. We were instantly a comedy of fisticuffs. We are all partzufim. We were arms and legs and bloody noses. Golems will be golems. In a chamber orchestra of Marxian proportions.[λ] We were a painful cavity with too many teeth. I soon lost two. Let us say I would have signalled for assistance but my hands were tongue-tied. In such a small casement, our bloody arm is an end in itself. There is no place to put it. I felt a weapon's thirst. What comes to hand? The soft end of a pencil? A volume of Talmudic ruminations, let us say. I pounded the word of God into a golem's mastoidal cabbage. I applied the sharp corner of my hardened prayers to the eye of the beholder. I rifled him an earful of paper cuts. I brandished high the dull pencil of my gleeful rage. Are you still at this? Am I a peddler? Must I go on like a peddler? Well, I should have. Gone on with it, I mean. Because to pause invites an underdog to focus. Not to mention a golem. The killer, given a painful moment's pause to reflect, soon remembers to press the grapes. Joey raised the knee of brotherly love. He seized the upper hand, I mean my hand and the pencil within its grasp, applied a writer's cramp, and lowered the volume.[μ] Faintly, I heard that familiar ringing sound between my ears. I took that and that. And that. I admit I may have expressed my discomfort, compensating for a lack of articulation with a certain degree of amplitude. And so would you. There was between us an objection. A refutation. An aquarium of bodily fluids. Shall we say that these Amoraim disagreed according to a difference of opinion? It was said thus and it was said thus : :

α Sanhedrin 112a

δ *Ir hanidachas*, a subverted city is a city in which all or a majority of the inhabitants practice idolatry. Deuteronomy 13:16

ε When did the generation of the Flood lose its share in the World to Come? When robbery became so woven into the social fabric that restitution, and hence the possibility of full repentance, became impossible. Robbery demonstrates callousness towards people, and God restrained his harsh decree until humans began to act harshly toward each other. Sanhedrin 108a

λ I mean the brothers, not that fatherly figure.

φ One attempts to brush them aside.

γ Habituate: to inure, to burn or brand in a flame.

η She followed the light of a camel into a lack of consciousness.

κ What do we mean when we say that he did not know what was on the mind of his animal? Sanhedrin 105b

μ Any description is a broken bicycle. And yet we go on pedalling.

With a Cafgu one may occasionally emerge from an electoral exercise to tumble through a flaming curtain of souls and back into the world. Perhaps you are thinking we should have broken off our wrestling match to extinguish the fire of Betty Boop's tribulation. Shall I say I was a failure to realize? An entanglement of boys will dispute anything. She had not come through with us. And shall we continue to embrace our mutual pain when all around us the voting population has become a to and fro of unextinguished cubicles? Already we lay in a pool of retribution.[α] I heard the alarm bells ringing. Joey declined to follow suit. Perhaps you think he might have been more attentive had I merely unclenched my few remaining teeth from his ear. Well what was he doing with the Other one? Do we need two? He should not have left it behind in that burning booth with his ballot. Thankfully, though no thanks were intended, a boot to my head by an upstanding citizen – to kick so hard one must be standing – gave a golem the back of the upper hand. And an inflammatory glance back into that furnace from which only two had emerged. His face was the sooty language of an emptied book. Shall we pause to read the Hebrew word for truth on a golem's forehead?

The people of Sodom became arrogant only because of the bounty that the Holy One, blessed is He, lavished upon them. They said, why do we need wayfarers? Come, let us cause the very concept of wayfaring to be forgotten in our land. There were four judges in Sodom: Shakrai, Shakrurai, Zaifai and Matzlei Dina. I mean: Liar, Outrageous Liar, Forger and Perverter of Justice. Someone struck his fellow's wife and she miscarried, those judges said: Husband, give your wife to the attacker, so that he may impregnate her for you. A person lopped off the ear of his fellow's donkey, those judges said: Give that donkey to the damager until that ear grows back. One who crossed the river on a ferry must pay four zuz, one who crossed in the water must pay eight. How long will you plot treacherously against man? How long will all of you murder with leaning wall, with toppled fence? In the darkness he burrows under houses; by day they seal themselves in, never knowing light. They allowed the naked to spend the night unclothed, no garment to shield against the co

What tumbling electoral exercise emerges after the orders were given? And in what language? That curtain flamed[η] back into the world. To extinguish Betty Boop's proleptic death. A howling strangulation was that calefacient chamber, that incendiary language, that burning bush. I meant book. Or pyrographic paragraph.[κ] We march those shadowy nouns across the page. A poem may vary this. Or theory bend it. Having chanted and breathed some life into those details and then disposed of a proper noun, which of the thirteen attributes of mercy might intervene?[λ] Perhaps we should have warned a reader before we came this far. Once embarked upon a paneful journey, there is no avoiding ashy death.[μ] We are the shadows of each other's sacred letters. We are always already partly each other's partzuf. And the glowing cinders of those charred numbers. We enter a room and a half in the mirror of a room and a half. How can a chamber of letters be both glowing and empt

אמת

Those lifeless eyes read our Betty Boop's proleptic death by fire. Let us say his mindlessness drifted momentarily. He lost interest in our electoral duality. Forgot to press his thumb into the other eye. What if we were Chananyah, Mishael and Azaryah, who were cast into the furnace?[δ] To escape a furnace the collective merit of three righteous persons is required. Perhaps Joey reflected more than I. If we were three righteous ones, why then had two emerged?[ε] Perhaps he'd lost interest in our murderous brotherhood and thought to leap into a blistered ballot box in hopes of rescuing Betty.[φ] He was a fishy gaze before that deflagration and already gone limp. Here was an opportunity to bear down on the soft rear end of a singed pencil and wipe the aleph from the face of Joey Cafgu. That took all the life out of him. Leaving only: מת. Shall we ascribe a final word to a dying golem?[γ] Mon frère, mon semblable. Later, after the fire, I confirmed this mutter in the mirror over a sink in the police station. That image was irreversible. I mean, I too bore the blackened sleeves of language on my own forehead. Have you checked lately?

אמת

So little is required to wipe the aleph from the face of the Other's face. In the mirror of our own room and a half. How should we act? He was silent. How long the shadows of those numbe

α God can bring a flood of water from between the heels of your feet. Sanhedrin 108b

δ Sanhedrin 93a

ε Did that girl's righteousness save a pair of boys, whereas our thoughtlessness condemned her?

φ What is the law concerning the hair of righteous women who live in a subverted city? Is it burned with all that city's property? Rava said: Excluded from this command is that which lacks separation and then gathering and burning. Sanhedrin 112a

γ Weakening of the effect when the end of the story begins. The world is conquered and we have watched it with open eyes. We can therefore quietly turn away and live on. F. Kafka *Diaries*

η What is the meaning of that which is written: flame is scorned by complacent dreams, destined to stumbling feet? Moses, to the Generation of Wilderness. Sanhedrin 108b

κ These are the ones who are executed by fire: a Boop and a book.

λ Hashem, Hashem, Almighty, Compassionate and Gracious, Slow to Anger, Abundant in Kindness and Truth, Preserver of Kindness for thousands of generations, Forgiver of Iniquity, Wilful Sin and Error, and Who Cleanses – but does not cleanse completely. God's Thirteen Attributes of Mercy. Sanhedrin 111a

μ Perhaps your initial reluctance to embark – you cannot have forgotten it – was fair warning enough.

Tere (two) = demut + zelem (image/likeness) = 160 + 450 = 610
The secret of two = 610 = representation.

Can there be impediments to the ear?
All turned out as had been expected.
Instead of. A fortuitous train of thoughtlessness.
Until they made a comparable replacement.
A song knows how to demand. There are one or more omissions.

No one is able to describe in writing anything which is spherical, but in its place one may draw a circle, and say in the book that this is an allusion and a sign for a sphere.

*I can only describe my feeling by the metaphor, that if a man could write a book on Ethics which really was a book on Ethics, this book would, with an explosion, destroy all the other books in the world.
L. Wittgenstein, Lecture on Ethics.

Those who have read this book have no place in the World to Come. It was necessary for this to be said. Meanwhile, what is England accomplishing? Who listens to an industry on the lips of glory? That area is possibly rusted.

Call 585-PITA

A solitude is necessary in order for there to be a freedom of beginning, the existent's mastery over existing – that is, in brief, in order for there to be an existent. These are the traits the existentialist analysis of solitude, pursued exclusively in terms of despair, has succeeded in effacing, making one forget all the themes of the Romantic and Byronic literature and psychology of proud, aristocratic and genial solitude.† The existent's solitude turns out to be insufficient (for its needs) and inferior (to ethical social life).

Ask Jim to fix this!

And if this cannot enter your mind, only the opposite way is reasonable! But say, it was not on this mind. To exclude. What is the novelty? What do you have to say? Someone. Anticipation. An elenctic. The one who saw it thought because of it. But this is not so. Who mentioned its name? What did you see? They laughed at it in the west. Is it necessary? They reached up to extend a hypotyposic hand. From the beginning, at the outset. A story to contradict. Just as in. And fr[om] from where you came, an a[...] great. The event which ha[...] [hap]pened, happened that wa[...] From where, but perhap[s...] cannot possibly think so[...] because. A retraction. P[...] difference. May it come[...] Up to here there is [...] How much more s[...] agrees with himself. [...] but he has no remedy. It[...] occur to you. It is difficult. [...] cast them. Such is not my ca[...] Should we rely on answers such as these? I heard. Hear from this, learn from this, conclude from this. Go down now to the end of the verse. And furthermore. And mine too, for that matter. A stroke of luck. And nothing more::

It is strictly forbidden to make any use whatsoever of the physical golem, which is merely a byproduct of the exercise.

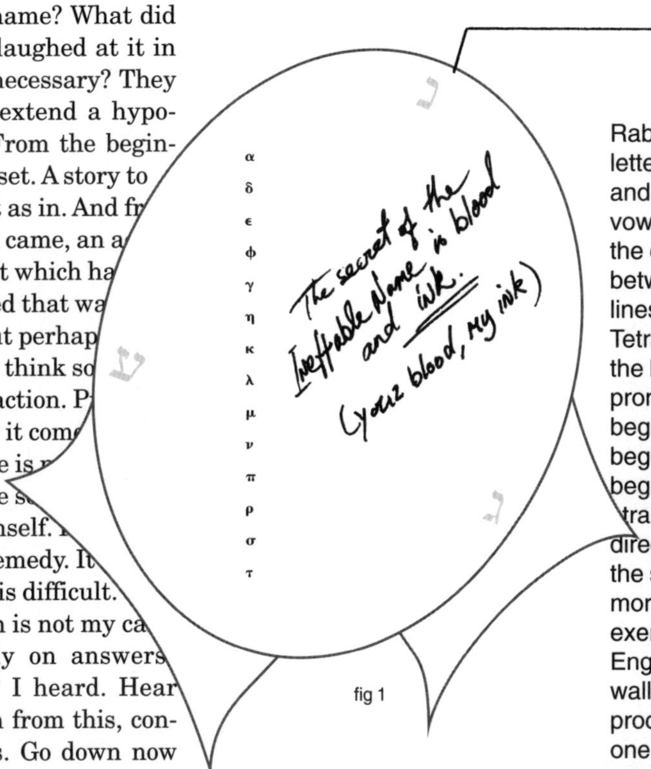

בלעז

†Amphibolous equivocation.

fig 1

Rabbi Abraham Abulafia taught: pronounce the 22 letters together with those of the Tetragrammaton and every possible combination of the five primary vowels. During the exercise, one is seated, facing the east. Between each letter, take a single breath, between pairs, no more than two breaths, between lines, no more than five, between each letter of the Tetragrammaton, no more than twenty-five. Make the head motions slowly and deliberately, while pronouncing each letter and exhaling. Cholam: begin straight ahead and raise the head. Kametz: begin at right and move head to left. Tzereh: begin at left and move head to right. Chirik: begin straight ahead and lower head. Shurek: move head directly forward. These motions correspond to the shapes of the vowels. The exercise requires more than 35 hours to complete. During the exercise, no interruption whatsoever may occur. Engrave them like a garden, carve them like a wall, deck them like a ceiling. An initiate must not proceed alone. One must be accompanied by one or two colleagues. All must purify themselves totally before engaging in this activity. They must wear clean white vestments. The soil must be virgin and kneaded with pure spring water. The purpose of the exercise is not primarily physical, but to ascend to a higher spiritual level. The highest spiritual level to which one can aspire is the Sefirah of Keter (Crown). The further one climbs, however, the more rarified the atmosphere, and the greater the spiritual danger. By a simple permutation the word Keter (כתר) becomes Karet (כרת), meaning excision, where a person is completely cut off spiritually and risks death. A novice attempting the exercise without a spiritual guide would be courting disaster

The numerical value of God's name אלהים (Elohim), the pure essence of the Divine, is eighty-six. It is the highest spiritual level attainable. The value of בלימה (Beli-mah), nothingness or the ineffable, is eighty-seven, one more than Elohim, and one stage beyond.

Until then, the Hebrew word Shabbat occurred only in compounds – Sabbath radiance, Sabbath candles – and he spelled it Sabbat. On 13 April, 1970, he wrote the final word of his last poem as Sabbath, with the last letter a silent h. He was living at 6 avenue Émile Zola, across from the quay Pont Mirabeau.
J. Felstiner, Paul Celan, Poet, Survivor, Jew.

The form of the letters is convex and the form of the eyes is convex, so that when one receives power from the letters in which the form protrudes, it is very thick and coarse.

Any day
now I

will begin

the

kitchen

A Note on the Type

The form of Apikoros Sleuth is based on that of the Talmud, in which a central sacred text is surrounded by the commentaries of scholars and sages accumulated over more than a thousand years. This layout evolved through centuries of copying by hand, and features narrow justified columns and dense pages. Using it in a modern design presented several challenges. The narrow columns in particular required more typographic adjustments than usual: for instance, increasing the number of hyphens, which medieval scribes used with abandon but some modern typographers have banished altogether. Every page is the same depth, although the number of words is different in each section of text. A degree of formal symmetry has been maintained between facing pages so that the book can be experienced as spreads rather than single pages. The demands of such a format required flexible interaction between editor, typographers and author, who sometimes changed words or phrases to fit the measure. This continual give-and-take between the restrictions of written English (with its many unbreakable words of six or seven characters), the given copy and the design requirements echoes the spirit of the tale itself.

The text face is Figural, an Expressionist font designed by Oldrich Menhart in 1940 and issued in a digital version in 1992. It has some of the strength and irregularity of nib-drawn forms. The face used for the versals, titles, running heads, folios and attributions is Legacy Sans, designed by Ronald Arnholm and also issued in 1992. It is an attempt to base a sans-serif font on Nicholas Jenson's roman of 1469.

A Note on the Author

Robert Majzels is the author of two novels, *Hellman's Scrapbook* (Cormorant Books, 1992) and *City of Forgetting* (The Mercury Press, 1997). Both have appeared in French translation, as *Le Cahier de Hellman* (Planète rebelle, 2004) and *Montréal barbare* (Les Intouchables, 2000) respectively. His full-length play *This Night the Kapo* was produced by Teatron Theatre (Toronto, 2004). He has also translated from the French four novels by France Daigle, a collection of short stories and a novella by Anne Dandurand and, with Erin Mouré, two books of poetry by Nicole Brossard. Robert Majzels lives in Quebec. Have mercy on these sentences.